THEO AND THE STOLEN LIBRARY

"BOOK OF THEO", VOLUME 3

MELANIE ANSLEY

Subscribe to the author's reader list to receive free books, exclusives, and giveaways:

This book is a work of fiction. Characters, names, locations, events and incidents described are products of the author's imagination. Any resemblance to actual events, locations, events, or persons, living or dead, is purely coincidental.

Cover design: Monika Zek

Cover image: istock.com/efilippou

For Sam.

CHAPTER 1

The arrows traced a fiery path across the night sky, brighter than the stars.

Indigo watched, dry-eyed, as her arrow found its target—a pile of oil-soaked wood and straw beneath a prone figure wrapped in white cloth.

> *In Aktu's balance*
> *Nothing is created*
> *Nothing is destroyed*
> *Through death shall be born life*
> *And through life shall be born the balance...*

As the wood smoked, then flamed into a blaze, she hardly heard the wizened priest's prayer for the dead. All she could think of was that Theo was gone.

> *Leave in joy and return to the earth*
> *May you re-enter Aktu in peace.*

The gathered crowd repeated the words after the priest, an ancient Grodlyn with wispy fur. Most of those gathered here on this sacred hill were Grodlyns, the short monkeys with rust-colored fur, or giant serpents, their scales shimmering in the firelight. Indigo could feel Brune's hulking presence by her side. The bear, she knew, had his own storm of emotions to grapple. He had been with her every step of the way, scouring every sandbar and turning every rock in search of the rabbit Theo. Though news of Theo's killing had spread far and hardened into fact, a part of her still refused to accept it.

Indigo had been kneeling on the rocky shore by a bend in the river, staring at a scrap of Theo's bloodied clothing in her paws, when her friend had found her. Brune had said nothing; he'd simply scooped her up in his giant paws and taken her back to the palace where she thought she'd fallen asleep for days, but later realized it had only been an hour or two.

The flames were roaring now, and she could feel the heat of the funeral pyre pressing through her fur, needling her skin. The rabbit of seventeen summers was no stranger to tragedy, death, or crushing loss. But a broken heart was an unfamiliar wound.

The straw and wood that had been bound in a rough semblance of a rabbit now caught flame and crackled in the fire's grip. The river had taken Theo whole, leaving nothing to burn, nothing to mourn but this crude bundle of straw and wood.

There's no body. Maybe he's not dead.

She forced the tiny voice aside, watching the flames rage then subside to a slow steady burn. The gathered crowd filed away, and Indigo noticed that the queen serpent, Mercusa, and her brother, Commander Lyusa, remained.

"He will always be remembered and honored in Jaipri, Princess Indigo," the queen said, her amber scales catching the firelight.

Lyusa looked at Brune. "Come join us at the funeral feast when you are ready."

"Thank you, old friend," the bear said.

Soon only Brune and Indigo remained at the smoldering

pyre, watching the embers spark and fade on the sacred funeral rock where Jaipri farewelled its dead.

Wordlessly, they turned and made their slow way back to the Jaipri palace, home of the giant serpents and the Grodlyns. The last thing Indigo felt like was a feast, but she knew that as the princess of Alvareth and a future member of the Order, she would be expected to attend and honor Theo's memory.

"I think we should leave Jaipri as soon as possible," Brune said.

Indigo nodded, relieved. Grief was best scoured clean with action, she knew. "I've heard that Ornox is headed for Nyatha. If we follow him, I'm sure we'll be able to find out how and where he's making black snow." The powerful powder that had nearly destroyed Jaipri had convinced some in Jaipri to give the enemy what they wanted: Theo. Whoever possessed black snow, Indigo reasoned, could turn the war.

The bear looked over at her, surprised. "I meant we should leave Jaipri for the Order, rejoin them in Hegg."

Indigo shook her head. "Theo spent his life looking for the greatest weapon in Mankahar, and black snow is the closest thing to it. If we find it, we'll be giving the Order the means to defeat the empire."

The bear chewed on this for a moment.

"I know you want to return to your home," Indigo said, "but we have a chance to defeat the empire."

"We cannot run off and fight this war by ourselves," the bear said, sharp. "That's what got Theo killed."

The words punched a hole in her, and her protest died in her throat.

Brune's expression softened. "Let's take the night to think on it. Big decisions shouldn't be made in small timeframes."

When they arrived at the palace of the serpents, the feast was well underway. With the somber rites of the funeral over, Jaipri tradition called for a joyous celebration of the dead. Oil lamps lit the royal dining hall, and the music of flutes, drums, and chimes overflowed into the hallways. Long, low tables held platters of food, and guests filled every available seat. Serpents coiled on lush pillows, while Grodlyns sat on small stools.

The queen, seeing Brune and Indigo enter the hall, gestured for them to join her. The two wove their way through diners and servers bearing giant platters of roasted yamba, elderberry wine, and grilled breads. They took their seats opposite the queen and her brother, and watched as Grodlyns hurried forward to fill their wine goblets.

"There is a gift beneath the table for both of you," the queen said, flicking her tongue between her teeth.

The bear frowned and bent his head to look. He pulled out a bundle wrapped in soft cloth that was as long as his arm and evidently heavy. He unwrapped it and revealed a gleaming axe head of fine metal, its handle carved from burnished pine. Pure joy lit his face.

"It's a thing of beauty," Brune said, and Indigo could tell he had a new infatuation.

"What did you receive, Indigo?"

Indigo had almost forgotten about hers. She peered under the table and pulled out a small box, similarly wrapped in cloth. She opened it to reveal an iron wrist guard, carved with patterns of the moon and stars.

"Thank you," Indigo said.

"You needn't have gotten us gifts," Brune protested.

"We didn't," Lyusa said.

At their confused looks, Mercusa the queen nodded behind them. "He did."

Brune and Indigo turned around to see a tall, broad-shouldered rabbit with a rust-red cloak and felt boots coming through the crowd. Two sets of iron rings pierced his wide ears, and his smoke-colored fur gleamed in the firelight. Two similarly dressed rabbits, their ears bearing only one ring each, flanked him as he arrived at the dining table and bowed.

"I am sorry I am late for the gift giving," the rabbit said. He had a curt, clipped manner of speaking, as if he disliked wasting breath on conversation.

"Princess Indigo, Brune of Hegg, may I introduce Prince Ebben of the Irontails," Queen Mercusa said.

Indigo nodded a greeting. She'd heard of the Irontails. Hard, toughened rabbits from the northeast, as flinty as the ore they mined.

"Thank you, Your Highness." The Irontail bowed. He turned to Brune and Indigo. "I trust you like the gifts?"

Brune rubbed the side of his new axe. "It's a work of art. Don't think I've seen anything like it myself."

Prince Ebben seemed unsurprised by the praise. "Irontail weapons are the best you can find in Mankahar." He turned to Indigo, expectant.

"It's a fine gift," she said politely. "And very generous." She didn't add that bringing gifts to a funeral, even a joyous one, seemed an odd custom to her. Perhaps it was an Irontail tradition.

Ebben appeared pleased with her thanks, however. "Good. Now, we should discuss my mission here, which is to carry the Order's message."

"You came from the Order?" Brune asked, surprised.

"Yes. I came to relay to you the Order's command that you return to Hegg at once."

Indigo's voice remained respectful but firm. "And we have encountered Lord Ornox's weapon, which we feel might tip the balance of the war. We can bring it to our own uses before Ornox strikes even harder."

If Brune disagreed with her, he was gracious enough to not voice it in front of Prince Ebben.

The prince's expression remained flat. "That's a decision for Lord Noshi and the other Order members. And I am told Princess Indigo would not disobey the Order's express wishes. Which is to return immediately."

"What can be so pressing that it's worth risking Ornox

building his defenses?" Indigo didn't care that her tone was no longer diplomatic.

The prince seemed unruffled. "Your marriage, Princess."

Indigo didn't know whether to laugh. "My marriage? There's some mistake."

"The Order wishes for you to marry, Princess, without delay."

"And just who am I supposed to marry?"

"Me."

At this, Indigo did laugh, and though she managed to cut it short, she knew she had, at last, ruffled the prince. His two followers looked shocked, and even Brune shot her a warning look.

"I think what Princess Indigo means is that this is sudden," Queen Mercusa cut in smoothly. "Perhaps you should explain why the Order arranged for this marriage?"

Prince Ebben nodded, mollified. "The siege of Hegg cost the Order much in terms of weaponry, armor, and fighting forces. The Irontails have iron to make the best weapons for the Order, and in return, we thought it would be mutually beneficial to unite two great tribes, the Irontails and the queendoms of Alvareth."

Indigo was incredulous. "No one consulted me on this."

Prince Ebben shrugged. "There was no time. And besides, your commitment to the Order is well known. No one thought you would object to anything that would help the Order."

"Thank you for your offer, Prince Ebben of the Irontails," Indigo said. "But we don't need your iron, and I don't need a husband."

The prince smiled condescendingly. "Ideals alone don't win wars. And as for needing a husband, well, I think most would agree that a marriage to an Irontail prince would be very rewarding. I'm glad I came to meet you myself. You are as... interesting as they say."

"I'm sorry, but I'm not leaving with you."

Though the music played on, a bubble of tense silence bloomed around the head table.

Prince Ebben's expression cooled. "It's the Order's rules. I know this is sudden, but I trust you will be ready to leave tomorrow following breakfast. Good evening. A pleasure to meet you, Princess Indigo."

And with that, the prince turned and swept away, back out the hall.

"Well, that was about as expected as hail in summer," Brune commented.

"He only arrived yesterday," Commander Lyusa said, "but insisted on not disturbing you until after the funeral."

Indigo turned to Brune. "You believe him? That the Order came up with this idea?"

Queen Mercusa flicked her tail in sympathy. "He had the Order's seal, so at the very least, he is here on their mission. I know it's a lot to digest, but I'm sure Lord Noshi and the Order would only suggest it if it was the best choice available."

At Indigo's heated look, Brune cut in. "May I speak to you, Princess?"

Indigo nodded, realizing that Brune was trying to save her from saying anything she might regret. She let him lean in close so that they could hear each other even with low voices. Queen Mercusa and her brother made a convincing show of being occupied in their own conversation.

"I'm not marrying him," Indigo said.

"I'm not saying you do. But we should return to the Order and argue against it. I'm sure Noshi has his reasons, and perhaps we can think of another solution."

"And while we're reasoning with Noshi, Ornox is making more black snow." Indigo shook her head in frustration. "No amount of iron is going to stand against that." She stood up from her chair and bowed to the queen and Lyusa. "Please excuse me. I'm feeling unwell and would rather spend the night in quiet."

The serpents nodded.

As she turned to leave, Brune growled, "Promise me you won't do anything rash."

"I promise," she said. *But what you call rash, I call necessary.*

* * *

THE UNDERGROUND PALACE was silent as Indigo double-checked her supplies and then stepped out of her room. She had a small water gourd, her sword, a light cloak, and enough dried yamba to last her until the next night, when she could forage. The iron wrist guard she left on her pillow.

The princess walked, silent, down the dark hallway, with nothing but the small oil lamp she had brought to light her way. She reached Brune's door and placed a paw on it, her resolve flickering. She wished she could have told him, but she couldn't risk his stopping her. She could not return to the Order and spend precious days debating this ridiculous marriage proposal when Ornox was busy somewhere, creating more black snow that could wipe out their already-diminished army.

Forgive me. She hurried upward through the maze of tunnels that led to the surface.

The serpent guards on duty didn't even question her, no doubt assuming the grieving princess wanted to visit her friend's funeral pyre one last time.

Indigo headed toward the sacred rock, but kept going after she reached the part of the path that wound up to the funeral site. She doubled back as quietly as possible and broke through the dense jungle to find the track that led to Jaipri's southern border. The direction Ornox had gone.

She was almost at the border, where she could see the jungle trees thinning and moonlight giving way to dawn, when she realized she was being followed. She heard the unmistakable breathing that was just too measured to be the wind, the rustle of leaves too loud to be caused by the usual night creatures.

The rabbit turned and drew her sword, searching the shadows.

"Step out. I know you're there."

A low growl came from the foliage behind her. Brune's helmet and the studs of his axe harness glinted in the moonlight spilling through the treetops.

"I thought we agreed. Nothing rash."

"If you're here to stop me," she said, "you'll have to fight me."

The bear snorted. "I'm not fool enough to take on the princess of Alvareth."

"But...?"

Brune sighed. "But I am fool enough to help you."

Indigo sheathed her sword, relieved. "To Nyatha?"

The bear nodded. "To Nyatha."

CHAPTER 2

The sound of horns from the walls of Nyatha told Lord Ornox that this visit would differ greatly from his last.

As he and his retinue rode toward the outer walls of the empire's northern trading post, the traders and merchants in the road ahead parted before him. Ornox saw the horn blowers lined along the top of the wall, where the gates had already been flung open.

People whispered and pointed, recognizing the crest on his saddle. Gradually, the whispers turned into applause, then cheers, before a hearty voice broke into song, and others joined in.

> *For Ornox is a mighty lord,*
> *The best we've had in the land,*
> *We lived in fear, but tall now we can stand.*
>
> *Theo Griffinrider rides no more,*
> *His shadow casts no fear.*
> *For Ornox came and cut him down,*
> *Saving all far and near.*

Ornox cut Theo down to save our mighty empire,
Now we spit on the cursed rogue,
And dance 'round his funeral pyre.

For Ornox is a mighty lord,
The best we've had in the land,
We lived in fear, but tall now we can stand.

The warlord allowed himself a smug smile beneath his helmet. His arched nose stuck out over a hard, wide mouth, and his dark eyes had an intensity that made men obey. He wore his thick black hair in a warrior's braid, its smooth surface broken here and there by the odd strand of silver. He rode his war charger with the straight back and wide shoulders of a man half his age, and the words of the surrounding people fanned not only *his* pride, but also that of his soldiers, he noticed.

His trusty aide, a thin, sharp-boned man of thirty-odd years named Yod, had a pleased smirk as he listened, and the soldiers' chins lifted a notch.

Not so long ago, no one wanted to be seen with Ornox, including the master of Nyatha, Ghazan. The emperor had stripped Ornox of his titles and left him a pauper, and that fair-weather ally Brel had left him in the cold. Ornox had dealt with Brel the same way he had dealt with that rabbit Theo: by use of a sword. And now, he was returning to the empire victorious, a hero. Things were right with the world once again. Or at least, they were about to be.

He urged his war charger to a faster clip and passed through the Nyatha gates into its courtyard. His men followed, and grooms rushed forward to take the horses.

Ghazan stood beside a woman at the entrance to the inner courtyards and the Nyatha mansion beyond. He was a portly man, and she a square, grinning woman, and they both wore fine linen dyed a melon green. Ghazan's collar bore the telltale coat of Nyatha's arms—a hand on the head of a lion. Next to the woman stood two children, a boy of some thirteen years and a girl who couldn't have been more than six. The girl was just an ordinary lass, dark-haired and wide-eyed, holding tight to her mother's hand. The boy had a wooden mask over the left side of his face, leaving visible only his right ear and the right side of his face from the eye down. Ornox had heard that Ghazan's son had been attacked by crows but hadn't realized the damage was so extensive. Clearly, the boy was useless at self-defense.

"Lord Ornox of Vyad! It is an honor to welcome you back to Nyatha!" Ghazan gestured toward the woman and children. "May I introduce you to my wife, Lady Tansha, and our children, Sarkus and Hassah."

They all bowed, one hand to their foreheads in a gesture of respect.

"Welcome, my Lord," the wife said. "It is an honor to host and serve you." Ornox found her crooked teeth and saccharine voice grating.

He dismounted and pulled off his gloves. "Thank you. It is good of you to receive me. Ghazan and I have much to discuss."

Ghazan beamed and gestured a fleshy hand toward the inner courtyard as the grooms began leading Ornox's men to their rooms and their horses to the stable. "Yes, indeed, growing rich together, eh, Lord Ornox? Come. Time enough for that after dinner. Tansha has prepared a wonderful pheasant."

Ornox gave his gloves and helmet to Yod. "I would like to see the alchemist first."

Both Ghazan and his wife looked perplexed. "Now?" Ghazan asked.

"Yes, now." One thing Ornox hated was saying things twice.

"But wouldn't you like some refresh—" Tansha fell into silence at Ornox's look.

"She isn't fit to be seen by your lordship. I told her to present herself at dinner," Ghazan explained.

"Then present me to her," Ornox said.

Ghazan hesitated, but quickly changed his tune at Ornox's expression. "Of course. At once."

Ghazan led him through several outdoor corridors, past a haphazard garden, and across a courtyard until they reached a nondescript dwelling with a tile roof and daubed walls. The windows were shuttered, and a pile of logs sat neatly on one side. A wide chimney silently disgorged thick, oily smoke.

Ghazan knocked on the door, to no answer. Flushing, Ghazan pounded harder, and this time, an impatient voice responded.

"Come in!"

Ghazan pushed open the door and motioned for Ornox to go first. The warlord had to stoop to avoid hitting his head.

Inside, the room was well lit, if pungent. A multitude of oil lamps hung from the rafters, while enough utensils and equipment to supply a village of alchemists covered the walls. Glass vials, brass tubes, tongs and pincers of varying sizes, spoons, ladles, and measuring cups hung from small to large. Jars of every hue were lined neatly in some logic that Ornox could not fathom. In one corner, a cage held an alchemist's canary, a common alchemist's tool to warn them in case their experiments mixing various potions turned the air toxic. The bird flitted about its cage, chirping loudly.

Sitting at a wide table in the middle of the room was a woman of debatable age, though certainly past childbearing. Her dark hair was meticulously braided and twisted around her head, and thick brows gave her a severe, distinctly unfeminine look. She seemed focused on pouring a small spoonful of yellow liquid into a vial and didn't even look toward her guests.

Ghazan coughed into his fist, displeased. "Ethana, this is our good patron, Lord Ornox."

The woman glanced up at them and reluctantly tore herself away from her table. She wiped her hands on her apron, then stood and came around to stand before Ornox and bowed with her hand to her forehead.

"You honor me, Lord Ornox, by visiting my workspace. I am sorry I am not presentable." She turned to the bird. "Quiet!" She pulled a blanket hanging over her chair and draped it over the cage, making the bird fall silent.

"Ethana, is it?" Ornox said when she had turned back to them. "Ghazan tells me you have discovered the mysteries of the black snow we gave you."

At this, the woman's face glowed with excitement, apparently transformed at the prospect of discussing her passion. She motioned toward the table and its jungle of tubes and glass jars, and chose one that looked indistinguishable from the others. "Black snow is a thing of wonder. Simply three ingredients, yet mixed in just the right amounts, they create a power and reaction that defies anything I've ever seen. I'd heard of black snow, of course. What alchemist hasn't? But to see it and recreate it and know its secret!"

She opened the jar and held it out to Ornox.

He took it and sniffed. "This is it?"

She nodded. "I made this batch. Look."

She pinched some between her forefinger and thumb, deposited it on a clay plate, and then fetched a piece of glowing wood from her hearth. Ornox and Ghazan instinctively stood back, and Ethana grinned.

"Not to worry. This'll be but a pop." She touched the burning ember to the powder, and as promised, there came a flash of fire and a popping noise, followed by that distinctive smell Ornox remembered.

"Dragon salt, flame rock, and charcoal are all that's needed to create this magic."

"That's all?" Ornox asked, surprised.

"I told you it was a thing of wonder."

Ornox held up the jar. "I shall take this with me."

"Of course, my lord." She bowed.

"How soon can you make me fifty barrels of it?"

Ghazan beamed, and Ornox could see he was trying to calculate the coin they would make when they sold it to the emperor. Good, Ornox thought. Let the thought of wealth motivate him. Ornox had no intention of revealing that it would never be sold to the emperor.

"I'll need three moons, if all goes well."

Ornox tried to rein in his frustration. "Three moons?"

"The dragon salt takes time to harvest, my lord, even on a farm as large as Nyatha." At his impatient look she continued, "We can make dragon salt from the manure of animals, but it takes time to ferment into the form we need for black snow. I can make enough for you to give samples to your buyers if you like? But for barrels, I will need more time."

"Samples would be a good start!" Ghazan nodded. "We'll have buyers lining out the door."

"Make sure there are fifty barrels in three months," Ornox said. "There is no issue of coin. Just see that it's done."

The woman raised her eyebrows but nodded. "Yes, my lord."

"And no one knows of your business here?"

Ethana glanced at Ghazan, who hurriedly said, "As you asked, we have kept Ethana's real work secret. People know she's an alchemist, but they think she's here to create a potion to restore my son's face."

Ornox nodded. "We don't want anyone knowing we have black snow, much less learning how to make it. Is that understood?"

"Of course, my lord," Ghazan agreed.

"Is that understood, woman?"

Ethana looked taken aback to be addressed as "woman," but at the look in Ornox's eyes, she nodded. "Understood. Master Ghazan has been very clear from the start. I will work day and night, my lord, and tell no one."

As they left the cottage, Ornox strode back to the manor with a light heart. His plans were bearing fruit, and in three moons, he could march on the empire's capital city. Once he had enough black snow, Kalyun-eh would fall to him within heartbeats.

* * *

IN THE EMPIRE'S capital city, the sun was melting into the horizon in a warm haze of gold and rose.

At this time of day, the city's activity surged. Traders made their way home, smiths did their last jobs, and taverns readied themselves for those seeking an ale to mark the end of work troubles and the start of home troubles. It was the time when tongues wagged and gossip flowed.

From the jutting balcony of the imposing castle overlooking the city, the empire's ruler stood and regarded his domain. From here, one could see the great city's spires and rooftops spread out below, and hear the constant din of carts, the shouts of merchants and cart drivers, and the music spilling from taverns.

Emperor Dorgun wore purple robes with gold trim, his hands resting on the balustrade. One eye squinted against the fading sun, while the other, a deadened orb of milky white that hadn't been able to see for decades, simply stared straight into the light. His clean-shaven jaw and neck showed his seventy-nine years, and his mouth showed his displeasure.

He was old, yes. But not losing his wits, as he knew some believed. And though even he had to admit he was losing his hearing, he could still catch the tune coming from one tavern that hugged the outer castle walls. There, on the fringes of where the city ended and the royal might of the empire's ruler began, a few taverns plied the castle servants who went in and out the servant gate with modestly priced ale and meals. And though he couldn't quite make out the words, Dorgun didn't have to. He knew the song already, for it seemed the city had sung nothing else for the last moon.

For Ornox is a mighty lord,

The best we've had in the land,
We lived in fear, but tall now we can stand.

And as it always did, Dorgun's blood grew hot. Ornox had disgraced the empire at the Battle of Ralgayan, and then brashly killed his top advisor, Brel. Dorgun couldn't say he was fond of any of his own advisors—he couldn't remember being fond of anyone, besides his father, whom he had killed—but it was the affront of the act more than anything that made Dorgun furious. Brel was not Ornox's to kill or even defy. And that Ornox had done so only made Dorgun suspect the warlord was planning to take the throne. Therefore, hearing Ornox celebrated as a hero in the streets—in *his* streets—was beyond galling. His ancestor Dakus, the first emperor of Mankahar, would never have suffered such a thing.

Perhaps it was time to cull the flock.

"Forgive us for disturbing you, Your Eminence."

The emperor gathered his thoughts and turned to see his three remaining advisors, Haegon, Unndoran, and Pridan, standing just behind him.

"Forgive us," Haegon repeated. "But we felt it wise to consult you."

Dorgun realized he had promised them an audience before sunset. "Speak then. You mentioned it was urgent."

Haegon stepped forward, his head cocked in the manner Dorgun had learned meant the advisor was nervous.

"The nobles wish to plan for the empire's well-being over the next few years, and—"

"This is about an heir." Dorgun cut past the idle talk.

Haegon hesitated and then bowed his head. "Yes, Your Eminence."

"Dogs," Dorgun muttered. "All the nobles are dogs who have forgotten who feeds them."

"Dogs need masters," Haegon murmured.

"Am I not their master?"

Haegon looked down, subservient. "Naturally, Your Eminence, you are the one and only emperor of Mankahar, rightful heir of the first emperor, Dakus. Invincible and eternal."

"Yet everyone is waiting for me to die, aren't they?"

All the advisors shook their heads vehemently. Haegon continued, "Of course not, Your Eminence. Never. But your eightieth birthday is soon, and empires are strong when they feel there is a continuation of rule, a steady hand that will steer the ship."

Dorgun digested this. "What unrest have you heard?" The advisors traded glances, which weren't lost on Dorgun. "Tell me."

"There have been whispers of rebellion, Your Eminence," Haegon said. "Whispers only, but they grow louder. Without an heir, the nobles have fanciful thoughts. Thoughts that they might become that heir, with or without your blessing."

"Fanciful thoughts, indeed. Is that all?"

The advisors again traded glances. Dorgun didn't have to wonder how much they discussed amongst themselves, what they told him and what they kept secret. Were they, too, hoping to pounce on his vacant throne once his body had withered enough?

Unndoran spoke this time. His carefully manicured beard bobbed as he spoke, the grooming wax he used in it so liberally making the hairs seem like one giant block protruding from his chin. "Your Eminence, the taxes from the war on the Order are necessary. Everyone knows that. But it means even the nobles are feeling the pinch. When the dog starves, the fleas die, as the saying goes, and the streets of Kalyun-eh are no longer safe for the lone or even the companioned traveler. The thieves are many, and the jails are full."

"And you bring me this problem because you haven't the wits between the three of you to figure it out?" Dorgun snapped. Unndoran blinked as if slapped. "This is not even a problem, but a blessing. Take the prisoners from the jails and sell them to the slavers. That will give us coin. And kill the ones you can't sell."

Pridan, always the silent one, looked alarmed. Haegon's eyes narrowed almost imperceptibly, while Unndoran looked to his companions for their reactions. For a split second, Dorgun missed Brel. The one formerly known as the Child had been a monstrosity, it was true, but he wouldn't have been as soft as these three.

"Your Eminence, while that will gain us coin, it is true," Haegon said slowly, "it may fan the flames of rebellion."

"Let them rebel." Dorgun moved away from the balcony and into the inner audience chamber. His advisors followed at a respectful distance. None but the closest of servants could approach too close to the emperor.

Dorgun turned to them and saw the suppressed surprise and fear on their faces. Let them think he had lost his wits. They would see. There was only one way to make sure Mankahar realized its ruler's fist had not weakened. That no one would sit on Dorgun's throne unless Dorgun himself put him there.

A fresh burst of song erupted from outside as the taverns filled and more voices joined in the chorus praising Ornox.

He dismissed his advisors and retired to his private chambers where the greatest secret of Mankahar lay buried—the stolen Library of Elshon. He drew the curtains, made sure he was alone, and then pressed the tiles in the floor of his bedchamber that opened the concealed door to the secret cavern below.

Dorgun would make an example of Kalyun-eh, destroy the city, and start again. He would let the whole of Mankahar see that he was still in power and that the emperor still had teeth. But how? An idea formed, but he knew he would need some time to research the details. Here in his library, he would devise a way to cleanse his empire of its rot.

CHAPTER 3

The blizzard washed everything in cold, white silence.

The giant birds, Irah and Hygra, flew as best they could through the knife-like winds, pushing their way higher up the jagged mountain face, toward the peak. There, Orjo had promised, was the Temple of Clouds. The place that might bring the rabbit Theo back to life.

Father Oaks tightened his stiff arms around his grandson's body. The large matriarch Proudfeather, Hygra, had suggested he and the muskrat Orjo devise some sort of strap so that they wouldn't fall off their respective Proudfeather's back. Oaks was grateful for that advice now. The snow and gales would have defeated them if they had relied on their own strength to hold on to the birds. Oaks had not been young for what seemed a lifetime now, and having to protect and shelter Theo's body was no easy task. He and Orjo had taken turns holding on to Theo, but even so, Father Oaks was exhausted. His whiskers were lined with ice, as were Orjo's, and he couldn't feel his feet. He wasn't sure if his paws would be able to unclench themselves from Theo's shroud should they ever reach this mysterious Temple of Clouds.

"There!"

The wind snatched Orjo's cry almost as soon as it left his lips. The muskrat was riding just ahead of him, on Hygra's daughter, Irah. Father Oaks squinted through the flurry of snow, but could see nothing.

"What?"

Orjo pointed. Through the clouds, Father Oaks dimly made out a glimmer of light above.

Encouraged, Hygra put on a fresh burst of speed, pumping her giant wings. Ahead, Orjo and Irah vanished, as if swallowed by the cloud bank, and Father Oaks felt a stab of fear. Where had they gone?

"Hygra! Stop!" He called out, but the words ripped away from him in the wind, and Hygra only flew faster, determined to catch up with her daughter. Before Father Oaks could shout again, they hurtled through some invisible barrier, and the snow was gone, as if by magic. It was still bitterly cold and windy, but here there was sunlight everywhere, reflected off the bed of clouds below and shimmering off tiles in the distance.

Father Oaks blinked, his breath forming small blooms before his whiskers. Ahead of him was Irah, Orjo astride her. And beyond them, a monastery rose into view, its walls painted a blinding white, its curved roof tiles shining blue and gold in the sun. He heard a tinkling, and as they drew closer, he could make out the glinting of tiny silver bells on the eaves.

"The Temple of Clouds," Father Oaks muttered, pulling his grandson's body closer to him. Some part of him had feared that Orjo had, true to his nature, lied, and that this place didn't exist. Seeing it flooded him with relief and hope that threatened to bring tears. "Hold on, lad. Just hold on."

Hygra followed her daughter over the monastery walls before nearly dropping straight down into the central courtyard. Irah, like her mother, was exhausted from their long journey from Jaipri. They had stopped only once, when the birds could no longer fly, and rested only as long as they needed to have a short sleep and meal. Orjo slid from Irah's back, clearly stiff and uncomfortable. Father Oaks waited for Hygra to fold her legs beneath her and shift to the side, allowing him to slide a shorter distance to the ground. He unwound the cloth strap he'd used to attach himself to Hygra, and keeping Theo's body above him, slid off the bird before gently supporting Theo's body to the ground.

Father Oaks heard running footsteps, the clacking of wood. He looked up to see two-dozen creatures—badgers, hares, and marmots—surrounding them. They all wore identical plain, cloth robes and simple wooden earrings, and held spears pointed toward the new arrivals. Father Oaks looked up at the monastery walls. Archers, also in identical plain robes and earrings, stood lining the ramparts, arrows trained on the intruders.

Orjo lifted his paws. His breath came out in clouds. "We mean no harm. We seek Zo."

The monks with spears didn't react. Father Oaks looked at Orjo, who seemed about to repeat his statement, when a voice sounded from the northern ramparts.

"Those who seek Zo are usually the desperate."

Father Oaks looked up. Among the archers stood a tall, imposing-looking polecat with night-black fur and a muscled body, a blue robe draped over her shoulders. Her words carried easily, as though she had not raised her voice at all.

Orjo grimaced. "Then we've come to the right place."

"Who are you, and why do you seek Zo?"

The muskrat indicated Theo's body. "We bring the Griffin-rider. He needs your help."

The polecat looked at Theo, then turned back to Orjo. "That answers why. Now, who are you?"

Father Oaks saw Orjo hesitate and stepped in.

"I'm the lad's grandfather, Father Oaks. And he's Orjo."

An almost imperceptible gasp followed the mention of Orjo's name, and paws tightened around spears. The only one unaffected by the information was the polecat in blue.

"Please, help him," Father Oaks said, chafing at this waste of valuable time. He needed them to act, needed to see if Zo could bring Theo back.

"Bring him in. But the birds stay here."

The monks withdrew their spears, and four mountain hares came forward to take Theo's body. They gently lifted him and, with a motion of their heads, indicated that Father Oaks and Orjo should follow them.

The hares led them through a circular gate into a wide reception room with a slate floor and a beamed ceiling. A large brazier burned in each of the room's four corners. A few monks came from a different chamber, bearing flat, round pillows, which they placed on the floor in the middle of the room. The hares who had brought Theo in laid the rabbit gently down on the pillows, then stepped back. Father Oaks looked at Theo's face, strangely peaceful in death despite the wounds inflicted on him—the swollen eye within its patch of black fur, the blood— and the makeshift shroud they had wrapped him in. Father Oaks' heart ached.

Please, Berjma, please, gods! Let Orjo be right! Let Zo be a miracle worker.

Where was Zo, anyway? Father Oaks looked around him. The hares and other monks had retreated to the far walls and stood with paws clasped.

Father Oaks turned to find the blue-robed polecat striding in, flanked by two badgers. Closer up, he could see that some of her hair had silvered around the brow, and she had sharp, white teeth that gleamed through black lips. She towered over Orjo and Oaks, her expression neutral.

"Please, where's the one called Zo?" Father Oaks broke in.

"I am she," the polecat said.

Father Oaks blinked, confused. "Yer younger n' I was expecting!"

"The original Zo lived hundreds of years ago," their host explained. "But he passed on all his knowledge of healing, and all his memories, to three disciples. From them, another Zo was chosen. This tradition has continued to today, and I am the current serving Zo."

Father Oaks stepped toward his grandson. "Can ye save him?"

The polecat came forward and glanced at Theo. "He is dead. There is nothing I can do.

"What about the cave?" Orjo asked. "The Cave of Light?"

Zo put her paws in her sleeves, contemplative. "You can try that. But you do know the price?"

"What?" Father Oaks cut in. "What Cave of Light? What price?"

Zo turned to him, patient. "Legend has it that the Cave of Light can perform miracles. It's why the temple was built here in the first place. It is a spot sacred to Aktu, and in time beyond time, it was believed to have magical healing powers. If the goddess Aktu deems Theo worthy, she will bring him back. If not, then he is gone forever."

"Then what are we waiting for?"

Orjo regarded him. "The price is that if Theo dies, the one who takes him into the cave dies with him."

"Real question is, does it work?" the old rabbit asked.

"You mean has anyone successfully brought someone back from the dead?" Zo paused. "Yes. Once."

Father Oaks didn't even glance at his grandson's lifeless body. "Where's this cave, then?"

* * *

THE AIR almost crackled with cold as the small party reached the broad promontory, a ledge in the mountainside with a large rock that had strange symbols carved into it. They paused to catch their breath after the steep climb up the mountainside.

"We are here," Zo said. "The Cave of Light." She motioned to the badgers, who had carried Theo up the mountain, and they moved forward and gently lay Theo's body down. They put their shoulders against the rock and heaved, sliding it open.

Father Oaks tried to ignore how watery his legs felt, his blood pounding in his head until he thought he'd burst, his lungs unable to get enough air up here.

"Take your time," Zo reassured him. "Do you need a rest?"

Father Oaks shook his head, willing his old body to push on. *We'll rest soon, old one. Soon.*

Zo motioned for the badgers to pull out the sash they had brought. They helped Father Oaks tie the sash around his back and positioned Theo in it. Father Oaks tried not to buckle under the weight.

"You will have to take him down some stairs and then through a broad tunnel," Zo explained. "You will see Aktu's womb of light. Put Theo in the waters there. We will wait until the third day. If we open the cave and you have not returned by then, we'll assume Aktu has called you to her." She stepped back, her breath hanging in the frigid air. "May Aktu be with you."

The other badgers bowed at the waist, both paws to the forehead, and repeated, "May Aktu be with you."

Father Oaks looked to Orjo, who nodded and held out an oil lamp.

The old rabbit took the lamp and squeezed his way into the cave, pulling his walking staff with him. The badgers began pushing the rock back in place, and soon, the cave was again dark and silent.

Inside, Father Oaks paused to let his eyes adjust. He held up the oil lamp to see better, then used his walking staff to make his way down, one laborious step at a time.

When he reached the bottom, he paused, panting, the sash that held his grandson cutting into his shoulders. Here, a ghostly glow emanated from a rock tunnel before him. As he drew closer to the light, he realized he no longer needed his lamp. Strings of blue-green globes hung like beads from the tunnel ceiling. Moon worms, the polecat had told him.

He kept walking through the glowing tunnel until he heard the gentle lapping of water. The tunnel widened into a vast cavern, at least thirty paces across from end to end, and here, every inch of the ceiling and walls were lit with the worms. In the middle of the cave floor was a shallow pool, about three times Theo's length and only waist high, from what Father Oaks could see. He moved closer and saw that it almost looked deliberately carved, its shape like some giant egg split down the middle. Its water glowed from within, the worms throwing light.

"The womb," Father Oaks muttered and knelt. He pulled at the sash lashed to his chest, and eased Theo's body off his back. He undid the robes they had used to wrap Theo. Zo had told him repeatedly that Theo had to appear before this goddess Aktu naked. Last season, he had never heard of Aktu. Now he was here, a supplicant for his dead grandson, hoping to all the gods that Aktu existed.

He summoned the last of his strength to lift Theo into the pool. The water was surprisingly warm, considering the cold in the cave. Father Oaks held his grandson, then let go, watching as the water closed over Theo's lifeless face.

Please, let him return.

CHAPTER 4

A scattering of firelight lit the edges of Nyatha's walls, the only parts visible through the deepening night fog that had descended. From the hill that led down to the main road into the trading post, Brune and Indigo paused, trying to survey the area, but the bear soon grunted in frustration.

"Can barely see my own paw in this."

Indigo nodded. "We'll have to get closer. Perhaps by then the fog will lift."

They began following the edge of the road down. One advantage they had, Indigo thought ruefully, was that no one would see them approach. And the fog had also kept travelers off the roads, which meant they didn't have to worry about running into Urzoks along the way.

Through the fog, the glow of fires along the walls grew closer until they could make out the dim silhouette of Nyatha before them.

"Perhaps we should wait for the fog to lift," Brune suggested.

They had traveled for days to get here, and the thought of having to wait on the whims of weather made her impatient.

"We can at least scout the perimeter, see how many other

entrances there are," she said. "Maybe even get a sense of how many sentries they have at each gate."

Brune nodded. "I'll take the north side; you take the south. I'll meet you back at this spot."

"Be safe," she said as she watched him disappear into the gloom. She headed south, keeping the perimeter walls on her right. She passed a side entrance with tall double doors but could see no smaller door for individual passage. And though she couldn't see them, she could hear the chatter of guards from above. This gate would be hard to sneak through, though not impossible. She continued.

Indigo had walked for quite some time without another access point when she thought she heard movement behind her. She was careful to not change her footfalls, instead swiveling her ears so that she could catch anything out of the ordinary.

She was just about to dismiss her worries as her imagination when something moved behind her. Her sword came out as she spun around and saw a set of yellow eyes in the fog. Then another. And another. She was surrounded.

One set of eyes narrowed, and the owner stepped forward. It was a large timber wolf, its salt-and-pepper fur blending in seamlessly with the fog.

"What's your business, rabbit?"

"I'm with the Order," she said, "here on behalf of Lord Noshi."

The wolf eyed her, wary. "You're a long way from the Order. The New Dawn patrol controls this area and the forest beyond. Whatever business you have, you need the Alpha's permission."

"The Alpha?" she asked. "Who is that?"

"He's the one who will decide if you live or die," the wolf chuckled, cold. "Come."

The wolves closed in around her, and Indigo weighed her odds. As if sensing her thoughts, the one with the salt-and-pepper fur growled, "I wouldn't recommend fighting. We've pack mates not far from here, and one howl from us will bring them on you."

Whether he was bluffing or not, taking down four wolves would be a challenge. And the more time she bought herself, the greater the chance that Brune would come looking for her. Indigo sheathed her sword. "Very well. Let's meet the Alpha."

They led her through the fog as if the night were clear as day. They had probably scent-marked these areas, Indigo realized, creating a mapped highway for themselves that only they could follow. The open ground of wild grasses gave way to a carpet of pine needles, and the arms of trees closed overhead. Though she considered making a run, she could hear the pad of a wolf nearby, far too near to allow escape.

They splashed through a stream and came up over a ridge in the forest, and Indigo saw the flicker of firelight ahead. The fog was lifting, giving the surrounding trees back their edges. The wolves picked up their pace, and soon, Indigo saw what looked like a small village. There were huts and drying racks, cooking pits and a clearing where the moonlight could struggle past the dissipating fog.

Standing in the middle of the clearing, surrounded by five wolves, was a figure that made Indigo's heart sink.

"Brune?"

The bear seemed just as disappointed to see her. "You too?"

The wolves formed a loose but alert circle around the clearing, watching the two prisoners. But what amazed Indigo was seeing a group of three rabbits emerge from one of the huts behind the wolves, glance at Brune and Indigo curiously, and continue walking away.

Brune frowned. "This night just became odder."

"What are rabbits doing living with wolves?" Indigo asked.

"We are allies in the fight against Nyatha," a voice said behind them.

Indigo and Brune turned. A giant wolf, ghost-white, stood there regarding them.

Recognition flickered in Indigo. "Argasar? Of the Blackmoons?"

The wolf's expression changed, and he studied her more closely. "You're royal," he said, his eyes on her tattooed ears. "From Alvareth. I knew a princess there once."

"I am she," Indigo said. This close, she could now see scars on his muzzle, a brand on his ear. None of those had been there when they'd last met on the steppe lands, and though in every other way the last alpha of the Blackmoons looked as she remembered, she sensed he had changed much since they had first met.

"You know each other?" Brune glanced from the wolf to the princess.

Argasar nodded. "We are both of the steppe lands. I tried to convince the princess's—aunt, was it?"

"Yes, the ruling regent," Indigo said, remembering.

"I tried to convince her aunt to fight the Urzok threat, the pacification that had taken over my pack. But she was unwilling."

"I thank you again for trying," Indigo said. She had been the one to plead that Argasar return with her to her queendom, to try to sway her aunt, their ruler, to do something, anything, in the fight against the empire. It still angered her that her aunt had refused.

"But if you're from the steppes," Brune asked, "then what are you doing all the way out here? With a village of rabbits?"

"I would first like to ask the same of you."

"We're here to find out where the warlord Ornox is making something called black snow."

"Black snow?"

"It's a powder that is so powerful, just a pawful can destroy a village when lit. We've seen it ourselves."

The wolf cocked his head. "And you think it's being made in Nyatha?"

Indigo nodded. "I know Ornox came through here, and this

is not on the way to his lands. I suspect he has an alchemist making black snow, and that alchemist is here. And if that's true, we need that alchemist. With black snow, we could win the war."

"Interesting," Argasar smiled. "So it seems we have similar goals."

"You wish to find the alchemist?" Brune asked.

Argasar shook his head. "We wish to take Nyatha. We could use experienced fighters. Join us, and you can find your alchemist."

"Take Nyatha?" Indigo repeated, surprised. Argasar was a seasoned wolf, but did he really think he could bring down an Urzok stronghold with a group of wolves and a village of rabbits?

Argasar smiled at her doubt. "We have a secret way in and a few advantages over the enemy. We have much to discuss and time to discuss it. Rest for the night. In the morning, I'll introduce you to the key to Nyatha's downfall."

* * *

INDIGO FORCED herself to sleep that night, despite all the buzzing questions in her mind. It was one of the more useful battle tactics her aunt, the queen regent, had taught her when she was young. One had to control the mind so that it did not prevent the body from resting. When dawn broke, she was up and had been to the stream to wash her face and paws. Brune was already causing a stir in the village, as rabbits awoke to the sight of the giant stranger in their midst.

Argasar arrived shortly after. Indigo noted how not just the wolves but also the rabbits seemed to defer to Argasar, calling him "Alpha." Though she was fast friends with a bear, she still found the sight of these rabbits and wolves living together strangely unsettling.

Indigo and Brune followed Argasar and his wolves down a well-worn path that wound through the trees to a clearing where several dirt-caked rabbits gathered around small oil lamps, leaning against makeshift pickaxes and taking swills of water from a barrel. In the middle of the clearing, set into a small knoll with a tree twisting out the top, was a yawning hole leading underground.

Several of the rabbits nodded greetings to Argasar as he and his wolves approached, murmuring "Alpha." Many studied Brune and Indigo with open curiosity.

Argasar said something to one of the rabbits, who immediately put down his pickaxe and went scurrying into the tunnel.

"Don't tell me you're digging all the way into Nyatha?" Brune asked, incredulous.

The large wolf grinned. "That's exactly what we're doing. Rabbits are excellent diggers, and we've been working day and night on this tunnel."

Indigo studied the worker rabbits. They looked exhausted, but not despondent. If anything, they seemed proud, and even prouder at Argasar's praise.

"If all goes well and we don't hit any other major obstacles or cave-ins," the wolf said, "we'll be inside Nyatha in a week."

"Storm it from the inside, then?" It was a slow and back-breaking endeavor, but Indigo wasn't convinced the element of surprise would be enough. "They will still surely outnumber us."

"There are over six hundred mercenaries guarding Nyatha," the wolf confirmed. "But they will surrender to us with barely a fight."

Brune raised an eyebrow. "How's that?"

"I'd like to introduce you to the rabbit who will guarantee Nyatha's surrender," Argasar said, nodding toward the tunnel. A thick-boned rabbit was emerging from the yawning gap in the earth, following the rabbit Argasar had sent in. Indigo could make out patches of fur, though what was dirt and what was original fur color was unclear. He had long, thick ears and protruding teeth, but a wide, honest face.

"Brune of Hegg, Princess Indigo, may I introduce you to Pozzi of Willago." Argasar turned to the black and white rabbit. "Pozzi, Indigo and Brune are experienced fighters with the Order. They were apparently trying to enter Nyatha when our night guard found them. I was telling them that we are digging a tunnel, and that you, Pozzi, know the inside of the manor." Argasar turned to Indigo and Brune. "Pozzi, along with Keeva and Walnut over there, were kept as pets of the Nyatha master's daughter, Hassah."

Argasar indicated a table to one side where a female rabbit with lush lavender fur and kind eyes stirred a pot of tea. Next to her was a young rabbit of brown fur and a mischievous face, helping ladle the tea and serve some sort of patty to the worker rabbits.

"He will help us secure Hassah, which will force the master to surrender."

The one called Pozzi looked from Brune to Indigo. "You're from the Order? You knew Theo then?"

Indigo's throat tightened as she nodded. *Knew.* She still couldn't quite fathom that it was all past, something that would never be again.

"Pozzi was a good friend of Theo's," Argasar explained.

Indigo glanced back at the unassuming rabbit. Theo had never mentioned Pozzi. In fact, he hadn't mentioned any of his friends or much about his home. So many questions that she would never have a chance to ask him now.

"You are eager to avenge your friend's death, are you not?" Argasar said.

"I'm eager to go home," the black-and-white rabbit replied.

The answer seemed to irk Argasar. There was a friction between the wolf and the rabbit that Indigo didn't understand. "And you will. But first, Pozzi will help us secure Hassah, the master of Nyatha's daughter."

"But she is not to be harmed," Pozzi said, firm.

"A promise is a promise. She and her family will be escorted out of Nyatha alive," Argasar said. His tone made it clear he'd had this conversation before, and it exasperated him.

Indigo wondered what it must have been like to be a pet in an Urzok household. Pozzi clearly cared about his former masters. Indigo had never cared for hostage taking. But she had another reason for wanting to make sure Argasar didn't unleash a vengeful pack of bloodthirsty wolves in Nyatha. "We need to find the alchemist," she said to Argasar. "Which means we kill as few as possible, because we can't afford to harm the alchemist if he's there."

Argasar looked amused. "It seems I am surrounded by pacifists. Very well. I will make sure everyone uses restraint. In the meantime, we'll show you the tunnel, and Pozzi will familiarize us with the insides of Nyatha until we know the layout better than our own paws."

CHAPTER 5

Theo floated in a green, blue glow.

Everywhere, warm light thrummed with an all-powerful energy, protective and unbreakable. There was nothing to do but drift and relish the omnipotent safety of the light. The pain he had felt before, the cold of the sword, the water in his lungs, the agonizing process of death itself—none of it mattered here. Indeed, none of it existed.

Wake up.

He couldn't define it, for it wasn't a voice. But the words were clear.

Wake up.

He sensed, rather than saw, a dark pinprick at the edge of his eye. Something told him that if he touched it, all this warmth, this safety, would shatter around him. He swam away, closer to where the light became so bright it felt almost white hot. Cleansing.

Stop.

The word came with such force that Theo paused.

Go back.

"Who are you?"

The light quivered around him, coalescing around itself until

35

it formed a vague outline—leathery face, trunk-like legs, and a giant ridged shell. Theo recognized the tortoise from the Sea of Petrified Waves, the one who also appeared in his dreams about the Library of Elshon.

I am a friend, Theo Griffinrider. And I'm telling you, you must go back.

"Go back?" Theo's thoughts hummed in the surrounding light. "Go back where?"

You must go back to Mankahar.

"Even if I wanted to, I can't." But deep down, he knew that wasn't true. The speck of darkness in the corner of his eye was growing, and he instinctively knew it led back to everything he wanted to forget.

Go back and find my greatest weapon.

Bitterness flooded him, and he resented its intrusion here in the light. "The Urzoks found a great weapon. Black snow."

Black snow is not Mankahar's greatest weapon.

"Then what is it?"

The tortoise smiled. *You already know.*

The light around him darkened and flickered until he was in a library, surrounded by towering shelves. He knew this library, even though he had only dreamed of it. It was the Library of Elshon, and from previous dreams, he knew what came next. The books began falling off the shelves, like birds diving for prey, and as they hit the floor, they transformed into versions of him. He tried to run, but his feet were rooted, and he watched as these identicals of him ran past him, intent on something behind him. Just as he was about to turn and look, the surroundings melted back into nebulous light, and he was looking at the great watery eyes of the tortoise.

The thought came, almost unwanted. "The *Book of Cures*. The *Book of Cures* is in the Library of Elshon. Am I right? And it explains how to reverse pacification, doesn't it?"

The Book of Cures *will heal Mankahar's body. Only you can heal Mankahar's soul.*

"I don't want to go back…"

The tortoise's face began to fade back into the light. *The choice is yours. But if you stay here, then those you love will die with you…*

"No! Wait!"

The tortoise vanished, and Theo now noticed that the black spot, which had been ever growing, was starting to shrink again. The warm light was enveloping him, wrapping him in its comfort. So welcoming. So easy…

He pushed back against it and swam for the dark hole beneath him that was shrinking breath by breath.

"Wait!" He wasn't sure whether he spoke, but he forced himself down, down toward the dark tunnel that led back to the world he had so wanted to leave behind. He kicked harder, pulling himself along until he was through the darkness and out to the other side.

* * *

THROUGH THE VIOLENT RETCHING, he heard a whoop of joy.

"I've got ye, lad, I've got ye…"

His body hurt all over and his throat was raw. As he opened his eyes, Theo blinked, confused at the tear-streaked, whiskered face before him. This was Father Oaks, missing an ear, it was true, but Theo had thought he would never see this face again.

"What happened to your ear?" Theo croaked, his voice ragged.

Father Oaks laughed and crushed his grandson to him until Theo cried out. "Never mind that, lad! Ye're alive!" Father Oaks wiped a tear away. "It took ye three days, but ye're alive. Aktu be praised."

Theo took in their surroundings—a glowing green-blue substance covered the cave walls, much like the light he had been cocooned in. The waist-deep water holding him also glowed—and close up, he could see that the blue-green glow was actually worms clinging to the sides of the rock pool.

"Ye must have more questions n' a dandelion has seeds," Father Oaks commented, "but let's get ye dry and dressed first."

Father Oaks helped Theo out of the water, steadying him on his shaky legs, then wrapped him in a robe, and gave him a pair of boots to keep his feet warm. Theo realized he was shivering, though perhaps not solely from the cold. His body felt like a stranger's to him, and he tested all his limbs and digits to make sure everything worked. He looked down at his chest and touched the ugly raised scar there.

"Ye had a hole in ye just yesterday," Father Oaks said softly.

The memories came back, sharp and crisp. The cliff by the river. Ornox with his sword. The look in the warlord's eye as he plunged the blade into Theo's chest, then pushed the rabbit into the swirling waters below.

"I was dead, wasn't I?" Theo asked. His voice was still hoarse, as if his throat resented being used.

"Aye, ye were."

"What about Indigo? Brune?" The memory of how he had last seen them, held down while he had been drugged and betrayed. What if he had come back too late?

"Time for all yer questions later," Father Oaks said, soothing. "Fer now, let's get ye warm and dry."

* * *

WHEN THE ROCK rolled back and they emerged from the cave, the group gathered outside looked as stunned as Theo felt. A large female polecat in thick, blue robes stood with the four badgers who had opened the rock door, and they all bowed low as Father Oaks emerged, supporting Theo. The only one who rushed forward, unabashed, was a wild-maned muskrat who squeezed Theo's shoulders with bruising force.

"Orjo?"

A mixture of surprise and anger bubbled up in Theo. The last time he had seen Orjo, the wily bastard had knocked Theo out and escaped with their mode of transport, leaving him, Brune, and Indigo stranded in the middle of nowhere. Theo felt the urge to punch the rat, but even as his arm made a move, he realized his newly revived body was much too weak.

Orjo looked hurt at Theo's frostiness. "Don't be sore. I ended up coming back and saving your life. Right, Oaks?"

Theo turned to his grandfather, who nodded grudgingly. "It's true. He told us of Zo, so we came here."

Theo frowned. "Zo? Zo of the Miraculous Cures?"

At this, the polecat seemed to shake off her shock and stepped forward. "You honor me that you know my name, Theo Griffinrider."

Theo was even more confused. "You're Zo?"

"Yes. Now let us get you down the mountain to the Temple of Clouds. This is a historic day."

The badgers wrapped Theo in another robe, and then led him, Oaks, and Orjo down the mountainside. One badger rushed ahead with news of Theo's arrival, and when they entered, all the monks they encountered lowered themselves to the ground. Theo gave up trying to convince them otherwise, and soon, a large crowd had gathered. Zo ordered a bath drawn, and the monks scurried to prepare food and a chamber for Theo.

After the monks had doused, scrubbed, dried, and wrapped Theo in clean plain robes, a badger monk led Theo through a hallway to a small dining room. The table held plates of rough barley bread, hard cheese, apples, and a thick vegetable stew of potatoes, wild dandelion, and thyme. Hot mead steamed in wooden mugs, which both Father Oaks and Orjo sipped appreciatively. Zo sat at the head of the table, and two monks waited on them.

"Please join us," Zo said, indicating opposite her at the other head of the table. Theo pulled out the stool there and sat. "You have been seven days dead. You must be famished."

"I'm not sure my stomach remembers how to eat," Theo said. And it was true. He didn't feel hungry, though how his body was still moving or working at all was a mystery.

"Ye should eat somethin'," Father Oaks insisted. "Start small." He spooned some stew for Theo and set it before his grandson.

"You are welcome in the Temple of Clouds for as long as you wish to stay," Zo said.

"Thank you," Theo replied. "But I must get to Kalyun-eh, and the Library there."

Orjo glanced at him as he chewed a piece of bread. "So, you figured it out."

Theo's anger flared. "You knew all along." This muskrat had led him and his friends around in circles, nowhere near Kalyun-eh where they were meant to be going.

Orjo swallowed his bread. "I did."

"Then why didn't you tell us? Many in Jaipri died because of you," Theo said, voice tight. "I died because of you."

Orjo's face clouded. "Perhaps that's true. And for that..." He cleared his throat, the next sentence evidently hard for him to say. "I'm sorry."

Theo didn't reply.

"What matters is I'm here now," the muskrat said. "And you can choose to let me help you or not. I've saved your life, and I'll help you find the Library if you want."

"Why?"

Orjo regarded him, and Theo could see the old muskrat had asked himself the same question before. "I guess I believe in you. And it seems Aktu does as well."

Theo couldn't detect any sarcasm or flippancy. "Then apology accepted."

Oaks cleared his throat. "Now that's out of the way, what d'ye think ye'll find in this Library?"

Theo noticed everyone looking at him with interest. He remembered his exchange with the tortoise. "Pacification came from a *Book of Ills*. I believe if there was a *Book of Ills*, there must be a *Book of Cures*. And if it exists, it'll be in the Library. We'll need to leave soon, as I must go to Jaipri first to find Indigo and Brune."

Orjo swallowed a mouthful of stew and pointed his spoon at Theo. "No. Absolutely no finding Brune or Indigo."

Theo frowned. "Why not?"

"No one can know you're alive."

Theo absorbed this. "You're not making sense."

"You being dead is the greatest, if not only, advantage we have," the muskrat replied with forced patience. "If the Urzoks think you're dead, they won't be looking for you. You do remember, don't you, that when you were alive, every bounty hunter and cure seeker wanted your blood?"

The muskrat had a point, though it felt strange to try to keep such a big secret.

Father Oaks turned to Zo. "Ye think it's possible? All the monks here know."

Zo bowed her head. "If you wish. Such a miracle cannot be a secret forever, but we are very remote and have few dealings with the rest of Mankahar. We should be able to keep this quiet for a while."

Orjo nodded. "Good."

"Indigo and Brune can be trusted." If they were even alive. But they had to be. The tortoise had said that if Theo didn't return, those he loved most might die. Which meant they must still be safe somewhere.

The muskrat shook his head at Theo. "We tell no one, rabbit. I mean it. Word gets out that you're alive, and there won't be a rock in Mankahar we could hide under. I'm not walking into Kalyun-eh with a target on my back." At Theo's hesitation, Orjo's face turned hard. "Ask yourself, Theo Griffinrider, do you want to win the battle, or win the war?"

Theo's throat tightened. "Very well. We'll let everyone think I'm dead."

Zo pondered this, nodding. "I will order a ban on all speaking of these last few days here. And begging your pardon, Theo Griffinrider, do you have a plan for getting into Kalyun-eh? Even if you are believed dead, almost everyone knows the color and markings of Theo Griffinrider."

He hadn't thought of that. He pushed the stew around in his bowl, thinking. "Then we'll need to sneak in. Which means we'll likely need the help of an Urzok. Someone we trust."

"Well, wherever ye're goin', I'm comin' too," Father Oaks said.

Theo glanced at his grandfather, who had aged lifetimes since he'd last seen him in Willago. His worry must have shown, for the old rabbit bristled.

"Listen, lad, I've traveled across Mankahar with Urzok slavers, and I've been through more n' I thought I'd ever see in seven lifetimes." He pointed at his stub of an ear. "I've survived this. I'm tougher n' most."

Theo had never won any arguments back home either, so he knew that he wasn't going to win this now.

"And I'll help you enter the Library," Orjo said. "You know it's in Kalyun-eh. But what you don't know is that it's beneath the emperor's private quarters."

There was a moment of stunned silence around the table. They would be going not just to the empire's heart, but right under the emperor's nose.

"We'll definitely need the help of an Urzok," Theo said, an idea forming. "And I think I know who."

CHAPTER 6

As he dismounted in the central Vyad courtyard, Lord Ornox surveyed the row of servants lined up beneath the main veranda, braving the pouring rain to greet him.

Despite the weather, they were wearing their best. The butlers and housekeepers who had linen or silk wore those, while the chambermaids, pages, and horse boys had clearly washed and scrubbed their clothing and used hot flat stones to drive out the creases. Days before Ornox's retinue had arrived, a Vyad messenger had told them that his ancestral home, and his household, would be ready and waiting with a warm welcome, despite the chilly autumn day.

Ornox was not foolish enough to think they loved him. He was iron-willed, exacting, and had a reputation for cruelty. But his disgrace and losing his title had meant that his household staff had become little more than slaves working for the deformed royal advisor Brel. So they welcomed their former master's return, for his reinstatement meant their reinstatement, and being able to hold their heads high.

He gave them a curt nod from where he sat on his horse, and his hand wandered to the Vyad keys that lay beneath his shirt.

"Your rightful lord is back. I hope you have not forgotten how to serve your true master."

He let a flock of servants take his muddy cloak and horse, and waved away the butler, who hurried forward with an oiled parasol for him. What was the point? He was already soaked. Besides, he wanted to take a moment to look at the castle that had raised him. Where he had raised his daughter. The castle that the emperor had taken from him, and that he had now taken back. Rain ran in sheets from the shingled roofs, pattering a song of welcome on the courtyard stones.

As he dismounted and passed the cellar door, its surface scarred from the countless arrows and short knives thrown at it in practice sessions, he tried not to think of his daughter. But once she entered his head, Agacheta was everywhere. She had chipped a milk tooth in this very courtyard, climbed the branches of the gnarled white oak in the courtyard's corner, mastered her archery on that cellar door, despite her nurse's scolding. Vyad, he realized, was full of painful memories that would root him in the past. He would rot if he stayed here. Even more reason to take over the empire and move to the capital, Kalyun-eh. Only then would Agacheta's death be meaningful.

"Yod!" His servant materialized by his side. "I want a new door there by tomorrow."

Yod bowed. "I shall see it done."

Lord Ornox nodded. "And have that tree cut down while you're at it. Bring me hot wine, bread. And any messages."

* * *

From his sitting room window, Lord Ornox watched the workmen mark out the tree and ready their saws. It felt good to be back, to have his household moving around him as stars moved around their sun.

A knock drew him away from the window. "Enter." Yod

appeared. The look on his face warned Ornox the news would not be welcome.

"An imperial messenger has arrived," Yod said.

How perfectly timed. That his own household messenger had not mentioned a visitor from the capital meant that the emperor's man had waited unannounced outside Vyad for the warlord's return. And with good reason. If Ornox had known a messenger from the emperor was here, he would have found an excuse to delay his return. But there was no escape now.

"Offer him a meal, and say I will see him after."

"He insists he sees you now, my lord."

Ornox felt a flicker of irritation. Best he did not rile the emperor for now. "Then what are you waiting for? Send him in."

Yod bowed and retreated, pulling the door closed behind him. Ornox had only just pulled off his soaking cloak to steam by the fire when the door opened again, and Yod ushered in a well-groomed man of medium build, wearing the red and purple of the emperor.

"Greetings, Lord Ornox," the man said. "The emperor sends his warmest wishes and is delighted to see Mankahar's greatest hero back safe."

"His delight is my delight, as my every wish is to serve him," Ornox said. Yod moved to the sideboard, where he picked up a waiting pitcher of warm wine and a goblet.

"His Eminence insists you come to the capital to celebrate your victory."

Ornox took the goblet of wine Yod offered. "That is unnecessary. His Eminence does me too much honor."

Yod offered their guest a goblet, but the man shook his head. Turning back to Lord Ornox, he said, "His Eminence will not hear of your refusing."

Ornox chose his words carefully. "Then I am humbled and will head to the capital as soon as I have put my household in order."

"The emperor is most eager to see you, Lord Ornox, and insists you come without delay. Tonight, as a matter of fact."

Ornox swallowed his anger along with his wine. The emperor was indeed eager to see him. So be it. "What the emperor wishes, no man may deny. Am I right?"

The messenger bowed in agreement.

And when this is all over, I shall be the one whom no one denies.

* * *

IT HAD TAKEN several sleepless nights of burning candles in the deep recesses of the buried library, but Dorgun had felt the heartbeat of a plan forming. It had been so delicious in its first formations that he had to restrain himself from calling his advisors right then and putting his plan into motion. But he forced himself to work out all the details, to research and plot until he knew he had accounted for every turn of events.

Only then did he summon his advisors to his audience chamber with its balcony overlooking the city. He could still hear the songs about Ornox being sung, but this time, the tune and the voices only excited him. Let them sing. Let Ornox have his time in the sun. Killing the powerful lion was, after all, so much more satisfying than slaying the timid deer.

After Haegon had arrived and prostrated himself, Dorgun said, "Send out invitations to all the noble families. We will host a feast on my birthday. Tell them I will announce my heir then."

Haegon raised an eyebrow at this. "Very good, Your Eminence. May I ask—"

"No." Dorgun wagged a finger. "Until the day, only I shall know who will rule Mankahar upon my death. Declare a public holiday, and arrange free food and drink for all in the streets. Entertainers, gifts, spectacles. Spare no expense, understood? But above all, make sure the noble families come to the feast."

Haegon bowed. "I will see to the messengers myself. Is that all, Your Eminence?"

"Send for the royal tailor. And bring me the city's best carpenter."

"Very good, Your Eminence," Haegon said, though the curiosity showed in his face. "Will this be for the day's entertainment?"

The emperor laughed, something he hadn't done for a long time. "Yes, Haegon. It will be for entertainment. The greatest entertainment Mankahar has ever seen."

CHAPTER 7

Theo tried not to scratch at the paint surrounding his eyes.

Orjo had insisted he disguise himself, as everyone in Mankahar now knew his markings. It had been easy enough to put on, but now that the mid-morning sun had dried it, his skin was beginning to itch.

"Think of somethin' else," his grandfather advised, walking next to him and Orjo. This advice proved easier than Theo thought, as there was much to look at in the city of New Hegg. Despite the war, Brune's birthplace was large and sprawling, and the wide grid streets spread away from steep cliff caves that rose to the west.

"That's the old Hegg, there," Orjo said, noticing Theo studying the cliffs. "Until the Urzoks destroyed it and built this new city."

They had entered through New Hegg's eastern gate and were now traveling to the northernmost section, where they had been told the lord's mansion was. The mansion and its gardens had been built by Urzoks, but now the Order had taken over. Many Urzoks, it seemed, had lived under their new rulers rather than escape to the southern cities, but the vast majority had fled, fearing that the Order's promises of equal treatment might be hollow. Thus the streets bustled with a mixed population—tall, lanky black bears, short golden sun bears, Urzoks of dark hair and face and those with lighter skin and reddish-brown braids. Tall, broad hares with impossibly long ears and legs, as well as badgers, stoats, and spiky porcupines made up the rest of the busy passersby in the streets. Hawkers shouted out their wares, and the smells of fried onion, cheese, weed soup, and barley porridge with cranberries mixed in the early autumn air.

Theo and Father Oaks wore non-descript traveler robes they had bartered for on the way. Zo had procured Orjo a few sets of fancier attire in their sizes, to help with their plan in Hegg. Irah and Hygra had flown them down from the Temple of Clouds once Zo had deemed Theo fit to travel, but the Proudfeathers had hinted that they wished to return home to their waiting family. And so they had said their goodbyes, with the Proud-feather matriarch promising that if they ever needed her help again, she would provide it.

The streets began sloping upward as they neared the lord's mansion, and Theo's pulse quickened at the thought of catching a glimpse of Lord Noshi. He would have loved to seek the wise man who led the Order, but Orjo had been adamant.

"Remember how you ended up dead in the first place? Sold out by your allies. Only those who need to know should be told. No one else."

As they drew closer to the hill on which the lord's mansion sat, they studied the various inns nearby until Orjo chose one that was respectable without being exorbitant. Orjo arranged for rooms on credit, citing his employer's arrival the next day, and the innkeeper judged Orjo to be trustworthy based on the fine weave of his robes. Once they had settled in, Orjo asked Theo again for the name he sought, and set off.

Father Oaks busied himself with washing off the dust of travel, and Theo debated about wiping away his face paint. But he found himself looking out the window at the lord's mansion just across the way. It was a gilded, monstrous thing, all twisted black iron tipped with gold, but inside it, he knew, the Order ruled their newly retaken city. He burned to go in, to see Lord Noshi and ask whether there had been any word of Indigo or Brune. His heart thudded. What if Indigo and Brune were here? It was possible. If they had survived Eluk's attack, they would come here, back to safety. This thought glued him to watching the mansion, scrutinizing everyone who went in or out, hoping yet dreading seeing either Indigo or Brune.

He was still by the window as dusk fell. When the innkeeper knocked to bring dinner, he was watching a large group of rabbits coming out of the manor, all tall and swaggering, with large plugs of metal in their ears. He had never seen rabbits like these.

"Who are those rabbits?" he asked the innkeeper, a short man with a ruddy mustache that covered half his mouth.

The man put down the tray of food before Father Oaks and came to the window. "Ah. Irontails. The word around is their prince is here to marry one of the Order. A princess in her own right, I heard. A warrior."

Theo felt a foreboding. "Princess Indigo?"

The innkeeper pointed a finger at Theo, as if he had won a prize. "That's the one."

The innkeeper left, closing the door behind him, and Theo stood rooted to the window.

Indigo was here. And to be married.

His thoughts fled in all directions, and a tightness squeezed his chest. It had only been a moon since he had died. How had she already met someone and arranged for marriage? Who was this groom to be, besides a prince? Did she love him? The possibility cut him to the core, making him too depressed to even pick at his food, which his grandfather noticed.

"The plan'll work, lad," Father Oaks reassured him, mistaking the reason for Theo's mood. "Orjo'll find him soon, ye'll see."

This, at least, proved true. As the night deepened and the

streets emptied, a firm double knock sounded on the door. Father Oaks looked at Theo, who nodded, then opened the door.

Orjo swept in, followed by a figure in a bright green-and-yellow cloak. He had aged since Theo lad last seen him, but Theo recognized the tall, thin man with the weathered face and the colorful cap. And he also recognized the red-furred monkey with the black face, known as a Grodlyn, sitting on Reenan's shoulder. Manneki had stowed away with Brune and Theo when they had first visited Jaipri, and ended up saving Theo's life when his brother Harlan had cast him down a well at Ralgayan. Theo couldn't help grinning at meeting his old friend again, but he cast a look at Orjo.

The muskrat shrugged. "The man insisted."

As soon as Father Oaks had closed the door, Reenan bowed to Theo and Father Oaks, no recognition on his face. "Your servant tells me you seek an entertainer, my lords? In which case you'll find none better than my partner and me right here. I'm Reenan of Reenan's Spectacular, and this is Manneki the Magnificent. May I know whose employ I have the honor of entering?"

"This is Father Oaks," Orjo said, gesturing at the old rabbit. "And I believe you've met the other one."

Reenan raised his eyebrows. "I have? I apologize, I don't recall."

Theo stepped closer. "Hello, Reenan."

Recognition flickered across the man's face before further confusion set in.

"It's me, Theo." The rabbit took a towel from the basin nearby and wiped the paint from his face.

Manneki shrieked and flew like an arrow from Reenan's shoulder, his paws barely touching the floor before his furry red arms wrapped around Theo's neck in a python-like grip.

"Theo! Theo, Theo, Theo!"

Theo managed to pat the little monkey's shoulder before gasping out, "I've died once already. Don't kill me with choking!"

"Or with that shriek," Orjo muttered, holding a paw to his ear.

The monkey let go and stared up at Theo, his black face beaming.

"But you're dead," Reenan exclaimed.

"Well, not anymore, it seems." Theo gave a rueful grin. "I'll tell you how later. For now, I have two favors to ask." At Reenan's expression, Theo's voice quietened. "I know. The last time you did me a favor it cost you much."

"And this time it won't?"

"It probably will."

Reenan sighed. "You sent me here, which likely saved my life. Lord Noshi has given me every protection and comfort I could ask for."

Theo nodded. "As Brune said he would."

"Go on then," Reenan said.

"The first favor is to tell no one I'm alive."

Reenan stared at him. "No one? What about Brune? Noshi? Or Indi—"

Theo's chest tightened, but before he could speak, Orjo broke in. "No one," the muskrat said and scowled at Manneki. "I didn't even want this fellow to know."

The Grodlyn glared back. Theo waded in, eager to avoid arguments. "The fewer who know, the better. So, you'll need to keep quiet about me and come up with another excuse for your leaving Hegg."

"Wait—leave Hegg?"

"Yes. Which brings me to the second favor. I need you to get me into a city, undetected."

"Dangerous, but not impossible."

"We need to enter Kalyun-eh."

The man's face blanched, and even Manneki's usual plucky demeanour cracked. "The capital? You wish to die twice?"

"The Library of Elshon is there, and we need it if we are to have any hope of saving ourselves. Of saving all this." Theo gestured outside the window.

"The empire is likely hunting for me," Reenan protested. "I would be foolish to enter the capital."

"More foolish than I?" Theo asked. Reenan looked away. "You're the only one I can ask," Theo pressed. "You're the only man I can trust, outside of Noshi, and he cannot leave the Order. The Order needs him here."

Reenan glanced at Theo and Father Oaks, hopeful. "If I die, can I be resurrected too?"

"Doubtful," Orjo said frankly.

"I thought not." He bit his lip, then looked from Theo to Manneki, who watched him, expectant. He sighed. "Well then, when do we leave?"

CHAPTER 8

The air around Pozzi felt hot and close, and he tried to calm his breathing. It was hard to not panic and take in deep lungfuls of air, but he was worried that would make him choke.

He felt a paw on his arm and looked back at Indigo's silhouette.

"Count your breaths. It'll help," she whispered.

He took her advice and found his heart settling. He was grateful the levelheaded princess with the strange tattoos was here on this day.

They were close now. He could tell by the gradual upward slope of the tunnel floor. He had helped dig out almost every pawful of this tunnel, and knew it well.

But today, he would not be digging.

Today would bring him, Keeva, and Walnut one step closer to going home. But to do so, he was helping a wolf and his forces capture a little girl.

Capture only, he reminded himself. He paused as Argasar's lieutenant in front of him, Nartah, stopped to listen. Behind him, Indigo also paused.

"What is it, Nartah?" Argasar growled.

The beta shook his head. "I thought I heard the bell."

"Too early," Pozzi insisted. But they needed to hasten. The bell would call the household to meals and signal the end of morning lessons for Hassah. The girl's governess would then, without fail, take her to the courtyard for play and exercise. Who did the girl play with, Pozzi wondered, now that he, Keeva, and Walnut were gone? The girl was but six summers, and though they had been her captives of sorts, Pozzi had a fondness for her that he knew Keeva and especially Walnut shared. He couldn't let anything happen to Hassah.

Nartah padded forward again, and Pozzi hurried to keep up. He could hear the tread of the hundred or more wolves behind him, the clicking of the wooden shin guards and head plates Keeva and the other rabbits had sewn together. The wolves moved two abreast, and again Pozzi marveled at what the rabbits had achieved: a tunnel five paces wide and over a league long. It was ingenious and crazed all at once.

Pozzi took a deep breath and regretted it. The tunnel smelled of damp earth, tepid breath, and something else Pozzi didn't like. Bloodlust.

The path sloped upward again, and Nartah stopped. Beneath his paws, Pozzi could feel the three ridges of wood that signaled there were only a hundred steps to the private chapel floor above. They had dug up through the private chapel on Pozzi's advice, as he knew Ghazan seldom used it. This meant it was empty and unguarded except for on holy days.

Everyone in the tunnel crouched and waited for the signal.

Up through the floor, to the hallway, down to the other end of the wing where the kitchens and the courtyards were. Where Hassah would be playing, as she did at this time every day. He, Argasar, Indigo, and Nartah were to secure Hassah. One team of wolves was to engage the inevitable guards they would encounter, while the other team would bolt for Nyatha's eastern gate. They were to open it so Brune could lead the rest of Argasar's forces who would subdue any remaining resistance.

But it wouldn't get to that if they had Hassah. Ghazan was many things, but he was a father, and he would not want to see his child harmed.

They waited in the dark, ears straining to hear the bell. And then he heard it: the faint pealing designed to be heard through the thickest walls. Pozzi held up a paw. They had to give the household time to respond to the bell. A moment passed. Two. But that was as long as Pozzi could hold them.

"Move!"

Argasar's snarl sent a current of excitement through the wolves in the tunnel, and Nartah barreled forward, using the flat of his head to push aside the large piece of slate that the rabbits had chiseled loose in the chapel floor. The square of slate fell to one side, and Nartah scrabbled out of the tunnel and up to the chapel.

Pozzi pulled himself up, followed by Indigo. Argasar leapt out in one fluid motion and waited as the wolves behind him scrabbled up and fanned out around the room. Pozzi looked around at the few pews and the statue of the emperor Dorgun against one window, staring down at them in silence.

Soon the small chapel was full of wolves, and Argasar was organizing them into various groups: one team for the gate; one team to cover the Hassah mission. When they were ready, Argasar nodded to Pozzi.

The rabbit helped Nartah and Indigo open the heavy chapel doors. The hallway was as he remembered it from his days as Hassah's pet, with long, thick carpets covering the floor. Left led to the audience hall and private quarters. Right led to the kitchens and the courtyard.

Pozzi listened for the usual sounds of activity and could hear chatter and laughter coming from the private chambers. He stole out to the right, willing his heart to stay in his chest.

Argasar padded at his heels, while Indigo brought up the rear with Nartah. A shout of surprise sounded behind them, and Pozzi turned to see a chambermaid drop her tray of cutlery.

A swarm of wolves pooled into the hallway from the chapel. The chambermaid spun around and screamed for help, running away from them. A few of the wolves gave chase, and Argasar nudged Pozzi with his snout.

"Hurry. The sooner we find Hassah, the quicker this ends."

Pozzi swallowed and rushed down the hallway, his paws remembering the way to the courtyard. Nartah followed alongside to shield Pozzi from anyone they might encounter, while Indigo and Argasar followed close behind.

They turned one corner to find themselves face to face with two guards bearing halberds. A skirmish ensued, and between the two wolves and Indigo, they brought the men down, but not before one of them landed a long gash across Indigo's arm.

"Are you all right?" Pozzi asked, but the princess waved him off.

"A tiny cut," she said. "Let's hurry. There'll be more guards soon."

They broke in upon the kitchens, and the staff there barely had time to register the wolves in their midst. Panicked cries broke out as the scullery maids fled, and the cook leapt up onto the bread table, a pan in one fist.

Pozzi and his throng ran past them and out the door to the courtyard. It was as Pozzi remembered—the fountain in the middle, the fish cistern at the side. The only thing missing was Hassah herself.

"Where is she?" Argasar asked, terse.

"I—I don't know," Pozzi said, confused. She was always here at this time of day. Where could she be?

By now, they could hear frenzied shouts from down the hall where the chambermaid had gone. She had alerted soldiers, and they heard the unmistakable clash of metal along with the thunder of boots as defenders grabbed weapons to repel Argasar's pack. There were howls of pain from wolves and humans alike. The carnage had begun.

"Think, Pozzi!" Argasar snapped.

Where could Hassah be?

"The staff will know," Indigo said, and she motioned for them to follow her.

Why hadn't he thought of that? They ran back into the kitchen, where the cook was clambering off the table, pan abandoned. She froze at the reappearance of the wolves, eyes darting toward the door.

"Where's the girl?" Argasar growled.

The cook blinked.

"Hassah!" Pozzi said. "Where's Mistress Hassah?"

Something seemed to click in the cook's mind, and she pointed out of the kitchens.

"North garden," she croaked. Pozzi rushed out, Indigo and the two wolves following. They crossed the courtyard and through an archway, down a flight of steps. and into a sunken garden. A few workers were hoeing the plots, and at the wolves' appearance, they gave shouts of alarm. Before Pozzi could stop them, Argasar had leaped on the closest man, and Nartah took down the second, their fangs sinking into flesh. Nartah's man escaped, stumbling and bleeding from his torn forearm as he fled to the kitchens, but Argasar's man went down and lay still, the surrounding ground darkening.

Pozzi stood, frozen in shock.

"Find the girl," Argasar snapped, lips bloodied.

"Come." Indigo was tugging on Pozzi's arm, and she pulled him with her past the garden beds of half-tilled vegetables, until they were into the children's garden beyond. It was called the children's garden because they had planted it with whatever took the children's fancy. Huckleberry and apple trees, sunflowers and nodding poppies grew in random patches, separated by a pebbled path.

At the end of the path was a bench tucked into a nook of ivy, where a little girl with curly black hair sat in a prim silk dress. Next to her stood a stout woman—the nursemaid Farriah had gained weight, Pozzi couldn't help but notice. A painter in a smock sat opposite Hassah, paintbrush poised over a canvas where a likeness of the girl was taking shape. His expression of annoyance at being interrupted twisted to fear when he saw the wolves.

"Pozzi?" The girl's tentative excitement at seeing him faded at the sight of the wolves, and Pozzi felt sick.

"Come with us, Hassah. I'll explain in a while."

"You're not taking her anywhere." Farriah's voice shook as she pulled the girl to her. "Get away."

Argasar bared his teeth. "Give us the girl, Urzok."

Farriah shook her head, but her face paled to ash. Hassah looked from Pozzi to the advancing wolves with growing fear. The painter made to run, but a sharp snarl from Nartah stopped him.

"Farriah," Pozzi pleaded. "We won't hurt her."

The nurse's eyes looked panicked. "The mistress should have pacified you when she had the chance."

Nartah made to leap, but Indigo held out an arm to stop him. "Farriah, is it? You have my word we won't harm either of you. But you must both come with us."

Argasar stepped forward, making the nurse recoil. "I came to take Nyatha, and I can take it with violence or I can take it with little bloodshed. Pozzi is offering you the choice to save lives."

"Please," Pozzi urged.

Farriah looked from them to Hassah. "Come, Hassah. It'll be all right."

"Yes, it will," Argasar said, then motioned to Nartah, who took up position behind Farriah and Hassah. They turned and rushed back out of the garden, leaving the painter frozen where he stood. They moved through the courtyard and into the now-deserted kitchen. In the hallway, they heard shouts and fighting from the main foyer. The Nyatha bell pealed again, this time in fast, desperate clangs rather than the usual calm, even tones.

"This way." Pozzi led Argasar, Indigo, and the prisoners up a flight of servants' stairs, then another, encountering only a dozen chambermaids fleeing the other way.

Pozzi, Indigo, and Argasar reached the upper landing, and Nartah drove Farriah and Hassah before him. Pozzi had picked this spot because it was high up, overlooking the main foyer where the battle had coalesced. Below them, they could see a tangle of wolves and Urzok soldiers, one side using teeth and claws and the other side using swords and spears. There were snarls and shouts to seal off corridors, and screams of pain punctuated by the crack of wood and bone.

Argasar's howl filled the foyer up to the rafters, making everyone below look up.

"Ghazan!" the wolf barked. "Tell Ghazan of Nyatha to surrender."

There were cries of defiance below, at which Argasar nodded to Nartah. The wolf gave Farriah a rough nudge. The nursemaid stepped toward the balustrade with Hassah, who looked to Pozzi for reassurance. He reached out and squeezed her hand.

"Ghazan," Argasar called out. "I have your daughter. Put down your arms now, and she lives."

There was a long, heavy silence. Maybe Ghazan wasn't there. But then the Urzok soldiers in the foyer below parted as someone shoved his way through their ranks. Pozzi recognized the melon-green clothes, the pudgy face.

"Let her go, wolf."

Argasar grinned. "Surrender Nyatha."

"Let him kill her, Father!"

Pozzi would recognize that voice anywhere. Hassah's brother emerged from the crowd, a carved wooden mask covering most of his face. But Pozzi knew the boy's soul was much more hideous than his face, and no mask would ever hide that. The rabbit squeezed Hassah's hand even harder, knowing her brother's statement had wounded her more than any cut she'd suffered so far.

"Silence, boy!" Ghazan's reprimand came with a sound cuffing to the boy's head. Sarkus glared at his father.

"You can't hope to hold Nyatha, wolf," Ghazan said, looking up. "The empire will be here before you can blink."

Argasar licked the blood from his lips, his grin even wider. "I hope so, Ghazan. Now, what's it to be? Your daughter? Or your surrender?"

Ghazan glared at the wolf, then shouted his command. "Drop your weapons."

As the Urzoks relinquished their weapons and the wolves formed bands to comb Nyatha and round up any remaining defenders, Pozzi tried to quell the disquiet he felt at Argasar's words. Did the wolf wish for an even bigger battle than this one? He looked at Indigo and saw a flicker of unease cross her features as well. At least he wasn't the only one worried.

CHAPTER 9

The road to Kalyun-eh was long, even with the pacified donkey and the sturdy cart Reenan had sourced.

Reenan had explained that the rich rode pacified horses between towns, but regular trader folk had mules or donkeys. They would attract less attention with a single donkey cart, and attention was something they hoped to avoid. Reenan drove the cart, with Manneki next to him, and Theo, Orjo, and Oaks bounced and jostled on the one thin bench inside. A threadbare cloth stretched over the cart's four poles kept the worst of the sun off the occupants. Traveling supplies and boxes of herbs and spices crammed every other unoccupied space, so that they could pose as spice traders.

When they'd ridden past Hegg's gates, Theo had felt a tug of pain. Would Indigo ride into these same gates in the next days? He was dead to her, and Manneki had, after much wrangling on Theo's part, admitted that Indigo's marriage to the Irontail prince Ebben was soon, though not yet set.

"It'll be all right, lad," Oaks said, seeing his expression. "Try not to look backward, but focus on what's ahead."

Theo took his grandfather's advice literally and climbed up

onto the seat next to Manneki and Reenan, turning his back on the gates of Hegg.

"What did you tell Noshi? About why you were leaving?" Theo asked.

"I told him I needed to see an old friend," the man replied. "Which isn't untrue."

"Thank you," Theo said. "I know you are again risking everything you have built just to help me."

Reenan looked over at him. "You and Brune and Indigo were the ones who gave me the chance to start over. So maybe I should thank you." The man indicated the little Grodlyn sitting squeezed between them. "I would never have met Manneki here otherwise, and he's the jewel of my new show."

The Grodlyn's black face broke into a proud grin.

Theo had forgotten how much he had missed the imp's smile. "I thought you wanted to become an Ihaktu, Manneki, a warrior of the Order like—like Indigo." He tried to cover his hesitation over her name, but thankfully, Manneki seemed too excited to notice.

"Manneki is top Ihaktu! For Reenan!"

At Theo's look, Reenan explained, "He performs fighting moves. Crowds love it. We're calling him 'Monkey Marvelous.'"

The Grodlyn glared up at him. "No, Manneki the Magnificent."

Reenan's expression said this was an old argument. "It's under discussion."

Theo looked away, hiding a smile. The cart had turned at a bend in the road as they left New Hegg, and now, the trampled dirt path wound up through sparsely populated hills. There were fewer travelers here, and the further away they drew from New Hegg, the more ramshackle the dwellings became. Signs of the fight for Hegg were still visible: scorched hills, burned out huts, and blackened stone walls. Some were being repaired by inhabitants bent by tragedy, while other homes had been abandoned. Everyone paid a price for this war with the Urzoks.

It has to end, Theo thought.

Just after midday, they stopped to tighten a loose front wheel. They let the donkey graze on a patch of grass near an old burned-out temple with a crumbling cottage attached to the back. While Reenan unhitched the donkey and took out tools to adjust the wheel, Theo helped Father Oaks step off the cart and stretch his legs. Orjo followed and gazed at the temple, assessing.

"Urzok," he stated.

"You sound happy," Theo said.

"Urzok temples often have a brewery, which means ale, or if we're lucky, mead." And with that, Orjo was off.

"Manneki don't like that muskrat," the red-furred Grodlyn confided to Theo. "Orjo the Terrible called Terrible for good reason."

"Yes, he's been terrible," Theo agreed. "But he's on our side now."

"Theo must be careful," Manneki said, black face scrunched. "Kalyun-eh is dangerous, but Orjo the Terrible worse."

The muskrat had betrayed Theo twice, tried to kill him once, and had been dishonest more times than Theo could count. But Theo somehow knew that he could trust Orjo with his life. There just wasn't a way to explain that to Manneki.

"If your rat friend is ready, we should get moving," Reenan said, testing the wheel bolts. From his tone, Theo could tell Reenan shared Manneki's misgivings. Orjo the Terrible had lived a long life, but his reputation seemed to have been around for a lot longer. Everyone knew the legend of the omatje sorcerer, one whose name was synonymous with ruthlessness.

"I'll go get him," Theo offered, seeing his grandfather and Manneki were busy helping Reenan check the other wheels. Theo set off, heading toward the blackened shell of the temple. The wood roof had almost completely burned away, with only blackened stumps to show where it once was. Soot caked the walls, and a wooden door teetered on its one intact metal hinge.

"Orjo!" Theo called. There was no answer. "We're leaving!"

When the muskrat didn't reply, Theo walked to the doorway and peered in. It was a small space, only ten steps in each direction. A blackened marble statue, its head half gone, stood in the middle of the temple, with cracked benches lining the walls. Theo had never been inside an Urzok temple, but he knew they worshipped the Emperor Dorgun. The first emperor had banned all other forms of worship.

"Orjo? Where are you?" Theo stepped in, trying to see if there was another room. When he reached the other side of the statue, he noticed a ring of fresh flowers leaning against the emperor's feet, with a doll slumped head down.

The doll was a rabbit made of gray fabric. Dread gnawed at him, but Theo couldn't help himself. He picked up the doll, its head flopping backward to reveal black eye patches and black paws.

Just like Theo's.

It *was* Theo. Or meant to be him, anyway.

A cow's bone, carved to look like a sword, was thrust through the rabbit's chest. The scar where Ornox's sword had gone through Theo tingled, as if remembering the feel of metal.

He dropped the doll, sickened.

"You should have seen the ones they made of me."

Theo turned and saw Orjo standing in the doorway.

"Why is it here? Why did they make it?"

"It's an offering," Orjo said, matter-of-factly. "A thanks. There are a lot of folks who are glad the Griffinrider's dead."

Theo felt queasy. To be the target of such hate was bewildering, and if this one was here, how many more were there?

"You better get used to it, Griffinrider," Orjo said, seeing Theo's expression. "We'll only be getting deeper into Urzok territory, and I suspect you'll be seeing more and more of this type of thing. Besides, that's not the worst part."

Theo frowned. "What?"

"I've looked in every cranny except under Blackhide's tail. There's no mead."

CHAPTER 10

*P*ozzi stood in Nyatha's main courtyard with Walnut, watching as Ghazan loaded a rustic cart with the few basic provisions Argasar had allowed his family—some dried foods, water, and blankets. Tansha stood with Sarkus, their faces sullen. Argasar and a dozen of his wolves, including Nartah, stood nearby, watching the proceedings with stony hostility. Hassah was the only one who looked a mixture of bewilderment and fear, her favorite doll under one arm, the other hand gripping her mother's. Pozzi's heart ached for her.

"I'll see you in Kalyun-eh," Ghazan said to his wife, squeezing her hand. He held both his children to him and then nudged them toward the cart. "Go now. Heed your mother, and I'll join you soon."

"I want to stay home," Hassah said.

Ghazan bent and took her hand. "You can't, my girl. But don't worry, Papa will be there before you know it."

Tansha seemed to be holding back tears, but at Ghazan's look, she hurried the children to the cart, clambering into the driver's seat and taking the reins.

Pozzi couldn't help but go forward and take Hassah's hand in his paw. "It's not safe for you here, Hassah. But everything will be all right. You'll see."

He didn't miss the cold look Tansha gave him, or the hateful one that Sarkus directed his way. Walnut clambered into the cart to hug Hassah.

"To think I saved you from the Cradles," Ghazan muttered bitterly to Pozzi, who stood next to him.

Anger flared in Pozzi. "I saved you from the wolves, so perhaps that makes us even."

"My pack will escort you out for a league or so," Argasar said to Tansha, stepping forward.

"I don't need your escort," the woman said stiffly.

"You may not need it, but you'll have it," the wolf insisted. "I don't want you secretly returning to Nyatha and attempting to free your husband."

With a last look at Ghazan, Tansha snapped the reins, and the donkey trotted forward. Nartah led three other wolves alongside the small family, out of the courtyard and through the open side gates of the Nyatha compound.

Pozzi watched the gates shut behind them, then squeezed Walnut's shoulders reassuringly.

"Where will she go, Pozzi?"

"I don't know. The capital, maybe. But she'll be all right, Walnut." He tamped down his misgivings. He had convinced Argasar to give Hassah, Tansha, and Sarkus their lives and freedom, he was powerless to do any more. On the point of Ghazan, Argasar had been immovable. He would keep Ghazan here to prevent him from joining and helping the empire's forces.

Having helped Argasar take Nyatha, they were free to leave. The thought warmed Pozzi, and even made the smoky destruction around them seem less ugly.

"Come, let's find Keeva," he told Walnut. "It's time to prepare ourselves for going home."

* * *

THE INFIRMARY HAD SPREAD from one chamber to three in order to accommodate the wounded. Wolves and rabbits alike had sustained cuts, broken bones, and arrow wounds from the siege, and Argasar's few healers were trying to cater as best they could. Pallets took up every available floor space, and the manor's curtains and linens had been stripped to make bandages. Curses and howls rang out as inexperienced healers tried to remove arrows or sew wounds.

Indigo observed all this from her cot, where she waited for treatment. Clearly, Argasar had planned out the attack, but not the aftermath. His forces were woefully unprepared for the demands for healing, rebuilding, and defenses that Nyatha would now need. For when the empire heard their northern-most trading post had fallen, they would come with a vendetta.

"I'm told we should wash that with this."

Indigo looked over. Keeva had appeared with a basin of bitter-smelling water and a clean towel. Indigo's cuts were just that, mere cuts, but Theo had taught her that the smallest wounds could kill if left untended.

"You look sad," Keeva commented, wringing out the towel and placing it against the gash on Indigo's arm.

"Just remembering someone."

Keeva smiled in sympathy. "I'm sure you've seen a lot of loss."

Indigo steered the conversation away. "How long have you and Pozzi been married?"

Keeva glanced up, her long silken ears flushing. "We're not married. And Walnut's not our son. His mother died, and Pozzi and I—I suppose we became a family of sorts."

Indigo wondered whether Keeva shared the adoration for Pozzi that Pozzi clearly had for Keeva. "I see. Argasar referred to you as his wife."

The lavender rabbit looked away, busying herself with the bandage. "My first marriage was... possibly the worst mistake of my life. I'm not keen to make a second." She looked at Indigo. "What about you? Is there a love in your life?"

Indigo prepared to brush the question off with a polite lie, but the words stuck. She hadn't talked about Theo—at least, her feelings for Theo—with anyone, not even Brune.

"There was someone. But he's dead."

"I'm sorry," Keeva stopped unrolling a bandage of linen, repentant. "And I am sorry to have asked."

"It's all right." Something about the doe made Indigo feel like confiding. Was it just that this was another female she could talk to? She hadn't had a female friend since she had left home. "And now I might be forced to marry a stranger. For political reasons."

"Perhaps an arranged marriage won't be as bad as you fear," Keeva said. "After all, I chose my husband, he was the worst choice possible."

"That terrible?"

Keeva's voice hardened. "Harlan betrayed us to the Urzoks. My husband was how we came to be in Nyatha in the first place."

Indigo had no words. She stayed silent as Keeva finished bandaging her cut.

Brune came through the infirmary door, helmet under one burly arm. He waded between the patients, and as he neared Indigo's bench, he motioned for her.

"Go ahead," Keeva said. "That should be all clean."

"Thank you," Indigo said, sincere. "And if it's not too bold…" She hesitated, then said, "Pozzi seems to have a good heart. I don't think he would be a mistake."

Keeva smiled at her. "I don't think so either."

Indigo picked her way through the patients and healers to Brune. "Ready to find some black snow?"

The bear grunted. "Let's hope it's here."

As they walked through the manor and down to the main hall, the heady euphoria sweeping Argasar's forces was evident. Nyatha's flags bearing Ghazan's crest were being piled for burning in the central courtyard, and many of the wolves and rabbits wore looted keepsakes like gold rings or gem bracelets.

"Boasts of victory are the seeds of defeat," Brune muttered.

"Do you think Argasar has thought about how he's going to hold Nyatha, now that he has it?" Indigo asked.

The bear shook his head. "Doubt it. That eastern door I came through during the attack caved with barely a knock of my fist. Nyatha's a trading post, not built for siege. There's no moat, no drawbridge. I don't want to be here when the empire arrives, crazed as a mama bear coming for her cubs."

The comparison, Indigo knew, was apt. On the first day, the victors had freed all the imprisoned animals and asked them to join Argasar. Almost all agreed, as most had no homes to return to, even if they were willing to turn down food, board, and a place in Argasar's growing army. The wolves had then imprisoned all the Urzoks in the newly vacant pens. Indigo had suggested Argasar assign over half his forces to cutting down trees and designing defense stakes around Nyatha's perimeter, but she saw no sign of action.

"The only thing that can save them is what can save us," she said. "Black snow."

Brune nodded. "Let's have a talk with Ghazan, shall we?"

* * *

THE FORMER HEAD OF NYATHA, once lord of the manor and all its inhabitants, seemed worn numb when Indigo and Brune arrived. Argasar had placed Ghazan in one of the high attic rooms of the manor, with one narrow window that offered only three things—fresh air, a view of the man's former lands, and a sharp plunge to death below should he decide to try to escape. The room had a pallet and a wooden chamber pot, but little else.

"What do you lot want now?" Ghazan asked as guards ushered the bear and rabbit in. Indigo closed the door behind them.

"I want to know what Ornox was doing here," Indigo said.

The man shrugged. "It's a trading post. Everyone comes here."

"What was Ornox trading?"

She caught a flicker of wariness in Ghazan's eye, and she knew she was about to hear a lie.

"He needed meat and supplies for his troops."

"He wasn't here to trade or resupply his black snow?"

"No."

Indigo pounced. "So you know what black snow is?"

"No! I didn't say that," Ghazan reddened. "I simply meant he was here trading meat and supplies. Nothing else."

Brune crossed his arms. "Argasar can make your life much worse if you don't tell us what you know."

Ghazan scowled. "And Ornox would do worse than that."

"Ornox isn't here right now," Brune added helpfully. "But Argasar is. And so am I."

The jowly trader looked from one to the other and sighed. "Ornox had me hire an alchemist. He came to see her and her progress."

Indigo's pulse quickened. She had been right. "Where is she?"

"She's dead." Ghazan rubbed his cheek, looking much older than the fifty years Indigo guessed he had seen. "I saw the wolves kill her when she tried to keep them out of her cottage."

"You're sure?" Brune asked.

The man nodded.

"Who else knows how to make black snow?" Indigo pressed.

"No one."

"No assistants?"

Ghazan shook his head. "I offered. But she works alone. No one but a pacified canary with her."

Indigo tried to hide her frustration. A dead end.

"How much black snow did the alchemist make?" Brune asked.

"Barely any. We were about to make more when you attacked."

Indigo thought on this. "How did you find your alchemist?"

Ghazan snorted. "I'm a merchant. I have my ways."

"This isn't a business dealing," Brune growled. "It's an interrogation. How did you find your alchemist?"

The man scowled at him. "I found Ethana through the alchemists' guild. She was the most recommended."

"And where would we find this guild?" Indigo pressed.

"I don't know." At Brune's threatening growl, Ghazan held up his hands, indignant. "The guild comes to you, you don't go to them. My chamberlain organized our meeting. He'll know how to contact them."

"And where's your chamberlain?" Brune asked.

Ghazan sniffed, bitter. "You tell me. Argasar's imprisoned everyone. If my chamberlain's alive, he'll be wherever Argasar's keeping them. My chamberlain has a horseshoe shaped scar here," Ghazan tapped his temple.

Brune nodded and glanced at Indigo. "I'll go search the prisoners."

When he had left, Ghazan turned back to Indigo. "Any more questions, or can I finally have some peace?"

"One more. Where's the alchemist's cottage?"

CHAPTER 11

*L*ady Tansha's first clue that something was amiss was when the wolves insisted she guide the donkey cart off the main road from Nyatha. The forest path that Tansha and her children now traveled along was little more than a dirt track, with pines and firs growing thick in a gully below it, and no other travelers to be seen.

"How much further do you intend to accompany us?" Tansha had asked several times. And the answer had always been the same from the lead wolf, the large-eyed one called Nartah.

"As long as it takes."

She tried not to buckle and sob. She had kept up a brave face for as long as she could, but she was at a loss without Ghazan, without her home. The tears welled and splashed her tight hands, which pulled the reins so taut that the donkey brayed repeatedly in protest. The children sat in tense silence behind her. Anger smoldered in Sarkus, as it normally did, close to the surface, while her daughter, Hassah, observed everything with an innocence that made all this even harder for Tansha. Once they were in Kalyun-eh, things would be better, she told herself. She'd find her sister. Her sister and her sister's husband would know what to do. They'd wait it out, until Ghazan could join them, drive out the horrid beasts and retake Nyatha. Things would go back to how they'd been. Ghazan, once freed, would make sure of it. She just had to make it to Kalyun-eh.

She was so preoccupied with these thoughts that she missed the nod between the wolves.

Nartah, the lead wolf who had always loped at a steady pace next to the cart, bolted forward. The donkey, more attuned to danger than Tansha, brayed and bucked as the wolf landed on its back and sank its fangs into the animal's shoulder below the neck.

Tansha screamed.

The cart jolted, then tipped as the donkey flailed, hooves scrabbling. Tansha instinctively reached back for her children, but found only air as the cart crashed to the ground. Something sharp slashed her hand and cheek, and she was in the dirt, but she could see Sarkus and Hassah pushing themselves to their feet, supplies and grain spilled around them.

"Sarkus!"

Her warning came too late. Sarkus went down as a hundred pounds of grey fur and teeth barreled into him. Desperation fired through Tansha, and she was on her feet, her hands grasping. She felt wood, and with a great effort snapped the spoke of the cart's wheel and threw herself upon her son's attacker. With a strength she didn't know she had, she brained the creature. Sarkus scrambled out from under the carcass, his wooden mask split.

"You all right?"

The boy nodded, and Tansha turned to her daughter. The girl stood, petrified, as the three remaining wolves advanced on them. From the corner of her eye, Tansha could see the donkey, dead where it lay on its side. Nartah stood on its body, muzzle bloodied, watching Tansha pull her children to her. She still had the club in one hand.

"Argasar promised us safe passage," she protested, her voice coming out as a squeak.

"Argasar changed his mind," Nartah grinned.

Tansha surveyed the remaining wolves, cold sweat chilling her.

She turned and ran, pulling her children with her, running as fast as she could. She knew she had but a dozen heartbeats before the wolves caught up.

"Run! Run, and don't look back!"

She let go of Hassah's hand and screamed at her to run before turning around, her club at the ready. The trees would have to protect her children now. The trees, the wooden spoke in her hands, and the precious seconds of time she could buy them.

* * *

Argasar, Indigo, and Brune, along with a few other rabbits, gathered at the main gate to bid Pozzi, Keeva, and Walnut farewell. The alpha wolf had offered the family a pacified mule to make better time, but neither Pozzi nor Keeva seemed comfortable looking after such a large beast, and told Argasar they preferred walking.

Pozzi bowed to Argasar. "I'll never forget you, Argasar. Thank you. And thank you for keeping your word to spare Hassah and her family."

The wolf nodded. "You are welcome. Are you sure you wouldn't like to stay? We could use every fighter we have, and the journey home will be dangerous."

Pozzi looked to Keeva and Walnut and shook his head. "We've never wanted anything but to return to Willago."

Argasar smiled. "Then safe travels, and may calm skies follow you home."

Brune and Indigo each said their goodbyes to the rabbits. Walnut's face lit up when Indigo presented him with a toy bow and arrow set. "I found this in the hunting storage and thought you might like it. I practiced with something similar when I was young. Protect Pozzi and Keeva with it."

The young rabbit grinned with pride. "Thank you. I mean, thank you, Princess."

While Walnut was busy testing the bowstring, Brune leaned in toward Pozzi and Keeva, keeping his voice low so Walnut wouldn't hear. "Avoid the busy roads and any Urzok settlements to the south. There are plenty of slavers out there who'd be thrilled as bees in pollen to capture unpacified creatures."

Pozzi nodded. "We will."

Keeva smiled at Indigo and Brune, then with a last wave, the three travelers passed through Nyatha's gate and onto the road beyond.

"May Aktu be with you," Brune murmured as the gates closed. "You'll need her help."

As Argasar and his followers turned back toward the manor, Indigo and Brune walked with them.

"We wanted to ask your wolves something, Alpha Argasar," Indigo said.

The wolf looked over, questioning.

"Whether they've come across Ghazan's chamberlain," Brune explained. "A man with a horseshoe scar at his temple. I've searched the prisoners, and he's not there."

Argasar frowned. "I thought you wanted the alchemist."

"Ghazan says he saw the alchemist killed by your wolves." Indigo hadn't meant to sound so accusatory, but her anger surfaced. She had been right to come here, right that the secret weapon that could help the Order was here. And in the end, they had made the one mistake she had warned Argasar against.

The alpha wolf made an apologetic sound. "I'm sorry, Princess. Sadly, those are the fickle fortunes of war. It is hard to ensure who lives and who dies."

"The chamberlain might know how to find another alchemist to make black snow," Indigo said, suppressing her anger and focusing on the now. "We'd like to ask your wolves if they've seen him."

"There's a chance he's still alive," Brune said.

Argasar regarded him for a moment. "I will make enquiries." He turned to leave.

"Not to be rude," Brune said, "but time's shorter than the teeth on a flea. Perhaps we can help with the enquiries."

Argasar's tone was firm. "My wolves are busy running Nyatha, I won't have them interrupted with endless questions. I have a few things to attend to, but I'll try to have an answer for you by nightfall."

The wolf and his entourage strode away, indicating the conversation was over. Indigo chewed the inside of her cheek, frustrated.

"I'm not sitting and waiting." She looked up at Brune. "Ghazan told me where the alchemist's cottage is. Perhaps we'll find some stored black snow. Or an idea of how to make it."

The bear raised one eyebrow. "Then what are we waiting for?"

CHAPTER 12

The cheers in the streets of Kalyun-eh both pleased and unsettled Lord Ornox of Vyad.

Flowers and sweet corn rained down from resident balconies, and the growing throngs in the streets sang the familiar Ornox song as he rode through on his charger, his retinue behind him. People waved scarves with the crest of Vyad on them, and others held aloft effigies of the grey-and-black rabbit impaled on stakes. Ornox's glacial progress toward the looming castle of Kalyun-eh slowed with the thickening crowds, but that suited the warlord. It gave him time to think.

Not that he hadn't been thinking all during the long journey to Kalyun-eh. In fact, he'd kept his pace slow, twice taking an extra day to rest because of some made-up illness or injury. For what he needed was time. Time for Ghazan's alchemist to make enough black snow for Ornox's purposes, and time for him to finesse his plan. And until his plan was in place, and he had enough black snow to flatten any enemies in his way, he was still vulnerable. Especially as Ornox didn't know how the emperor would receive him, given that he had killed the favored advisor Brel.

By the time he reached the Great Square outside the castle,

the crowds had forced Ornox's retinue to a crawl. Once they'd made their way through, horns from the ramparts blasted nine long notes, the welcome for victors.

Ornox looked up at the immense castle, its drawbridge lowering to connect with the giant square. A row of guards helped keep the crowds back as Ornox and his retinue rode onto the drawbridge and through the barbican, a long tunnel with murder holes in the ceiling that allowed defenders to loose arrows on attackers below. Ornox admired the design, as he always did, in this castle that would be his.

Servants hurried forward and took charge, organizing for horses to be stabled and Ornox's traveling household to be seen to. A wiry butler with oiled hair, felt boots, and manicured hands bowed to Ornox as he dismounted.

"A very warm welcome, Lord Ornox," the butler said. "His Eminence is waiting for you. But first, I apologize and ask that you leave all weapons with your men."

Ornox unbuckled his sword and pulled out the dirk at his waist. He handed them to Yod, who had come forth to take them.

"A thousand apologies, but I am sworn to make sure no one comes armed to His Eminence."

Ornox submitted himself to being searched. The butler moved efficiently, then gave a curt nod and a smile.

"A thousand thanks. Please follow me."

Ornox followed the man through the main castle courtyard, and beyond a set of stone arches and exterior corridors.

"I will not be paying my respects in the audience chamber?" Ornox knew Dorgun usually greeted guests in the reception hall on the second floor.

"His Eminence has ordered a special event in your honor," the butler replied, dipping his head but not slowing his pace.

Ornox kept his unease in check.

They walked on until the open-air corridor ended at a giant

playing field with a luxurious cover of perfectly trimmed grass. He knew where he was now. The castle's own horseball field. On the far left were the imperial viewing boxes, where the emperor sat amidst a gathering of courtiers, nobles, guests, and civil servants.

At Ornox's arrival on the field, the emperor stood and began gently clapping his hands.

"Ah, the returning hero, Lord Ornox of Vyad!" the emperor said, his painted eyebrows raised.

The other nobles in the box dutifully followed suit, clapping as Ornox went through the prostration of respect for the emperor.

"Rise, Ornox, and come join me." He turned to the butler. "Tell the Game Master to begin the match."

Ornox climbed the steps to the emperor's box, noting who was here. A few of the most powerful nobles were in attendance, observing the emperor's every move with practiced disinterest. No doubt they wanted to see what the ruler's attitude toward Ornox was, to decide how they should deal with the reinstated warlord. Flanked behind the emperor stood his imperial guards, twelve of them, all men except for one. They attended the emperor everywhere outside of his private chambers, and rumor had it they could hear an arrow nock from within five hundred paces. As if to prove this prowess and their untouchability, none of them wore helmets.

"Sit down, Ornox," the Emperor Dorgun said. "I've reserved this seat for you. Would you care for wine?"

Ornox held up a hand to decline the tray of goblets a servant was offering. Dorgun took one and sipped.

"I do enjoy a game of horseball. It's been too long since we've held a game." Dorgun watched the players ride onto the field, their long wooden clubs in their hands. Game boys were setting up the tiered rings, biggest to smallest, on each end of the field. Putting the ball through different-sized rings garnered different points.

"It is an honor to return and be able to share your favorite game, Your Eminence," Ornox replied.

Dorgun smiled. "I realize that when you left, it was not on amicable terms."

An understatement, the warlord knew. He wanted to throttle the emperor, but now was not the time. Besides, ears were listening. "Your Eminence had every right to be disappointed in me, and punish me."

The emperor nodded in agreement, which only made Ornox's blood simmer. The riders were now lined up in rows and ready to play. Ornox observed that today's "ball" was the corpse of a small goat, trussed together by the legs and lying in the middle of the field. At a signal from the emperor, the riders spurred their horses forward, hoofs churning turf as they raced for the ball and hit it into play.

"I'm glad we see eye to eye and that you have no ill will," the emperor said. "Though I must admit, your killing my chief advisor Brel upset me greatly. How do you explain your flagrant disregard for my servant and my laws?"

Ornox had practiced this response during his journey here, and he leaned forward for a cup of wine. Drinking would help him hide his response from any curious onlookers who had the skill of reading lips. "I hate to bring such news, but Brel was a traitor to you, Your Eminence."

"Oh?" Dorgun clapped his hands as one team sent the goat carcass through one of the smaller holes, earning a point amid loud cheers from the onlookers. Dorgun's face showed nothing but enjoyment for the game, and for a moment, Ornox wondered if he had even understood what Ornox said.

"He tried to bribe me to assassinate you, Your Eminence," Ornox continued. "He thought I'd bear Your Eminence a grudge and be eager for treason. But when I refused, he threatened my life, as he didn't want news of his plan reaching other ears. I had no choice but to kill him."

Dorgun smiled, though it wasn't clear whether his mirth was

at Ornox's story or the opposite team, who had just scored a goal. "Then it seems you are doubly the hero this hour. For ridding me of a traitor *and* killing the Griffinrider."

Ornox dipped his head, careful to maintain humility. "I serve you and the empire."

"So it is true, then, that the Griffinrider is dead by your hand?"

"Most certainly. I watched him die."

"Good. Though one thing bothers me."

Ornox maintained his guard despite Dorgun's casual tone. "Yes, Your Eminence?"

"The Griffinrider's body. I would have liked to put it on display."

"I was unable to retrieve it from the river. But everyone in my regiment saw him die. If you doubt me, you are free to ask any of my soldiers."

"I already have," Dorgun said smoothly. "They all say the same thing, and attest to the Griffinrider's death." He turned to the warlord, his milky eye now fully visible. "They sing of you in the streets, and the empire thanks you for your heroism."

Ornox bowed his head. "I only do my duty toward my emperor."

"Of course. I am glad you have returned, for I wanted to personally invite you to my birthday festivities next moon. It will be a city holiday, and I will announce my heir." He smiled and leaned close. "I think you will be very pleased to hear who I name heir."

Was the emperor hinting he might name Ornox as his heir? Ornox tried to still his blood and bowed his head again. "Your Eminence is wise in all things, and I will swear loyalty to whomever Your Eminence names."

"Make sure you attend," the emperor said.

A rider bearing the colors of a messenger rode in from the outer courtyard and dismounted at the edge of the field. He hurried up the steps to the imperial box and then prostrated himself before the emperor.

Dorgun frowned at the man. "Can it not wait until the end of the game?"

"I come from the warlord Chagen, Your Eminence." He pulled out a seal and showed it to the emperor.

This piqued Ornox's curiosity. An urgent message from the leader of the Imperial Army must be important indeed.

"Nyatha has fallen, Your Eminence."

Ornox stiffened. If Nyatha had fallen, then his alchemist was in enemy hands. And he needed his alchemist, and her black snow, to win the empire.

"When?" Dorgun asked.

"Two days ago."

"To the Order?"

"It appears to be rebels outside Nyatha, Your Eminence."

Ornox cursed inwardly. Two days during which Nyatha had been in enemy clutches. It would take several days to gather a large enough force to take the place back, even if it wasn't a well-defended fortress. But he had to be the one to regain the post. He couldn't afford to have Chagen or some other warlord liberate Nyatha and possibly find out about black snow.

"Your Eminence," Ornox said, leaning over. "Forgive me, but may I suggest I win Nyatha back for the empire?"

Dorgun considered him, as if only just aware that he was present. Ornox stifled his impatience. The old man really did seem to shift between clarity and confusion in heartbeats.

"You?"

"As the killer of the Griffinrider, I can strike fear into the enemy's heart better than any of your warlords." Ornox pressed his point home. "I crushed the Griffinrider, and I will crush these rebels. Once and for all."

The crowd had risen to its feet. During their conversation, the teams had scored numerous goals, and now the winning goal was in sight. Dorgun remained seated, contemplating Ornox.

"Tell me, Ornox. What would you do if you were emperor?"

Ornox tried to read Dorgun's expression. Was this a test? He had to answer well, but still convince the emperor to let him march on Nyatha. "I would order my most reliable warlord, in this case me, to take a force to Nyatha, and then assign Chagen to take another unit and recapture Hegg. If these rebels in Nyatha are being inspired by the Order, then it's best we deal a double blow and show them the empire tolerates no resistance."

The crowd had settled back down with groans of disappointment. It seemed the rider had missed the winning goal, and a few of the spectators jeered.

"Very well," the emperor nodded. "I admire your eagerness to prove yourself. I will be waiting for news, especially as I hope that you and Chagen can retake both New Hegg and Nyatha in time for my birthday festivities."

Was that another hint? Ornox couldn't be sure. But best to be safe and ensure he regained Nyatha.

"As I said, Your Eminence, I wouldn't miss your birthday for the whole of Mankahar. I shall return victorious, or not at all."

* * *

WHEN THE GAME was finally over and Dorgun had reached the audience chamber, his advisors were waiting for him as asked. He dismissed all the attendants.

"Do we have a man on Ornox?"

The lead advisor bowed. "Yes, Your Eminence. We will follow him at all hours and report his every move to you."

The emperor nodded. "Good." Perhaps the warlord would die in battle, and he'd be rid of Mankahar's latest hero. Ornox was plotting against him somehow, the emperor sensed. He just didn't know how. Never mind. Dorgun had some plots of his own. "Is the carpenter here?"

At the advisor's nod, Dorgun motioned for the guest to be shown in. The advisors bowed and left, and shortly afterward, the heavy door opened again, allowing in a weathered man of medium build and square proportions. The city's best carpenter looked like he himself had been chiseled from a block of wood. He had a square jaw and square hands, and his clothing was of plain colors and patterns. The man prostrated himself and waited for the emperor's permission to rise.

"Stand. Is the ship on schedule?"

The man stood. "Yes, Your Eminence. I have my best men working on it without rest."

"Just make sure your men are trustworthy and can keep their tongues."

The carpenter bowed. "I know each man personally, Your Eminence."

"Good. Because if word does leak, I will have each one of you flogged and then put to death. Understood?"

The man's face lost a shade of color. "If word leaks, Your Eminence, it won't be from my men."

The emperor regarded him for a moment. "Regardless, each one of you will pay the price."

The carpenter looked ill, but nodded.

"Let me know when the ship is finished."

As the door closed behind the carpenter, Dorgun walked out onto the balcony and looked over his city, inhaling its smoke and smells. He would clean this city. Purify it of all its pests.

CHAPTER 13

Theo was on a cliff, a rushing river below. Everything was silent—the river, the birds, the trees. Something was wrong, and a dread built in him. He could sense something malignant just behind him. He didn't want to turn, but his body wouldn't obey him.

A tall Urzok, his face obscured by his helmet with its sharp curves and unforgiving edges, was coming for him. He was a bear of a man, with a sword, and menace surrounded him like a tangible thing. Theo couldn't move, even though in his mind, he screamed for his feet to run. And then the man split in two, and then four, and then split again, until there were too many to count, and they were all coming at him with their swords. He felt the metal pierce him in multiple places, felt the panic as he tried to fight back, but the enemy pierced him again and again and—

His teeth rattled in his head, and something gripped his shoulder.

He felt a paw over his mouth, severe dark eyes beneath bushy eyebrows looking down at him.

"Stop it, Griffinrider!" The voice came as a hiss. "You're dreaming aloud again. Control yourself."

He blinked, the panic ebbing as he felt his limbs and moved them. A dream. He pushed Orjo's paw away and sat up. The donkey cart was dark, with nothing but moonlight and stars to see by, but Theo could make out his grandfather's sleeping form next to him. Reenan and Manneki had bunked under the cart, and Theo saw the donkey's silhouette nearby.

The muskrat handed him a water jug. "Drink."

Theo took it and drank deeply. He nearly spat out the contents. "What is this?"

"Don't rightly know," Orjo replied. "But it's strong. Siphoned it off that chatty trader we met on the road today."

Theo passed the jug back. He wouldn't be getting to sleep again with that taste in his mouth. He rubbed a paw over his face. How long had it been since he'd slept through the night? Four days? No, five. When he had seen that first rabbit doll.

It hadn't been the last. Every day, they had seen more and more of them: wooden puppets, rag dolls, straw effigies, all crudely resembling Theo, all with swords through them. Some hung from trees, others were staked to tavern doors, and there had even been a larger one propped by the side of the road. Father Oaks had tried to tell Theo to look away and ignore them, but how could he? Instead, he observed each one, their details seared into his mind. And the closer they drew to Kalyun-eh, the closer he drew to the heart of this hatred for him.

"You know what crocodiles are?"

Orjo's words cut into Theo's thoughts. "Father Oaks told me of them once. Never seen one. Why?"

The muskrat settled himself back against the cart wall, making it creak. "They grow to the size of large bulls. Can kill a baby dragon if it comes to the water's edge. Jaws that can snap tree trunks in two like scissors going through cloth. But it's not the biggest ones that are the most dangerous. You know which ones you ought to fear?" Orjo didn't wait for a reply. "It's the ones you can't see. They lie beneath the water without even a ripple, and you don't even know they're there. The crocodile that doesn't exist is the one who gets his prey."

"I'm afraid of enough things without adding crocodiles," Theo said, exasperated.

"That's your problem, Griffinrider," Orjo replied. "You don't realize you are the crocodile. The silent one beneath the water. The Urzoks think you're dead, and that's the most powerful weapon you have right now. Don't look at those silly toys and feel fear. It's just proof that they don't suspect we're coming. I was never safer than when everyone thought me dead. You can think on that for the rest of the night, it's your shift."

Orjo turned over on the cart, pulling his cloak over his face and his wild mane of hair. Theo sat for a long time in the dark, but even before dawn broke, he was seeing things in a new light.

* * *

TEN DAYS AFTER LEAVING HEGG, the travelers sighted the first spires of Kalyun-eh. The landlocked Urzok capital spread out over the valley in concentric squares, overflowing with towers and laneways. And above all, Urzoks.

Theo felt a familiar trepidation as Reenan brought the cart to a halt at the top of a hill, letting Manneki, Orjo, Father Oaks, and Theo take in the sprawling mass that was Kalyun-eh.

Theo had thought that Doria, where he'd met Reenan, was large. But this made Doria look like a hamlet. From here, he could see countless buildings that were three or four stories tall, large, manicured patches of orchards and gardens, and private grazing grounds. A cloud of smoke and ash from the city's countless fires hovered over the city like some possessive ghost, a haze that sucked in the sun's rays. In the city's center stood a tall, sprawling castle, with grasping, thin spires.

"That's where the Library is?" Theo asked.

Orjo nodded. "Right in the center."

Reenan turned to Orjo and Oaks. "Remember what I told you."

Father Oaks sniffed. "Do little. Say less. Never felt so useless in me life."

"The important thing is to blend in," Orjo said. "Most non-Urzoks here are pacified, except for those who are slaves or will work for less pay than Urzoks."

"Here, you need a fresh coat of paint." Reenan held out a jar of reddish-brown clay to Theo.

The stuff itched when dry, but Theo knew Reenan was right. He couldn't chance anyone seeing his true fur color, and as Orjo said, he needed to make sure that Theo the Griffinrider stayed dead.

They began the descent toward the capital city, joining the throngs of horse carts, noble folk, courtiers, priests, and peddlers on their way to the heart of the empire. The roads grew dust choked as they neared the city gates, which loomed larger and larger the closer they got. Soon, they could make out the towering immensity of the city wall, its limestone stacked high and sanded until it rivaled the smoothest eggshell. Flags of all sizes and colors flew from rooftops, and the sounds of hooves and chatter filled the air.

Theo, Father Oaks, and Orjo rode in the cart, trying to stay inconspicuous. They watched streams of Urzoks going in the other direction: merchants with wagons piled high, traveling entourages bound for distant cities, messengers on fleet-footed horses, impatiently weaving past slower travelers. Carts full of pacified ducks, geese, chickens, and pigs drove by, and Theo knew without asking that they were meant for slaughter.

As they drew closer to the gates, the pace slowed. Theo chanced a peek out at the arched entry to the city and saw that the city wall was at least fifty paces thick. Just outside the wall was a long table staffed by a dozen Urzoks, all processing those entering.

"I don't see anyone like us," Father Oaks muttered next to Theo.

Theo had also been examining every animal that came or went, and within the crowds, he had so far only seen a few that weren't pacified: a tiger who was clearly protection for a rich merchant, a messenger hawk sitting high and haughty on a nobleman's shoulders, a few miserable-looking monkeys following a milliner's cart piled with hats and fabrics. Who were these animals, and how had they agreed to a life like this with Urzoks? Then again, Theo reasoned, those same animals were probably asking the same question about him and his companions.

It was their turn at the gate. A stocky guard motioned them forward.

"Business?"

"Here to trade some fine spices."

The guard glanced over their cart and peered inside, giving a cursory glance at the neatly arranged goods. He eyed the Grodlyn, rabbits, and muskrat. "You trade in animals too?"

Reenan scoffed. "This lot? I'd be lucky to get a copper piece each. No, no, they work for me. Skilled with shelling seeds and grinding spices. The monkey attracts business."

"No weapons?"

Reenan shook his head. "We keep to the busy roads, helps avoid brigands, so we don't need arms."

The guard searched the underside of the cart, just to be sure, then seemed to accept Reenan's explanation. "You'll need permit tokens for them. Don't let them wander off alone. If they don't have a token on them to show they've a patron, then anyone can catch or kill them, understood?"

Manneki looked like he was suppressing a hiss, and Theo grew hot with anger. Orjo remained unruffled. Reenan nodded. "What do I owe you?"

"Three bits for the lot."

Reenan dug out some money from his pocket and leaned over to hand it to the guard. "Good day to you."

The guard handed four round clay tokens to Reenan, who slipped them into his pocket and clicked his tongue to the donkey. The guard motioned to the next in line, having already forgotten about them.

They rolled past the wall and into the city. Theo tried to keep from gaping as they entered a flat expanse that seemed to ring the city proper. Here, blacksmiths and farmers and butchers dominated, the hammering of metal interspersed with the bleating of sheep and the screams of pigs. Theo saw an Urzok wrestle a calf into a narrow pen where a boy waited with a wet knife. In a few seconds, it was over and another calf was being pushed in, but Theo knew he would remember the look of terror on the calf's face, and the casualness of the boy in the blood-spattered boots, for the rest of his life.

"Don't stare," Orjo said, and Theo noticed his grandfather had turned away. "There's nothing you can do but draw attention. And if it's any comfort, they're pacified already."

Theo forced himself to look at nothing but Reenan's back. The man glanced over his shoulder, then slapped the reins to urge the donkey into a trot.

What seemed an eternity later, they had left the outer rings of the city and were now on higher ground, away from the sounds and smells of the smithies and butchers. Here, Theo chanced a look outside and saw small houses and shops lining the streets. The smell of bread, soap, teas, and spices mixed with the stench of scraps and discarded slops. Urzoks dressed in multi-colored clothing pressed in on all sides, and as they traveled, the dress became finer and more elaborate. They had entered a wealthier part of the city, Theo realized. Here, the shops were cleaner and the streets kept free of debris. Regularly spaced troughs of water were available for the pacified horses that the nobles rode, and garlands of flowers on the balconies kept unpleasant smells at bay. But no matter how the neighborhoods changed, one thing did not. Soldiers roamed the streets, and Theo watched one nervous raccoon being questioned, his token examined thoroughly before the guards waved him on.

"This is a terrible place," Father Oaks muttered.

"You'd best have your tokens on at all times," Reenan advised, pulling them out and handing them over. Manneki rummaged for some string and made four thongs, then strung the tokens. The four of them each took one and slipped the thongs over their necks.

Being out in the open like this made them all the more eager to reach their destination. "Where is your friend's house?" Theo asked Reenan. The man had refused to say much about where they would stay.

"Not far."

Theo couldn't be sure, but he thought Reenan sounded nervous. They continued through the city, winding their way through a maze of streets. They reached a large central square with a bubbling water fountain. Here, Urzoks of every type and hue thronged the streets. The travelers also got their first good look at the castle of Kalyun-eh, for at the north end of the square the moat to the castle began. The castle towered over the city like some giant, omnipresent god, dark and imposing. It emanated power, defying any to penetrate its walls. Theo couldn't help an involuntary shiver.

"The library's under all that?" Oaks asked.

"We just have to get in and find the door," Orjo said drily.

The cart turned, and the castle became obstructed by the crowding of buildings around them. The streets grew narrower and poorer again, more haphazard, until they had reached a small ring of three-story houses that stood so close together Theo had the impression the buildings couldn't breathe. All were tidy but in varying stages of disrepair, with cracks and peeling paint and chipped windows everywhere he looked. Barefoot Urzok children ran here and there, and a halfhearted knife sharpener wandered by, calling out for clients over the clattering of whetstones at his belt.

Reenan stopped the cart and hopped off. "Here we are."

Theo helped Oaks down. Orjo jumped out, nimble despite his impossibly old age.

"Which door is your friend's?" Theo asked, looking around.

"The blue one," Reenan replied, pointing. Manneki leaped onto Reenan's shoulder and sat, peering around.

"Aren't you going to knock?" Theo asked, when Reenan made no move.

"Of course." Reenan coughed into his hand, but again he hesitated. "It's been a while."

"You said your friend would not turn us away," Orjo said sharply.

"Oh, she won't." Reenan took a breath and knocked. "The real question is whether she'll kill me."

CHAPTER 14

Theo didn't have time to ask Reenan why before the door swung open. Standing there was an Urzok woman with a thick build and lush black hair coiled atop her head. She wasn't so much plump, Theo realized, as she was solid, with a smooth, round face and unassuming eyes. The thing that made Theo take an instant liking to her, however, was the lily-pad shaped birthmark that ran over one eye and cheek. It reminded him of his own eye patches, coloring which he'd never seen on an Urzok. She felt safe and familiar, and her smile was warm.

"Reenan! What a surprise."

There was an awkward pause before Reenan gestured at Manneki, Theo, Oaks, and Orjo. "Everyone, meet Hizarah. Hiz, I've come with some friends."

"I see that," the woman said, beaming. If the sight of unpacified animals surprised her, she didn't show it. "Come in. That cart yours? It's safe there, not to worry." She stepped back and motioned them inside.

They filed into the house, a cozy if cluttered space that had a hearth on one end and a staircase leading upstairs at the other. Wool bales of all colors hung from the ceiling, and the shelves overflowed with various spinning tools like wool combs, spindles, and clay whorls. A large wooden spinning wheel sat near the staircase. Orjo looked around with practiced curiosity. Theo knew the creature was marking all possible exits, anything that could be a weapon, anywhere that could be a hiding spot. The old rat hadn't survived this long without a honed sense of caution.

Theo wondered whether Reenan had been attempting humor when he said his friend might kill him. She was all smiles as she glanced outside before shutting the door and pulling the latch.

"Hiz, let me—"

When the punch came, it knocked Reenan straight to the ground. In the shake of a whisker, Orjo had two knives from the kitchen table in his paws, and Manneki had leapt to the rafters. Reenan motioned for them all to stay back, gingerly feeling his jaw.

"I'm glad you came back," Hizarah said, rubbing her knuckles.

Reenan moved his mouth. There didn't seem to be blood, Theo was relieved to see.

"If it helps, he's here because of us," Theo said.

Hizarah raised an eyebrow, and Reenan's panicked expression told him he'd said the wrong thing.

"Oh. So you're not here to apologize for lying to me?"

"Well yes, that too, but—"

"And this is how you apologize?" Hizarah's voice dropped to an angry whisper. "By coming back as a wanted outlaw, having helped the Griffinrider escape Doria? Why don't you go the full distance? Might as well bring the Griffinrider right into my home."

At their expressions, her face turned darker. "What? Why are you all looking at me like that?"

"You seem someone who deeply values honesty and hates lies," Orjo said slowly, still holding the table knives. "So my opinion is, it's best we're honest with you." He pointed one knife at Theo. "This is the Griffinrider. My name is Orjo, possibly the only one with a worse reputation than the Griffinrider. And this one-eared fellow is Father Oaks. He's an omatje like Theo and me. So really, outside of that Grodlyn there, we're all wanted outlaws, and the fact that we're in your house is enough to have you strung from the castle pillars at dawn."

A crushing silence fell.

Hizarah frowned. "But the Griffinrider is dead. Everyone knows."

"So you know how he died?" Theo asked. "Where the sword went in?"

Hizarah nodded, suspicious. "Of course. Every toy in town has a sword going right through here." She pointed to the center of her chest.

Theo pulled his shirt down until it revealed the same spot, the grey fur marred by the ridged scar there. "You mean here?"

Her eyes widened, and she shot Reenan a suspicious look. "Is this some sort of trick? I've seen some good theater work with paints and gum in my day."

Reenan shook his head. "It's real, Hiz."

"Will you help us?" Theo asked.

"Or if you won't," Orjo said, "can we be assured of your silence?"

There was a long pause, and Hizarah contemplated them one by one. "You're threatening to kill me?"

"No," Orjo said, "I'm asking if we have to."

Her eyes settled back on Reenan. "That depends. Reenan and I have some unfinished business."

"Clearly," Orjo agreed. "We will leave you two to negotiate." He turned to Manneki, Oaks, and Theo. "Let's wait outside in the cart."

* * *

Dusk was falling, and Theo thought that Hizarah had indeed killed Reenan. They had heard shouting, the smashing of plates, but Orjo had shaken his head in a gesture for patience. Then the door opened and Reenan, looking tired but relieved, motioned them inside.

Hizarah was sweeping up broken crockery and putting the kettle on, humming gently as she went.

"Sorted it out, did you?" Orjo commented.

Reenan nodded, and Theo noticed he looked happy. "I thought it impossible, but yes."

Theo and Oaks helped Hizarah put out cups and stools, looking for animosity in her face but finding none. When everyone had a seat and a steaming tea before them, Hizarah wasted no time.

"Reenan tells me you're wanting to get into the castle."

"Has he told you everything?" Theo asked.

"About you coming back to life? About the lost Library of Elshon under the emperor's private quarters, and how you're planning to bring down the empire? Yes. We've been through all that."

"And ye're willing to help us?" Oaks asked.

"You brought us back together. That's worth a thousand empires." She smiled at Reenan.

"A thousand deaths," Reenan added, looking at her.

Orjo wrinkled his nose as if someone had loosed a stench, but Theo was glad for Reenan. At least one of them could be with the one he loved.

"So how are you getting in?" Hizarah asked.

"I think swimming the moat and scaling the walls at night might be the best tactic," Orjo said.

"Fine for Orjo. Orjo is muskrat," Manneki pointed out, "But Theo can't climb." At Theo's look, he shrugged. "It is truth, Manneki had to help Theo down a tree, remember."

Theo sighed. "He's right. Those walls will be hard to scale

unnoticed." He didn't bother adding that for a rabbit, the idea of swimming a moat held even less appeal.

"Nightshade then," Orjo said. "Easy enough to slip to the guards."

Oaks looked at him aghast. "Poison? I'm a healer; I'll not stoop to poison."

"What do you want to do, old one?" The muskrat scoffed. "Cure them to death?"

"What about—" Hizarah began.

Father Oaks made a disparaging sound. "There's poppy milk."

Theo shook his head. "It wears off. We need at least a week to find what we need."

Hizarah refilled their cups. "If you're all done, I know a laundress at the castle."

This made everyone pause.

"Laundresses would know a castle's inner workings," Orjo admitted. "Do you think she could get us in?"

"And risk her life?" Hizarah asked drily. "Not likely. But she knows the castle, and the routines, and likely who has access to the emperor's chambers. All the laundresses gather at the alehouse by the eastern well after work."

"That's a start," Theo said.

Reenan nodded. "Hizarah, Manneki, and I will go to the alehouse tonight and keep our ears open, see if this friend is there."

"And you three better stay indoors and out of sight as much as you can," Hizarah said to the two rabbits and muskrat. "No point drawing attention to ourselves as the only house on the street with unpacified animals."

A shout arose from outside, along with the crack of a whip. Theo, Orjo, and Reenan went to the window and peered out from behind the curtains, while Oaks stayed at the table.

"Careful, lad," Oaks cautioned Theo.

But the younger rabbit didn't answer, observing the scene

outside. A few dozen Urzoks walked by in chains, led by an imperial soldier at the front and pushed forward by another from behind. Both soldiers carried whips and waved them at slow-moving captives or any passersby in their way. The prisoners all had shorn heads, dull eyes, and multiple bruises.

"Slaves," Hizarah said, her quiet voice bitter.

"Your people do this to your own kind?" Theo had thought that the Urzoks were cruel to others, but he hadn't known they could treat their own this way.

Reenan shook his head. "The cities do this to pacified animals, yes, but I've never seen this."

"Kalyun-eh has changed since you left, Ree." Hizarah gathered the cups. "Part of the reason I gave up the theater and went into spinning yarn for the fabric guilds. The war and the tales of the Griffinrider all made the rich afraid, and they either hoarded their coin or they put it into armies and weapons to keep the empire safe. So the poor became poorer. And when you're poor, the noose of the law has its way of finding you. And once the prisons were full, the emperor made slaves of the rest."

Something twisted in Theo's gut. This was the reason he was hated—these prisoners had lost everything, even their freedom, and they blamed him for it. Blamed him and the Order for fighting back against the empire. His resolve hardened. He had to find the *Book of Cures*, and show Mankahar that the problem was not the Griffinrider, but the emperor.

* * *

THE SMALL, unassuming cottage that sat between the pacification cradles and the yards seemed too homey to be an alchemist's workshop, but it matched Ghazan's description. The door took some convincing, but in the end, Brune's shoulder won out.

The cottage's smell hit them first. It wasn't unpleasant,

simply a heady mix of unusual scents such as beeswax, smoke, copper, and clay.

An overturned birdcage lay in one corner, its door open. Smashed jars lay in puddles on the floor, along with pawprints of ash from the hearth.

"This definitely looks like an alchemist's workshop," Indigo said.

Brune sniffed. "More smells in here than there are scales on a salmon. Won't be easy to sniff out black snow."

Indigo knew bears had much keener noses than most other creatures. "We'll just have to use the traditional way then. Search everything."

Indigo surveyed the room and its shelves of substances. She began going through the intact jars one by one, opening them and peering inside. Many contained black powders, but none of them had the distinctive smell of black snow that she remembered so clearly from when she, Orjo, Brune, and Theo were escaping Orjo's island.

Brune flipped up the pallet on the raised bedframe and began searching the baskets underneath. He stood up and sniffed again. "Wait. I smell blood."

Indigo recorked a jar and took a new one off the shelf. "The wolves likely spilled blood when they came in here. They probably dragged the alchemist out."

The bear frowned. "That was days ago. I smell blood that's…." He trailed off.

Indigo waited. "That's what?"

"That's…" He paused. "That's new."

They shared a look. They looked around the room, but could see no one. A small scraping sound, so faint she almost missed it, came from the wall by the bed, and Indigo noticed the cupboard there.

"Hello?" Indigo called.

There was no answer.

Brune approached the cupboard, sniffed again, and turned to

nod at Indigo. Someone was inside. "We won't hurt you. You can come out."

Only silence greeted them.

"I'm going to open the door," Brune said. "Don't be frightened, all right?" He reached out a paw and slowly pulled one of the cupboard doors open. Sitting up on the top shelf was a canary, one wing limp and bleeding.

"Must be the pacified canary Ghazan mentioned," Brune said.

The canary burst into tears, quiet sobs shaking its body. "Please, don't kill me."

The bear and rabbit shared a look of surprise. Brune's voice was reassuring. "We're from the Order, we're not here to kill you. This is Indigo, and I'm Brune. What's your name?"

The bird hesitated, as if this was a trap.

"I give my word we won't hurt you," Indigo said.

"Kestrel," the bird conceded. "I'm the alchemist's canary."

Brune growled. "I thought alchemists only kept pacified birds."

Kestrel cocked her head. "Ethana was lonely and saved me from pacification."

Indigo's mind leapt at what this might mean, and what Kestrel might know, but she kept her thoughts to herself for the moment. "Well, Kestrel, you must be hungry after hiding here for two days with barely food or water."

The canary said nothing, but trembled at the mention of food.

Indigo nodded. "I'll get you something to eat, and we'll see to fixing your wing."

As she left for the kitchens, she tried to keep her excitement down. If Kestrel had been with the alchemist all this time, then she might know the secret to black snow.

When Indigo returned with food and water, the bird was sitting in an improvised nest of blankets on the bed. Brune was bandaging Kestrel's wing with a strip of linen. Kestrel fell upon the food, pecking away at the pile of grains and nuts Indigo had found. Brune and Indigo let her finish eating before speaking again.

"We know Ethana was making black snow," Indigo said.

The bird seemed to curl in on herself. The rabbit tried a different tack. "If you know how to make black snow, we can protect you. Can you make it?"

The bird hesitated, then nodded.

Brune smiled. "Paint me yellow and call me a bee."

"Can you make it here?" Indigo asked.

Kestrel looked around. "I don't know. So much is destroyed." She cocked her head. "If I make it, will you let me go?"

The plaintiveness in the question made Indigo's heart ache.

"It may not seem like it," Brune said, "but we don't want to keep you prisoner. We're asking for your help, Kestrel."

The bird thought on this, then nodded. "If I do, I need you to promise me something."

"What's that?" the bear asked.

"Don't tell anyone else I'm here. Please. I'll make your black snow, and you get me out with no one knowing."

Indigo and Brune looked at each other. "Why? The wolves won't harm a non-pacified animal."

The bird drew her head in, defensive. "I don't trust the wolves. That's my condition."

Indigo nodded. "Very well. We'll bring you food and supplies, but you'll have to keep silent and out of sight here."

CHAPTER 15

*I*t was the fourth night Hizarah had been to the alehouses, and when she returned, Theo could tell from her expression the trip had revealed little.

"All anyone wants to talk about is Feast Day," she complained, unwrapping her shawl and gratefully taking a cup of water from Father Oaks.

A shout sounded from outside, cutting short their conversation. Running footsteps followed, before the door burst open and a boy, no older than fourteen summers by the look of him, stumbled in and shouldered the door shut behind him, yanking the latch.

"Reenan, I thought you were going to fix the door latch?" Hizarah snapped.

The boy held a bloodied finger to his lips, his eyes desperate. His head, Theo noticed, was freshly shorn, and his arms bore several angry-looking welts where they'd felt the whip. His left trouser leg was dark and sticking to his leg, the floor below speckled with blood.

"Aktu curse it, he's a slave," Orjo hissed. "We have to get him out of here."

The boy looked at the muskrat, clearly not expecting unpacified animals. More shouts sounded outside, as well as fists pounding on doors, angry voices demanding entry.

Making a decision, Theo grasped the boy's hand and pulled him toward the stairs. "Father Oaks, help me stitch him up. Reenan, you'd better clean up the blood and deal with the soldiers. Orjo, try not to kill anyone."

He led the boy, one painful step at a time, upstairs and to the room he shared with Orjo and Oaks. It was more of a storage room, with enough cleared floor space for a pallet, with a cracked wash basin and pitcher to one side, and a small window that looked out onto the street below.

The boy collapsed on the pallet and suppressed a scream when Theo ripped the trousers from his leg. Father Oaks poured water in the basin and fetched some towels, which he used to clean the wound. The boy yelped and put an arm to his mouth.

"Bite on this," Theo said, twisting up a rag and holding it out. The boy obediently took it, wincing as Theo and Father Oaks rinsed the wound.

"Spear, I'd say." Father Oaks examined the gash and then rummaged in a cupboard. "Here it is." He pulled out a dark bottle and uncorked it, pouring a generous amount of a sharp-smelling alcohol on the boy's leg.

Angry knocking came from below, and Theo motioned for the boy to be quiet. They heard the door open, and then Hizarah's voice.

"Evening. What's the commotion?"

"We're looking for a runaway slave. He been through here?" The flinty voice made it clear Hizarah's charm was falling on deaf ears.

"Sounds dangerous," Hizarah answered. "But you're welcome to come in and search."

Theo, Father Oaks, and the boy stiffened. There was the sound of boots, then a loud cough from Reenan.

"I forgot to say," Hizarah added, "it's best you're quick and don't touch too much around the house."

"Why? What's wrong with him?"

"My brother's got the wasting sickness."

There was a quick intake of breath, then the hurried slam of the door and the receding boot falls of the soldiers as they moved on.

A few moments later, Hizarah, Reenan, Manneki, and Orjo appeared in the doorway.

"Is he dead yet?" Orjo asked. The boy glared at him.

"We'll need some needle and thread," Theo told them. "And bring me a lit candle."

As Reenan and Hizarah hurried off, Orjo spied the dark bottle of alcohol. "By Aktu, you used my liquor on him?"

"Be useful," Father Oaks snapped. "Somewhere else."

Orjo snarled but walked away.

Theo shot the boy an apologetic look and found the runaway slave studying him with wary curiosity.

"You're safe for now," Theo said, staunching the blood and willing Hizarah to hurry. "And it's not a death wound."

Reenan appeared with a lit candle on a holder, and Hizarah and Manneki were close behind. She placed two spools of thread and some needles on the pallet next to Theo and Father Oaks.

"Thinnest I have," she said.

Father Oaks waved them out. "It'll do. Now give us some space."

The man and the Grodlyn dutifully left. Hizarah followed once she had closed the shutters to the window.

Theo ran the needle through the flame and threaded it, then offered it to Father Oaks. The old rabbit shook his head. "My paws aren't as steady as they once were, lad."

Theo looked to the boy, who drew a deep breath and then nodded. Theo pushed the needle in, drawing a shocked gasp, and began to sew, trying not to hurry despite the boy's obvious pain. Careless haste now would only slow the healing later.

When he had finished, he bit the thread and dropped the

bloody needle in the basin of water. Father Oaks picked it up and wordlessly went to empty it.

The boy's face was slick with sweat, but his eyes were clear. "My thanks for not sending me back to the slavers."

"You're welcome," Theo said, wiping his paws and cleaning up the leftover thread and needles.

"I'm Xandru. What's your name?"

Theo hesitated. "It doesn't matter."

"I've never met an unpacified before," the boy said. "What are you doing in Kalyun-eh?"

"Rest and heal," Theo urged, avoiding the question.

"You're the Griffinrider."

Theo glimpsed himself in the mirror on the wall and cursed. The reddish-brown paint he had donned this morning, as he did every day, had come off in the basin of water and when he had wiped his brow with his forearm. His eye patches, and swabs of his natural grey fur, showed through the brown.

"I'm not the Griffinrider," he said, a little too firmly. He hoped that saving this boy from the slavers hadn't just doomed him to something worse. Perhaps doomed them all to something worse.

"It's all right," Xandru said. "I won't tell no one."

"There's nothing to tell, as you're mistaken."

"Is it true your blood cures anything?"

At this, Theo's voice dropped low. "I am not the Griffinrider. And no one's blood cures everything." His saving of Indigo during the battle of Ralgayan had turned into a tall tale of how his blood was magic, a cure for pacification and every other ill under the sun. That rumor had made sure nearly everyone in the land, not just the empire, wished to capture Theo. "Now stay here, and rest."

Theo rushed from the room and down the stairs, straight into everyone else gathered there. It was clear they had overheard most of the exchange.

"I told you, he's a liability," Orjo said, cold.

Hizarah bit her lip. "If he knows, he might sell us out to the empire."

"He's on the run, like us," Theo said. "He won't tell anyone."

The others shared dubious looks, and Orjo looked as if he wanted to march up and kill Xandru right then.

"Well, he can't get far on that leg," Oaks pointed out. "He's not going anywhere fer now."

But the next morning, when Theo went to check on the boy, the room window was swinging open in the breeze, and Xandru was gone.

CHAPTER 16

$\mathcal{H}$izarah's laundress friend proved harder to find than she had thought. The woman had apparently left to be married in her hometown and would not be back for several days.

"I'll try to find out what I can from the other laundresses," Hizarah promised as she left for the alehouse again.

Theo sat down by the hearth, trying to busy himself with drying burdock root for his grandfather, who drank the tea. The mention of marriage had reminded him of Indigo and her marriage to the prince. Was she already lost to him, even now?

"That Keeva was never the one fer ye, lad."

Theo looked over. Father Oaks had just returned from outside with a log under his arm and sat down next to Theo on the bench to push the wood into the fire.

"What?"

Father Oaks grunted. "That look on yer face," he said softly, so the others couldn't hear. "Ye were thinkin' of someone, and I know about yer feelings towards Keeva."

Theo almost laughed. His grandfather had missed so much of his life, and there was so much Theo had to tell him that he didn't know where to begin. Theo now knew Keeva was a childish infatuation, but he was surprised that his grandfather knew about it at all.

"She was a fool," Father Oaks said. "If ye needed proof, look at who she married."

Theo said nothing. Harlan had been many things to him—bully, brother, enemy, and competitor for Keeva's affections. But even so, Theo wished things had been different. Wished he hadn't had to fight his brother at Ralgayan. Perhaps Harlan was right. Perhaps Theo had made Harlan the rabbit he was, mean and resentful. He wondered where his brother was now, after having been branded and sent from the Order for his role in helping Ornox's army breach the castle at Ralgayan. Theo took a seat next to his grandfather.

"Father Oaks, there's something I have to tell you," he said, quiet. "About Harlan and the fire."

His grandfather didn't look up. "What fire?"

"The one that nearly burned down the medicine shed."

Father Oaks glanced at him. "Ye goin' t' tell me it wasn't Harlan's fault?"

Theo nodded. "It was my fault. I was releasing words from one of your books, and I wasn't watching the pot. But I put the blame on him, and you sent him to Gawelt afterward."

"I knew it was yer fault. But I didn't send Harlan to Gawelt because of that."

"You didn't?" Theo looked over in surprise. "Then why?"

Father Oaks prodded the fire without saying anything for a while. "Harlan needed harsher discipline than I could give. Even before the fire, I decided the only one who might knock some sense into that rabbit was Gawelt." Father Oaks sighed. "I was wrong. Gawelt knocked too hard, and Harlan never forgave either of us fer it."

Theo took this in, both confused and relieved. All this time, he'd been carrying the guilt of thinking his lie had sent Harlan to the harsh paws of the village brewer, when his fate had been determined beforehand.

Wherever he is, I hope he's found a new life, and peace.

* * *

POZZI, Keeva, and Walnut had been traveling several days now, and though the way was rough and they slept on hard ground, Pozzi felt happier than he had ever been since that fateful day in Willago when the Urzoks had arrived and destroyed their village. They were on their way home. With Keeva and Walnut by his side, the two he loved most in the world. Especially since Theo was gone.

A pang of sadness for his best friend stabbed him. Were all the rumors about Theo true? He didn't know, and he probably never would. After their ordeal the last few seasons, he'd probably go to his deathbed with more questions than answers. But for now, he was safe with Keeva and Walnut. That's what mattered.

As they decamped one evening, after sleeping by day to avoid encountering other travelers, Keeva asked Walnut if he was feeling all right. Pozzi noticed that Walnut's eyes looked clouded, and he hadn't eaten his ration of elderberries and wild onion that Pozzi had managed to forage for them. Walnut's appetite, Pozzi had learned, was the best indicator of Walnut's well-being.

"I'm hot," Walnut complained.

Keeva felt his ears and paws. "You've a slight fever. But not too bad."

"Can you walk, Walnut?" Pozzi asked. "Or do you want to rest awhile?"

"Rest," Walnut answered sleepily. "Just a while longer."

Keeva took off her cloak and laid it over the young rabbit, rubbing his back until he was asleep again, which didn't take long.

By the middle of the night, though, Walnut's ears had turned dry and pink with heat, and his body was shivering.

"What do we do?" Keeva asked, worried.

"There's not much we can do," Pozzi said. "Perhaps the fever will break and pass. We'll wait until morning."

But the morning brought a turn for the worse. Walnut was stiff and twitching, his breath coming in rattling gasps.

"We cannot stay here," Keeva said, her voice strained. "We have to find help."

Pozzi was torn. Traveling by day would be dangerous, but Walnut clearly didn't have the luxury of waiting. They devised a sling out of their cloaks, and Keeva helped Pozzi strap the young rabbit to his back. They ventured out of the forest, keeping a keen eye for any sign of habitation, of any shelter where they could ask for help. After half a day's journey, during which Keeva constantly checked on Walnut, they spied a wisp of white in the distance.

Pozzi was bone tired from carrying Walnut all this way, and the sling chafed his neck raw. But he picked up his pace.

"What if they're Urzok?" Keeva asked.

"We'll have to take our chances," Pozzi said. "Walnut cannot sleep outside again, or go long without a healer."

Just after midday, they reached a tidy farmer's hut, sitting amidst a patch of cabbage and potato plots. Pozzi eased Walnut to the ground, looking for signs of the inhabitants.

"Over there," Keeva said, pointing out a girl who was coming from around the back of the hut with a basket of washing. The girl looked over, spied them, and slowed, seeing their clothes and recognizing them as unpacified.

Pozzi raised his paw in greeting. "We are just passing. But we have need of a healer. Would you know where we could find one?"

The girl hesitated, then looked at Walnut. She nodded and pointed in the direction of two hills some distance away. "There's a village over there. You'll reach it by nightfall. They've a healer there, and a rabbit at the temple brewery who might help you."

Pozzi nodded, grateful. "Thank you."

The girl pushed at a wisp of hair. "But take care. There are those there who dislike unpacifieds."

Keeva helped Pozzi get Walnut onto his back, and they set off again, keeping the hills in sight. The girl's warning echoed in Pozzi's mind as they walked, but he pushed it away. Worry would not make his options any easier.

* * *

THE VILLAGE TURNED out to be a medium-sized town, with a simple rustic inn at the north. As they passed the inn door, it flew open. An innkeeper bustled out to take the two lanterns in for lighting, but he stopped at the sight of the rabbits.

"We don't serve unpacifieds here," the innkeeper said gruffly, and motioned with his meaty hand for them to be off.

"We're not asking to be served, we're just looking for the temple—"

The innkeeper frowned, then jerked his head down the street. "Down the hill, around the baker's." He retreated into the inn and closed the door behind him.

Keeva pointed at a high bell tower at the south end of the village that denoted a temple. "I can see it. A fellow rabbit will likely be kinder."

They walked downhill and around the corner, and at the edge of the village, they found the temple. Pozzi knocked hesitantly on the door, and when there was no answer, he pounded.

"Keeva?"

They turned at the voice behind them and saw someone standing silhouetted in the setting sun, near a cottage attached to the temple's side.

Pozzi blinked, trying to see. The voice was strangely familiar, but looking into the sun, he couldn't make out the features of the rabbit standing there. For it was a rabbit. Tall. And when he stepped closer, Pozzi nearly dropped Walnut. Keeva stared.

"Harlan?"

The rabbit's appearance was a far cry from when Pozzi had last seen him, when they had all been on the forced march led by the Urzok general, Agacheta. His fur had turned from its former rich-honey shade to a dusty straw, and he had a purplish brand burned onto his cheek. But even so, there was no mistaking Harlan, Theo's brother. And Keeva's husband.

Harlan rushed forward and crushed Keeva in an embrace. Pozzi flushed, tempted to stop him, but held back. Keeva, after her initial shock, managed to push him away, gently but firmly, while shooting an embarrassed glance at Pozzi.

Harlan looked at him and the small rabbit on his back. "I'm sorry. It's just—I never thought I'd see you again. Pozzi? And Walnut? What are you doing here?"

Pozzi shifted the small rabbit, protective. Harlan must have seen the wary expression on his face, for he shook his head, paws out. "You and I parted on bad terms, but what's past is past. Just how are you all the way out here?"

Pozzi boiled with anger, but Keeva quickly cut in, "Questions can wait. For now, we need a healer. Walnut's very sick."

Harlan glanced at the youngster and nodded. "Come, you can stay in my rooms, and I'll fetch you the healer."

CHAPTER 17

While Theo and his friends waited for news from Hizarah, Father Oaks assigned himself the task of sorting out Hizarah's clutter—a task Hizarah clearly didn't appreciate. But Theo grew restless at being cooped up with Orjo in the spinner's house. They didn't want to risk being discovered any more than they had to, especially after the slave-escape incident, and had taken only two trips with Reenan to walk around the Kalyun-eh castle perimeter, memorizing each entrance and exit. And while stuck inside, Orjo proved himself a difficult housemate, as he was used to living on his own in exile and became irritable at every little habit everyone else had. Hizarah was careful to tell any inquisitive neighbors coming to buy her thread that the animals were kept inside sewing and mending goods for Reenan, a distant relative come to trade.

When Hizarah returned from the tavern on the sixth night, her news was discouraging. Not only was the emperor's private chamber heavily guarded at all hours, but only those with a special gold seal were allowed in, and even then, they had to be accompanied by a guard.

"We maybe steal a seal," Manneki suggested.

"I thought of that. But apparently, any missing seal has to be reported," Hizarah said, "and then, all seals are destroyed and new ones made. They told me of someone who had lost her seal and received twelve lashes and a dock in pay besides. No one loses their seal."

"Even if we got ahold of one, we can't go searching for the Library with a guard on our backs," Orjo pointed out. "This whole plan is daft. I say we do it the old-fashioned way—scale the wall, break in, and break out."

"We've walked around that castle many times," Theo said. "You've seen it. It's designed to withstand exactly that. Smooth walls, a wide moat. If we want to get in, we have to think of a way they're not expecting." They needed to understand the castle's rhythm and flows. From there, they'd be able to figure out a way in and out. Maybe.

On the eighth night, Theo could tell Hizarah had news from the way she latched the door and didn't bother to take off her cloak before motioning them all to the table.

"Stop fussing and sit," she told Oaks, who grunted but obediently put down the colored wool he'd been sorting into neat piles. Theo and Orjo sat, followed by Oaks. Reenan leaned against the wall, while Manneki perched on one of the rafters above.

"One of the girls from the castle was in a talkative mood," Hizarah said, clearly excited. "She'd been given a tongue lashing from the head laundress apparently, and was in a hurry to complain to anyone who would listen. She burned a small hole when ironing the sheets for the emperor, so the sheet had to be thrown out."

Orjo sighed. "Scintillating."

Hizarah shot him a chilly look. "To patience goes the prize, as they say. Now the reason why throwing out sheets is such a fuss is because the emperor only sleeps on silk sheets. And not just any silk sheets, but silk sheets from one particular tailor who makes it from a secret process only he knows."

"You're saying we could sneak in with the tailor's sheets?" Theo asked.

Orjo drummed one claw against the table. "Or even pretend to be the tailor."

Hizarah nodded. "Precisely."

Father Oaks looked confused. "I don't follow. Reenan'd play tailor?"

The man shrugged. "Or maybe just the tailor's staff. We could deliver the new sheets into the castle, and once inside, get you into the imperial chambers."

"What about getting out?" Theo asked. "We'll need several days inside the library."

Hizarah shook her head. "The most we can give you is one." At Theo's confused look, she elaborated. "How do you expect to survive with no food, water, or lamp oil in there? We can't run provisions in and out, it's far too dangerous."

"So, how would you manage to come back the next day? The tailor doesn't deliver sheets every day, surely?" Orjo asked.

"We'll say we delivered the wrong ones," Hizarah said. "The guards at the gate will be too busy to confirm everything. They'll just send us in to the head of household and let us sort it out. Returning once might work. Returning multiple times will arouse suspicion."

"Then we'll have to find the *Book of Cures* in a day," Theo said, resigned. "But even assuming this plan works, we still haven't solved how we get into the emperor's chambers. Didn't you say we need a special seal?"

Hizarah nodded. "None of the laundresses have a seal for entering the emperor's chambers. They pass all linen to the head chamber woman, who can only enter with the chamberlain."

"And how do we take this seal without having all the seals changed?" Theo asked.

"We don't," Orjo said, thinking. "I have an idea."

* * *

"I can't do it. I can't make black snow."

In the days after discovering Kestrel, Indigo and Brune had taken turns to discreetly bring food and water to the alchemist's cottage, as well as come up with excuses to keep an eye on the hiding place to make sure no one else was curious enough to investigate.

Today, they had slipped into the cottage to ask Kestrel about her progress. The bird had been careful to not tidy anything, in case someone other than Indigo or Brune entered.

"Do you need equipment?" Brune asked. "We can try to find replacements."

"Or your wing?" Indigo added. They had devised a splint for the bird's injured wing, and stopped the bleeding, but it made movement and getting up and down tables difficult for the small canary.

Kestrel shook her small head. "It's the ingredients. Black snow is made from three things."

"That sounds easy," Brune commented. "I was worried it would be dozens. So what are we looking for?"

"Charcoal, flame rock. And dragon salt."

Brune whistled. "Charcoal and flame rock are easy enough. But dragon salt?"

Kestrel nodded.

"That's the white powder found in dragon caves?" Indigo asked. "Do dragons even exist anymore?"

"Legend has it there are a few remaining." Brune frowned. "Closest would be Doom Hollow. But where did you find dragon salt? There are no dragon caves nearby?"

The bird shook her head. "Ethana distilled it from manure. But it took several months."

"We don't have several months," Indigo said. "Is dragon salt the only thing that works?"

The bird nodded. "It needs dragon salt to catch fire."

Brune ran a paw over his head. "Then I guess we'll have to find a dragon's cave."

"And defeat a dragon," Indigo said, thinking. "Where's Doom Hollow?"

"West," Brune said, "some ways south of Hegg."

"Looks like we'll be leaving Nyatha sooner than we thought," the rabbit said. "Kestrel, you should pack anything you need to bring. I'll go speak to Argasar to let him know we're leaving."

At this, Kestrel shifted nervously. "You won't tell him about me?"

Indigo paused. "If you'd prefer, I'll only tell him that Brune and I are leaving to see if we can find Ornox and black snow. How's that?"

The bird nodded, seemingly mollified.

"I'll get our own things together," Brune said to Indigo, following her out.

It was a short jog across the open oval and past the prisons to the main manor.

"She really mistrusts the wolves," Brune commented.

"Can't say I blame her," Indigo replied. "They took over Nyatha and killed her only friend. We're lucky she's speaking to us."

"Let's just hope Argasar doesn't find out about her," the bear muttered. "Something like this might get his fur in a ruffle."

The sound of screams and snarls coming from the prisons made them both fall silent.

Indigo broke into a run, Brune close behind, and they reached the prison gate just as a pack of forty wolves emerged.

She froze at the sight of the blood on their chests and muzzles, and something twisted in her stomach.

"What have you done?" She demanded of the first wolf she encountered, a silvered grey with a scarred nose.

He looked at her and Brune with disinterest. "Argasar's orders." He didn't bother explaining, instead following his pack mates toward the manor.

Brune rushed to the prison gate and stopped, staring. Indigo joined him, and the scene within made her cover her nose and mouth. Urzok bodies were everywhere. It had been a massacre, with no one left alive.

Argasar's orders…

"Ghazan," Brune growled.

"They'll kill him too," Indigo realized.

They bolted from the prison gates, running past the unhurried wolf pack and into the manor hall. Indigo took the stairs three at a time, her lungs burning, but she didn't care. At the top of the turret, she and Brune pushed past the wolf guards before they could stop them, through the open door of Ghazan's room.

Argasar was standing over the man, who lay face down, one arm flung out. Indigo could tell from the pooling blood that he was dead.

The white alpha looked at them. "Hello, Princess."

A thousand words rushed through her head, but she only managed to get one out. "Why?"

"The alchemist is dead," the wolf said, matter-of-factly. "We had no more use for the prisoners."

"And that justifies killing them?" Brune growled.

"I can't risk rebellion from the inside," Argasar replied, calm. "And what supplies we have I need for feeding my pack, not prisoners."

"But now you've lost your pack's only bargaining tool," Brune argued. "The empire will show no mercy when it comes for Nyatha."

"And we'll be ready," the wolf replied calmly.

A chill slithered through Indigo. For the first time, she sensed that Argasar's thirst for vengeance made him a danger not just to the Urzoks, but to those he claimed to defend. The wolf didn't care if he died, perhaps even yearned for death, and planned to take down as many other lives as possible.

"I said, did you find anything useful in the alchemist's cottage?"

The rabbit realized the wolf had been speaking to her. Indigo's throat closed, and Brune answered for her. "No. We found nothing."

"Then if you've no other business with me, I have matters to see to." Argasar made a move to step past them, but Indigo stood her ground.

"Now that the alchemist is dead, we shall leave in search of the alchemists' guild."

The wolf flicked his ears and looked from one to the other. "I'm afraid I can't allow that."

"What?" Brune growled.

Argasar looked unruffled. "I need every fighter we have. I can't have my army seeing you two fleeing. It will encourage deserters."

"We're not fleeing," Indigo said hotly. "We came to find the secret to black snow, and now that the trail's dead here, we can't stay."

The wolf smiled. "I'm afraid I must insist you do. If you leave, there will be consequences."

Indigo forced herself to stay silent as Argasar left. But when she was alone with Brune, they shared a look, and she knew he was thinking the same thing. They were prisoners, and if they wanted to reach Doom Hollow with Kestrel, they would have to think of a way to secretly escape.

CHAPTER 18

The marketplace was doing a roaring noonday business. Merchants, business folk, and errand boys choked the laneways, while buyers hurried to favorite shops or allowed themselves to slow and be enticed by the various wares pushed in their path.

Reenan wove through the crowd with Manneki perched on his shoulder, seemingly absorbed in cracking seeds between his teeth and spitting them expertly so they didn't land on passersby. But Manneki kept one keen eye on their real target, using his tail, which rested on Reenan's shoulder, to alert him whenever they needed to turn left or right.

The man was short, which would have made it hard to keep track of him in the crowd if not for the bright cap he wore. It also helped that Reenan and Manneki knew where the man was headed. Today was payday, and the man was dutifully taking his earnings home to his wife and daughter, as he did every week.

The alley was within sight now. At a nod from Reenan, the Grodlyn clambered down his side and leapt nimbly to the ground, disappearing among the forest of legs. Reenan turned to the right abruptly and cut his way across the crowd, disappearing into a nearby laneway. He hurried down the narrow street, then took a left. One, two, three, four laneways later, he paused to listen, expectant.

A shout cut through the market hubbub, and there were several exclamations of alarm.

"Thief! Thief!"

Manneki had struck. Reenan sprinted down the next alleyway where a pottery hawker's mat was laid out, a few small wares displayed. The potter looked up, flashing him a welcoming smile as she kneaded the soft clay in her hands.

"Care for a nice jug? Or bowl?" the woman asked.

Reenan hunkered down, as if examining Hizarah's wares. Within a heartbeat, Manneki came tearing around the corner, something clutched to his chest. A few passersby yelped as he sped past their legs, and then Manneki was crashing through the pottery wares, sending bowls and plates flying. As Hizarah shouted in a show of anger and tried to save what she could, Manneki deftly passed his cargo to Reenan—a healthy coin purse, and a silver seal on a rope.

Reenan knelt, as if helping gather the broken pottery, while Manneki shimmied up a nearby drainpipe, disappearing over a neighboring roof. Reenan quickly pressed the seal to the soft clay Hizarah had been kneading, then pulled it free and turned the clay over on the ground. Hizarah swept it up and placed it in her wares basket, expertly flicking a cloth to cover the whole thing.

Reenan wiped the seal to remove any clay, then stood, purse and seal in hand, just as a disheveled and distraught man with a bright cap appeared at the alley entry.

"Thief!"

"Is this yours?" Reenan held up the purse and the seal.

The man looked so relieved that Reenan was worried he would cry. But the man's emotions quickly turned to anger.

"Where's the little beast?"

"I'm afraid I couldn't catch him," Reenan said, apologetic.

"But this was all he had on him. He dropped it when he crashed into the pots."

"Everything! He broke everything!" Hizarah moaned.

The short man came forward and took the purse and seal with shaking hands. "Thank you." He didn't even check the coins in the purse, but instead, felt the seal over and over, as if to make sure it was real.

"No need for thanks, but you must be careful of thieves, they're everywhere," Reenan said.

"Yes, we wouldn't have this problem if animals were banned from the capital," the short man said gruffly. He turned to Hizarah, who was picking up pieces of pottery to see if any could be salvaged. "Let me pay for your wares. It's the least I can do."

A look of surprise flitted across Hizarah's face. She and Reenan hadn't expected Dorgun's chamberlain to be generous. But Hizarah quickly recovered.

"Indeed, that's only fair, isn't it? My thanks. Five coin, I could have made."

Reenan winced inwardly, but knew that Hizarah had to play the part of the wronged and opportunistic vendor, or the chamberlain might suspect something.

The man seemed happy to pay. What were five coins to a lashing and losing one's job, Reenan reasoned. The chamberlain handed the money to Hizarah, thanked them both, and then placed his coin purse and seal deep inside his shirt pockets. No one was going to rob him again today.

When he had gone, Hizarah picked up her basket and pocketed the coin. "Perhaps we should rob another chamberlain."

Reenan shot her a look, but she had already pulled the hood over her face, hiding her smile.

* * *

JUST AS HE began to worry that the trio had failed, Theo heard Manneki slip into the house via the upstairs window, then patter down the stairs. The exultant look on Manneki's face told him that the Grodlyn's part, at least, had gone well.

Father Oaks stirred the pot of metal at the hearth, while Orjo kept the fire stoked.

"Is it ready?" Theo asked.

Orjo grunted in exasperation. "If you don't stop asking, I'll—"

The door opened and Hizarah entered, pushing her hood off her head.

"Where's Reenan?" Theo asked.

"We took different routes to be safe," Hizarah answered. "He should be here soon." She set her basket down and pulled the cloth away, reaching in to withdraw the clay mold.

"Any trouble?" Theo asked. He couldn't help worrying for both Reenan and Hizarah's safety. They were risking everything, and while Manneki would surely be punished, the couple would pay dearly for turning against their own kind.

"Easy as getting wet in the rain. Even made some coin." Hizarah motioned for the wooden bread paddle leaning against the hearth, and Manneki brought it. She placed the mold on the paddle and held it to the flame to harden the mold.

By the time it had set and they were ready to pour the metal in, Reenan came through the door, then latched it behind him.

"Are we officially chamberlains yet?"

Orjo grunted. "Nearly. Now be quiet while I pour."

Hizarah positioned the paddle holding the clay mold on the ground, and Orjo took a pair of mitts to handle the kettle on the fire. Everyone stood back as Orjo carefully poured the contents out and into the mold, stopping before it could overflow.

"Where'd you learn metal smithing?" Theo asked. The metal smiths of Willago took years to hone their craft.

Orjo hung the kettle back on the hook and pulled off his mitts. "Living as an exile, I had to learn a few things. Made quite a few of my own weapons." He motioned for Manneki to bring a jug of water, which the Grodlyn did. Orjo poured the water over the clay mold, and the hot metal steamed angrily.

When the air had cleared, everyone leaned forward. Orjo motioned for a hammer lying on a table nearby, and Father Oaks handed it to him. The muskrat took it and smashed the clay, then held up the bronze metal seal for them to see. Between his claws was what, at first, looked like a coin, but ridged along the sides. Its surface had an intricate design of a horse on it, the fine strands of its mane and tail a complex web that would have been painstakingly carved.

"Color's different, but otherwise, it's like the real thing," Reenan said. "So far this is easy as getting wet in the rain."

Orjo shook his head at the two people. "You two really are a couple."

Theo hefted the seal. "Now for the hard part."

* * *

THE TAILOR'S was a luxurious building, even compared to other ornate establishments. This part of town was the fashion district, Hizarah had explained to Theo, where the well-heeled and well-coined came to have their hats, britches, vests, gowns, and even undergarments made.

He could imagine it during the day, a bustle of activity as silks, cottons, muslins, and furs flowed in and out of these shops, their fronts decorated with bright signs showing the specialties to be found in each. But now, under a sliver of moon, the streets were quiet but for the occasional city guards, tavern goers, and musicians off to their next stop.

From across the road and hidden in an alleyway, Theo examined the tailor's building again. It was painted an attractive apple green with yellow-rimmed windows and shutters. Unlike the other shops, it had no sign at the front, simply an ornate gate that declared it was important, and that if you didn't know its business, then you had no business there. It was a two-story place, with a wide carriageway curving around its back.

A small shadow slipped from this carriageway and hurried across the street to the alleyway where Theo and Hizarah waited. Orjo nodded toward the shop.

"The watch has gone to bed."

Hizarah opened her basket and held it while Theo and Orjo took out what they needed: rope for Orjo, and a wooden tube that Theo slung over his body. He checked its contents, then nodded to Orjo.

"Ready? In and out, remember. Easy as getting wet in the rain."

Hizarah closed the basket, and Theo and Orjo looked up and down the street. An ale-soaked man was warbling his way through a melody while trying to navigate the stairs up to another street, but besides that, the fashion area was deserted. Orjo led the way, with Theo following, the leather tube on his back.

They squeezed in through the ornate gates, then slipped around the back of the building. The grandeur of the house sloped down to a rougher building with double doors and one shuttered window. Theo heard the neigh of horses from inside.

They had scouted the shop multiple nights and had not found a way into the stables. Their only option was to go via the shop's main chimney, which led into the workroom, and from there enter the stables.

Orjo pushed back his robe, then slung the rope over his shoulders and shimmied up a drainpipe with an ease Theo envied. Orjo was ancient, but clearly still agile.

The muskrat disappeared for a moment, two. Then the rope came tumbling down over the roof edge, landing at Theo's feet. Orjo's impatient face appeared a moment later, clearly annoyed at his taking so long.

The rabbit took a breath. As much as he dreaded this task, it was time to pull his weight, literally. He made sure the tube was secure to his back, then reached up with both paws and began the ascent. Rabbits, he thought for the hundredth time, were not built to climb.

Theo had barely made the halfway mark when Orjo lost patience and began pulling on the rope to try to help him. When Theo finally grasped the edge of the roof with raw, burning paws, Orjo was huffing as he pulled the rabbit up and onto the roof tiles.

"By Aktu, we should have devised a pulley," Orjo grumbled. Theo stepped onto a roof tile that cracked in the silence, and both of them froze, ears alert to any hint that they had woken the watch.

On their scouting trips, the night watch had seemed a sound sleeper. He hadn't awoken or investigated when they had tossed pebbles against the roof and windows to test his slumber. But this cracking of the tile had been loud.

The tapping of a cane against the cobblestones reached them. The agreed signal with Hizarah to let them know all was clear, and that she could see no candlelight in the windows to indicate someone had woken.

Heart thudding, Theo made his way to the chimney and peered in. Total darkness. Orjo had tied one end of his rope in a girth hitch around the chimney and now brought the rest of it up onto the roof. He fashioned the other end into a loop and tied it under Theo's arms and waist.

"Ready?"

There was no point in saying he wasn't. Theo took a steadying breath, then straddled the edge of the chimney. Orjo held on to the rope and gave a mock salute, as if to say *Good luck*.

Theo began lowering himself in, cursing his own lack of strength. If he'd been stronger than Orjo, then their roles would have been reversed, and he wouldn't be going into this yawning, dark cavern.

As he worked his way down the soot- and cobweb-covered chimney, the moonlight faded. His eyes tried to adjust, but it was too dark. He felt his way down, bit by bit, his paws and toes feeling for secure holds in the crevices. His confidence grew as he navigated more and more of the chimney, and when he passed what he guessed must be the halfway mark, he gave a silent thanks, while begging his limbs to not give way. He didn't want to think about how he was going to get back up.

He focused on one brick at a time, all the while trying to make as little sound as possible. If he woke the boy on watch, they would have to abandon the mission and try another night.

The thought of coming back made him try to hurry, which was a mistake. His paw slipped, scraping him along one side as he slid unchecked down the chimney. Terror made him reach out with his back legs, but this only earned him a bruising blow to his backside and resulted in his landing shoulder first on the hearth floor.

He couldn't help a groan from escaping. A silhouette appeared at the top of the chimney.

Orjo gave a soft owl's hoot from above.

Theo stood and checked his bones. Bruised, and his fur had been scraped off in a few places, but otherwise he seemed all right. He gave three short tugs on the rope, the signal for everything being all right. He untangled himself from the rope, then looked about him, and in the dark, could just make out that he seemed to be in a display room. Bolts of cloth leaned against one wall, while a long, stuffed stool ran the length of the room. Closed double doors on the north side led to the front of the shop, while another set of plain double doors led to the south.

Theo headed for the southern doors. Hizarah had given him the lay of the land when she'd come pretending to be a customer. These doors led to a hallway, at the end of which were the stables for delivering orders to buyers. Theo went through this hallway now and into the stables.

The smell of leather, tack, metal, and straw hit his nose. A skylight let in a single shaft of moonlight, and Theo could see and hear the horses on the right side of the stables. To the left was the tailor's carriage.

He circled the vehicle, examining the white needle threaded through a garland of green flowers painted on one side. He opened his tube and pulled out two pots of ink, one white and one green, and two brushes made of donkey hair, along with a beige linen sheet.

He started with the white needle on the carriage's side, and painted the white ink onto it, careful to stay true to the lines. He then switched to green, and painted in the green flowers. He had to work fast, before the paint dried.

When he was done, he unrolled the beige linen sheet and pressed it to the carriage. He counted to twenty, then to thirty just to be sure. When he peeled the linen away, the paint came away onto it. Theo knew he had little time to admire his handiwork, however. He pulled a cloth from his tube, and dipped the cloth in the horse's trough, then returned and wiped off the excess paint left behind on the carriage.

He checked to see that the linen was dry, then carefully rolled it up and placed it back in the tube, along with the stoppered pots of paint and the brushes, which he wrapped in his cloth. Shouldering the tube, he left the stables and made his way back to the chimney.

He pulled the rope loops around his arms, then secured the rest around his body. He would be happy to get out of this place. He gave the rope three short tugs to signal he was ready.

There was no answering tug.

When he tugged again, a voice behind him made him jump.

"We're both climbing the chimney now."

He whirled, heart hammering, to see Orjo standing behind him. "What are you doing down here?" he hissed.

"Solving a problem." The muskrat pushed past him and wiped his paws on the rope, then began the climb up the chimney.

It took Theo a moment to realize what was bothering him—

besides the fact that Orjo was not on the roof. Why wasn't Orjo whispering?

"What problem?" Theo dreaded the answer.

"The watch woke up," Orjo said simply.

Theo's gut twisted. The watch might have been Urzok, but that didn't mean he deserved to die. "Did you have to kill him?"

"We can discuss morality when we get back to Hizarah's," the muskrat called down. "Now climb, or you'll have us both in the empire's clutches by morning."

CHAPTER 19

*V*aliant, but completely ineffective, Ornox concluded as he surveyed the trading post's defenses from the small knoll to Nyatha's west.

A half moat had been dug around the walls, with sharpened spikes to deter attackers. But Ornox knew this only defended the main entry point. The trading post had one other gateway, much smaller than the main gate, true, but both were designed for trade, not siege. Which meant none of the entries had barbicans, or murder holes.

Ornox looked out at his army camp, set a safe distance away from Nyatha, out of range of any long bows or catapults the occupiers might have obtained. What farmhouses and huts dotted the landscape outside Nyatha were deserted, as the residents smelled war and knew better than to stay. An imperial army meant giving up all their carefully saved foodstuffs and livestock to feed the soldiers. So they had fled, leaving Ornox's army to pick and forage what was left.

Ordinarily, taking Nyatha would be easy, almost a skirmish one could assign an inexperienced warlord. With no defenses to speak of, Nyatha would fall within hours with a few catapults, perhaps at most a fire-arrow barrage. But Ornox could do neither of these things. Not without information.

He needed his alchemist alive, and he could not risk her dying from some stray arrow or being crushed beneath catapulted boulders. He also needed to make sure he was fighting a ragtag group of upstarts, and not the more organized forces of the Order.

Yod came plodding up the knoll from the camp, where cooking fires were already being lit.

"The messenger returned, Lord Ornox."

"The answer?"

"No surrender."

Though he had expected this answer, he had still hoped they might be intimidated into submission. He had instructed his generals to set two campfires for every soldier in their army, to make the defenders think he had a bigger force than he did. Creating fear in the enemy might just make them surrender without a fight. And for the first time in his career, Ornox didn't want a fight.

"What of prisoners?"

Yod's jaw twitched. "It seems they were all killed. Massacred."

Ornox digested this unexpected piece of news. "No survivors?"

"None."

This changed everything. The good news was this was not the Order's work. They wouldn't be foolish enough to kill every hostage and leave themselves no room for barter. The bad news was, it looked like he might have lost his alchemist, and his weapon for taking the throne. It was this that made Ornox's blood run hot.

"Have every man ready to attack at nightfall. Have all the catapults primed. We strike when the sun sets, and we take no prisoners. Kill every last one, except for their leader. I want to skin him myself."

* * *

INDIGO HAD, like everyone else, watched the arrival of Ornox's forces the day before from the walls of Nyatha. Though the appearance of the enemy had brought a current of unease to the other defenders, Argasar seemed elated. He had sent Ornox's messenger back with a sound rejection of any surrender and sprung into a frenzy of organizing defenses and rousing the rabbits to dig pits and barricades near the main gates.

"It's a death sentence," Brune said grimly, looking out over the growing smudge on the horizon. "Argasar's got fire, but he's as outmatched as a candle in a blizzard."

Indigo nodded, heart heavy. She couldn't bring herself to voice her thoughts, that everyone here was as good as dead. They had killed Ornox's prize alchemist and his business partner Ghazan. There would be no mercy.

"We have to get Kestrel out," she said. "Before Ornox attacks."

Brune nodded. "We'll need a new plan."

They'd intended to hide Kestrel in Brune's satchel, then get themselves onto the outer moat crews, and from there, sneak away. But now that Ornox's troops had arrived, they were trapped, as work on the moats had to be abandoned. The only way past the warlord's troops was above them, through them, or around them.

Or under them.

"The tunnel," Indigo said. At Brune's look she explained, "We can get out through the tunnel without Ornox knowing."

"Good thinking." The bear turned back to watch the enemy amass beyond the walls, frowning. "Best to leave at night, before it's too late."

* * *

DARKNESS HAD SCARCELY FALLEN, but Indigo chafed at every minute wasted. She excused herself from her assigned task of drilling the archers and went to seek Brune, who was similarly extricating himself from hauling water for the fire-defense team.

Brune put down his empty bucket, adjusted his helmet, and motioned at the cottage. "Let's go, Princess."

They walked through the central yard, trying not to hurry, past the prisons and to the cottage. Indigo looked around to make sure no one was watching before opening the door and entering. They found Kestrel perched on the windowsill, peering out.

"I thought we agreed you wouldn't go near the windows!" Indigo said, worried.

"I heard shouting. What is happening?"

"We're leaving," Brune said simply.

The canary jumped down onto a small satchel they'd given her to keep for when they left. Brune held the satchel open for the bird to climb in.

"It'll be uncomfortable," Indigo said, "but it's only until we reach the tunnel."

The canary nodded.

Brune closed the satchel and slung it over his shoulder. "Try to stay still," he advised. He then picked up a sack filled with cloth and hefted it over his shoulder.

Indigo led the way out, heading toward the manor. Argasar had warned that Ornox might decide against siege, and that everyone should be ready for attack at any time. The entire force of rabbits, wolves, and other liberated Nyatha animals had leapt into action to ready stakes, rocks, pitch for fire arrows, and other lines of defense. Any who glanced at Brune and his bulging sack would assume he was carrying sand or rocks to the outer perimeter. Hopefully, they would ignore the satchel holding Kestrel.

Inside the manor, the hallways were nearly deserted and steeped in darkness, all lamp oil conserved for the battle, and all the ground-floor windows boarded up in case the defenders had to retreat to Nyatha's heart. Brune and Indigo passed the great hall, then turned down the corridor that led to the chapel, where they had entered the manor what seemed a lifetime ago.

"Just a little further," Brune reassured Kestrel. Indigo turned into the chapel, Brune behind her, but once inside both stopped in their tracks.

"The battle is outside, Princess. Not here."

Standing on the other side of the tunnel entrance was Argasar, with three of his betas surrounding him, including Nartah. A few pews lined the walls, and the statue of the emperor looked down at them all from his pedestal by the window.

Indigo turned, ready to flee back out the door, but another wolf had filled the space, a great tawny female with blackened teeth.

"Your entire pack should go through this tunnel," Indigo said. "If you don't, it'll be a slaughter."

The alpha cocked his head, disappointed. "I had thought you braver than this. The Alvareth queendoms are famed for their fearlessness."

"This is not fear," Brune growled. "This is good sense."

"Then why don't you leave your bundle and save yourselves?" the wolf replied.

Indigo and Brune stood silent, unmoving.

"I thought not." Argasar gave the rabbit a wry smile. "You lied to me about not finding anything in the alchemist's cottage. Show me what you found."

Brune slipped the sack to the floor, and let it fall open. Loose blankets and tools fell to the floor. "Just some supplies for the road."

The wolf smiled. "I meant the satchel."

At the bear's hesitation, Argasar barked at his wolves, "Tear it open."

"No!" Indigo shouted. Then looked to Brune. He reluctantly slipped the satchel off his shoulder and placed it on the ground, then opened the flap to reveal Kestrel's bright yellow feathers and scared face.

"What is this?" Argasar asked.

"The alchemist's canary," the rabbit said. "She's our one chance at making black snow and defeating the empire."

"Sounds like an important ally," the wolf agreed. "Someone with such knowledge cannot be let out of Nyatha, and I am disappointed to learn you would keep this from me." He turned to the wolves. "Take the bird to the turret upstairs. And put these two in the prisons."

"Argasar, this is a mistake," Brune growled.

"Ornox will attack at any moment," Indigo added. "If he gets ahold of her, we'll never be able to defeat him."

"I'm not inclined to trust deserters," Argasar said coolly. "Now place your weapons here. You won't be needing them."

Indigo looked to Brune, uncertain. She was tempted to fight, but Brune gave a short shake of the head. There were too many of them. She pulled her sword from its sheath and sent it clattering to the floor at Argasar's paws.

"Good. Now you, bear."

Brune looked pained as he pulled the axe from his holster.

"Now," Argasar snapped.

The bear bent to put down his axe, when horn blasts sounded from outside, and a bell began pealing. Everyone looked out the chapel windows.

"It's Ornox," Indigo said. "He's attacking!"

No sooner were the words out than a giant rumble echoed through the manor. Shouts and the sound of splintering wood followed.

"Nartah, with me!" Argasar snapped, his decision made. "The rest of you, get these three to the turret and lock them there!" The alpha swept from the room, Nartah following, while the other three—a silver, a grey, and Blackteeth—closed ranks around their prisoners.

Indigo's heart thudded as the tension thickened. The wolves were less confident, but still outnumbered them.

"Drop your axe, bear!" Blackteeth snarled behind them.

Brune went very still, clearly calculating.

"I said drop—"

Brune hefted his weapon and threw. The axe blade cleaved deep into the silver wolf's head, dropping him instantly. The grey leaped, while Indigo dove for her sword. She reached it just as the grey snapped its jaws at where her head had been, but she rolled and scrambled to her feet.

"Into the tunnel!" She yelled at Kestrel.

"Where is it?" the bird cried, flapping her wings and skittering out of the way of claws and teeth.

"Middle of the room! Look for a loose slate!" Indigo brought her sword up to defend against the grey's renewed attack. He snaked in from the side, teeth bared, but she darted behind the emperor's statue. The wolf brought his full weight against the statue. Indigo rolled out of the way just as it crashed to the ground, shattering with a roar. She brought her sword up at the charging wolf and slashed a straight line across his shoulder. The wolf stumbled and tried to turn around to regroup, but she sank her sword past his ribs and into his heart. The wolf was dead before she freed her blade.

She looked over to see Brune standing over Blackteeth, who lay motionless on the ground, her head at an odd angle, rubble scattered around them. The square in the floor had not been moved, and Indigo hurriedly looked around.

"Kestrel?"

A chirp came from under a pew and Kestrel appeared, still shaking.

"Are you all right?" Indigo asked.

The bird nodded. Indigo looked over at Brune. "You?"

The bear retrieved his axe and placed it back in its holster. "I'll be better when we're far from here." He moved to the loose square floor, and worked it free, then pushed it to one side. He grabbed the satchel and opened it for Kestrel, who hopped inside. Brune closed the satchel.

The sounds of the battle were growing louder, the horns and crashes more strident.

"Let's go," Indigo said, dropping into the tunnel. "Nyatha won't stand long."

CHAPTER 20

"You are lucky you brought him here when you did." The Urzok healer, a short man with a long braid and a kind face, gave Pozzi and Keeva an encouraging smile. "Any later, and I couldn't have helped him."

It had been a day of no sleep, of sitting by Walnut's bedside and having the healer come in each hour with a grave expression. Harlan had given up his room, a small but comfortable hut next to the temple's brewery, and they'd wrapped a stiff and shivering Walnut into the bed there.

"We cannot thank you enough," Keeva said. "Let us do something for you."

"No need. Harlan has taken care of it," the healer said. "Two barrels of his fine mead are payment aplenty."

Keeva turned to Harlan, who stood in the doorway. "Thank you."

Harlan smiled a smile that Pozzi remembered well.

"No need to thank me. Anything for a fellow villager."

Pozzi wondered again at whether the rabbit could possibly have changed. The Harlan he had known refused to even share his moldy bread ration with Walnut when they had been on their forced march to Nyatha. Seeming to sense Pozzi's hesitation, Harlan pulled a stool and sat down after the healer stepped out.

"I know you and I traded some harsh words, Pozzi. I was an angry and very frightened soul when you both last knew me." He reached out for Keeva's paw but she pretended not to see and bent to tuck Walnut's blanket in. Harlan withdrew his paw. "But I did much of it to make sure you and the rest of Willago were freed. And I've suffered my fair share." He touched the scar on his face.

A tense silence fell, and he must have seen their expressions. He looked from one to the other.

"They didn't free us," Pozzi said, bitter. "They took us to their farms. Most of Willago is dead."

Harlan stared. "Is this a jest? If so, it's cruel."

"No jest," Pozzi said, voice low. "I said then and I say now, the cat doesn't bargain with the mouse. You sold Theo out for nothing."

Harlan turned to Keeva. "Is that true?"

She avoided his eyes. "We were only saved because we were kept as pets. The three of us are just now escaping from Nyatha, on our way back to Willago." She told him of everything they had been through, first in halting sentences, and then in an outpour. From the journey to Nyatha, to being kept as playthings, to learning of the Cradles that turned thinking creatures into passive, mindless ones, she told Harlan everything.

Harlan sat still, his face a mix of anger and disbelief. He had genuinely thought he'd saved their lives by helping Agacheta and her father, Pozzi realized incredulously. Harlan had genuinely believed himself the hero of Willago.

"I don't know what to say," Harlan finally said, looking up at them. "They lied to me, and I believed them. I'm sorry."

He seemed to hope they would contradict him. When the silence stretched, Pozzi asked the question that had been on his mind ever since they first saw him.

"How did you come to be here, Harlan? Living with people?"

"They took me in when no one else would. They learned of my brewing skills and said I could work and live here among them."

"If you thought we'd been freed, why didn't you return to Willago?" *To your wife*, Pozzi almost added, but couldn't. He thought he caught a flash of the old Harlan in the rabbit's eye, that familiar contempt, but then it was gone.

"It's a dangerous journey back without a safe-passage token," Harlan answered. "I was attacked many a time. I knew I couldn't make it home by myself." He paused. "But now, maybe we can. Together."

The idea of making the journey back to Willago with Harlan was more unpleasant for Pozzi than facing the Urzoks on the way. Pozzi would have willingly traded his right paw if it would guarantee returning home without Harlan.

"Unless…you don't want me with you," Harlan said, despondent.

"That's not it," Keeva was quick to say. Hurting feelings, for Keeva, was against her nature. She would do anything to avoid it, and the cynical side of Pozzi wondered if Harlan had been counting on it.

"No, I understand," Harlan said, low. "You still blame me for what happened."

Yes! Pozzi screamed inwardly, but bit his lip. *If you hadn't betrayed Theo and all of us, if you hadn't trusted the Urzoks, if you had listened to Father Oaks. If, if, if!*

"You're welcome to come with us," Keeva said. "Right, Pozzi?"

Oh gods help him. "If that's what you want."

Harlan smiled. "I've changed, Pozzi, you'll see."

"We all have," Pozzi said, glancing at Keeva. When they had still been imprisoned, she had said marrying Harlan had been a mistake. Did she still feel that way now?

"My time here at the temple has given me a chance to think." Harlan seemed to be addressing Keeva now, eager to convince her more than Pozzi. "I've dreamed of having a second chance at being better. At everything, including being a husband."

He reached out again, and this time, Keeva purposefully drew her paw away. "Harlan, there's something you need to know." She looked at Pozzi, and his heart thudded. He made to stand and leave, but Keeva shook her head for him to stay. "You've changed, but so have I. Things cannot go back to what they were. Pozzi and I…"

Harlan glanced at Pozzi, a look of incredulity quickly suppressed. "But we're married. Does that not count for anything?"

Keeva's ears flushed, and Pozzi was tempted to smack Harlan. Keeva was trying to tell him her feelings, and all Harlan could think to do was to make her feel guilty.

"So much has happened, Harlan. That was then. This is now."

"I see," Harlan said, in a way that Pozzi felt meant he didn't see at all. Harlan had always been the strongest, the best looking, the most prized. Despite the brand burned onto his face, he no doubt still expected to be adored.

"Do you still want to leave all this behind?" Keeva asked.

Harlan nodded. "'Course I do. Home is home. And if you've chosen Pozzi, then I must respect that, mustn't I?" An awkward silence fell. "I'd better see to the healer's mead."

He left the room, clearly as eager to be away from them as they were from him. Keeva stood and slipped her paw into Pozzi's, and his heart danced a little, as it always did.

"Do you think he's really changed?" Pozzi couldn't help asking.

"Anything is possible," Keeva answered, leaning her head on his shoulder and looking down at the sleeping Walnut.

Yes, anything is possible, Pozzi thought. But instead of making him hopeful, the thought made him even more uneasy.

CHAPTER 21

Ornox stepped through the shattered doors, then to the audience hall with its dais and Ghazan's chair, which he knew well. It was here he'd come to strike his deal with Ghazan, and neither had known that within half a year, Ornox would have to battle his way back through the gate.

"Double-check for survivors, and bring any to the trade hall next door," Ornox commanded Yod, who was ever by his side. "Has anyone found Ghazan yet?"

Yod shook his head. "We assume they're all dead, my lord. I'll have the men dig up and search the bodies."

Ornox nodded and took the opportunity to slip through the corridors to the courtyard. Much was destroyed or in disarray, with captured animals, dead and alive, being organized into piles or groups, respectively. But Ornox prided himself on his memory of people and places, and he found his way easily enough to the cottage by the Cradles. Inside, he could see that the place had been ransacked, though much remained untouched on the higher shelves. He picked his way through the room, looking for traces of black snow, or anything that might indicate the occupiers had known about the alchemist's project. But all he could determine was that the cottage was a mess, and if there was by any chance a small cache of black snow some-where, it was well hidden.

"My lord, we've found no surviving people."

He turned and followed Yod out of the cottage and back up to the manor. He wasn't in the habit of bargaining with gods, but he found himself asking some unknown being to grant him this wish. That by some miracle his alchemist was alive, that Yod was wrong.

"Show me the dead," he said finally.

Yod hesitated. "The bodies haven't all been gathered yet. But we found Ghazan's body."

Blackhide curse it. "Find some trusted men, only our own, search the bodies. I'm looking for a middle-aged woman with a high nose and long brown hair. I need to see anyone that matches, even if only vaguely."

Yod nodded and hastened to give instructions to the men. Ornox strode away down the corridor, wanting to find some quiet in this chaos so he could think. Was Ethana dead? If so, his plans for the throne were severely dashed. And the only one he could ask, the only one who even knew who Ethana was, was Ghazan. And he was dead.

He decided all he could do for now was wait. Destroy those who had resisted him, and wait.

Ornox's men cleared out the main chambers for Ornox's use, and he had them bring him a basic meal and wine. By the time he'd finished, Yod had appeared in the doorway, his expression telling Ornox the man had unwelcome news.

"We may have found her, my lord."

Ornox wiped his mouth and stood. He followed Yod down to the ground floor and to the audience hall, where two soldiers stood over a body, a piece of cloth obscuring her face. Ornox pulled the covering back and stared down at the lifeless features.

She was bloodied, bruised, and she looked smaller in death than in life. But there was no mistaking the alchemist.

Ornox tried to quiet his emotions, to not let his anger show.

A great warlord did not give up the battle when facing a more powerful enemy. No, a great warlord would know that if you can't overpower your opponent, then step back and find another route. Ornox would still take the throne, with or without the alchemist. He just needed to think of an alternative to black snow. But for now, he needed an outlet for his frustration.

"Bring me the wolf," Ornox said. "The alpha."

Yod nodded and left. The remaining soldiers looked uncomfortable, clearly unwilling to be near their master when his mood was palpably foul.

Yod returned with two soldiers who had poles attached to a metal collar on the white wolf. The creature was matted with blood, one eye swollen shut.

"You the one they call Argasar?"

The wolf flashed his fangs in a humorless smile. "Alpha Argasar."

"Leave us," Ornox told his men.

The soldiers put down the poles holding the wolf's collar and backed out of the room, and Yod closed the door after them before standing to one side, waiting.

"Did one of yours do this?" Ornox asked the wolf, indicating Ethana's body.

"I hope so." Argasar's reply was regal and considered, given his situation.

"Do you know who she is?"

"A dead Urzok," the wolf replied, flat.

Ornox considered him, trying to see if the beast was playing games. "She was an alchemist. My alchemist."

"If she was of worth to you, then I'm glad she's dead."

He had to give the wolf credit for his courage. "Relish your victory, wolf, for it ends now. Did you have any requests before we proceed? Leniency for your followers?"

Argasar laughed. "Why, would you give it?"

"No," Ornox replied, honest.

"Then let's get this over with." Argasar's snarl returned, and he leapt.

Though Ornox hadn't expected the move, his instincts kicked in. He brought up his armored left arm while his right hand reached for the dirk he kept strapped to his chest. The poles and metal collar dragged behind the beast, but his fangs still gripped Ornox's arm with a bruising force.

The warlord went down, but his dirk came out, and as the wolf let go to lunge for Ornox's face, the man drove his dirk home in three precise stabs—two to the throat and one to the ribs. Yod reached forward and hauled the wolf off his master using the metal collar. Ornox sat up and checked his face for cuts, while the great white beast jerked and then went still, a pool of red staining his chest and paws.

Satisfied he was unscathed, Ornox stood and called in the soldiers. "Kill all the unpacified animals, and make sure all the men have meat tonight. Let them feast and drink."

The soldiers brightened at this and rushed to spread the news. Yod looked to his master. "What would you like done with the bodies, my lord?"

Ornox glanced at the wolf. "Place his head on a spike in the courtyard. And have a tanner bring me his pelt." Yod nodded and called for men to help remove the beast's body.

His anger satiated, Ornox returned to his rooms. He needed time to think. And devise how he'd take the throne, now that he'd lost his black snow.

THE NEXT DAY brought with it the cumbersome tasks of dealing with cleanup and reestablishing order at Nyatha. Ornox had his troops hoist the empire's flag above each corner of Nyatha's walls so that the farmers and residents, as well as any lingering enemies, would know Nyatha was under rightful rule once more. With all the former inhabitants slain, Ornox would have to organize a garrison of troops to stay and hold the post to keep it running while he prepared to return to the capital. Victorious once more.

The trickle of returnees started by midday. Ornox was interrupted in his overseeing the damages to horses and weaponry when Yod appeared discreetly at his elbow.

"Our soldiers have found some survivors, my lord."

"Anyone useful?" He didn't need more mouths. Ideally, they had found women who could clean up the manor or soldiers who could defend the fort.

"Perhaps. They're Ghazan's children, my lord."

Ornox sighed. So they had escaped. Though they were now fatherless. Traditionally, they would be the rightful heirs to Nyatha, and he would have to see to their safety. Another drain on his resources and time.

"Show them to the audience hall," he told Yod. "I'll meet them there."

He hoped the two brats would not require too much attention. Perhaps he could assign one of his older soldiers to play chaperone and make sure they stayed out of his way.

The two children who stood waiting for him in the audience hall could not have been more opposite. Both had been cleaned up, but they still bore the marks of some brutal time in the wild, it seemed. The girl had scratches on her face and neck, bruising on one cheek, and a frightened, dazed look in her eyes that Ornox had seen many times in war. The boy had lost his mask, and his mutilated face was on display for all to see—a drooping eyelid, a twisted mouth where vengeful crows had, according to the stories, pecked and tore until the face was unrecognizable. Both children had been given new clothes.

"My name is Lord Ornox of Vyad. I knew your father."

"I know who you are, my lord," the boy said. "I am Sarkus, son of Ghazan. And I know my father is dead."

Ornox nodded. "Good. There's no putting it nicely. And

you're not the first children to lose your parents to war. But you're lucky you escaped and returned."

"We came back as soon as we saw the flag flying," Sarkus said. "I am rightful heir to Nyatha now, am I not?"

The warlord considered him, cool. "You are. But there are formalities. So for now, I am in charge here. Do you understand?"

The boy's mouth twisted, and Ornox was unsure whether it was a grimace or a smile. "My lord, I'd like to be in your employ."

The girl looked like she might say something, but Sarkus silenced her with a glare.

It was Ornox's turn to grimace. "Me? Employ you?"

"My lord, I wish to learn to be a warlord like you," Sarkus said. "You are respected, feared, powerful. I have no father to teach me these things, so I'd like to submit myself to you."

"I am not in search of fatherhood," Ornox said sharply.

"Then an apprentice. A servant, even. I will work for my keep."

"I have need of men, not boys."

Sarkus stepped closer. "I'm not a boy, my Lord. I am heir to Nyatha. Surely, that is worth something. I simply ask to serve you, to learn from you. Take me with you to the capital. I don't want to be a common trader like my father."

Ornox considered this. The boy had spirit. But spirit untested was like an unbroken horse: useless. Best to get rid of the boy, and he had an idea for how to do just that.

"Very well," Ornox said. The boy broke into a wide sneer, which Ornox took as a grin. "But you must prove yourself."

"Anything, my lord."

"I won't have a boy who can't even fight off common crows. If you want to join me, you have to show me your mettle."

The boy's skin mottled at the mention of the crows, but his chin remained high. "Who would you have me fight?"

Ornox called for Yod. "Yod, who's the biggest soldier we have?"

"That would be Neth, my lord."

"Bring Neth in, and take Ghazan's daughter out." He smiled at her. "She might not want to see this."

Yod bowed and motioned for the girl to follow him. She shot her brother a frightened look, but to his credit, the youth didn't back down, and instead, motioned impatiently at her. "Go."

She followed Yod out, glancing one last time behind her before the doors closed.

Yod returned, this time without the sister but with a large, hulking man following. Neth had wiry long hair in a messy braid, a nose that looked like it had been hammered flat, and stood a good head taller than Ornox, which was in itself a feat.

Ornox could sense Sarkus shifting, nervous. The warlord turned to the boy. "If you can make Neth submit, then I shall grant your request and take you under my wing."

"And if not?" Sarkus asked.

Ornox shrugged. "Then I'm guessing your face will seem a minor injury compared to what Neth will deal you."

Neth looked from Sarkus to Ornox. "You want me to fight the child, my lord?"

Sarkus reddened with anger.

"Yes," Ornox said. "Do you have qualms about hurting children?"

Neth shrugged. "No, my lord. Quicker job, really."

"I trust you have weapons on you?"

Neth nodded. "The usual."

"Good." Ornox looked from the boy to Neth. "You may choose one weapon each. Neth may choose first, the boy second. Yod will take your other weapons."

Neth grinned and dutifully handed over a dirk, his soldier's vest of hardened hide, and long sword. He kept a modest skinning knife. At Ornox's raised eyebrows, Neth shrugged. "Don't need a big sword for a small job."

"Your turn to choose a weapon, boy," Ornox said, taking a seat on Ghazan's audience chair, which he knew was the height of insult for the son.

Sarkus glanced at him, but then moved forward to look over the displayed weapons. He hesitated, then snatched up the dirk.

"Begin."

Neth stepped toward Sarkus, gauging. The boy seemed wary, but at a loss, like a chicken facing a fox. Neth lunged with his skinning knife, and Sarkus darted. They circled again, and Neth made another strike, but again Sarkus moved out of reach, clutching his dirk. Neth advanced on him, more determined this time, trying to move his quarry into a corner. He sliced with the knife and drew blood across the boy's chest, but Sarkus still managed to dart out from under the big man.

"I said you'd have to fight him, boy," Ornox snapped. "Not dodge him. If you don't stop running away like a coward, I will consider you forfeit."

Sarkus eyed Neth, his shirt blooming with a ribbon of blood, then reluctantly came away from the walls, his dirk gripped tight. The two circled each other again.

The boy rushed close, as if charging the large man. Ornox supposed the boy had some ridiculous notion that he could take the giant man by surprise. His head went into his opponent's gut, and his dirk went in to stab Neth in the side, but Neth was more experienced. Neth clamped one hand around the arm that held the dirk and twisted.

Sarkus buckled to his knees and howled in pain, the weapon clattering to the ground.

Neth drew his skinning knife back, ready to plunge it into the boy. Sarkus pulled back, Ornox assumed to escape the knife. But then Sarkus's free arm was down at his boot, and there was a flash of metal as his hand yanked something free. A paring knife.

The look of surprise on Neth's face quickly turned to agony

as the boy's arm shot up, propelling the knife straight into the space between Neth's inner thigh and his groin.

The howl brought several soldiers running, their swords drawn. Neth dropped the boy and fell to the floor, gasping like a fish while blood stained his pants and began pooling onto the floor.

Ornox sat up, impressed despite himself. He nodded to one of the soldiers, who rushed forward and placed his hands on the wound to try to stop the bleeding. Another soldier left, shouting for a healer.

The warlord motioned to Yod. "Take Neth out." The giant was already going pale, and Ornox's guess was he wouldn't last the night.

Ornox turned to Sarkus, frowning. "You cheated."

Sarkus glowered. "You said I could choose a weapon. You didn't say anything about giving up my own."

"I never said cheating was a bad thing." Ornox regarded him, thinking, then nodded. "From now on, you serve Vyad."

* * *

EVEN FROM THE safety of the Redwood Forest, they could see that Nyatha was lost. Smoke rose in billowing plumes over the treetops, visible from Argasar's abandoned village where Brune, Indigo, and Kestrel had come after emerging from the tunnel.

Indigo forced herself to look away and not dwell on all of those who had died needlessly with Argasar.

The rabbit took stock of the bird sitting perched on a boulder nearby. Kestrel appeared exhausted, and in pain, but also relieved.

"You all right?"

The bird nodded her yellow head.

"We'll follow the Bear Star north and west," Brune said, clapping his helmet on. "It'll be a long journey." He paused and held out a paw to Kestrel. She hopped on, then made her way up to his shoulder, dragging her injured wing.

"Now let's make tracks. We don't want to be anywhere Ornox might be."

The bear set off with Kestrel on his shoulder, and the rabbit followed, bound for the renowned dragon's cave known as Doom Hollow.

CHAPTER 22

The threat of rain from the low summer clouds made people in the streets scurry, anxious to get their business done. Reenan hitched the donkey to the cart, which was newly painted with the tailor's crest Theo had brought back. Hizarah was loading the cart with sheets, linens, and a bundle of finer clothes for Reenan.

Theo's anger toward Orjo had cooled, though he still felt a nagging resentment that the muskrat sensed but seemed to accept. Upon learning what had happened, Oaks had also berated Orjo until Hizarah had intervened.

"Theo was in danger, and Orjo had to do what needed to be done." She looked at Theo and Oaks. "I dislike bloodshed as much as anyone, but when you choose a path, you walk it. You don't complain about every pebble and ditch."

And though Theo hated to admit it, he realized Hizarah was right. He had chosen to come here and find the Library, despite the risk it brought to everyone. He had no right to condemn Orjo for making a decision to protect them, even if the decision was a drastic one.

Reenan helped Theo and Orjo into the cart. Manneki brought them their bag of supplies, which Orjo checked.

"Everything there, yes?" the Grodlyn asked, wary. His mistrust of Orjo had eased, but seemed to have returned with the news of his killing the watch.

Orjo nodded. "Now, let's hope this scheme works."

"Everyone ready?" Theo asked.

"Almost," Oaks said. "I'm comin' with ye."

"To the castle?" Theo asked, surprised.

The old rabbit shook his head. "Into the Library."

Orjo guffawed, earning a cold glare from Father Oaks. "There's no time to be polite, so I'll just say it. You've more aches than bones, and you'd be a liability. I'm not going in with you. You'll get us killed."

Father Oaks' voice was icy. "Way I remember, last time we were in a bind, it was me who saved yer hide."

Theo had heard the story of Father Oaks and Orjo being captured by the Proudfeathers and nearly eaten. In the end, it was Father Oaks' healer skills, and his insistence that Orjo was Theo's friend, that saved the muskrat.

Orjo waved a paw dismissively. "I would have found my own way out."

Father Oaks snorted. "Aye, by way of some Proudfeather's stomach and backside. Now if ye need to find a book, and find it fast, then ye need every word catcher ye have. And that includes me."

"Father Oaks—" Theo began.

"That goes fer you too," his grandfather said. "Ye were lyin' dead, and it was me who brought ye back. So there's no sayin' no."

Theo digested this, then nodded. "Very well."

"You're both mad," Orjo muttered.

"We don't know how many books the Library has," Theo said. "And we have only a day to find the *Book of Cures*. Every omatje we have increases our chances."

Orjo scowled and waved a paw in exasperation. He lay down in the cart bed, while Theo helped Father Oaks into the cart.

Hizarah piled thick linens over the trio. Then Reenan, Hizarah, and Manneki boarded the wagon and they set off, the wheels creaking over the cobblestones as they made their way to the castle.

Theo tried to keep calm as they neared the heart of the city. Orjo's bulk squeezed him uncomfortably on one side, but he didn't want to lean too hard the other way on the frail form of his grandfather. So he sat in the middle, stiff in mind and body.

The cart jolted onto wood. They must have started across the drawbridge that allowed supplies in and out of the east bailey. The wheels rumbled before the donkey came to a braying halt.

"Not the usual jig today?" a voice asked.

"Broken wheel," Theo heard Reenan reply easily. "Might be in the shop for a few days, so we're using this instead."

The cart jerked forward again. Theo let out a breath he hadn't realized he'd been holding, and was grateful when the contraption stopped and the linens lifted, revealing Hizarah's face. She'd already wrapped her hair in a chambermaid's kerchief, and she had pulled off her cloak, revealing her laundress's clothing underneath. She helped Orjo, then Theo, then Oaks out, and they clambered down to find themselves in a small courtyard that was mercifully deserted.

Reenan pulled out a jacket with the royal household emblem sewn on it, and shrugged it on. Manneki helped him pull a basket from the cart before motioning for the three omatjes to get in. They did so, Theo again trying to make as much room for his grandfather as possible, though the old rabbit didn't complain. Reenan gave them a rucksack each with dried food, water, an hourglass to keep time, along with tools they would need overnight.

"Good luck," Manneki said to Theo before piling the sheets they had brought on top of the three stowaways.

We'll need it, Theo thought.

The basket heaved as Hizarah and Reenan picked it up and

began moving. Theo peered through the weave of the basket, trying to see what he could of where they were going.

They had passed into another courtyard, this one busier with servants bustling to and fro. Theo caught a glimpse of the great pyramid Orjo had described to him. A giant structure right in the center of the castle grounds. Carved stairs, with guards stationed at the bottom, went all the way to the top to the emperor's private chambers. Before he could study it further, they turned and were indoors again, climbing up a carpeted staircase. The angle meant that the three occupants were pressed against each other, and Theo could feel Orjo's elbow and hip digging painfully into his side. Reenan had to pause at one point, putting down the basket.

"Gods, you're heavy," he muttered.

They reached the top of the stairwell, and Theo was grateful for the basket being level again. Reenan and Hizarah hefted it down a hallway, where they stopped and put it down. Theo could just make out a pair of shiny leather boots and heard the sound of Hizarah pulling something out of her pocket. The seal.

"It's not the usual sheet-changing day," a voice said.

"His Eminence complained of a rash," Reenan answered. "Wanted the sheets changed."

There was a pause. Theo wondered if the soldier was examining the seal.

"Come with me," the voice said. Theo heard the sound of a door swinging open, and Reenan and Hizarah picked up the basket and began moving again. They were in another hallway, Theo could see, with a carpet woven in red and purple. They must be in one of the two sky bridges. Hizarah had described to them how these elevated hallways connected the emperor's private chambers on two sides to the second floor of the main palace.

There was the sound of jangling keys, and then a lock being opened. Hizarah and Reenan brought the basket into a room, which from Theo's view looked like a foyer, then onward through to a bedroom. Reenan and Hizarah placed the basket on the floor with a relieved thump, and Theo gritted his teeth to stop from crying out as Orjo's knee rammed him.

"You guards get the day off for the emperor's Feast Day?" Hizarah asked cheerily. A layer of sheet flew off the top of the basket, and Theo braced himself.

"Only the lesser ranked," the guard replied, not without a hint of pride.

Hizarah clucked, and Theo could hear the sound of sheets being smoothed. "Pity. It'll be free food and drink in the streets, along with all sorts of entertainment."

"Nothing like the feasts of the castle, I imagine."

"Now I wouldn't say that," Hizarah argued. "Word is there'll be shows from all over Mankahar. Things you've never seen in the castle, I dare say."

Theo felt another sheet lifted off the basket.

"Like what?" The guard's voice held a touch of curiosity.

Hizarah began rattling off various acts of magic and wonder, and then Reenan was pulling the final sheet from the basket. He unfolded it and held it up, as if to examine it for marks, in the process blocking the basket from the guard's view.

At this cue, Theo and Orjo climbed out, pulling their rucksacks with them. Orjo crawled under the bed, and Theo shoved both sacks in after him. He then turned and helped Oaks out, and they both clambered to join Orjo. Theo's heart pounded as he watched the three sets of feet from his hiding spot, and prayed to any god who would listen for the guard to not notice their presence.

"...sawed a man in half and put him together again."

The guard grunted his disbelief.

"Saw it with my own eyes," Hizarah insisted. "Anyhow, look at me talking the morning away. We best get back. More chores than time in the day." She picked up the basket with the dirty linen, and Theo watched the three sets of feet leave the room, followed by the sound of the guard's key in the lock.

Theo and Oaks looked to Orjo, whose short ears were cocked, listening. When the last sounds of Hizarah's voice had faded away, the muskrat nodded, and they each slid out from under the wide bed.

Theo looked about, stunned by the room's opulence. Tapestries of war and hunting hung on the walls, and an oversized fireplace yawned from one side. A red and purple mosaic covered the center of the chamber's floor, just at the foot of the grand canopied bed they had been hiding under. Through one door, Theo could see a bathing chamber with a sunken bath, towel racks, and various bath furniture. Opposite this door were glass doors that led onto an expansive balcony overlooking the courtyard below, where he'd noticed the stairs leading up to this very balcony.

Theo moved into the foyer, which had doors on each end. They must have entered through the left, Theo realized, while the right seemed to lead to another sky bridge that connected with the main castle. The foyer itself looked like a sitting or reception area, with leather couches that had bone armrests sprouting from them. Theo's skin crawled at the sight of a bearskin rug, complete with head and splayed before another oversized fireplace. A portrait of a man with dark hair and an even darker expression hung over the mantel. Theo knew without being told that this was the first emperor. He tried to shake off the feeling of being watched.

"Two exits," Orjo said, interrupting Theo's thoughts. "I've barred both of them so we're undisturbed. We should close the drapes over those balcony doors too." He pointed into the bedchamber.

Oaks joined them in the foyer. "Then let's find this Library, eh?"

Theo nodded. "The entry must be in the floor; none of the walls are thick enough to contain a staircase or passageway. I'll take the bedroom. Father Oaks, search the bathroom. Orjo, can you search the foyer?"

Orjo pulled up the bear skin while Theo went into the bedroom and Oaks made his way to the attached bathing chamber. Theo methodically scanned the floor closest to the walls, pressing the tiles to search for trap doors. When he had gone around the perimeter, he stood and scanned the center of the room.

He looked again at the elaborate floor mosaic, caught in a memory.

He'd seen one like it, in Elshon where the original Library had been. There, the floor mosaic had opened into a subterranean chamber. Could the first Urzok emperor have built an identical entry here? To hide the Library he had stolen?

"By Aktu, it's in plain sight." Orjo had materialized beside him. The muskrat looked down at the pattern, walking around it.

Father Oaks hurried out of the bathing chamber, having heard Orjo's words. They all stared down at the pattern of interlocking dragons forming a ring about five paces wide. There were twenty-seven dragons in total, each clutching a glyph from the Forbidden Language in their claws.

"A word puzzle," Theo muttered. He was starting to tire of word puzzles.

"What's a word puzzle?" Father Oaks asked, mystified.

"Pressing the right glyphs will unlock the door," Orjo said.

"But how do we—"

"Shh!" Orjo put a digit to his lips and motioned toward the foyer. At first, Theo heard nothing, but then there came the scrape of the key in the lock, followed by a mutter of surprise.

"I just used this key."

There was a hard push against the door before another voice said, "It's barred. From the inside."

"But no one's…" There was a curse, then a fist pounded on the door.

Orjo pulled out his dagger and hefted it. "Figure it out, preferably soon."

He raced from the bedroom to the foyer, and Theo turned back to the mosaic. *Think, Theo!*

Father Oaks pressed on one glyph, and it gave way, but no door opened. What word would the emperor use? Theo could hear footsteps, calls for soldiers.

Could the secret word be Mankahar? Theo pushed down the relevant glyphs, but again nothing happened. The shouts were growing louder now.

"What word would the emperor use?" Theo muttered. "Kalyun-eh? Dorgun?" He tried these but again the glyphs simply slid back up into place after he pressed them.

"I still don't understand how this thing works," Oaks grumbled, frustrated.

"Hurry!" Orjo called. "They're coming up the pyramid stairs as well."

"There's a word that will unlock this door," Theo explained impatiently. Already, he could hear the wood of the foyer door cracking.

Father Oaks grunted. "If we're goin' to stand around and make guesses..." He leaned forward and pressed several glyphs down. A loud click sounded below them and then Theo felt the floor beneath him give way. The mosaic shifted on its axis, one side tilting up while the other tilted down, revealing a stairway that descended into darkness.

"'Calgornan'? How'd you—"

"Those tiles're faded. Because they're pressed the most. 'Calgornan.' What kind of name is that?"

Theo didn't have time to admire his grandfather's thinking, or give him an introduction to the bard poet Calgornan. They could hear the splintering of the door. Theo pulled both their packs and threw them down the staircase, his grandfather descending first. "Orjo!"

The shouts now sounded as if they were almost within the foyer. The muskrat rushed in, then closed and locked the heavy doors to the bedchamber behind him.

"We haven't long." Orjo grabbed his pack from where it was lying on the floor and tossed it at Theo.

Theo caught the pack. "What are you doing? Get in! I'll close the door behind us."

Orjo shook his head. "This is where we part."

Theo heard the outer door give way, and then the soldiers were at the bedchamber door, banging loudly.

"But what—"

Theo had forgotten the muskrat could move so quickly. Orjo's paw clamped hard over Theo's mouth, and the old omatje's whiskered cheek was suddenly right next to Theo's ear. His voice was calm.

"They know about me," he whispered, "but they don't know about you. Remember… crocodiles."

And with that, the muskrat shoved Theo down the stairway, where he saw Father Oaks peering up, confused.

"Orjo, no!" Theo reached for him.

But with a last salute, the muskrat brought his foot down hard, and the round door locked into place.

Theo and Father Oaks were shut in, with Orjo trapped above.

CHAPTER 23

*H*aegon burst through the doors to the audience chamber, unannounced. The emperor had asked not to be disturbed while he met with the imperial sail maker, and he therefore gave Haegon a cold glare.

"Your Eminence, there's been a breach."

"Leave us, and wait until you're called," Dorgun said. The sail maker bowed and gathered his various fabrics, retreating from the room.

"Speak," Dorgun commanded, once they were alone.

"Someone snuck into your bedchamber, Your Eminence," Haegon said.

"Do we know the man's clan?"

"It's not a man. Or a woman. It's an unpacified. A muskrat."

Dorgun's eyebrows rose. "Who is its sponsor?"

"Not just any muskrat, Your Eminence," Haegon replied.

Dorgun frowned. "What do you mean?"

The answer came as a hushed whisper. "It's Orjo, Your Eminence."

Dorgun looked at his advisor. And everyone thought *he* was losing his wits. "Impossible."

"Of course, Your Eminence, it's impossible. But nevertheless, Orjo the Terrible is here."

* * *

WHEN THEY NEARED THE DUNGEONS, Haegon held out a sweet-smelling kerchief to Dorgun, but the emperor waved it away. If he really was about to question Orjo, he wanted his words to be clear, not muffled by cloth.

A guard unlocked a padlocked gate and bowed as they came through. They stepped down a flight of stairs to a long corridor with cells on each side, lit by torches in the walls. The private dungeons were home to only a few this day, Dorgun noted. Haegon led him all the way to the end, to the last cell.

Inside, what looked like a matted lump of fur sat against the wall, forehead caked in blood and paws chained to a metal ring embedded in the ground. Dorgun's first instinct was to laugh, for the creature was barely higher than his knee, but something about the look in the animal's eye, the face, the tail, made Dorgun realize his advisor had not been wrong. The laughter died in his throat.

Orjo.

He must have spoken aloud, for the creature said, "The one and only."

"I am burning with curiosity to know how you are still alive after a century. More."

"It's a good story."

Dorgun nodded, clasping his hands behind his back, trying to make sense of what he was seeing and hearing. "I'm sure. But I'll have to satisfy that itch another time. Right now, I'd like to know why you were in my bedchamber."

The muskrat snorted. "Why do you think, One Eye?"

Haegon cocked his head and glowered, but Dorgun waved him back impatiently. He searched the muskrat's face for a hint of what he knew. "Haegon, leave us."

"But Your Eminence, he has—"

"Leave us, I said."

Haegon bowed, his curiosity clearly making him reluctant to go. Only when the advisor was out of earshot did Dorgun return his smile on Orjo.

"You want the Library," he said softly, so only the muskrat could hear. "You're here to steal from me."

The muskrat chuckled. "You stole it first. Or rather, your ancestor did." Orjo grinned through a split lip. "You're a right bastard, but compared to him, you're just watered-down wine."

Dorgun let the words flow past him, refusing to take the bait. The old rogue either had no fear, or he wanted to die.

"How did you get in?" he asked. "Who helped you?"

Orjo regarded him with distaste. "I'm Orjo the Terrible. I don't need help."

The emperor considered this. Orjo was notorious for being the lone wolf of the lone wolves. Legend had it that Orjo had betrayed almost every friend who had been foolish enough to trust him.

"Even a lone player like yourself can't expect to cart off an entire library."

"Who says I wanted the entire library? Just wanted to see if you had some rare editions of the bard Calgornan's songs."

"You broke into my castle…for poetry?"

"Exile gets dull. Calgornan was the best that ever lived." The muskrat felt around in his mouth, wincing, and worked a tooth out, spitting it to the floor.

"If you won't tell me the truth, I will have to kill you."

"You'll kill me anyway," the muskrat replied, nonchalant.

"Have a think about your future, Orjo," Dorgun said. "When I come back, you may want to give me a believable explanation, and tell me about anyone who came with you."

Dorgun headed straight for his bedchamber, followed by Haegon, and found a team of servants busily trying to clean up the blood and disarray.

"Get out, all of you," he snapped. The servants hurried to obey.

He surveyed his room, annoyed that the servants had likely erased many clues as to what exactly had happened here.

"Find out which servants visited my bedchamber—chandlers, maids, anyone. Question them."

After Haegon left, Dorgun closed the doors to his private chambers, surveying each room with an angry eye.

In the foyer, the portrait of his ancestor was torn, and blood spotted the floor. He entered his bedchamber and contemplated the mosaic. Had Orjo known where the Library was? Had he tried to get in but couldn't? The muskrat had seemed defiant, as if he had won. He didn't seem like someone who had snuck his way into a castle only to be foiled at the door to his prize.

He knelt, ignoring the creaks in his body. His fingers found their way to the familiar tiles in the floor mosaic. He pushed the door open and stepped down into the stairway, listening.

He walked the rest of the way down and took a lamp and flints from where he kept them on a shelf on the wall. Once lit, he swept the space with the lamp's light. His ancestor's war helmet sat, silent and stoic, on its stone pillar, and Dorgun walked up to it.

"I hope no one has been disturbing you," he murmured, running one finger down a curved, sharp horn that decorated the top of the headpiece.

Dorgun walked down the wide corridor, shining the light into each room and peering in. The Library seemed untouched. He walked to where he kept his plans, but everything was undisturbed, just as he'd left it. There was no sign that the muskrat, or anyone else, had been here.

He walked back to the stairs, blowing out the lamp and returning it to its place, then climbed back up to his bedchamber, deep in thought as he sealed the Library.

When Haegon returned to his chambers in response to the

emperor's summons, Dorgun said, "Put Orjo in the Forgetting Well. Let the most notorious figure of Mankahar be forgotten forever."

CHAPTER 24

Theo didn't know how long he and Father Oaks sat by the door after Orjo closed it, listening in horror to the sounds of fighting up above, never knowing if they were listening to Orjo's last movements. After a while, all went silent, and they had no way of knowing whether Orjo had escaped, or died. Tears of anger pricked Theo's eyes.

"We can't help him now," Oaks said into the dark. "Orjo's bought us time, let's make sure it wasn't fer nothing." He fumbled in his pack, and Theo heard the sound of flints as his grandfather tried to get a light going. When his small oil lamp flared to life, Theo saw his grandfather's concerned face looking at him.

Theo sat on the stairs, silent in his shock and trying to tell himself that Orjo would be all right. He was Orjo the Terrible. He had found his way out of countless dead-end situations, and he would again. He had to. The quicker Theo found the *Book of Cures*, the sooner they could get out and help Orjo. Theo refused to dwell on the possibility that Orjo might already be dead.

The younger rabbit stood and looked around him. Oaks had lit the lamp from Theo's bag as well and held it out to his grandson. Theo took it, then looked upon the Library for the first time.

The staircase led down to a large rectangular space, with over a dozen open archways on the left and right. Stepping off the stairs to investigate, he passed a stone pedestal with a war helmet on it, and in the dim light, it looked like some shrunken skull observing them.

"The Library's bigger than I imagined," Father Oaks said, walking the length of the wide corridor. "Where do we start?"

Theo opened his pack and pulled out the hourglass, then flipped it. "I don't know, but we start now."

Theo heard the distant click of the round door and froze.

Someone was entering the Library.

Theo blew out their lamps, plunging the windowless chamber into darkness. He pulled his grandfather through the first archway and rolled under a bookcase, the dust beneath it thick enough to be a carpet.

He carefully pulled their packs in as well, and held his breath.

They heard the sound of footsteps. Then a pause, a striking of flints to light an oil lamp, and a shuffling walk.

Theo's mind raced. Had they left paw prints? Moved anything? How good was the emperor's sense of hearing, or smell?

His heart thudded, and he could almost hear his grandfather's next to him.

"I hope no one has been disturbing you," an ancient voice muttered.

Theo swallowed. Had the emperor found them out? Was he speaking to them? But the voice went quiet.

After what seemed an eternity, the footsteps came closer, then moved further down the corridor.

Theo held his breath. One moment. Two.

Eventually, the footsteps started again, this time, returning up the stairs. The click of the door shutting was the sweetest sound Theo had heard all day, and he let out the breath he had been holding.

"That was whisker close," Father Oaks grumbled as he struggled out from under the bookcase, batting the dust from himself and coughing.

Theo had to agree. Trying to find the Library's greatest weapon was hard enough without having to worry about being discovered at any moment by the emperor himself.

"I'll try searching the books on magic, you search the medicine section," Theo said, sloughing dust off himself. "It has to be in one of those."

His grandfather relit his lamp and wiped cobwebs from his whiskers. "At least the place is organized."

Theo wondered how accurately, if at all, the first emperor had replicated the original Library. The rooms were labeled with simple wooden plaques: sciences, literature, music, art, ballads, mathematics, magic, and history. Within each room, the bookshelves seemed to be divided further into subcategories, theoretically making it easier to find a book. But even so, each subcategory had hundreds of books that they would have to go through.

Theo turned the hourglass, starting the sand on its journey back. Only twenty-three turns of the glass left before Hizarah and Reenan would come back to the chambers for them.

Theo settled himself and his lamp in front of the shelf with books on magic and began poring over the titles one by one. His mind was soon swimming with all the different titles and subjects, with words he didn't even know. Most of it was theoretical, and Theo soon lost all hope of making sense of any of it. A scan of twenty books revealed nothing that mentioned pacification or how to reverse it.

When he had turned the hourglass another two times and combed the magic section once more just to be sure, Father Oaks appeared with his lamp, rubbing at his eyes.

"Find anything?" Theo asked.

Oaks grunted. "Not about a cure. But I found some urns at the back, full of ashes."

"Dorgun's ancestors?" Theo guessed.

"Don't know," Father Oaks said. "But they made a good latrine."

Theo stared at his grandfather.

The old rabbit shrugged sheepishly. "We've got to go somewhere, an' we don't need the emperor sniffin' us out."

Theo walked down the corridor to the room marked "Sciences." Like the other rooms, this one had two levels of bookcases, with a ladder to reach the top ones. Like the other rooms, it had a single armchair in the middle. But unlike the other rooms, this one had a wide desk in it, with a matching wooden chair. A sheaf of papers lay bound with twine on the desk, next to two pots, one with quills and one with ink. In the center of the desk, several open books lay stacked on one another.

Curious, Theo lifted the top book and looked at the cover, then examined the books beneath it. One was about silk production and quality, while another was open to a diagram of a giant ship with towering masts.

While cooped up at Hizarah's, Theo had tried to learn as much as he could from the woman about the city, the Urzoks, and the empire's history. Kalyun-eh was a land-locked city, with the nearest port a day's travel away. For all their hunger for power, Mankahar's rulers had never had any desire to explore or conquer the lands beyond the sea. Why would the emperor be interested in shipbuilding?

He put the books back, careful to replace them as he found them, then glanced over at the sheaf of papers next to the books. The top sheet had rows of measurements and calculations, and notes about a ship's capacity and holds. Theo's breath caught when he noticed "pacification" scrawled across the bottom.

Pulling back the first sheet, Theo tried to read what he could on the sheet under it. This had scrawled observations about seasons and weather patterns, with a map of Mankahar on it.

Theo frowned, trying to connect the pieces to see what Dorgun saw. Was he taking pacification powder to sea? To other lands? That had to be it. But then why were there wind and weather patterns jotted over a map of Mankahar, and specifically over the capital city? Why study land weather patterns for a seafaring ship? And why did the emperor need to hide his studies down in the Library, away from his advisors' eyes? Something didn't make sense, but Theo was certain of one thing. The emperor had something terrible planned.

Theo had to get out of the Library alive to warn everyone. Of what, he didn't know. He glanced at the hourglass. Only fourteen hours left.

He went back to the shelves of books, even more determined. He had to find the *Book of Cures*. He had to.

He searched for hours, dutifully turning the hourglass to mark their remaining time. His task was hampered by the fact that many books had faded or illegible covers, so those he put aside to look through once he'd pored through the clearly labeled books. They had already burned through half their time, and Theo was struggling to keep his eyes from closing.

Father Oaks returned, looking as exhausted as Theo felt. The old rabbit offered him a drink from the waterskin. "Nothin' in Medicines. Ye find anything here?"

Theo shook his head. "I've one shelf left."

"Why don't I help ye."

Theo began at one end, Father Oaks at the other. Theo's eyes were gritty, but he forced himself to keep going. He picked up a nondescript volume bound in goat skin. This one also had no visible title, but when Theo's paw passed over the cover, he paused and looked closer. The surface had been rubbed flat in places, as if someone had deliberately taken a chisel or sandpaper to it, so that parts of the cover felt grainier than the rest. Theo opened the book and skimmed the pages.

"Father Oaks, can you make sense of this?" Theo passed the

book over to his grandfather, who squinted at the tiny script within.

"I've seen some o' this before. It's Old Mankahar script," Father Oaks said. "Similar to what you and I know, just takes a bit longer t' read."

Theo took the book back and traced the rubbed parts of the cover. He frowned. These were not random scrapings on the book cover. The roughened areas formed glyphs. He felt the areas with his paws and managed to make out the title: *Book of Cures.*

"This is it!" He stood up and opened the book again. He flipped through some of the pages, then glanced at the hourglass. They had turned it twenty-two times, and the sand was already halfway through this hour. "No time to look through it now—Reenan and Hizarah will be back in the chambers above soon." *I hope.*

* * *

As the cart's wheels creaked over the drawbridge, Hizarah slapped Reenan's hand.

"Stop fidgeting."

"I don't fidget."

"Reenan does," Manneki confirmed from where he was perched on Reenan's other side. "He twists fingers in the reins."

"I don't think they'll let us in," Reenan whispered.

"We don't know that," Hizarah answered, keeping her voice low as well.

Reenan indicated several people who were walking back from the castle bailey, disgruntled looks on their faces. "They're being turned away. They've closed the castle."

Yesterday had gone as smoothly as they could have dared hoped. They had dropped the trio off in the bedchamber, then returned to their cart where Manneki had been waiting, then driven off through the bailey and back home, taking pains to tell the guards they had brought the wrong sheets and would have to return on the morrow.

But when Hizarah had gone to the alehouse and found none of the castle laundresses there, she had realized something was very wrong. And when the innkeeper had passed on the news that the castle had shut down due to an intruder, Hizarah, Reenan, and Manneki had spent the night debating what to do. In the end, they decided they had to stick to their plan, if only because it was the best chance they had of not leaving the three omatjes stranded in the castle.

They reached the guards on duty at the castle gate.

"Business?"

"The emperor's linen delivery," Hizarah said in her sweetest voice.

"Not today. Come back in a week. Like I told the other merchant, it's orders."

"A week?" Hizarah echoed.

"What're more essential than linens?" Reenan argued. "Unwashed linens mean bedbugs, and bedbugs—"

"I'm telling you, the castle is closed to everyone but imperial messengers. Now go."

Hizarah tried one last tack. "Perhaps you can ask the head of household, she'll—"

"I've said it several times, no one's allowed in or out!" The guard had clearly lost his patience. "Now get going before I make you."

Reenan reluctantly turned the donkey around and steered the cart back over the bridge. When they were safely out of earshot, Hizarah voiced what they were all thinking.

"What do we do now? We can't even come back tomorrow."

"We could use the seals," Reenan said. "Get in saying I'm the chamberlain."

Manneki shook his head. "No one allowed in or out, not even the laundresses or chamberlain. How Reenan and Hizarah leave?"

"Good point," Reenan said.

"So we just abandon them?" Hizarah asked, incredulous.

"I don't see much choice right now," Reenan said, glancing over his shoulder at the castle and its high, smooth walls. "And we're not doing much good here. Best we head home and think of options."

* * *

FROM UNDER THE royal bed in Dorgun's chamber, Theo watched the last of the sand disappear from one bulb of the hourglass to the other. He had turned it twice now after the agreed time in midafternoon, but Reenan and Hizarah had not appeared.

Next to him, Father Oaks shifted, stifling his groan. Lying like this on the hard floor under a bed for several hours was not easy on Theo, much less his grandfather. But they couldn't afford to miss the chance that their friends might make it.

Theo had wondered what the consequences of Orjo's heroism might be, and he guessed that regardless of whether Orjo was dead or alive, security had been tightened. And if security had been tightened, then Reenan, Hizarah, and Manneki were not coming for him and Father Oaks today. Perhaps not ever.

His throat went dry. Not only were they trapped in the empire's most secure fortress, but they also had to get out without help.

At least he had the *Book of Cures*, which surely held the secret to reversing pacification. The tortoise had said the book would heal all Mankahar's physical ills. His paw strayed to the pack next to him, with the bulging *Book of Cures*.

"They're not comin'," Father Oaks muttered, looking up at the bed frame above them.

"We'll have to spend the night in the Library. Come back same time tomorrow."

"They won't be here tomorrow either," his grandfather said.

Though he was reluctant to admit it, he knew Father Oaks was right. "Then we'll have to make our own way out."

"Ye have a plan?"

"I will tomorrow," Theo promised. They needed some miraculous way of getting out of this Urzok fortress. Alive.

CHAPTER 25

By the fifth day, Walnut had strengthened enough to sit up in bed, though the healer still insisted he take foods sparingly and not try to walk yet. Keeva and Pozzi took turns watching over him until the healer assured them that Walnut was past the worst.

"The healer says Walnut should be able to travel in a couple of days," Harlan said over dinner one night, downing a generous goblet of mead. "So we can all soon be on our way."

Keeva looked joyous at this, while Pozzi tried to bury his mixed emotions by focusing on the plate of food before him. The thought of journeying with Harlan had only grown more distasteful, especially as he saw more signs of the old Harlan surfacing, including a possessive air toward Keeva.

Harlan leaned in, as if to impart a secret to both of them. "And I have a surprise." He fished in his pocket and pulled out a pouch that clattered.

"What is it?" Keeva asked.

Harlan reached forward to empty the pouch on the table. Pozzi didn't miss the fact that Harlan's arm brushed against Keeva's as he did so. Four wooden tokens fell out, their surfaces carved with rabbit heads on one side and the empire's insignia of a horse on the other.

"These," Harlan said with a flourish, "are our tokens for safe passage across Mankahar."

Keeva gasped and reached out a paw to touch one.

"Where did you get them?" Pozzi asked.

Harlan made a dismissive gesture. "I know someone who knows someone. I had a bit of coin saved up, and I'm just grateful I could use it for getting us all home." Pozzi was about to reach for one when Harlan gathered them back into the pouch.

"Thank you," Keeva said. "For everything."

"You all being safe is thanks enough." Harlan directed this at Keeva, despite the use of the word "all," and her ears flushed. If they traveled with Harlan back to Willago, the journey would make everything Pozzi had endured at Nyatha seem pleasurable in comparison.

* * *

"I don't think we should go to Willago with him."

Pozzi had accompanied Keeva to draw water from the village well, as the bucket and pulley were built for Urzoks and needed two rabbits to operate. They had just filled their two jugs when Pozzi finally blurted out what had been weighing on him since dinner the night before.

Keeva looked at him, puzzled. "Where should we go?"

"No, I mean we should return by ourselves."

Keeva's eyes twinkled, and her ears flicked playfully. "Is this you being jealous?"

"No!" Pozzi knew his tone said otherwise.

Keeva sighed, a hint of exasperation edging her voice. "I know you don't like Harlan. And you have good reason not to. But this is about getting home. He has a right to go home."

"And he can! Just not with us. I don't trust him. Never have."

"He bought tokens for us," Keeva argued. "He spent his coin to give us all safe passage. Maybe he's changed."

Pozzi scowled. "That's what he wants you to think! He did it only to win you!"

At this, Keeva looked taken aback. "Even if that were true, Pozzi, and I doubt it is, he's our best chance to travel home safely. You'd throw that away?"

The accusation pained him, precisely because it held a certain amount of truth. The words spilled out before he could stop them. "You said yourself, you've always been a fool for your husband. Perhaps you wish to return to him?"

At her wounded expression, he immediately regretted the words.

"This is not about Harlan. It's about getting us home. And if you can't see that, then maybe Harlan's not the problem. Maybe the problem is you."

She picked up her jug and walked away, stiff, leaving Pozzi feeling ill. He took a deep breath, but just as he was about to call out and apologize, Harlan appeared around the corner, offering to take her water jug. She accepted, and without a backward glance at Pozzi, walked with Harlan back to the brewery.

* * *

THROUGHOUT THE DAY, Pozzi worked under a dark cloud. Stubbornness and resentment made him hesitate to seek Keeva out and apologize, but Keeva never gave him a chance to be alone with her either. She busied herself mending their clothes, packs, and shoes for the journey, and kept Walnut close by, sharpening their knives and flints. Pozzi felt ashamed for what he'd said, but he knew he'd said them because he feared Keeva really did still harbor feelings for her husband.

That evening, Harlan suggested they join him to have a celebratory drink in the brewery, as the priests would come to say their goodbyes. Pozzi started to make an excuse to not attend, but when he saw Harlan's face light up and his glance at Keeva, Pozzi found himself saying he'd be there. He would not give Harlan the satisfaction of an evening alone with Keeva and Walnut.

And so that night, Pozzi stepped out of Harlan's hut, having prepared what little he owned for the next day's journey, and headed for the brewery. The door was open, and through it, Pozzi could see giant barrels lining one wall, and the middle was filled with a vat of bubbling liquid, as big around as four rabbits holding paws. Several Urzok priests in their robes stood about, laughing and chatting, holding cups of mead.

Harlan stood among them, with Keeva and Walnut, laughing at something a priest had said.

"Pozzi!" Harlan smiled, looking genuinely pleased to see him. "Come join us."

Pozzi approached, hesitant. Keeva glanced at him, but then a priest was speaking to her, and she turned toward him, her back to Pozzi. Harlan made his way to Pozzi, motioning for him to follow.

"This is much bigger than Gawelt's back in Willago."

Harlan laughed. "My master back in Willago could only dream of such a brewery. But I shan't bore you with details. The proof is in the tasting." He led Pozzi to one of the barrels, pulled a new cup from a stack on a nearby stool, and siphoned off a rich amber mead into it. He held it out. "Try some?"

Pozzi shook his head. "Maybe later."

Harlan's smile slipped. "Just a taste? I opened a special cask."

"No thanks."

"That's all right. More for the rest of us." Harlan downed the mead himself, smacking his lips in appreciation. "Everything all right between you and Keeva?"

Pozzi felt his ears grow hot. "Of course. Why?"

Harlan shrugged, and poured himself another mead. "Oh nothing. You two seem a little cold toward each other today. You seemed to be arguing by the well."

Pozzi glared at him. "You were spying on us?"

Harlan held up his paws. "I'm simply a concerned friend."

Pozzi was about to give his opinion on the worth of Harlan's friendship, when a banging against the beer vat drowned out all conversation. Everyone turned to see one of the priests, a short man with wild black hair, holding a cup of mead in one hand.

When he had everyone's attention, he raised his cup. "Friends! A toast! Harlan, does everyone have a drink?"

Harlan refilled his cup and then again offered another cup to Pozzi. When Pozzi declined, the priest making the toast guffawed, "Who are you that you won't toast your friend?"

Several priests joined in, heckling.

Pozzi started to give a curt reply, but then he noticed Keeva's eyes on him. Refusing to toast Harlan would only cement her view that he was being unreasonable. He grudgingly accepted the cup from Harlan, who beamed.

The priest held up his mead. "That's better! Now tonight, we say farewell to the best brewmaster this temple has had in years. We will miss you—"

"But mostly, we'll miss your brew!" someone shouted, and the crowd laughed.

The priest waited for the laughter to die down, then continued. "We'll miss you, but we wish you speed on the road and happiness at your destination. To Harlan Brewwell."

Everyone cheered, then raised their cups and drank, and Pozzi with them. Keeva smiled at him, and he felt warmed, despite the surprising bitterness of the mead in his mouth.

Harlan gave a few words of thanks, which Pozzi barely heard, for he was trying to catch Keeva's eye again. The gathered guests clapped and shouted encouragement, then Harlan appeared back at his side.

"I've got to move a few casks back to the inn," Harlan said, wiping his paws on his apron. "Pozzi, I hate to ask, but would you be willing to lend me a paw rolling some barrels over? The innkeeper made me promise I'd bring them back tonight."

Pozzi glanced at Keeva, who was busy helping gather empty cups and plates as the celebration wound down. His head was feeling fuzzy, and the last thing he wanted was to push barrels up a hill, but Harlan was looking at him expectantly. He helped Harlan cart three barrels of mead out the door, then lay them on their sides to roll them up the street. The effort of it brought sweat to Pozzi's paws.

"Thanks, Pozzi, I appreciate it."

The two rabbits walked abreast of each other, the sun now nearly invisible behind the horizon. The barrels were heavy enough, but pushing their cargo up inclined streets made it that much worse. Along the way, a few villagers called out farewells to Harlan, who cheerfully answered back.

"Seems you've a good life here," Pozzi commented. "You sure you want to leave it?"

Harlan grinned at him. "Admit it, Bucktooth. You want me to stay."

Pozzi shook his head, annoyed at Harlan's needling, but couldn't think of a reply. His head was pounding now. The barrel was indeed heavy, but he was surprised at how winded he felt.

"…just over there."

He realized Harlan was turning, rolling his barrel into the barn at the back of the inn and motioning Pozzi to follow him. Pozzi rubbed his forehead and began pushing his keg in, unwilling to let Harlan see his discomfort, but as soon as he was inside, he felt his vision go grey and his legs gave out.

The last thing he remembered seeing was Harlan's concerned face bent over him, asking if he was all right.

CHAPTER 26

Theo comforted himself that his escape plan was the best possible. But that was also because it was the only plan possible.

There were only two ways out of the bedchamber; either through the foyer doors, past the guards, and into the castle proper, or from the balcony down the stairs to the courtyard, which would be fully visible. Not to mention that guards patrolled the bottom of that staircase. When they'd been hiding under the emperor's bed, Theo's keen ears could hear them even from within the bedchamber. And from there, it would be a long way to any of the castle perimeters because the emperor's private chambers were at its heart. Between what Hizarah had told him of the castle layout and a blueprint he'd ferreted out in the Library, he figured they would have to make their way undetected either toward the front of the castle and its moat, or through the living quarters and granary at the side. The granary was their best bet, for it had a sloping roof from which they could reach the inner bailey wall, and from there, the outer bailey wall and the northern postern gate.

He and Oaks had debated the plan at length throughout the previous night, until they'd decided they could get out onto the balcony unseen, and avoid the stairs to the courtyard by using the ledges of the raised hallways that connected the royal chambers with the castle proper. Theo himself had been daunted by the physical demands of such an escape, and he knew it was asking much of his grandfather. But he didn't see another way, and they were running out of food and water.

Father Oaks had sighed and nodded. "Promise me somethin', lad. If anything happens to me, leave me be. Don't look back, don't come back. Ye hear?"

"Nothing will happen to you."

"I'm serious," Father Oaks said, eyes hard. "Ye get out of here and ye show the empire what's what. Understand me?"

Theo had nodded, chest squeezing at the thought that they might not both make it out of Kalyun-eh castle. "I understand," he had said.

Now, standing at the base of the Library stairs, ready to head up to the bedchamber, they used the light of their one lit lamp to check and make sure they had what little they needed to take. Theo had the *Book of Cures*, along with the knife he had brought. Everything else, they had shoved into the urns at the back of the Library, as every extra bit of equipment would only weigh them down in their escape.

"Are you ready?"

The old rabbit nodded, and Theo picked up the lamp.

They moved toward the stairs, ears primed for noises above. The night before, Dorgun had not entered the Library until late, and Theo was counting on the emperor having a routine. If the Library was secret, then chances were Dorgun only entered at night before bed, when he wouldn't be disturbed. But for Father Oaks and Theo, leaving during the day would have meant being spotted, so they had to escape between nightfall and when Dorgun visited his underground vault. This they estimated to be about an hour from now, but there was no way to be sure since the Library had no windows by which they could judge sun or moonlight.

He was so intent on watching the door above, worried that Dorgun would open it at any moment, that he scraped his arm against the old helmet as he passed it. The helmet shifted, and Theo carefully moved it back. Dorgun was bound to notice if it was out of place.

They climbed the stairs to the door, and Theo pressed his ear against it. Hearing only silence, Theo felt along the wall until his paw brushed the lever that opened the door. He had learned of it the first time Dorgun had come and left, and heard the emperor opening the door from the inside. Theo pulled on this lever now, and heard a loud click. He pushed up on the round door and sprang out, then turned and helped Father Oaks up the stairs.

The bedchamber was dark, with only the faint light of the moon coming through the balcony doors. Theo said a silent goodbye to the Library, then carefully pushed the disc back into place, clicking it closed as softly as he could. He and Father Oaks stood, listening. Satisfied, Theo motioned for his grandfather to wait while he crept to the balcony door.

The weather, at least, seemed to be favoring them. The sickle moon drifted in and out from behind the low clouds, leaving most of the castle grounds in shadow. From his spot by the doors to the balcony, Theo could see it was empty. But his ears picked up the scuff of the guards' boots and the soft tap of a staff at the bottom of the pyramid stairs.

He motioned to his grandfather, and Father Oaks snuck over. Theo pulled the catch on the door, then reached up toward the high door handles, having to stretch on his toes to get a proper grip. He eased the handle down and pulled the door open, then slipped out into the night.

From the balcony, he could see the guards standing at the bottom of the pyramid stairs. He adjusted his pack on his back so that it wouldn't slip, then pressed himself flat to the stone floor and scurried over to the left side, where the balcony ended. He peered through the balustrade to make sure no patrols were below, then signaled his grandfather.

If they could get to the sky bridge and sneak across to the main castle, maybe they could find another way out of the castle grounds. As Father Oaks made his way over to him, Theo contemplated the challenge they faced. There was a gap between the edge of the balcony and the sky bridge began, a space of about a stone's throw. He knew he might be able to jump it, but not his grandfather. His first escape plan was already unworkable.

"Go," his grandfather hissed. "Leave me."

Theo shook his head and took off his boots, then socks .

"What're ye doin'?"

"I have an idea," Theo whispered. He quickly tugged his socks over his front paws, then put his boots back on and swung himself over the railing, making sure his pack was secure on his back. He stood on the small ledge on the other side and motioned for Father Oaks to do the same. "We certainly can't just walk down the pyramid steps. We have to slide."

Father Oaks looked down the side of the pyramid, dubious. Theo had forced himself to not look once he had made his decision, for he loathed heights. But he had made it down a towering tree to escape the Blackwings. He could slide down the smooth face of a pyramid, and his grandfather would have to as well.

"Ye serious?"

Theo nodded, sat down on the balcony ledge, and leaned back. "Lie on top of me."

Father Oaks hesitated, then began climbing over the railing. Theo scanned the area below, making sure they were still undetected.

"Hold tight," Theo whispered and leaned back as flat as he could. Father Oaks wrapped his thin arms around Theo's neck, lying belly down on Theo. Theo took a deep breath and pushed his fear away. He eased himself off the edge, paws outstretched and boot soles flat against the pyramid, in the hope of controlling the slide.

The downward rush made his stomach coil. Even through

the socks, the pyramid surface scraped Theo's paws raw as he tried to slow himself. The pack on his back rode up until his lower spine was rubbing against the rough surface, and he was worried he would crack a vertebra. But then the ground was there, its solid, flat surface welcome after what felt like an unchecked fall.

He didn't have time to dwell on any injuries. His grandfather was pulling him up with urgent paws, and now, he could hear the sound of guards coming.

Theo forced himself to his feet and followed Father Oaks' lead as they darted across the courtyard to the shelter of a doorway. From the shadows, they watched as one of the guards walked by the perimeter, searching. The man peered up the pyramid face, then along the raised corridor, but then turned and headed back.

Theo pulled his socks from his paws and shoved them in his pockets. He was scraped in a dozen places, but the backpack had saved him from the worst of the slide. He glanced out and waited for a group of priests finishing evening prayers to pass.

Once they had gone, the rabbits crept along the courtyard walls, keeping to the shadows, making their way toward the granary and the inner bailey.

So far, their luck was holding. *Just a little longer*, Theo prayed.

DORGUN ENTERED his bedchamber and sent his servants away without their usual ritual of disrobing him and helping him with his bath. Something was bothering him, and he had no patience to put up with his attendants' numbingly slow and exact ministrations.

He glanced at the empty space where the portrait of his ancestor had hung. It had been sent out to be repaired, and he felt its absence. But that was not what was bothering him.

No, it was the muskrat. What exactly he had been looking for?

A notorious killer such as Orjo did not reappear from exile for no reason. He would only show himself, risk breaking into the heart of the empire, for something very special. Magical or no, a muskrat couldn't steal an entire library. So what had he been looking for? Something told Dorgun that the answer was important.

He closed the doors to the bedchamber and noticed the light spilling in from the balcony doors. Cursed chambermaids must have forgotten to close the curtains, as he preferred. He yanked the curtains shut, then knelt by the mosaic and let his fingers find the tiles.

The circular door in the floor pivoted open, and Dorgun stood, taking a nearby candelabrum from his bedside and walking down the steps.

He stood still, scanning every visible surface and letting his ears and nose try to detect anything out of place. Everything seemed as usual, and yet…

The emperor shuffled forward and reached out his hand toward his ancestor's helmet. "Good evening, Dakus. Am I simply imagining things now that I'm old?"

There was, of course, no answer. But just as Dorgun was about to pull his hand away, he paused.

Something was stuck to the helmet's lower cheek guard. The piece of metal curved in red and gold, sharpening to a point like tusks beyond the wearer's face to keep swords or other weapons from crushing the skull. Dorgun frowned and then plucked the object from the tusk.

It was fur. A rabbit's fur. He held it up to the lantern and saw its unmistakable grey color. Clutching it in his fist, he rushed as fast as his heart and legs would take him, up the stairs and back to his bedchamber. He was screaming for the guards before the Library door had completely shut.

"Search the castle," he told the head guard. "Every corner,

every inch of this place."

"Yes, Your Eminence." The guard bowed, then hesitated. "What are we looking for?"

"A rabbit," Dorgun said. "A grey rabbit."

The guard frowned. "A grey—?"

"Just do it, and now!" the emperor shrilled, his voice unrecognizable even to him. The guard retreated, shouting for his men and rousing the castle.

* * *

THEO HAD JUST HELPED his grandfather up onto the roof of the granary when he heard the sound of boots. There were too many of them, accompanied by too many shouts, to be simply routine guard movement. No, these were the sounds of a hunt.

Theo pulled himself up one of the poles supporting the granary and then reached out for the ledge of the roof. With a heave, he managed to swing himself up, where his grandfather waited with his pack. There, they could reach the inner bailey wall, and below that was the shorter outer bailey wall, which led to the moat, and freedom. If they could swim it.

Theo took his grandfather's paw, helping to steady the older rabbit as they crept along the thatched granary roof, careful not to slip on its sloped surface. The thatch crackled as loud as whips to Theo's ears, but the soldiers on the bailey wall were still focused on the commands coming from their superiors. Theo and Father Oaks huddled just inside the inner bailey wall, and Theo peeked over the side.

The inner bailey was connected to the outer bailey by a perpendicular wall, which Theo estimated to be fifty steps away from them. The inner wall's closest patrol point was a guard tower further down, and the outer wall had a matching tower. Theo could make out two guards in the closer tower, and four in the one further away.

"We have to run," Theo whispered to his grandfather. "Keep low, and don't stop. I'll be right behind you."

Father Oaks nodded. Theo shouldered his pack, then watched until the guards were looking away. He pulled himself up and over the inner bailey wall, checking to make sure he hadn't been seen, and then reached up to help his grandfather over. Theo could tell the movements pained the old rabbit, but Oaks uttered no complaint.

They crept along to the connecting wall, careful to keep their heads low and out of sight. The inner bailey guards were busy conferring with a superior who had just arrived, but the outer guards, Theo could hear, were splitting up and spreading across the outer wall.

Theo glanced at his grandfather. They were unarmed and completely visible. If they were going to make it, they'd have to run now, before the guards reached this connecting wall and spotted them.

Father Oaks nodded to signal he was ready, then ran as quickly as he could. Theo followed, back bent so that he had some protection from the connecting wall. Shouts from the guards told him they'd been spotted.

The outer wall ledge was close now, only a few heartbeats away. Something hissed by Theo's ear. An arrow. He didn't have time to gauge its direction. Instead, he sprinted even faster, willing Father Oaks to do the same.

Five steps, and they'd be there.

Four.

Another arrow flew, and this one grazed his pack. He pushed Father Oaks ahead of him onto the ledge, then scrabbled up beside him. The edge of the wall ended in a heart-stopping drop below into a blackness he could only assume was the moat water. He turned to take his grandfather's paw, heart hammering. The soldiers were running toward them, even the ones from the inner wall. Several were nocking more arrows.

"Just close your eyes and jump with me," Theo said. "Ready?"

His grandfather gave a grunt of surprise. And that's when Theo saw the long slender wood protruding from the old rabbit's back.

"No..." Theo stood rooted to the spot.

Father Oaks gripped his shoulders. His voice was pained. "Go. Remember yer promise."

The old rabbit pulled him into a fierce hug, then pushed with an unexpected strength, sending Theo backward over the ledge and into the moat.

Theo's scream was cut short when he hit the water with a bone-smashing jolt. The pack was like a weight on him, part of the cold, hungry water trying to suck him down. But he couldn't let go. He had to save the *Book of Cures*. He kicked his legs, struggling toward the surface while fighting the panic inside him. He clawed with every ounce of strength until his head at last broke the surface. Arrows peppered the water around him as he gulped mouthfuls of night air. Theo struggled toward the moat edge that led up to the grand square, and clung there against the rocks to catch his breath.

He heard shouts above and looked behind him at the water. For a moment, he indulged the desperate hope that Father Oaks had followed him over. But he saw no one in the water. He looked up at the castle ramparts and saw his grandfather's face. The old rabbit smiled at the sight of his grandson before his eyes went blank in death.

At this, Theo nearly sank back into the water, but he remembered his promise, the impossibly heavy pack on his back that held the book he had risked everything for. With shaking limbs, Theo clawed his way up the stone embankment and to the sprawling square above. Shivering from wet and shock, he stumbled to his feet, shouldered the pack and hurried along what shadows he could find in the square.

Distraught as he was, he didn't see the soldiers' superior on the ramparts, watching him leave and noting the direction he took.

CHAPTER 27

"*H*e really didn't tell you where he was going?"

Keeva cleared the breakfast plates, trying to ease her anxiety with chores. Walnut was outside gathering stones for an improvised slingshot he said he'd use to protect them on the journey home.

Harlan shook his head and wiped his mouth. "Not a word. As I said, he stayed at the inn after helping me with the mead and said he needed a walk alone."

"That doesn't sound like him," Keeva said. "To just walk off on the night before we were to leave." She paused, mentally revisiting their argument at the well. Could he have disliked Harlan so much that he would simply leave without a goodbye? Another thought struck her. "What if slavers caught him?"

Harlan stood and came to put a comforting paw on her shoulder. "I'll admit that's possible. But let's not jump to conclusions."

"What else could it be?"

Harlan took a deep breath and glanced outside, as if to make sure Walnut wasn't in earshot. "Well...he asked me whether I wouldn't rather stay here."

Keeva stared at him, not understanding.

"I wasn't going to tell you, but Pozzi asked that I not go to Willago. Demanded, actually."

Keeva stiffened. "He did?"

Harlan nodded. "He said if I went, he wouldn't. And some heated words were said. But in the end, I told him I had a right to go home. And that if he didn't want to go, that was his choice, but I didn't think it fair for him to make me stay."

Keeva swallowed, her thoughts in a tangle. "You think he abandoned us?"

Harlan shrugged. "I didn't say that, Keev. But my gut was… that he hates me so much he just wanted to leave. Even if that meant leaving you."

"It just…doesn't sound like him." Though Harlan was saying almost exactly what Pozzi had said, she couldn't quite believe he would just go, without one word. She felt a cold queasiness in her stomach and willed herself to not cry in front of Harlan. She had come to think of Pozzi as the rock she had always wanted.

"Look, if you don't want to leave yet," Harlan said, gentle, "we can stay, see if anyone's seen him. Or maybe he'll come back."

Keeva thought on this. Her disappointment had turned into anger. She'd always had terrible judgment in partners. She had just been sure Pozzi was different. "No. We planned to leave today, and we'll leave today. If Pozzi wants to come with us, he can find us."

* * *

THE FIRST THING Pozzi awoke to was heat. A burning heat on one side of him, while the other side was icy cold. And his throat was dry as a day-old biscuit.

He reached back for the last memory he could muster. Keeva. Harlan. Walnut. Then he remembered—the mead that was too bitter, the brewery, collapsing in the barn, and Harlan's face—

He became aware of whistling and cracked one eye open. He was at a campfire, lying outdoors under the stars. A cheerful fire burned in a pit, and opposite him was an Urzok of around sixty years, wiry, and with hair cropped short at the neck. He was whittling something, a pipe clamped between his lips, and behind him, Pozzi could see a mule and cart.

He went to stand up, but something clanked around his ankles. Chains.

"Ah. You're awake," the man said, his voice cheerful and friendly. "I've dinner for you. And even some ale if you fancy that."

"Why am I chained?" Pozzi asked, a knot of dread forming in his stomach. "Who are you?"

"I'm Joseb, best toymaker in these parts," the man said, unaffected by Pozzi's obvious distress. "And I'm wagering you didn't know you were being sold."

"Sold?" Pozzi repeated, though part of him had expected this answer. "I'm not for sale. I have to get back. I have a family—"

"We all do, rabbit," Joseb said, matter-of-fact. "Here, have some dinner. You'll feel better on a full stomach."

"I don't want a full stomach. I want to go back!" Pozzi shouted. All his rage burst from him as he tried to run. He tripped over his chains and fell hard, biting his tongue as he went crashing to the ground.

"Easy now, Pozzi," Joseb said, still seated.

The use of his name made the rabbit stop. "How do you know my name?"

Joseb set aside his half-carved toy and pulled some tobacco from his pocket. "The brewer. He said you were a good carver, which is what I need." He filled his pipe and lit it.

Pozzi's stomach lurched. Harlan had planned this. Was it because he wanted Keeva? Or because of their bad blood? Or both? When Pozzi got back, he would throttle the bastard. "Joseb, is it? Please, let me go."

The man let smoke trickle out of his nose. "I'm afraid I can't. I paid good coin for you, Pozzi, and unless you can pay me back right here, right now, I'd be short."

"I'll repay you, just let me get back."

Joseb took a draw on his pipe, his eyes genuinely sympathetic. "If I did that every time I heard it, I'd have as much coin as a pauper's pocket."

Pozzi looked about him. He could see something dark and winding a few paces away under the moonlight. A road. He had never been the best at reading the stars, but if he could find out which way they'd gone, he could likely follow the road back to the temple, and to Keeva and Walnut.

"I wouldn't try to escape," Joseb said helpfully. "This stretch here is all empire territory, where an unpacified like you would need a token to move freely. Otherwise, you'd just end up sold again. To someone worse." Joseb held out the plate once more. "But if you're determined to escape, you won't want to do it on an empty stomach."

Pozzi returned reluctantly to the fireside, his mouth full of more than just the taste of blood. He had to think. He took the plate and sat, sniffing the food.

Joseb looked insulted. "It's not that bad. My assistant eats what I eat. Fair's fair."

"And what am I supposed to be assisting you with?" Pozzi asked. The more information he gleaned, he reasoned, the better he'd be able to figure his way out of this mess and back to Keeva. He didn't want to think about whether Harlan had harmed her, whether he had sold her and Walnut to someone else.

Joseb beamed, as if they were now friends. "Making these." He pulled a wooden carving out of a sack nearby, and Pozzi saw that, unlike the one he had been whittling, this one was polished and refined, all the details painted on. He also realized it was in the shape of a rabbit. A rabbit that looked strangely familiar. "These statues of the dead Griffinrider are selling everywhere, and with the emperor's birthday festival coming up, there'll be roaring business to be had in the capital markets." He held the figure out to Pozzi, and Pozzi tentatively took it.

The Griffinrider. A sick realization dawned on Pozzi that he was looking at a carving of Theo—the black eye patches over the grey face, the black paws, with a removable sword that could be slid in and out of a hole in the rabbit's chest. He stared, unable to look away.

"I've made a hundred of these that are in the cart, and I'll need to make at least a hundred more," Joseb said.

"These…are toys?"

Joseb nodded. "The Griffinrider. You've heard of him, surely? He was a terror of the empire, but no more, thanks to the great Lord Ornox." Joseb began to sing,

> *Theo Griffinrider rides no more,*
> *His shadow casts no fear.*
> *For Ornox came and cut him down,*
> *Saving all far and near.*

Pozzi stared at him, disgusted. Theo dead, and here was this man rejoicing. The injustice of it all made tears well, and he didn't even know they were falling until he realized the singing had stopped. He wiped his eyes and saw Joseb looking at him, sheepish.

"Listen, I'm sorry. I forgot you might have sympathies for the other side." Joseb waited for a reply, but when none came, he pressed on. "I meant it that I'm a better master than others."

Indignation flared in Pozzi. "Where I come from, no one owns another. A master, good or bad, is still a master."

Joseb poked at the fire. "Well, you can't move a mountain, you can only walk around it. People own animals, that's just a fact. The sooner you get used to the idea, the easier it will be. Why don't you get some sleep? Sleep on a full stomach will make you a bit happier in the morning."

Joseb shook out a blanket and a rolled-up shirt, while Pozzi sat and ate, watching him. When Pozzi was done, Joseb took his plate and began whistling as he scraped the plates and rinsed their utensils from a kettle. Pozzi's eyes drifted to the statues of Theo.

"What if I could make you a hundred and fifty of those?"

Joseb turned, eyebrows raised. "What do you mean?"

"What if I could make you one hundred and fifty of those, by the time we reached Kalyun-eh?" Pozzi said. "Would you let me go free then?"

Joseb broke into an indulgent smile. "You'd have to work day and night."

"Would you let me go free?"

Joseb crossed his arms, regarding him. "Two hundred."

"You're scared of losing?" Pozzi goaded.

Joseb chuckled. "No, I'm simply a good businessman. The sale of two hundred figurines will pay me back for your buy price, your food and keep, and give me a profit."

Pozzi took a deep breath. Two hundred carvings would be nearly impossible. But nearly impossible was still possible. "Very well. You will keep your word?"

Joseb bowed. "Let no one say Joseb breaks his word."

"Then pass me your knife."

Joseb nodded. "Aye. Guess you'd better start now if you want a fair chance." The man handed Pozzi his carving blade, along with a chunk of wood and a finished figurine. "Try to make yours exactly like mine. And don't start a new one until my say so."

Pozzi turned the carving of Theo over and over in his paws, before picking up the knife and starting to work. He tried not to envy Joseb, who bedded down and was soon snoring. For Pozzi, there would be little to no sleep until he won back his freedom.

CHAPTER 28

By the time Theo reached Hizarah's house, the street's usual morning bustle had already started. Theo hadn't had the strength to go straight there after leaving the moat, having instead spent the night hiding in the back entrance of a birder's shop.

Dazed, frozen, and in shock, he had heard the sounds of birds from the street, and instinct had made him duck inside the alley next to them. He peeled off his wet clothes and pack, then slumped against the wall before the sobs overtook him. He couldn't remember the last time he had cried, but the tears came now, uncontrollable. The sounds of the birds flitting in their cages at least gave him cover, and he needed some moments to gather his thoughts and catch his breath.

He ached, inside and out, and his mind was still raw with disbelief. Once the weeping had left, wringing him dry, he forced himself to think and take stock. Night was giving way to dawn, but the streets were still empty, save for the occasional vendor heading to some market, and bakers opening up for the day. Just another day for them, but for Theo the world had turned darker.

Theo knew he needed to hurry to Hizarah's with the priceless book in his pack, while the city streets were mostly deserted. He focused on finding his way back, and by dawn, found himself on her street.

He checked for anyone who might be following or watching, then walked at a deliberate, unhurried pace to the door and knocked. One, then four together, then one again.

The door opened, revealing Hizarah. She welcomed him in, for all the world acting like he was simply an early-morning visitor. Once the door was closed behind her, however, she knelt down and helped strip him of his pack and damp clothes. Reenan appeared in the stairwell, Manneki on his shoulder.

"Theo! You're all right!" Reenan looked like he hadn't slept for the last few days.

"Father Oaks is dead," Theo whispered. "Where's Orjo?"

The couple looked at each other, grim.

"He's not here?" Theo asked, hopes falling.

"He never came out of the castle," Hizarah said softly, wrapping him in new robes.

Theo sat heavily on a stool. He had never wanted so badly to simply lie down and sleep. Sleep forever, so that he didn't have to feel the pain that flooded through him now. He longed to be back in the rock pool, surrounded by that comforting light.

"Orjo wily," Manneki offered, coming and sitting at Theo's side. "He probably find a way out and just hiding somewhere."

Hizarah offered Theo a cup of something steaming. "Drink this."

Theo didn't want to, but her stern look made him sip it.

"Did you find the *Book of Cures?*" Reenan asked.

"Reenan!" Hizarah said sharply. "Give him time."

"It's all right," Theo said. He'd rather talk about anything other than Orjo and Father Oaks' death. He pulled the book from his pack and opened the wrapping. The book was wet, but perhaps salvageable. He spread it open before the fire as Hizarah, Manneki, and Reenan crowded around.

"Let's hope there's not too much damage," Theo said.

"This is it?" Reenan asked, looking at the volume critically. Many of the pages were crinkled with water, and several looked stuck together. "The greatest weapon in Mankahar?"

"It should have the cure for pacification," Theo said. "And speaking of pacification, I think the emperor is planning something big. Involving a ship."

"A new pacification center?" Reenan suggested. "Perhaps he's sending pacification up via the coast."

"No," Hizarah shook her head. "Pacification is moved around every day, the emperor has ministers of transport and a well-oiled system in place."

"Exactly," Theo agreed. "He wouldn't see to it himself and have all these books about winds and ship building if he didn't have something unusual planned. Something no one else knows. We have to find out what it is."

Something shattered the window and hit the pillar by the fireplace. A flaming arrow.

Hizarah cried out as another arrow followed, and then another, all lit. The flames began licking up the mantelpiece, delighted at finding dry wood.

"Imperial soldiers!" Reenan hissed, from where he'd crept to the window. "There's a whole regiment of them!"

Cries of alarm were sounding from the neighboring buildings, and Theo could hear doors and windows opening, people shouting.

Smoke was filling the cottage, and both Manneki and Theo were trying to douse the fires with what water or blankets they had. But the flames only hissed at the water and ate at the blankets, spreading up to the roof and lapping at the ceiling. Reenan was shoring up the door with furniture, while Hizarah grabbed a purse that clinked from a hidden drawer in the pantry.

"You have a fugitive in your midst," a commanding voice shouted from outside. "Surrender now, and we will grant you merciful deaths. Resist, and you shall die by flame."

"Not much of a choice, is it?" Hizarah muttered, coughing as she brought her arm over her mouth. "Up the stairs! Now!"

Manneki darted up, followed by Hizarah. Theo grabbed the book by the fire, and was about to run up when he heard Reenan cry out.

Theo ran through the thickening smoke to the man, who was leaning on a chair, an arrow protruding from the back of his leg. "Get down!"

Theo managed to pull his friend down to the floor as more arrows found their way into the walls, the furniture, the rugs. He pushed Reenan ahead of him, the book still under one arm.

"Go up!" he shouted.

Soon Hizarah was there as well, having come down to help. She reached out and pulled Reenan to the bottom of the stairs as another arrow narrowly missed her head. She hauled Reenan up into the comparative safety of the stairwell, Theo following.

They rushed up to the second floor, to the room where they'd healed Xandru. Reenan limped along, but Manneki was already at the open window, his face fearful.

Theo realized why when Manneki pointed outside, and Theo snuck a peek. Two soldiers, swords drawn, were down in the alley below, clearly waiting in case any of them tried to flee out the back door. He closed the shutters.

"We'll have to try to go over the roof next door," Theo said. He looked at Reenan's leg. "We should break that arrow shaft, so it's easier for you to move."

Reenan nodded and closed his eyes as Theo placed the book on a nearby chest, then with one paw, held the shaft firm near where it entered Reenan's calf, and with the other paw, broke it clean off, leaving a short stub. The man gasped in pain. The arrowhead remained embedded, but they'd deal with that later.

"Can you make it?" Hizarah asked.

"I'll have to," Reenan said through gritted teeth. Hizarah squeezed his hand. Smoke had started to seep under the bedroom door, and they heard crashing as the staircase collapsed.

"Manneki go first and help you up," the Grodlyn said. Theo nodded, but as they opened the shutters all of them froze. The window in the building opposite them, no more than three paces away, was open. And standing there was a teenager with a fuzzy layer of new hair.

"Xandru?" Theo said, incredulous.

The teen put a finger to his lips, then motioned for them to come across to him. It couldn't have been more than three steps away if they were on level ground, but the drop was long. Xandru pulled up two nightsoil chamber pots and placed them on the window ledge.

In moves so practiced Theo knew he had done this many times before, Xandru picked up one pot, aimed, and threw, then picked up the other and did the same. Both dropped like boulders, smashing squarely onto the soldiers' heads. The two fell to the ground, one already unconscious and the other clearly too stunned to stand.

Xandru produced a ladder on his side and pushed it out the window so that the opposite end landed on their window. "Hurry! Come over!" the boy hissed.

"What if he betrays us?" Reenan whispered to Theo.

"I think we have to take our chances," Theo said. Manneki scampered across the ladder first. Hizarah and Theo helped Reenan up and onto the ladder. He moved across as best he could on all fours, trying to lift his injured leg to avoid it catching on the ladder rungs. Theo could tell from the man's stiffened back that the pain was immense, but he made it across. Next, it was Hizarah's turn, and despite her heavy skirts, she clambered across easily, gripping Xandru's arm and stepping into the building opposite. The team turned back to Theo.

"Hurry!" Xandru urged.

Theo grabbed the book from where he had placed it on the chest, climbed up the windowsill, and tossed the book to

Xandru. The boy caught it and set it down before motioning frantically to Theo. The rabbit crawled across the ladder, doing his best to not look at the street below. To Xandru's credit, the ladder was light but solid. He was relieved when he made it over and Hizarah pulled him safely through the window.

Xandru pulled the ladder in, then closed the shutters and rushed to the opposite side of the room. They were in a dusty, cluttered attic, full of disused furniture. Hizarah had an arm around Reenan's waist, and Manneki was peering out the window that Xandru had opened on the far side. Theo retrieved the book and joined the boy. Xandru peered out the open window to make sure all was clear, then fetched the ladder and repeated his placement, this time on a lower window in the house opposite.

"Quickly!" the boy urged.

Manneki went first again, and Theo looked back to Reenan. Hizarah nodded to him. "I'll help him. You go."

Theo took a breath, then climbed across the ladder, clutching the book to him, again determined not to look down. When Theo reached the other side, he and Manneki held the ladder as Hizarah and Reenan took turns climbing across, followed by Xandru, who pulled the ladder in after them and shut the window.

"This way," Xandru said, carting the ladder down a staircase and into another room, where he opened another window and pushed the ladder out to rest it on a balcony railing. "And be quiet. We don't want the residents finding us. We're almost there."

"Almost" turned out to mean another six houses, and each time, Xandru pulled their ladder after them and placed it against an adjoining building. With each building they crossed to, Reenan deflated a little more with the effort. But after they had they managed to make it to the roof of a plain brick home, they could see Hizarah's house several streets down, engulfed in flames. Hizarah gazed at it, disbelieving.

Theo touched Hizarah's hand. "I'm sorry."

She turned a look on him that made him flinch, but then her expression softened. "You've nothing to be sorry about. It's the empire that did this."

"We have to keep moving," Xandru insisted, hefting the ladder under his arm. "I can keep you safe, but only if you come now."

Xandru led them across several house roofs, Reenan helped along by Hizarah, before arriving at one with a hatch door that opened upward. Xandru pulled out a loose brick from the chimney next to the hatch, then fished out a key. He unlocked the hatch and pulled it up, then lowered the ladder and motioned them inside.

They climbed the short distance down, with Hizarah and Xandru helping Reenan negotiate the rungs with his injured leg. They were in a spacious attic, with neatly stacked woven carpets, shelves of yarn, and spindles. Hizarah and Xandru lowered Reenan in, his forehead damp with sweat, then sat him down against a rolled-up carpet. Manneki discovered a pillow and brought it to help prop up his wounded friend.

"What is this place?" Theo asked, still gripping the *Book of Cures* to him.

"Gerdene has one of the biggest loom businesses in this area," Xandru explained. "The noise of her looms going all day will hide any sounds you make up here. She's like a mother to me, so you're safe for now. I'll get her to bring some healing supplies for that leg, but whatever you do, don't leave this room."

And with that, he was gone, disappearing through the hatch in the roof and locking it behind him.

$\mathcal{A}$ week after the fire, Reenan's leg was strong enough for him to limp around their attic space. Theo had, with a scalpel and much liquor, managed to pull the arrowhead out, clean the wound, and bandage it. The widow Gerdene, who'd they met on their first night when she brought up bandages, water, food, medicine, and clothing, had encouraged Reenan to scream as much as he wished. The constant clacking of the looms in her workshops below would drown out all sounds, and all the girls working the looms were devoutly loyal to her.

Though they hadn't seen Xandru since he'd brought them here, they had grown to trust Gerdene. The woman had seen at least sixty summers, and the others hadn't yet noticed, but Theo detected a slight tremor in her hands and head that he suspected was the early onset of shaking sickness. Other than that, she seemed an image of vitality, moving with the gait of someone far younger, and speaking with the calm, measured tones of someone far older. She wore the same pressed, woven dress of cream white every day, and each evening after the shop closed, she rapped on the trap door leading from the rooms below and brought up meals, clean linens, soap, water, and most important, news.

"Three of the houses were gutted," she told them the day after the fire. "But it seems they think there are no survivors. The city's been talking of little else."

At Hizarah's expression, the older woman had given an encouraging smile. "Houses can be rebuilt. Hearts can be healed. But lives cannot be regained."

Theo knew she had said this to comfort Hizarah, but she couldn't have known how many had already paid with their lives. The wound of losing both his grandfather and Orjo still bled, raw and new. Theo threw himself into deciphering the *Book of Cures* in an effort to avoid his grief, but even so, there were too many pockets of time between catching words and falling asleep, between waking and realizing anew that Orjo and Father Oaks were gone. Added to this was the growing frustration with the *Book of Cures*, which was proving dense. Theo often looked up after struggling through a page to find that an hour had passed, with no further clues as to how to reverse pacification.

On the eighth day after the fire, Xandru returned to the attic. He hid his fuzzy scalp under a cap and brought a bundle with him.

"How's the leg?" he asked Reenan.

"The wound will hound me in my old age, I'm wagering," Reenan shrugged. "But at least I get to have an old age."

Xandru nodded, then sat down on a rug. In the week they had lived in the attic, they had taken Gerdene's advice and rearranged some of the carpets and pillows into a semblance of a living space: a sitting area in the middle, with rolled-up blankets along the sides of the attic where they slept. Now, Xandru invited them to sit with him.

"I'm sure you have questions," he said, looking at each of them. "But I'll start with some of the obvious ones. My name is Xandru, but some call me the Magpie."

"The Magpie?" Hizarah raised an eyebrow. "You're the city's most famous thief?"

Xandru bowed his head, clearly flattered. "We're the biggest guild of thieves in the city, so we know the rooftops and alleyways like we know our own faces. I've had my friends keep an eye on you, in case you needed our help." He looked at Theo then. "I know you're Theo Griffinrider, and as long as I'm alive, my boys and our guild will all make sure you're safe."

"Thank you," Theo said. There had been no point in denying his name. Gerdene had seemed unsurprised to see the *Book of Cures*, and never said a word when she saw Theo poring over it whenever she came up to the attic. "So, we are trapped here?" Realizing he had offended Xandru, Theo corrected himself. "I mean, we should stay here? For how long?"

"For a little while longer," Xandru said. "Things are quietening down, but the empire is still combing the city, asking about you, especially as those soldiers out back have told anyone who will listen that they were attacked. So, it's best you stay out of sight."

Theo considered this. Though they were grateful for the shelter, he didn't relish hiding. Not just because the long days and longer nights here allowed his thoughts to dwell on Orjo and Father Oaks, but because he wanted to find out more about the ship and the emperor's plans.

Theo ventured to ask, "You say you know the city well. How well, exactly?"

"I know every alley and back street, every roof and every chimney. Why?"

"The emperor is planning something terrible for everyone, Urzok or no. I need to find out what it is and warn Kalyun-eh."

"Even if you did find out, how would you make anyone believe it?" Xandru asked. "No one would trust the Magpie's word, and you're not even supposed to be alive."

"What if Theo had proof?" Hizarah asked.

Xandru shrugged. "Like what?"

"Like a ship," Theo said. "I need you to find a ship."

* * *

"Presenting to Your Eminence, His Lordship of Vyad, Ornox."

The servant stayed prostrate as Ornox walked forward and then similarly laid himself down on the floor. Then at some unseen gesture of the emperor's, the servant left, closing the great doors with a quiet hushing sound.

There was the sound of cutlery, the scrape of a chair.

"Rise, rise, Ornox. We do not make the empire's heroes kneel or prostrate for too long, do we?"

Ornox rose and bowed his head once. "Thank you, Your Eminence."

"Come, sit down." The emperor motioned to one of his advisors, who pulled out a chair. Ornox wasn't sure which advisor it was, as he didn't bother keeping track of their names. They were all like Brel, a plague on the empire, a lichen to be scraped off one's brickwork.

The table was heavily laden with delicacies and drink, all in the finest holders. Ornox sat, halfway down the table from the old ruler of Mankahar. The advisor poured wine into a goblet and placed it before him, while another came forward with a plate.

"You honor me with a place at your table, Your Eminence."

The emperor smiled. "The empire owes you thanks and congratulations, yet again. I would not dream of welcoming you back without a feast and gifts."

Ornox didn't voice aloud that this feast was very poorly attended. Whatever the emperor wanted to gift him, or say to him, was apparently going to be given in private. "The service to my emperor is reward enough."

"Of course," the emperor's smooth voice purred. "But we are generous to those who serve us well. Those who bring back lost posts such as Nyatha deserve rich things. But before I get into that, won't you eat?"

It wouldn't do to refuse, though he couldn't stand the heaviness of the emperor's tastes. Ornox helped himself to a modest portion of the meat in front of him, as well as something else that smelled of spices.

"You haven't been in the capital for some time, so you probably haven't heard yet," the emperor said, picking up a pastry and nibbling it. "But there's been a new rumor. About a ghost."

Ornox's attention snapped back to the emperor. Was this the reason the emperor had summoned him to a private dinner? "A ghost, Your Eminence?"

The emperor shrugged. "I say a ghost. The talk is that Theo Griffinrider is not dead, but alive and well in our capital."

Ornox studied the emperor's face, trying to gauge whether this was a jest. "Your Eminence, you and I both know those rumors are ridiculous."

"Of course," Dorgun said, swallowing the rest of the pastry and flicking a crumb away. "Lies, I am sure. But I can't quite figure out who started them, or why they would take hold."

"People always need something to fear."

"True." The emperor smiled. "There really is no way the rumors could have merit, is there?"

"I killed him myself," Ornox replied, firm. "If there are rumors in the city that Theo Griffinrider is alive, those rumors are being spread either by malicious traitors or those with more gossip than sense."

The emperor nodded. "I thought as much. But I wanted to know your views on it. You are the hero of the empire, you have proven your worth. Your loyalty. Which is why I have had my men prepare you a gift of fine eastern horses, which you are welcome to take with you. They are the best from the stable. I chose them myself."

Ornox inclined his head. "Your Eminence is much too kind."

The emperor took a bite of meat from his plate, his hand giving a dismissive flutter. "That is only the beginning. I will, of course, also pay you handsomely from the royal coffers, a sum befitting such a successful warlord. And I think, Ornox, it is time you had help with your affairs, no?"

"My household is sufficient for my needs," Ornox replied.

The emperor smiled. "Of course. But you are young. In the prime of life. A strong warlord, like a strong emperor, needs heirs."

At this, Ornox stiffened. Was the emperor actually—?

"I've brokered a marriage between you and the daughter of the lord of Harkwin, which will see you owner of all those lands when the old lord dies and his titles pass to his daughter. Who, I might add, is young and, by most accounts, quite attractive." The emperor leaned forward, as if imparting a secret. "I need a man I can trust to make sure the outer edges of the empire stay loyal, Ornox. Remember, anyone who wishes to rule Mankahar must have power, and an heir."

Ornox inclined his head again, trying to contain his surprise. He had no stomach or fondness for marriage. His first had been like this, an arrangement his father had made when he was twenty and could no longer sustain arguments of wanting to marry later in order to bring war glory to Vyad. He had been chained to a woman for whom he hadn't a shred of attraction, with whom he had nothing in common. The only pleasure she had ever given him was his daughter Agacheta, and now, even that was gone.

Now, the prospect of marriage itself was repugnant, but the benefits that came with such a marriage were great, as were the implications of why Dorgun would insist Ornox needed an heir. Harkwin was on the southern border of Mankahar, rich in grain, cotton, and timber. The lord of Harkwin was one of the richest nobles at court, and as such, his daughter was a prize that every eligible bachelor was vying for. The Harkwin coffers were one of the few in Mankahar that had suffered the taxes of war without seeing much of a dent. For the emperor to offer this on a platter to Ornox was a great prize, one of the strongest possible shows of favor.

"Your Eminence again does me too much honor. I would humbly accept your bounty."

The emperor drank from his goblet and wiped his thin lips. "Of course you will. Just sleep with a dagger close by, for when the news gets out, I expect there will be many unhappy suitors. I shall notify Harkwin at once, an alliance between a great military house such as Vyad and a rich house such as Harkwin will be a strong, unbeatable union. We'll have the wedding after my Feast Day."

Ornox inclined his head again, still stunned by the emperor's move. Was this a trick? Birds did not fall out of skies, and fish did not leap into nets. But if the emperor was setting a trap, what was it? His gaze wandered over the twelve imperial guards who attended the emperor. As always, they kept stony countenances, as if deaf to all conversations around them.

"Speaking of," the emperor continued, wiping his lips, "I look forward to seeing you at my birthday festivities. It wouldn't be right without you there, as I am announcing my heir."

"As I said, I wouldn't miss it for all of Mankahar's treasure, Your Eminence."

Later, as Ornox left the inner castle and crossed the courtyard to the outer gates on his way out, he mulled over his conversation with the emperor, trying to dissect every word and meaning.

"Yod," he said to his man as they reached the outer bailey where grooms waited with their horses, "find me someone with knowledge of those in the emperor's imperial guard." All signs pointed to the emperor naming Ornox heir. But it always paid to be prepared. Just in case.

"Very well, my lord. Is that all?"

"Look into the rumors about Theo Griffinrider being alive," Ornox said. "Do it personally." All lies, Ornox was sure. But he had learned that rumors were like flies. They bred best where something was rotten, and he intended to find out what that was.

* * *

THEO FROWNED at the crude map he had been perusing. With Xandru's drawing skills, Theo had put together a rough depiction of Mankahar, with its different districts and the ports where Xandru had been inquiring about the ship. He had written down the names of each of the ports, and each time Xandru came, he brought news of whether they had found any information. The answer had always been the same.

"There's nothing of that size being built in the ports. There hasn't been one of that size built in decades, I'm told. It would be hard to hide."

Theo was hoping tonight would be the night for good news. But when Xandru entered from the roof, he had the same weary expression. He dropped into the room with a hemp sack and shook his head. "We've been over all the ports twice. There's no sign of a ship like the one in your drawings."

Theo surveyed his map, trying to contain his frustration. No leads on the ship, and so far nothing in the *Book of Cures* on how to reverse pacification. "We must be overlooking something."

"What about looking in the obvious place?" Hizarah asked. Everyone turned to her. "Here. Right in Kalyun-eh."

Xandru frowned, skeptical. "But there aren't any shipbuilders in Kalyun-eh."

"What if it's not meant for the sea?" Theo asked. "It wouldn't have to be built in a port."

Xandru thought on this. "I suppose that's possible."

"No one would expect a ship to be built in Kalyun-eh," Reenan added.

"I haven't heard of anything, but I'll search the carpentry district," Xandru agreed. "In the meantime, can I ask you something?"

"Anything," Theo said.

Xandru upended his bag, revealing a small knife, a bowl, and a water skin. Theo and his companions watched Xandru line them up on the floor.

"What's this?" Hizarah asked.

Xandru looked up. "I'm sure you've noticed that Gerdene is sick."

Theo nodded. "She says it's a chill, but I think it might be the shaking sickness."

The boy nodded. "The healers say she'll lose control of her limbs, then eventually her organs and mind."

"I am so sorry, Xandru," Theo said, sincere. "They also told you that it's not curable?"

Xandru looked down, seeming to gather himself. He then looked up at Theo. "Are you sure about that?"

"I've never heard of a cure."

"What about your blood?" Xandru asked quietly.

Theo tried not to look at the knife. "The story of what I did at Ralgayan is a myth. My blood is not magic. It won't cure the shaking disease."

Xandru seemed to struggle between despair and suspicion. "She's like a mother to me, and I would do anything to save her."

"I understand," Theo said, "but I promise you my blood won't help her."

Xandru frowned. "Then how did you save your friend at Ralgayan?"

"I used the Forbidden Language," Theo explained. "I had a book that told of a cure, a changing of the blood."

"Like the *Book of Cures*?" Xandru asked.

"Yes. Like that. So she wasn't saved because of my blood, she was saved because I learned of a cure."

Xandru's shoulders slumped, and Hizarah reached out to squeeze his shoulder.

"I am sorry, Xandru," Theo said. "I would do anything to save Gerdene."

The boy looked at the *Book of Cures*, lying open on the pillow next to Theo. "Maybe there's something in there."

Theo put a paw on the boy's shoulder. "I'll work faster. If I find anything, you'll be first to know."

"I'd like to help you."

"The only way you'd be able to help is if you knew the Forbidden Language."

"Then I'd like to learn it."

At first, Theo was too surprised to reply. No one had ever asked to learn the Forbidden Language. "It's taboo. You could be sentenced to death."

The boy shrugged. "I'm an escaped slave. They'll do worse if they find me. If you won't give me your blood, then give me what helped you save someone you loved. Perhaps I'll find a cure to the shaking disease in there."

Theo found himself unwilling to reject the boy twice. "Very well. I'll teach you as we read. We'll need slate and chalk."

CHAPTER 30

The great western dragon-salt cave was like an ugly frog's mouth—wide, squat, and dark. It was half hidden in a scrubby plateau where the beaten earth lay parched and the air smelled of heat, scorched vegetation, and something slightly unpleasant.

Brune and Indigo peered out from the shelter of the nearby trees, straining to see any signs of the fabled monster that was supposed to guard this place.

"You sure it's here?" Indigo asked Brune.

Kestrel, on a nearby branch where Brune had placed her, tilted her beak into the air. "I can smell it."

Brune nodded. "So can I. There's dragon salt here, and lots of it."

"I don't see a dragon," Indigo commented. "In fact, I don't see any life at all."

"That's what worries me," Brune growled. "No lizards, birds. Nothing. Quiet and still as hibernation, this."

"Perhaps it's inside?" Kestrel suggested.

"Only one way to find out," Brune said, pulling his axe from his holster and giving a cocky smile to the others. "Ready?"

Indigo turned to Kestrel and pointed at an outcropping of rock behind them. "Hide there and wait for us."

"What if you don't come out?" Kestrel asked, eyes dark with worry.

"Then run if you can," Brune answered, somber for once. "And don't come back."

Kestrel helped them find dried branches and grasses to make torches. Brune and Indigo lit them with flints, then nodded up at Kestrel before heading into the cave.

"Be careful," the bird said.

"We'll be back soon," Indigo promised and watched the bird hop back behind some leaves, now well hidden.

Inside Doom Hollow, it was cool, and just as still. Brune and Indigo paused at the lip of the cave, as if waiting for the monster to come out of the dark and seize them.

But nothing happened.

"Perhaps he's gone to get himself lunch," Brune said lightly.

Indigo tried to share his levity. They could use some good luck for a change, but it seemed a tall ask that the dragon might have died a quiet death in its own cave. They continued onward, and the cave began to widen into a long corridor with jagged spires of rock rising from the floor, and matching rock fangs jutting down from the ceiling. Some of them were broken off, as if smashed by a great force. The odd scrap of clothing or pile of bones hinted at the others who had come before, and never left. The light from the mouth of the cave faded the deeper they went, and soon, both the rabbit and the bear were grateful for the light of their torches.

They walked on like this until the walls turned glistening. Indigo stepped closer and saw layers of ashen crystals, glowing white and wet.

"This what we're looking for?" Brune asked.

Indigo ran a paw along it and tasted it. The salt had a bitter, smoky tinge. She nodded, excited. "I think so."

Brune grinned, ecstatic. "And no monster."

The words had barely finished before the air around them heated rapidly.

"Down!" Brune shouted, diving to the ground and pulling her with him. A wall of flame shot out just over their heads. A burning smell hit her, and Indigo realized her fur was singed.

"Looks like someone's home!" Brune was back on his feet with his axe drawn in the time it took Indigo to push herself onto her arms and feel the vibrations of something big—very big —pounding its way toward them from the cave's depths.

A giant red maw full of yellowed teeth snapped closed where her head had been. She rolled toward the monster and heard Brune grunt as the dragon slammed the bear into the cave wall with a flick of its front claws. She scrambled to work her sword free, but the beast's spined tail came whipping back, smashing several stalagmites before bludgeoning her in the side with a force that sent her flying.

In the light of their fallen torches, she could make out flashes of green, gold, and something else that flashed metallic. She heard the crash of metal chains and saw mean-looking spines along a huge back. The dragon spewed another river of flame at Brune, who dove for the beast's foreleg and bit down.

The dragon roared, and Indigo caught sight of the tight noose of chain around its neck. She took this opening to clamber up its tail and onto its back, using its spines as footholds. It was instinctively trying to bring its great leathery wings into play, but the cave was too small for it to turn around effectively. And as long as Brune and Indigo were close to the dragon's body, it couldn't spit fire for fear of injuring itself. She slipped on the dragon's scales but caught one spine with her paw. The dragon rippled its back, trying to shake her off, but she scrambled until she was up near the neck.

This only seemed to drive the dragon mad, and it flung its head about, in attempts to dislodge her, while trying to shake Brune off its foreleg.

Indigo clung on, barely able to grip the dragon's two horns

and slippery neck muscles, much less get a sword free to wield it.

"Axe! Use your axe!"

But a resounding thud told her that the dragon had managed to shake Brune free, and she saw the bear fly into the cave wall. The dragon gave a triumphant scream and lowered its head to try to swipe her off with its foreclaw.

"Stop! We're here to free you!"

The dragon's shift was slight, but Indigo felt it. The beast had heard. Brune growled at Indigo, but she gave him a look. *Trust me.*

"We can take off your chain, but we need dragon salt to do it."

She felt a ripple course through the giant beneath her.

"Why would you do that?" the dragon asked, suspicious.

"Because we need dragon salt, and lots of it." Indigo cautiously slid down to where she could look the dragon in the eye. "We'd be willing to free you, if you let us have the salt."

The dragon glanced at Brune, a low growl in its throat. "Chains cannot be broken by axe. Or by fire. Morr has tried."

"Is that your name? Morr?" Indigo asked. The dragon's voice sounded male. "We need this dragon salt to help save our lands from the emperor, Morr. You know of him? And the Urzok Empire?"

"Morr doesn't care about emperors. Morr cares about leaving this cave."

"Of course," Brune said, putting his axe away and making a show of displaying his empty paws. "And we can break the chains with black snow, but to make it, we need dragon salt, see?"

The dragon drew up to his full height, head against the cave ceiling, and glared at them, wary. "Morr is listening."

"Let us take the salt," Indigo said. "We'll be back as soon as we have made enough to break the chains."

The dragon frowned, smoke seeping from between his teeth.

"How do I know you won't just leave? That you aren't just tricking me?"

Brune stepped forward, pulling his axe from its holster and putting it down. "I'll stay here with you. If Indigo here doesn't return, then I die here."

The dragon hesitated, unmoving. They waited for a moment, two.

"You really can break my chains?"

Indigo smiled. "Absolutely. You'll see."

The dragon finally nodded and enfolded Brune in his tail. "If you don't come back, the bear dies."

Indigo looked to Brune, who attempted a carefree grin. "I'm counting on you, Princess."

She nodded, then picked up a great chunk of dragon salt that had fallen to the ground during the fight. She ran back through the cave toward the mouth, and Kestrel.

EVEN WITH INDIGO'S HELP, it took Kestrel two days to make enough black snow. The princess worked at not only gathering materials and tools, and creating a large bonfire for charcoal, but also at taking enough food into the cave to keep Brune from starving.

Kestrel showed her how to hollow a branch out into a tube, and what trees provided a sap that when chewed, turned into a malleable gum that could be pushed into tubes, where they hardened into a plug. Toward dusk, they had managed to mix enough dragon salt, charcoal, and the flame rock they had brought with them from Nyatha to fill a wooden tube the length of Indigo's arm.

"No chain will withstand that," Kestrel said, cocking her head in satisfaction at their work. "Just don't stand too close when it's lit. You could easily lose a limb."

Indigo nodded and took the tube, as well as a lit torch, into the cave.

Brune's eyes lit up at the sight of the tube in her paws, while Morr's scaled face looked skeptical.

"Trust us," Indigo said. She made Morr stand, then examined the chain to choose the best spot to ignite the black snow without injuring the dragon. The chain around the dragon's neck looped through a large ring by its jaw, such that whenever he tried to move toward the cave entrance, it choked him. She had seen similar "choke collars" on pacified animals. The other end of the chain was welded to a metal plate in the cave floor.

"Whoever did this did it well," Indigo murmured.

The dragon lashed his tail. "A village sorcerer chained Morr here."

"Well, once you're free," Brune said, "my advice is to leave that village alone."

Indigo placed the tube of black snow into one of the chain's links closest to the metal plate in the floor. Each link was the size of her torso and as thick as her arm, and she hoped Kestrel hadn't underestimated how much black snow was needed. Morr didn't strike her as patient, so they would likely only have one chance to free him before he decided to kill them in retaliation.

"Stand back as far as you can," she told the dragon, who shifted until the chain was taut. Indigo picked up the torch she had left burning on the ground and looked to Brune and Morr. "Ready?"

"Like salmon in spring," Brune growled.

Indigo touched the torch to the oiled wick Kestrel had made her weave, and once she had it lit, she retreated back to join Morr and Brune. She folded and covered her ears and saw Morr flatten his and close his eyes.

The blast, when it came, sounded like a pop that sent dust raining down on them. But when the debris cleared, they could see that where the chain plate had been was now a blackened hole, and the chain that had been welded there was now broken, lying on the cave floor in a mess of jagged metal.

Brune let out a whoop.

Morr opened his eyes, and upon seeing the broken chain, pulled it to him with trembling foreclaws. "You broke it. You really broke it."

Indigo smiled. "You're free, Morr."

With Brune's help, the dragon pulled the broken chain through the ring near his neck, and slipped free. The dragon shook his head, clearly relishing the feel. In the torchlight, Indigo saw the scars where the chain had rubbed Morr's neck raw and then healed over into calluses. She felt a stab of pity for the large beast.

The dragon raced out of the cave. Brune and Indigo followed, watching as the great beast spread his leathery wings and took to the sky. He wobbled and dipped at first, his wings clearly unused to flight after his imprisonment in the cave. He circled higher and higher, a dark smudge against the blue, then came plummeting back to land before the cave.

"Thank you," Morr said sincerely, and then stood for a moment, smoke trickling through his nose.

"What's wrong?" Brune asked.

"Morr is unsure where to go."

"Anywhere you want," Indigo said. "You're free."

Morr thought on this. He marched back into the cave, leaving Brune and Indigo confused. But in a moment, the dragon reemerged, a leather thong with an object hanging from it clenched in his teeth. He held it out to Brune and dropped it into the bear's paw.

"Take this. It's a whistle one of the thieves left behind, and Morr kept it. Blow on it if you need Morr, and Morr will come."

Brune took it. "I'd have to blow pretty hard for you to hear me."

Morr shook his head. "Dragons have very good hearing. No matter how softly you blow, Morr will hear."

Brune slipped the thong and whistle over his neck. "Thank you, friend. Safe travels."

The creature nodded to them. And with a great rush of wings, he was aloft, shaking the trees with mighty bellows of joy.

* * *

IN THE DAYS after they encountered Morr, the three of them worked long and hard to create a production system for black snow. Though Kestrel's injured wing was almost completely healed, Indigo insisted the bird avoid any physical labor that might endanger her recovery. So the bird supervised and instructed with a keen eye, while Brune made sure they had an endless supply of wood to make the charcoal.

"What will you do after this?" Indigo asked Kestrel as she mixed wood ash with dragon salt according to the bird's strict measurements. "You'll be ready to fly in two days, I think."

The bird fluffed her feathers. "I'm not sure, exactly."

"Hegg, and the Order, could use an alchemist," Brune suggested. "You're more than welcome to come with us."

Kestrel smiled and dipped her head. "Thank you. Ethana taught me all she knew of alchemy, and she was one of the best in the land. But I don't want to be an alchemist one day more than I have to."

Indigo and Brune shared a look. "So where will you go?" the rabbit asked.

The canary stretched her wing. "Home." Her eyes softened. "I haven't returned since I was a chick."

The bear nodded, sympathetic, and Indigo felt her own pang of homesickness for the steppes of Alvareth.

"If you change your mind, you'll find us in Hegg," Brune said.

The bird bobbed her head. "Thank you."

By the end of the first week, Kestrel's wing had improved enough that she managed several short flights around their campgrounds. They had also managed to make several tubefuls of black snow, all stoppered with the gum resin that Kestrel had first shown Indigo.

"We won't be able to carry much more back," Indigo said. "Just enough to show the Order the possibilities. We'll return with more forces once they see us demonstrate it."

Brune nodded. "We should leave tomorrow. The sooner we get help to bring back, the sooner the Order has this advantage against the empire."

Indigo couldn't agree more. They would set out at first light. As Indigo prepared her own bed, she watched Kestrel settle down to sleep in the nest the bird had made herself. Tomorrow, they would part ways, with Indigo and Brune traveling to Hegg, and Kestrel to her home. Indigo knew she would be in for a strict tongue lashing from Noshi and the rest of the Order for disobeying, but she hoped the tubes of black snow she brought back would make up for it. Turning the tide of war would have to win her some grace. Wouldn't it?

* * *

THEO CAUGHT another word on the slate and watched Xandru and Reenan dutifully copy them.

What had started as a private lesson for Xandru had grown to include Reenan and Hizarah, who had gradually drawn closer to the lesson each day, until they both also picked up charcoal pieces and began practicing. Manneki was the only one they thought could risk venturing outside, and he spent his days wandering the rooftops, on the lookout for spies or imperial soldiers.

The attic space had thus been converted into a teaching space. Xandru had brought up a larger slate so Theo could write for everyone to see. Manneki had pilfered other bits of slate for Reenan and Hizarah to use, and there was always plenty of charcoal from Gerdene's fireplaces downstairs.

Theo found himself glad for a break from reading the

ancient text of the *Book of Cures*. He was three-fourths through and had still found nothing about curing pacification or the shaking sickness, and his frustration was mounting.

Every night before lessons started, Theo would ask Xandru whether there was any news on the emperor's ship. Each night Xandru shook his head.

Just as they had with the ports of Mankahar, Theo drew up a map of Kalyun-eh and crossed off each area where Xandru and his guild of thieves had thoroughly searched. The number of patches of neighborhoods with thick crosses marked on them grew every day, until Theo despaired that the whole city map would soon be crossed out with nothing to show for it.

That night, while others slept, he pored over his map again, trying to squeeze some overlooked information from it. They had checked the carpenter districts, the furniture makers, and carriage builders, and none had shown any indication of building something resembling a ship.

When his eyes began to blur and he had burned several candles down to nubs, he shoved the map aside. He would burst from restlessness if he didn't escape the room. He normally would not risk being out on the rooftops, where he could be seen, but he felt that if he didn't sit under the open sky tonight, his frustration and despair would eat him from within. Besides, by now, the night had deepened and the sounds of the city had subsided to near silence. There'd hardly be anyone on the deserted streets at this hour.

He glanced over to make sure his companions were asleep, then gently opened the roof hatch and climbed out, finding himself a spot on the tiles and taking a welcome breath of night air.

Theo wasn't sure how long he had been sitting there, looking at the moon, when Reenan poked his head out of the hatch.

"Theo? You all right?" the man whispered.

Theo nodded. "I just needed to be outside. I don't know how much longer I can stand this imprisonment."

Reenan pulled himself out and sat down next to Theo. For a while, they simply gazed at the stars in silence, wrapped in the chilly night air. The castle lights glowed in the distance, like a dozen cat eyes watching over the city. He thought back to his time in the Cave of Light, the tortoise.

"Reenan, do you believe there is a life beyond this one?"

"Some things we cannot ever know." Reenan looked at him. "And some things you cannot blame yourself for, like your grandfather's death. Or Orjo's. They chose for themselves."

"But I've failed them."

"I doubt they'd see it that way."

"I was sure the Library would have the weapon we needed," Theo said. "I was so sure that the *Book of Cures* was it. Something to reverse pacification and return Mankahar to what it was, but there's nothing about that in it. Even after days of releasing words." His throat closed at the thought. His grandfather had died for this book, died for Theo. Died for a collection of old, useless words.

"First of all, Mankahar can probably never be what it once was," Reenan said. "It is different now. You cannot expect to be able to restore it to what it was. And second, what makes you so sure you were meant to find the *Book of Cures?*"

"I don't follow," Theo said, frowning.

"Maybe you weren't meant to find a weapon *against* the empire," Reenan said. "Maybe you were meant to find out what the *empire's* weapon would be against us. And now that you know, you just have to find it and stop it."

Theo mulled on this. The silence stretched again.

"I know you've lost your grandfather, and Orjo." The man gazed out at the stars, eyes sad. "But don't lose your hope too." He stood. "Don't give up, rabbit. Every entertainer like me knows that no success ever comes before steady failure. So take comfort in that the more you fail, the closer you are to the prize. True failure comes only when you stop trying."

CHAPTER 31

The fighting oval was little more than a mud pool in the rain, and the dogs locked together there were almost indistinguishable in the muck. Not that Ornox minded. He wasn't here for the dogs. Or at least, not the ones that fought in the ring.

He looked about him at the men gathered there for the sport. They stank of ale and greasy foods and had the air of the mean and the desperate about them. None of them were real fighters. Otherwise, they'd be in the ring themselves. No, Ornox knew this sort. They liked watching others fight, seeing other's blood flow, while they themselves would probably go down at his first punch. Such were men who enjoyed dog fighting.

"Good blow!"

Ornox regarded his new ward, who clearly relished blood-sport. Sarkus had taken to Ornox's employ like a limpet to a rock. He followed Ornox whenever he was allowed, observed everything from behind that new wooden mask of his, and seemed particularly keen to memorize every detail of how Ornox disciplined and punished his men when needed. The boy had a very dark streak, Ornox decided, as evidenced by his clear excitement at the death match held here.

As if sensing his sponsor's gaze, Sarkus tore his attention away from the entertainment and looked up. "Who are we waiting for, my lord?"

"Someone with information."

Sarkus turned back to scan the crowd. Everyone seemed intent on the match, with no one showing any interest in the warlord and his page.

A man jostled Ornox's elbow as he maneuvered to a place at the front. "Some room, if you please."

The man's long braid was plainly knotted but clean, his cloak mud-spattered and old, but still well made to go with the sturdy boots on his feet. Ornox made out a sharp nose, thick lips, and a wide brow beneath the hat.

"Wet weather favors the smaller hound," the man said, surveying the fight.

Ornox nodded. "I agree. Though the bigger one has my bet." Sarkus glanced over at the two of them, but was smart enough to keep his mouth shut.

The man leaned against the barrier that separated them from the more enthusiastic crowds below, who were pressing against the ropes in their eagerness to see the competition. Up here in the stands was where the more reserved sat, the ones who had greater money on the game but less risk in who lost.

"What is it you want to know then?" the man asked, his eye still on the fight. The smaller hound was indeed gaining the advantage, proving the agreed-upon code words the man spoke.

"Who is a soft link in the emperor's imperial guard?"

A sardonic grin worked the man's lips. "Depends. What do you want them to do?"

"I don't need a kill. I just need them to be...partial to my views."

The man glanced at him then. "If it's the ear of the emperor you want, then you should seek the advisors."

Ornox shook his head. A great cheer rose from the crowd as the small dog scored a bloody tear across the larger dog. He eyed

Sarkus, who was cheering with the rest, and waited for the noise to abate. "I don't need persuasion with the emperor. I simply need this guard to be in my pay."

The man was silent for a while, and Ornox wondered whether he had heard him. But then the man leaned over toward him, as if to get a better view around a tall patron up front. "You've two choices then. The youngest one and the woman. The youngest comes from a rich noble's family, but he's keen to prove himself. He'll do anything that gets him more status if you can offer him something."

"Young means inexperienced," Ornox said. "I saw him, he can't be more than twenty summers."

The man shrugged. "Then your next bet is the woman. She is tough as all the men here, barely speaks, and comes from a poor family."

"She'd want coin?"

"No," the man answered. "She's incorruptible. Honest to the point of stupidity."

"Then I don't see how I would be interested in her."

"Her mother has a lame leg."

Ornox weighed this, trying to see the man's logic.

"She loves her mother. Every cent she earns goes back to that woman, and the woman can't move beyond the house without help now. Some might say she's a ripe target."

Ornox nodded. "I'll pay her a visit."

* * *

On the far reaches of the other side of Kalyun-eh, Yod sat and sipped his watery ale. He hated ale normally, but this job called for it.

The Archer's Table was an unpretentious haunt, full of petty servants, small-time traders, and soldiers looking for a way to spend their coin. But it was also a place where scraps of gossip fell as freely as spilled beer.

The bar was well attended tonight, with rowdy celebrants toasting each other over some new job, and another group of quieter patrons sitting in relative silence. Yod had stayed in the center, near the long ale-soaked table where the bartender and his wife slung glasses of mead, sour wine, and bread soaked in oil and salt to disguise the fact it was stale.

He had already had some interesting brushes with rumors about the rabbit, but none that seemed worth pursuing. He wore the clothes of a common page, and the crowd of the place meant that he could still sit near enough to people to overhear their conversations without being conspicuous. He bantered with an imperial soldier who was just this side of drunk and heard the theory that Theo Griffinrider had risen from the dead and had an army of animals to take Kalyun-eh. Yod tried to trace where the man had heard this, but couldn't get further than the statement that the rumor was everywhere.

Just as Yod was about to pay his debt and leave for another tavern, a red-faced young soldier stumbled in with his three companions. They had had a few, and were clearly merry, but still had command of their senses. They made their way to a table near the bar, occasionally elbowing each other in good-natured jest as they sat down. They called for the waitress. Yod stood and tossed coin on the counter, and as he passed their seats, he caught a snippet of their conversation.

"…as burned out as Blackhide's oven."

"Aye, any bones would be ash. Don't know why we're still doing these rounds."

"We get paid. That's why."

"Well, I'm sick of hunting some phantom rabbit."

Yod's ears pricked up. He looked over and saw the man who had just spoken impatiently calling the waitress again. She was either ignoring them or simply run off her feet.

"Are you a barmaid or a piece of furniture?" the soldier hollered.

"Let me help," Yod said, and taking two steps over, he

touched the waitress's elbow. "We're needing four ales here. On me."

Yod sat down at their table, and the soldiers looked at him appreciatively.

"Hard work, being a soldier," Yod said. "Least I can do is buy you lot a drink."

Grins all around. "What're you then?" The young leader of the pack had a coin he kept passing between his thick fingers.

Yod shrugged. "Just a patriot who admires those who keep the city safe. Can't have thieves running free and burning houses."

A short soldier with oily hair scoffed. "We don't hunt common thieves. That's for the sheriff's lads."

"Oh?" Yod said. "You go after the bigger fish, then?"

"That's the usual," a large-boned soldier with meaty hands said. The dissatisfaction in his voice drew Yod.

"So this isn't the usual?"

Oily Hair snorted. "Hunting some unpacified rabbit who probably died in the fire?" At a glower from the other three, Oily Hair rolled his shoulders. "What? Everyone this side of the square knows."

"Seems a lot of trouble for just one unpacified rabbit," Yod said. "What does he look like?"

The lead soldier transferred his coin to the other hand. "Doesn't matter. All rabbits are to be rounded up and taken in."

The ales arrived, and Yod paused as he let the men slake their thirst. When they had sated themselves on their first mouthfuls, he waded back in. "You mentioned a fire. Where, exactly?"

CHAPTER 32

Ornox kept his eye on the woman in front of him. She walked surely and quickly, and he followed some paces behind.

The market hummed with its usual business, as vendors and buyers made their way through the clogged alleys. Smells of spices, manure, and animals mingled with the stale stench of sweat and the sweeter smells of perfumeries and candle wax.

She turned down a side street, and Ornox quickened his pace, keeping his face hidden under his cloak's hood. He turned at the same corner and found himself slammed against the side of a wall, a knife hovering at his throat.

"Why are you following me?"

He pushed his hood back and smiled. "I just wanted a talk."

"Lord Ornox." Her eyes narrowed in recognition. She stepped back but didn't sheath her blade. "Then whatever you'd like to say, kindly say it now."

"Why don't we walk," Ornox suggested. "I promise I didn't mean disrespect, and you have my oath that I will not harm you."

She measured him, apparently amused by his suggestion that he might harm her. Sheathing her knife, she followed him out of the alley.

"I don't wish to waste your time," Ornox said. "So I'll be blunt. I like rewarding people of skill. Which I think you are, Volchega."

She gave him a look as if she resented his using her name. "I am not in your employ."

"I am proposing we change that. You probably have heard of my daughter, the only female warlord to ever have lived in Mankahar?"

"Yes," Volchega said. "I'm sorry for your loss."

"I bring her up not for sympathy," the warlord said sharply. "I simply want to prove to you that unlike most men, I believe women soldiers can be leaders. Can be promoted."

She glanced at him then, assessing. "What does that have to do with me?"

"I'm offering to make you a general, much more than just a private guard. I'd like to pay you double and have you captain my entire forces."

"You are trying to steal from the emperor. Some might call this treason."

"Treason is betrayal. Changing employers is simply a matter of coin. I see no offense in offering the emperor's staff a better wage."

"The answer is no. My thanks, Lord Ornox."

Volchega was about to walk off, but Ornox kept pace.

"Let me rephrase my offer."

She stopped then and faced him. "I have told you, I'm not interested in your offer. Loyalty is worth more than any pay or any position."

Ornox nodded. "I admire loyalty. But I'd like to ask you, is loyalty worth more than family?" At her puzzled look, he pointed over her shoulder. "You have your mother's eyes, you know. Though she insisted you get your height from your father."

She turned and looked where he pointed. In a vendor's tent

some distance away, a middle-aged woman sat on a chair, her hair piled on her head and covered with a woven cloth. An attendant was showing her various samples of beads and jewelry. Sarkus, wearing his wooden mask, stood behind her, holding a crutch for walking. He bowed toward Volchega.

"I think you may have misunderstood me," Lord Ornox continued. "Of course I'd rather you'd made the choice of your own will, but if you won't—and I admire your loyalty, it's one of the reasons I chose you—then I'll need to use a less gentle approach."

"You are vile," Volchega said, her voice poisonous.

Ornox shrugged. "Perhaps. But I need to know I can count on you. Your mother needs to know she can count on you."

Volchega glanced again at her mother, and then turned back to Ornox, her face stony. But Ornox could feel the fear rippling beneath her expression, and his heart gladdened. Another piece of his plan was falling into place.

"What do you want from me?" she asked.

* * *

IN THE KALYUN-EH CASTLE, Dorgun listened to the unending rounds of musicians being brought before him. Music for such a momentous occasion was something he wanted to choose personally, rather than leave to the uncultured ears of his advisors. And the minstrels were all talented enough, but none of them had the distinct flavor Dorgun was looking for. Something befitting a rebirth of an empire. He again envied his ancestor Dakus, who had lived to hear the bard Calgornan sing.

As he dismissed the latest gaggle of flute players, a servant came and whispered in his ear. He nodded.

"Send him in."

The man who entered was slender, with jet-black hair and a remarkably forgettable face. Dorgun had chosen him personally for this task, for the man was gifted with average, forgettable looks that meant he could as easily be a baker as a thug, a minstrel or a blacksmith.

The man prostrated himself. Dorgun motioned him closer, so that they could speak in softer tones.

"Ornox had words with one of your guards today, Your Eminence."

"Who?"

"Volchega of Harbet."

Dorgun raised one painted eyebrow. Interesting. The one woman. He doubted Ornox was a man of any passion. Volchega certainly had never shown any interest in men—or women, for that matter. If they had exchanged words, it was of the business kind.

"Do you know what was said?"

"No," the man answered. "But she didn't seem happy about whatever Ornox was telling her."

Interesting. If they were allies, it seemed one, at least, was unwilling. But an unwilling traitor was still a traitor.

"Anything else?"

The man bobbed his head. "Only a minor curiosity, Your Eminence. I don't know if it's of import."

"Tell me and I will decide."

"There've been a lot of questions asked around the ports of late."

"What questions?"

"Questions about a ship being built."

Dorgun stilled, his heart slowing. "What are they asking?"

"About any large ships being commissioned. They're not asking directly, which is why it's suspicious. They're asking about who might need a large supply of wood, or tar for caulking. They've been seeking out gossip at the wood yards and the tool sellers, trying to find out who's building and what." At the emperor's lack of reaction, the man cleared his throat. "Do you want me to bring in some of these inquisitive folk? For a few questions of our own?"

Dorgun shook his head. "No. Don't go anywhere near them. If you let the minnows feed, soon you'll attract the trout. We will wait, for the prize catch will swim into our nets soon."

CHAPTER 33

Theo was setting up the implements for the day's lesson when Xandru arrived through the roof hatch, breathless.

"I've found it. The ship."

Theo's heart thudded. "Where?"

"As Hizarah said, it was here. But not in the carpentry areas. A friend who works with a set maker that does all types of fancy work for the rich folk told me he delivered a great helm to a theatre workshop here."

"A helm?" Theo repeated.

Xandru nodded, excited. "He saw part of a hull when he delivered it, a hull bigger than any he's never seen, he said. The carpenter in charge has hired all the best in the area. It's made of light, unsealed wood, they said, which would never last in water, so it's not meant for sea."

Reenan frowned. "So he's making a prop? For a show?"

Xandru nodded. "Seems so. My friend overheard someone say it has to be ready for the emperor's birthday feast."

Theo's mind worked at this. "But if it's for a play, why all the study of winds and weather?"

"And what will he do with all the pacification powder?" Hizarah asked.

The rabbit paced the length of the room, then shook his head. "Where is this workshop?"

"In the western part of the city, in the theater district. It's crawling with workers during the day, and at night, it's locked."

"Can you get me in?" Theo asked.

Xandru pursed his lips. "I can get you in anywhere. But give me a day or so. I'll have to see what the security is like."

Theo nodded. "Do it quickly. We don't know how much time we have."

* * *

THE TWO-STORY HOUSE lay in blackened ruins, a charred husk of its former self. Rubble and wood stuck through the debris like broken bones, but the place was deserted except for a few optimistic street dogs.

And Yod.

Yod observed the house from a distance for a while. It was in a poor neighborhood inhabited mostly by lowly weavers and cloth merchants. There was the occasional tavern worker, but most of the residents seemed to be spinsters, seamstresses, loom operators, and wool merchants. If this house had been like its neighbors, then it had housed someone similar. The dwellings were crowded together, some of them with only an arm's length between them.

Yod walked up to the remains of the burned house for a closer look. Two of the walls still stood, blackened and crumbling, but the roof had collapsed completely, and the only intact structure was the ground-floor hearth and its chimney, which stood naked to the elements. Yod pushed aside a piece of rubble with his boot, seeing evidence everywhere that others had done the same thing.

"There's nothin' to find here," snapped a voice nearby. Yod

looked up and saw an elderly woman in a neighboring doorway, her hair swept into coils on her head, her mouth pinched in disapproval. "Thieves better than you've come and picked everything clean." She indicated the dogs with her broom. "Even they won't find nothin' no more."

"What about bodies?" Yod asked. "They find those too?"

The woman shot him a suspicious look. "You a body thief?" He understood the disgust. Thieves stole things, and sold them. Body thieves robbed the dead for parts to be used by the more secretive healers, witches, and other types. It was not an envied profession, regardless of pay.

He shook his head. "Just heard my family was here."

The woman's expression softened. "You Hizarah's kin?"

Hizarah. Yod mentally tucked the name away. "Yes. Would you know where Hizarah went?"

"The soldiers were searching for someone. They burned the place down but then combed the neighborhood, asking everyone all sorts of things like who lived there and whatnot. If you're related, you might want to keep quiet about it."

Yod nodded. "Appreciate the warning."

The woman nodded, anxious to leave now that she'd done a good deed but needn't be caught conversing with him.

Yod looked at the house again. So the soldiers had thought someone might have escaped. Were they after the one named Hizarah? And what did she have to do with the soldiers hunting a rabbit? He walked to the back alley and looked around at the other houses. Many of the second stories had windows, or roofs that were merely a large step apart. Was it possible the inhabitants, and maybe a rabbit, had escaped over the rooftops? And if so, where had they gone? Could they have gone far without being noticed? Unlikely, for if the soldiers had been thorough, it would have been hard to get on a cart or travel without being questioned. But what if they were close, hiding?

Yod turned back to look at the house again. It was time to explore the neighborhood.

* * *

Theo and Xandru were double-checking their supplies when Gerdene arrived. They had filled two packs with what they would need to steal into the theatre workshop—rope, a grappling hook, a whistle, and a knife. Reenan and Hizarah helped him while Manneki kept up an insistent chatter about wanting to come. But Theo was adamant.

"I'm not risking losing anyone else."

Manneki was extremely put out, and his face remained thunderous throughout Theo's preparations.

Gerdene knocked twice, then three times, their agreed code. She pushed the trap door open, and Xandru helped her up.

"I wish you good luck," she said and patted Xandru's face with a quivering hand. "Be careful."

He nodded, grasping her hand in his. "Am I ever not?"

She gave him a disapproving frown. "I mean it. Theo here has said it, and I agree with him. Whatever this shipbuilding business is, it involves the emperor, which means it will be well guarded and you're poking a hornet's nest."

She watched them leave through the roof window, then turned as a bell sounded from below. Gerdene frowned. "Strange. We've closed. I'd better see who it is. Stay quiet, in case."

Hizarah, Reenan, and Manneki nodded, then helped her down and shut the trap door.

* * *

"We're closed, young man," Gerdene called out to the visitor, stepping off the last stair onto the shop floor.

A reception counter divided the customer area from the looms, which stood in rows, all silent now and waiting for their workers to return at dawn. The man was just on this side of her trading counter, which was unusual. Most patrons waited out of courtesy on the customer side.

The figure turned. He was in his thirties perhaps, averagely dressed, and everything about him was knife-like, from the cheekbones to the shape of the eyes, to the pointed chin. Gerdene's instincts kicked in. Something about the man's hawkish eyes and overly broad smile put her on guard.

"I was hoping to buy some cloth. Something fine, for the emperor's birthday feast."

"I'll be happy to help you tomorrow."

The man shrugged his bony shoulders. "My master's keen to get his wardrobe sorted. I'd be very appreciative if you could let me see just two or three bolts of cloth."

She said nothing, then nodded and walked behind the stairs into a back room. While she was there, she kept her ears primed. Her hands were not what they were, but there was nothing wrong with her hearing. She heard the telltale slide of shoes across the floor, the whispering creak of the staircase. She swept up three bolts of cloth, pocketed a pair of fabric shears hanging from the wall, and stepped back out to the shop floor.

"That's the girls' quarters, young man."

He turned from where he stood at the staircase, again giving that overly broad smile. "Sorry, I thought perhaps there was more merchandise above. I didn't mean to offend."

As he stepped back past the counter, she took in his clothing, noting the fabric. He wasn't from Kalyun-eh, she was sure. The cut of his clothing was more popular to the north, a style no one in the capital emulated.

She spread the fabrics out for him and cursed her hands for the tremor in them. She caught his keen glance, saw him gauging her, like a snake gauging a mouse. She turned her head, making sure to not try and control the quiver there, as she usually did.

"I have the shaking sickness," she said.

The man nodded with a show of sympathy, and some of the tension went out of him. An old woman with the shaking sickness was hardly a threat. He turned back to the cloths spread before him. One was a fine gold, another a deep blue and the third a rich white that seemed spun of clouds.

"Any of these strike you?" she asked.

He passed a hand over the cloths. "Hm. A hard choice. My master wishes to impress the emperor, without seeming vain."

"I'd go with the blue then."

He examined the cloth, picking at a stray thread. "So hard to please my employer. Especially as we lost his first order of clothing in that fire nearby."

Gerdene regarded him, her expression neutral. "Very unfortunate."

"Though at least it didn't spread far. I suppose there couldn't have been any survivors."

"I wasn't there, so I can't say," Gerdene answered. She fingered the metal of the shears in her pocket.

"A terrible way to die. One of my friends was in the fire. Hizarah."

Gerdene nodded in a show of sympathy, but said nothing. She could feel him examining her.

"Though," he said, as if he had just thought of it, "the houses are so thick together here, it might be possible for someone, especially someone with a light build, to go onto the roofs? Escape to the neighboring houses. Perhaps even to this one? Come to think of it, this is where I would hide. It must be loud during the day. You could live upstairs and no one would know."

She met his gaze then, and the look, unlike her hands, was unwavering. "I've been in the loom business now since I was a wee child, barely able to walk, yet I could shuttle a loom. And you learn one or two things in that time. I've learned that you can make a blanket with mountains on it, clear as day, snow on the peaks, clouds around the top. And one customer will see the hills, and another will see the waves of the ocean. Each sees what they want to see."

"Very right," the man said. "It doesn't do to have fanciful imaginations. I'll take the blue one, thank you."

Gerdene nodded and pulled out her shears. In short order, she had cut the cloth with expert precision and folded it into a neat square with sharp corners, then tied the bundle in string. He paid her coin and bowed as he turned toward the door.

"Let me help you out," she said, following. "The door can get a little stuck from this side."

He reached for the handle, his back to her. "I'm sure I can—"

But he never finished his sentence.

Instead, he sank to the floor, the fabric shears protruding from the base of his neck. Gerdene watched him fall, before sliding the lock on the door.

CHAPTER 34

Theo and Xandru traveled across multiple rooftops, eventually leaving Gerdene's neighborhood. Next to her loom district was the tailor district, where Theo had broken into the tailor's, and after that came the neighborhood of household goods and wares. They skirted the rowdier areas, the taverns and entertainment quarters where people were out and about and leisurely eyes might see a young lad traveling with a short figure in a cloak.

Theo had to admire Xandru's familiarity with the city. He seemed to know it intimately and would expertly navigate shortcuts that allowed them to avoid passersby. He also knew the exact moment the timekeepers would walk their rounds, sounding the gongs that marked the hour.

Eventually, they found themselves in the theatre district. They crossed several wide boulevards, then made their way to the outskirts, where a large sprawling theatre sat. A tall wall with two giant sliding doors encircled the area, and behind them, Theo could smell the warm scent of freshly cut wood and the sharper odors of paint.

Xandru motioned for Theo to crouch down with him behind a water barrel outside the doors.

"I don't see any guards," Theo said, wary. He had expected any place hoarding the emperor's secrets to be heavily guarded.

"There are at least six guards during the day, but at night, there's only one," Xandru answered quietly. "Six guards for an old theatre would seem very unusual."

"How are we getting in?" Theo asked.

Xandru held up a thin piece of metal. "With this." He snuck forward to the tall doors and looked around for any signs of the guard. Theo also scanned the area, expecting at any moment to see the flash of lanterns and be surrounded by imperial soldiers. But none appeared.

Before long, the lock clicked in surrender, and with a grin, Xandru motioned for Theo to follow him. The door slid sideways on rusty tracks, and Xandru immediately pulled out a small container of oil. He sprinkled it generously on the rollers, then motioned for Theo to help him. Together, they opened it just enough for the two of them to slip through, and then carefully pulled the rolling door closed again.

Inside, Theo could see they were in a large workshop at the back of the theatre. Moonlight flooded in through the side windows, revealing woodworking stations set up around the area. Axes and lathes covered one wall, and in the middle of it all was the towering silhouette of a ship. Its hull rose over their heads like a multi-story house, and he and Xandru walked around it, taking it in.

"I've never seen a ship this big," Xandru breathed.

But its size didn't puzzle Theo as much as the lack of sails, or even any mast. Perhaps they hadn't been added yet. The portholes were there, and the ship had been painted in the royal colors of red and purple, with steps leading up to the deck.

Theo looked around, then began climbing the steps, Xandru following. On the deck, where the mast should have been, was a giant chimney.

"I thought cooking hearths were usually in the holds?" Theo asked.

Xandru looked just as puzzled. "No idea. Maybe there's going to be another level above it?"

But Theo doubted that. He could see no rudder or helm, which was odd. He moved to the edge and examined a large copper ring welded to the ship's side. There were six of them, and when he checked the other side, he saw an identical row of six.

"What are these, do you think?" Theo asked Xandru. The boy came and had a look.

"I'd say for anchors." The boy cocked his head. "But then if it's not meant for water, why bother with anchors?"

"And why six?" Theo frowned. "I'm going to look below deck."

"I'll stay up here and see if I can find a mast, or evidence of a sail. If you hear a bird call, hide."

Theo nodded, then took the ladder that led below deck. Here, the darkness reigned, for barely any moonlight filtered in through the row of portholes along the ship's side. He fumbled for the lamp and flints he had brought in his bag, and pulled them out. He soon had his lamp going, and he held it aloft to look around.

It was a giant hold. Big enough to hold all the villagers of Willago, and more. He walked around, trying to find a clue as to what it could be used for. The wood was thin, and the walls hadn't been caulked, something he knew was necessary for water vessels from when he had traveled in a boat to find Orjo. He also noticed a giant line running the length of the floor, as well as a pulley at one end. He bent to examine the line and realized it wasn't a line at all, but a seam formed from two separate slats of wood. Walking to the side of the ship, he realized he wasn't standing on a floor, but a giant trap door.

He looked over at the pulley, thinking. Walking over, he took the pulley's handle in both paws and pushed. At first, nothing happened, but when he strained and put his shoulders into it, the cog finally turned, and a creaking of wood sounded as the bottom of the ship cracked open.

He stopped, letting this information sink in. Why would you make a ship with a bottom that could open? It didn't make any sense. Unless...was the emperor going to drop the pacification powder over Mankahar? But that would mean the ship would have to fly.

That's exactly what he's going to do.

He didn't know how, but Theo was sure Dorgun planned to make the ship take to the air. He ran back to the ladder leading to the deck, extinguished his lamp, and began climbing. He pulled himself onto the deck, but saw no sign of Xandru.

"Xandru?" He said, as loudly as he dared.

No answer. He went to one end of the ship and looked over the side, toward the gate they had entered. All appeared as they'd left it. He turned to check the other side of the ship and found himself surrounded by a group of Urzok soldiers, their swords drawn.

Before Theo could run, two of the soldiers threw a large, weighted net over him and rushed him. He struggled, but was soon overpowered. One of the soldiers trussed his arms and legs while another blindfolded and gagged him.

"There's someone who's been very eager to meet you," a gruff voice said before Theo felt himself lifted over a shoulder and carried off the deck.

CHAPTER 35

The theater door slid open, and six burly figures came out. Two of them had sacks over their shoulders, one much smaller than the other. They loaded their cargo into the waiting wagon before banging on its side, signaling the driver to go.

Manneki watched from the rooftop of the nearby scrap-processing shed as the wagon headed off in the direction of the castle. When he was sure no one had spotted him, he began making his way back over the rooftops as fast as he could, through the various neighborhoods and back to the widow Gerdene's house.

When he finally reached the hatch, he pulled it open and dropped into the attic, the words pouring from him before both feet had touched the floor.

"They've caught Theo and Xandru! They take them away in wagon!"

But the attic was empty. Baffled, Manneki saw the open door in the floor, and was about to close it when he heard Hizarah's and Reenan's low voices downstairs. He cautiously descended to the shop floor, where Gerdene, Hizarah, and Reenan stood in heated debate over a burlap bag with something large and angular inside.

Reenan noticed him. "Manneki, what are you—"

Manneki jumped about, almost exploding with nerves. "They were taken! Taken by emperor's guards! Manneki followed them like Gerdene asked!"

A silence fell, and everyone's faces paled. With a sense of foreboding, Manneki asked, "What's that?"

"An enemy," Gerdene said, then took command. "Manneki's news changes things. You must go, Reenan."

"And you with us, you can't stay in this house," Hizarah insisted.

Gerdene shook her head. "No, I mean you must leave Kalyun-eh and get help."

"Help?" Hizarah asked. "We have no one to turn to now."

"The Order!" Manneki leapt up onto Reenan's shoulder, tail lashing. "The Order will help if they know Theo is prisoner."

"That's days away," Reenan protested. "Besides, this is all my fault. Noshi will blame me for lying to him and bringing Theo here."

"What choice is there?" Hizarah said, grim.

"I'll take care of the body," Gerdene said, "and let what's left of Xandru's guild know what's happened. They may be able to find out where they've been taken. The man had a horse. Ride it and go."

"You'll make faster time without me," Hizarah said to Reenan. "I'll stay here and help Gerdene. You and Manneki go."

Reenan looked torn. "I cannot leave you here."

She smiled and put a hand on his face. "You did once, and you came back. I know you will again. Now go!"

Reenan gave one last glance at Gerdene, who reassured him, "She'll be here when you return. You have my word. Now make haste, before whoever this dead man worked for comes looking for him."

* * *

BRUNE AND INDIGO had parted with Kestrel near a stream that wound north, for though the bird's wing was mostly healed, she was not used to flying long distances and needed to stay close to a water source. They'd exchanged their goodbyes and thanks, then watched Kestrel disappear amongst the trees, before hefting their own tubes of black snow and turning toward Hegg.

In the days that followed, Indigo tried not to think of how much she wished Theo were here. He had given his life to find the weapon to free Mankahar, and now, they were bringing the mightiest weapon they knew back to Hegg. But he wasn't here to see it.

Today, they knew they should reach Hegg by noon. Their steps quickened, and they felt the prospect of friends and sanctuary giving them strength. But as they neared, Brune seemed increasingly unsettled.

"What is it, Brune?"

"Strange. The city outline should be visible by now."

"Could we have mistaken our whereabouts?" Indigo asked.

"I've more chance of mistaking where my nose is." Brune quickened his pace, and Indigo followed close behind.

A sense of dread crept in as they noticed out-of-place objects along the road into the city: an abandoned shoe, a broken staff, a donkey cart missing two wheels, a burned-out wagon.

"Something's wrong," Brune growled, and they broke into a run. When Indigo couldn't keep up, Brune swept her onto his back, then set off as fast as he could while she clung to his hackles.

At the outer gates of Hegg, the bear slowed to a horrified stop, and they both stared.

The city's gates were blackened and peeling, hanging off their hinges in the outer walls. Rubble lay around the outer wall, scars of war everywhere they looked—caved roofs, abandoned carts and belongings strewn. Indigo slipped off Brune's back at the sight of a large mound of fresh earth in one yard, and choked back her shock.

A mass grave. Rocks had been laid in a circle around it, to denote Aktu's balance. When Brune joined her, he sucked in a pained breath.

"I didn't see anyone," Indigo said. "Do you?"

Brune shook his head. "This grave proves someone's survived. Question is whether they're still here."

They combed the city, glancing into gutted homes and shops. Brune stopped and pointed. Indigo looked and saw a large, sprawling structure on the top of a hill.

"The governing lord's manor," Brune explained. "Strongest building here. If there are survivors, that's where they'd shelter."

They followed the main street up to the manor. Here too, the gates had been smashed in, and much of the building was blackened and cracked. When they entered the central foyer, where a wide staircase led to the upper and lower levels, they found that the main building still seemed intact, though the floor was strewn with a mess of smashed furniture, broken weapons, and armor.

Brune's paw hit a dented helmet, sending it clattering across the floor.

"Hello?" Indigo called.

Nothing stirred.

"You go down. I'll go up," Brune said. They were about to part ways when several figures appeared at the head of the stairs. A man in flowing robes was flanked by a giant timber wolf on one side, and a team of six badgers on the other, all bearing short spears.

"Noshi!" Brune rushed up the steps and crushed the man in an embrace. Noshi patted his arm and stepped back, trying to muster a smile. The man seemed to have aged ten years.

"We couldn't hold them back," the old leader said. "There

were too many, and the humans who lived here decided it was best to surrender than to fight."

Indigo looked to the timber wolf, Tarq. The quiet commander of the Order's forces looked haggard, and she noticed new scars on an already heavily scarred muzzle. "How many are left?"

"A few hundred, but almost half are wounded," the wolf replied.

At Brune's and Indigo's shock, Noshi said quietly, "Commander Tarq here lost most of his best fighters. And Lord Ibwa, among others."

Guilt coursed through Indigo. "I am sorry for not returning when you ordered. I—"

The old man raised a hand, his eyes closing briefly. "Don't waste time treading that path, Princess. There was a time when I and the rest of the Order felt you were being impetuous and childish. But now, I'm glad you and Brune were not here for Hegg's fall. It means you are alive."

"Is the enemy still here?" Brune growled. "We didn't see them on our way in."

Tarq shook his head. "They came to kill, not conquer."

"They've left us and the city to die," spat one of the larger badgers, stepping forward.

"They likely thought us destroyed. But we have survived, and Aktu must have spared us so that we can build out of the ashes and start anew, no matter how dark the times may seem." Noshi looked at Brune, his eyes watering. "Certainly you are both a welcome sight."

"We have brought something that might help the Order," Indigo said, unslinging her wooden tube. "Though I know it's too late to save Hegg. It's black snow, and what we lack in numbers we can perhaps make up for with its power. If we can take everyone remaining and go to the dragon cave—"

Noshi held up a hand. "Black snow?"

They heard a bird's cry from the entry and turned to see a hawk perched on the lintel of the doorframe.

Noshi frowned. "Are there others with you?"

"No," Brune said, pulling out his axe. The badgers raised their spears.

"Then Hectram has spotted an intruder," Tarq growled, hackles up.

Indigo turned to Noshi. "Brune and I will see who it is. I think it's best everyone else stays here, out of sight."

She and Brune went out the manor door and down the steps. They snuck their way through the streets, looking for a high vantage point. They found one in the city's central square, a pedestal that had once held a statue but now had only a vandalized stump. Brune shaded his eyes.

"Urzok. On horseback."

Indigo squinted. "A man, I think."

"And someone small," Brune added. "A rabbit? Stoat?"

"Let's get a better look," Indigo said. The two of them ran lightly down the city street and climbed up to the roof of an inn. From there, she saw the small figure was a Grodlyn.

Something in his motions seemed familiar. He chattered something to his companion, and then, as if sensing Brune and Indigo, turned to look up at the inn, giving them a clear view of his face.

"Manneki?" Indigo cried.

The Grodlyn spotted her and shaded his eyes, then waved his arms wildly and chattered. The man on the horse threw back his hood.

"It's Reenan!" Brune said.

Manneki leaped back up onto the horse in front of Reenan, and then they were galloping toward the inn.

Indigo and Brune raced down the stairs to meet them at the bottom, and though there was joy at seeing each other, Indigo could tell from Reenan's pinched expression that he bore bad news.

"What's wrong?" she asked.

He shook his head. "I'll tell you and Noshi together. Is he here? The Order?"

Brune nodded. "Follow us."

Brune and Indigo led Reenan and Manneki back to the manor, where Noshi and Tarq came out to greet them.

"Good to see you, Reenan," Noshi said, embracing the man.

"And same to you, Lord Noshi," Reenan answered. "We had hoped to come here for help, but it looks like the Order has its own troubles."

"What kind of help?" Brune asked.

Reenan took a breath, searching for words, but Manneki burst out, "We need to save Theo!"

Indigo thought she had misheard, and everyone else stood in stunned silence. "Theo?"

Reenan looked pained. "Theo's alive, but the empire has him in Kalyun-eh."

"I don't understand," Indigo said slowly.

"Theo wanted to tell Princess, but he couldn't," Manneki cut in.

"Why not?" Brune asked.

"Orjo thought—"

"He's with Orjo?" Brune bristled.

None of this is making sense, Indigo thought.

"What's important right now," Reenan said, "is that he needs us. He's been captured by imperial forces, and they'll kill him."

Indigo wasn't sure what to feel, except that she didn't want the sudden tendril of hope in her to go away. "Then we must go to Kalyun-eh. Now."

"You can't just march into Kalyun-eh," Noshi warned. "Think wisely."

"We don't have time!" Brune growled.

"He's right. But we do have black snow," Indigo said. "The four of us will get him back." Indigo sensed Noshi was about to protest. "Please, we don't have time to move everyone. We'll be faster as a small group."

Noshi sighed, then nodded. "Aktu be with you. I will gather our remaining forces, let them know that Theo is alive, and follow as soon as we can."

Brune nodded. "Thank you, Lord Noshi. We cannot lose Theo a second time."

CHAPTER 36

It could have been two days, it could have been five. Here in the sunless dark, there was no way for Theo to know how long he had been imprisoned.

On the night the guards took him, he had been thrown into this small airless cell that stank of fear and excrement. He didn't know where he was, except that he must be somewhere in the castle's deeper keeps. The soldiers that appeared at his door were all in uniforms that bore the imperial crest, and they were all armored to the teeth, eyes full of suspicion.

Perhaps they knew who he was. He would have laughed at their apprehension of the Griffinrider, had he not been so fearful of what would come next. He was surrounded by limestone walls with no windows. A plank bolted into one wall served as bed and chair. The only other items were a foul chamber pot and ominous-looking metal loops in the ceiling that seemed designed for chains.

He quickly realized there was no way to escape, so there was nothing to do but wait, and try to figure out what was coming for him next.

On the fourth or fifth day, he couldn't be sure, he heard the distinct marching of multiple boots outside his door, echoing down the corridor. This was unusual, because so far, only two guards at a time had come, to give water and food. Theo tensed as the key scraped in the lock and the door swung open.

The guards moved in before he could even form a question. They gripped him, one at each arm, their gloved fingers tight. They locked shackles on his ankles, then half dragged, half-marched him out and along the corridor. Torches lit the way, and before long, they were sweeping up a staircase. Someone threw open a door, and all of a sudden, they were in harsh, blinding sunlight that made his eyes ache.

His guards hauled him through several courtyards and into a grassy expanse. Theo had never seen such luxurious grass, so evenly trimmed it looked like the surface of water.

Standing in the middle of it was a figure in red and purple robes, a wizened man with a milky eye and painted eyebrows. Beyond him, two-dozen workers were erecting what looked like a large silk tent on a wooden platform. The breeze played with the silks, whipping them about as the workers tried to fasten them to slender poles.

Theo heard shouts and the thunder of hooves, and looked to the right. The field had been set up for some sort of game, and a dozen riders were storming down the field, their horses churning the grass and their wooden mallets raised in the air as they descended on the ball.

"You may leave him," Dorgun said to the guards. They bowed and stepped back. Dorgun waited until they were out of earshot, then turned back to the game. Theo knew he couldn't escape, even if his legs hadn't been chained. Though they were far away, he could see a ring of two dozen archers encircling the grassy area, eyes trained on his every move.

"You're Emperor Dorgun," Theo said simply. He wasn't sure what he had expected. He'd never gotten a good look when they were in the Library, as he had only heard Dorgun's shuffling of feet, his breathing, and been able to smell the faint hint of perfume that the emperor favored.

"I am. And I finally meet the great Griffinrider." The emperor regarded him, appraising. "You do not look like a scourge that could bring down my empire. But I suppose I don't look like a man who commands everything in Mankahar. From who lives and dies to who grows wealthy or poor, who lives free and who bends to the whip." He smiled. "You and I are similar, Theo Griffinrider. We are not warlords, but we have power. Because of the Forbidden Language." Dorgun pulled something from his pocket. Theo watched as Dorgun came forward and held something out to Theo's face. A tuft of fur that he knew matched his own, despite the days of grime and filth hiding it. "That's why you were in my Library. You must be curious about the ship."

"You plan on flying it over the city and pacifying everyone."

"That's missing a few details, but yes."

Though he'd suspected it, to hear Dorgun speak of it not only calmly, but with relish, chilled him. "You really want to pacify your own people? Why?"

"Even the cleanest of houses can become infested with pests," Dorgun said mildly. "So in a week's time, at my birthday celebrations, you and that street thief with you will die in a game of horseball here. I cannot think of a better way to send you off than in my favorite sport."

He motioned to the guards, and they came to take Theo by the arms again.

"Don't be sore, Theo Griffinrider," Dorgun said gently. "My ancestors and I have been smarter and stronger than you for generations. You cannot expect to win over those bigger and mightier than you. So submit, and rest assured knowing that you tried. That's what all heroes want in the end, isn't it? To know that even if they failed, they tried?"

Theo wanted to rush up and scratch the smile off the emperor's sallow face, even if he was killed doing it, but the guards held him firm.

"Goodbye, Theo Griffinrider," Dorgun said.

Theo couldn't fight off the guards as they dragged him back

to the prisons. This time, however, they didn't take him to the same cell, but turned off at another hallway. Theo was confused. What was happening? This dungeon had rougher walls, no light, and smells that curdled the blood. Screams echoed from some unknown chamber.

He was thrown into a bare, windowless cell that made his last one seem well furnished by comparison. The door locked behind him, plunging him into darkness. He could hear faint scrabbling and singing from one side, and he put his ear to the wall, incredulous.

"Orjo!" he cried. "Orjo, is that you?"

The singing stopped abruptly. "Griffinrider?"

Theo thought he would cry and laugh all at once. "You're alive!"

"I'm alive," Orjo said. "Though I'll admit, death seems attractive some days."

"Theo!" Came another voice, and Theo turned to the other wall.

"Xandru?"

"Are you all right?"

Theo wasn't sure that question was worth answering truthfully. "We have to find a way out. Dorgun is going to put us in the horseball game next week."

Orjo sighed. "Thank Aktu."

"You're giving up, Orjo?" Theo asked, fearful.

"No. But there are only two ways out of here, the hard way and the easy way. Hard way is to escape when they take us somewhere."

Theo thought on this. "And the easy way?"

"We die."

CHAPTER 37

For the period leading up to Dorgun's birthday, Ornox had decided not to return to Vyad, but to rent a manor in the affluent northern district of the capital city. Here, he could keep a close eye on the emperor's activities and also let Yod look into these rumors of Theo being alive.

But when Yod didn't return for five nights running, Ornox knew something was wrong. He sent a few trusted men looking for information, but none seemed able to find Yod's whereabouts.

Yod's disappearance rattled Ornox more than he cared to admit. Of course, Yod was no fighter, and it could have been that as he poked his nose in and around the more unsavory parts of town, he had stirred someone to anger and gotten himself killed. Perhaps sending Yod had not been the most appropriate choice. But the worry nagged him: what if Yod's disappearance was not due to some random stranger's anger? Or some tavern accident? Then Ornox would have to look further into these supposed rumors about Theo being alive. If the emperor really was going to name Ornox as his heir, then Ornox didn't need any of these rumors changing the emperor's mind. Another possibility occurred to him. What if the emperor was jealous and worried about Ornox's favor and fame? If Dorgun could sow the seeds of doubt that Ornox had killed the feared Griffinrider, then Dorgun could cut Ornox's power off at the knees, humiliate him publicly, and name someone else heir.

Is that your plan? It won't work, old one, Ornox thought to himself as he dressed for the day. *I will take this throne, with or without your blessing, and I will make a new dynasty rise.*

"My lord?"

Ornox turned to see Sarkus at his bedchamber door. "What is it?"

"It's about Yod, my lord."

Ornox immediately focused entirely on the boy. "Is he back?"

Sarkus shook his head. "His horse was spotted several towns from here, on the road to Hegg. "

Ornox digested this. "And Yod?"

"No sign of him, just the horse, my lord."

"Who had the horse?"

"Don't know."

"Well, find out," Ornox said coolly. "If you don't use that ugly head of yours, I might as well remove it, no?"

The part of Sarkus's face that was visible beneath his mask blanched before he bowed and retreated.

Ornox reined in his frustration. This was unlike Yod, to simply disappear and chase a lead without giving his master information. Yod's horse had been stolen, and if Yod hadn't returned, he was likely dead or injured somewhere. Ornox felt genuine regret at this, for to lose Yod was like losing one's best hound, something that could be replaced only with time and effort. Sarkus, as much as he tried, was no Yod. The question was, did Yod find out something to do with the Griffinrider that got him killed? Or was this all simply a coincidental price of nosing about in the capital, where everyone had secrets?

Ornox didn't have time to find out. Tomorrow was Feast Day, and he had to put his plan into motion. But first, he would take precautions.

He changed out of his chosen clothes and opted for a peasant tunic and plain, comfortable boots. He would take nothing with the House of Vyad arms, for he didn't want to be recognized. He also didn't bother taking his horse. Instead, he walked the markets, which were filled with at least double the usual crowd. Kalyun-eh was already bursting with visitors here to celebrate the emperor's birthday. Even so, he found what he was looking for within moments: a stall selling all manner of necklaces, lucky charms, and accessories.

He took his time, examining each necklace he picked up. He was only interested in ones with lockets made of wood that opened and shut tight like a clam. At last, he found one that suited him, one of the largest. A palm-sized locket made of thin cherry wood and strung on a chain.

"Excellent choice, sir," the vendor said encouragingly. "This will hold a great amount of tobacco and keep it dry. And for you, only five gold bits."

Ornox was about to protest the exorbitant price, if only out of principle, but then noticed the carving on the back of the locket. A phoenix rose from flames, its head craned skyward, wings curved around the locket edges. He couldn't help but feel it was the gods giving him a sign. He would be the phoenix, struck low only to rise out of the flames and conquer the empire. Life and new blood would emerge from the decay of the current reign. It wouldn't do to be stingy with destiny.

"Here, you may keep the change."

* * *

DORGUN WATCHED from the sidelines of the expansive green field as workers scurried around the great pile of silk, following the shouted instructions of the headman, who pointed and gestured. Workers with giant bellows rolled forward and began to prop the triple-layered silk balloon up on giant stilts over the ship. A long line of servants carried kindling up onto the deck and piled it next to the chimney, where a raging fire was already burning.

Dorgun waited patiently, knowing it would likely be some time before the great contraption came to life. But eventually, it did, and the silken balloon expanded. It was stitched together with strong cord and made from the supplest, strongest multi-layered silk coin could buy. Dorgun watched as it grew and grew, a giant turgid belly that began pulling on the great ropes holding it to the ship. The vessel creaked as it lifted off the ground, and had it not been for the anchor staked into the earth, the great contraption would have left for the skies.

Dorgun allowed himself a satisfied smile. It was beautiful, as he knew it would be. The ship that would cleanse Mankahar was the finest masterpiece he had ever seen.

"Your Eminence, your staff is ready for inspection."

Dorgun reluctantly turned away from the great ship and looked at his advisors, who had joined him on the field.

"You have told the others their instructions for the day?"

His taller advisor bowed. "Yes, Your Eminence. They know to stay within the quarters assigned to them on pain of death. No opening doors or windows until they are summoned. As a precaution, we will lock the doors."

Dorgun nodded. "Very good. Did you have difficulty finding new staff?"

The advisor shook his head. "We doubled their salary. Payable at the end of the festivities, of course."

Dorgun smiled. "Yes. Of course." None of them would receive that pay. "This is going to be a birthday to remember, I think."

The advisors bowed and left, leaving Dorgun to turn back and admire his ship. He watched as a line of horse-drawn carts, loaded with cargo covered in tarpaulins, began making their way to the ship's open hold. All the drivers had cloth bandanas over their faces, and the workers who helped unload the cart's contents of oilskin sacks also wore scarves covering their noses and mouths. There was a panicked shout as someone discovered a hole in the bag, and several workers rushed forward to help seal it before its contents could escape.

They were right to be cautious. A lungful of the fine pacification powder they were handling would transform them. Dorgun smiled. Tomorrow, these same workers would all be as mindless as the horses on the field. Tomorrow, Dorgun would cross a new year. And tomorrow, a new Mankahar would be born out of the ashes of this rotting city.

Pozzi knew that he would never forget the sights, sounds, and smells of Kalyun-eh as long as he lived.

The crowds of festival goers began thickening far outside the city limits, forming a floodtide. Revelers and merchants, peddlers and children, beggars and thieves, all converged on this city that Joseb had described to him as the center of the empire's might.

"The best of everything's there," the trader had told him excitedly as they swayed to the donkey cart's movement through the rutted roads, surrounded on all sides by other travelers. "Food, drink, fine silks, the best inns and taverns and entertainment."

And my freedom, Pozzi thought. He had realized that his quickest way back to Keeva and Walnut was to keep his bargain with Joseb: produce two hundred of these wood carvings of Theo, let Joseb make his money, and in exchange, receive a token for free passage back across Mankahar. Pozzi had early on tamped down his rage at the unfairness, at the impotent anger he held toward Joseb, instead focusing all his energy on making the dolls.

And he had. He had stayed up late every night, barely taken

the time to eat meals. The first few attempts Joseb had casually thrown away, much to Pozzi's anger, dismissing them as not of good enough quality or imitation. A few had broken under Pozzi's unpracticed paws, for he had never had to make the fine, thin details of a toy before. All his experience had been with bowls, plates, and other everyday items. But Joseb was an exacting master when it came to his product, and he inspected each finished doll Pozzi produced with a meticulous and uncompromising eye.

Pozzi had been nothing if not determined, however. He concentrated on learning Joseb's craft and kept a bucket of cold water nearby at night, which he plunged his feet into whenever he was in danger of falling asleep. And one by one, he had carved the dolls. And with each doll, Joseb's admiration had grown.

Now, with their imminent arrival in Kalyun-eh, Pozzi was close to his goal. He had only one more doll to go, and then he would be free. As the wagon jolted along, he looked into the baskets in the back, at the last half-carved toy that he still needed to finish. His paws were chafed raw, he had several nasty cuts from handling the shaving knife, and his eyes were bloodshot from lack of sleep. Yet he still itched to get back to this last doll and finish it. But he'd learned that trying to carve a toy on a moving cart was a sure way to mistakes, and he'd do better to wait for them to stop at mealtime.

As they neared the gates of Kalyun-eh on Feast Day, the choked roads forced their cart to a crawl.

Pozzi craned his head. "What's keeping us? Is there a toll?"

Joseb chuckled. "No, there's no toll. Today the gates are open to all. The whole of Mankahar has come!"

They made their sluggish way toward the city walls, and even from this distance Pozzi could hear the trill of flutes, the beating of drums, the celebratory singing and dancing.

Joseb stopped the cart just outside the gates when he noticed the donkey limping. He guided the cart to the side and jumped off, and finding a stone in the donkey's hoof, he pulled out his pocketknife to pry it out. Unwilling to waste a single moment, Pozzi took up his last doll and his carving knife and began work. He had to finish off the sword and the head, and then he would be done.

Joseb eyed him as he came back to the wagon. "Looks like you're nearly finished."

Pozzi nodded. "And then you'll give me my freedom, as promised?"

A glint of disappointment flashed in Joseb's eyes. "So you're still wanting to go back then? I could pay you, as you're a fine carver." At the look on Pozzi's face the man sighed. "As you wish, Pozzi. Let it never be said that Joseb breaks his word."

The toymaker clucked at the donkey, and they trotted back into the river of traffic flowing into the city.

* * *

JOSEB CIRCLED a few city streets before choosing his spot, a corner where two main thoroughfares met just before the large square leading to the castle. Other peddlers had long ago claimed the streets closest to the square and the main festivities, and they firmly shooed Joseb and his cart away. He now set up his table and banners in the back of the cart, after providing the donkey a feed bag to make sure it stayed still.

Despite the distractions of the city, the noise and tumult, the music and fanfare, Pozzi focused on the task in his paws. He carved carefully, making sure to not chip the wood and sentence himself to starting over. Joseb set out the dolls on a tray and began calling in a booming voice.

"Griffinrider! Griffinrider toys! Everyone gets a chance to stab the Griffinrider right here! Half a silver only. Come, children, have a look!"

A gaggle of children and parents soon surrounded the cart.

Pozzi kept his head bent, intent on the figurine he was working on. He heard Joseb suck in a breath.

"By Blackhide, it's him!"

The excitement in Joseb's voice made Pozzi look up. A crowd was cheering and parting for a man on a tall, dark horse, his entourage following behind him. The man had raven-black hair shot with silver, and shoulders as broad as a bull's. He was wearing fine clothing and a thick, red cloak, with a large locket resting on his chest.

The man's features seemed disturbingly familiar, but Pozzi couldn't place him. He watched as Joseb grabbed a figurine from the tray and rushed forward to the man on the horse.

"Lord Ornox! Savior of Mankahar, may our emperor's blessings fall upon you," Joseb said, bowing. "It is such an honor. Please, please accept a small gift to express my and all of Mankahar's gratitude."

Joseb offered up the figurine with both hands, and the man named Ornox looked down on it, impassive.

He jerked his head toward someone behind him.

"Sarkus, take the gift and thank the man."

Pozzi's hackles rose at the name. A short figure emerged from Ornox's men, and even without the wooden mask Pozzi would have recognized the boy anywhere. Sarkus took the figurine Joseb handed him before his eyes fell on Pozzi.

"Wait," he said. "Is that your stall?"

"It is!" Joseb seemed flattered at the boy's interest. "Would you like something? A special price to anyone in Lord Ornox's retinue."

"How much for the rabbit there?"

Pozzi's blood turned cold, and he was gripping the figurine in his paws so tightly that the ear cracked.

Joseb looked at Pozzi, and at the figurine, hesitating.

"I'll pay you five gold coins for him," Sarkus said.

Five coins! A fortune. Pozzi considered running, but without a token of passage he would be imprisoned by day's end.

"He's not for sale," Joseb answered.

"Ten!" Sarkus snarled.

Joseb looked taken aback at this, then spread his hands apologetically. "It's not about price. I freed him just today, so he's not for sale."

Though the wooden mask hid most of his face, Sarkus's neck flushed, and he looked like he might leap onto the cart and drag Pozzi away. He stopped only at Ornox's voice.

"Sarkus. You heard the man. Come away."

Ornox kicked his horse forward, and Sarkus, clearly unwilling to disobey, shot one last hateful look Pozzi's way before following his master and disappearing into the crowd.

When Joseb came back, Pozzi said, "Thank you."

The man shrugged. "You looked terrified. Let no one say that Joseb is a cruel man."

CHAPTER 39

By the time Indigo, Brune, Reenan, and Manneki reached Kalyun-eh at midday, the festivities were in full swing. Every lantern was lit, and free food was dispensed from the uncharacteristically generous castle. Wine flowed, as did song and conversation, and all of the Urzoks acted as if they had just emerged victorious from war times.

At the city gates, Indigo and her companions realized that one thing they didn't have to worry about was arousing suspicion. The emperor's birthday and largesse meant that everyone from all over the empire, animal or Urzok, had traveled far and wide to be here and revel in the rare holiday. Traders had come to avail themselves of the crowd, entertainers jostled each other for space on every corner, and children in festive clothing ran through the streets trying to find sweets or flags being given away.

At Indigo's suggestion, they had tied the dead man's horse to an inn's hitching post several towns outside Kalyun-eh. If the horse had belonged to someone powerful, then it would be recognized. They had bought another horse, older and slower but sturdy. Even at the slower pace, they'd still made good time, but still Indigo felt ill at the thought of Theo trapped in the castle, and their being too late.

Now, deep into the city, being on horseback was problematic as they tried to maneuver through the throngs of people. They tried to stick to back streets and alleyways and finally emerged in a small square far from the city center. But even here, revelers filled the streets. Reenan led them up to a nondescript door, tied up the horse, and knocked. An old, but well-groomed lady opened the door, and at the sight of Reenan and his friends, she ushered them in with a shaking hand.

"Is Hizarah here?" Reenan asked.

But before the woman could answer, a younger woman swept down the stairs. She had a pleasant face with a large birthmark along the side, and she hugged Reenan tightly, then bent to tousle Manneki's head.

"This is Hizarah, and Gerdene," Reenan said, introducing the two women to his companions. "Meet Indigo and Brune, old friends from the Order."

"Thank goodness you're back!" Hizarah looked at Indigo and Brune. "Where is the rest of the Order?"

Brune grimaced. "I'm afraid we're the only ones here for now. Hegg has been destroyed."

"We heard rumors after you left," Hizarah said, "but weren't sure whether to believe them."

Gerdene looked from Reenan to Brune. "I've alerted Xandru's friends, but there's little they can do. They're young and more used to picking pockets than fighting open battles. But if they can help, they will."

Indigo nodded. "We'll need a wagon brought to the castle drawbridge. If we manage to find Theo and get him out, we'll need to leave in a hurry." She turned to Hizarah. "Reenan tells us you can get us in with our weapons?"

Hizarah glanced at Reenan and nodded. "I have some ideas."

Brune snorted. "I don't have to dance, do I?"

Indigo knew Brune hadn't enjoyed the last time Reenan had

helped them escape a city, when Brune had to perform in front of an official.

"No," Hizarah shook her head, "But you may have to push a cart."

"Manneki and Reenan, we'll need you two to take some tubes of our black snow and wait up in the drawbridge bailey," Indigo said.

Manneki nodded, eager. "Manneki will fight and destroy many soldiers!"

Indigo shook her head. "That's not what I want you to do. I need you to have the black snow primed and waiting. When you see us running out, destroy the chains so that the drawbridge can't be raised."

"And I'll have another tube for when we escape," Reenan explained. "We'll collapse the gate arch once we're out so that no one can follow."

The Grodlyn's face brightened with understanding.

"Just remember to be careful with the stuff. A pawful of it will do a lot of damage," Indigo said. She turned to Gerdene. "We brought a horse with us that you can use. How long will it take to source a horse cart?"

"I should be able to find one within the hour."

Brune nodded. "In that case, we'll all leave first and enter the castle. Just make sure you're stationed outside the drawbridge when we need you. We'll likely be coming out like bees from a flaming hive." He turned to Hizarah. "Now, let's hear your ideas about how we get in."

Hizarah explained her plan to the group, while Gerdene left to source a cart from the few who remained in Xandru's guild.

Hizarah soon had multiple items gathered for their infiltration of the castle: a vendor's pushcart painted yellow and red, bright vendor hats and vests, and several sacks of dried sunflower and melon seeds. She set Manneki to folding paper cones that could be used for scooping seeds, while Reenan gathered flints and a small oil lamp, which he placed in a satchel.

Brune adjusted his vest to hide a thin tube of black snow. "Just in case," he'd said. When they were ready, they triple-checked that everything was in place before all of them set off for the castle.

As they strode through the city, Brune pushing the cart full of seeds, Indigo kept her ears primed for any whispers of a public execution. She saw no gallows, no blocks for beheading, only crisp new imperial flags flying from every roof and window. She wasn't sure whether to be relieved or even more anxious. If the emperor was going to kill Theo, it would make sense to do it on a public day like today's Feast Day, somewhere everyone could witness. He was either not to be executed today, or he was already dead. Indigo felt cold at the possibility.

"Don't miss it, good citizens of Kalyun-eh. Don't hide inside today of all days, for Emperor Dorgun has a surprise attraction, a feat of such magnitude that you will be telling your children and your grandchildren for years to come!" The imperial crier was dressed in bright red leggings under a purple silk tunic, and his voice carried over the crowds. "Make sure you are out here to see it, anywhere in the city, anywhere at all, simply step out and look to the heavens..."

Indigo leaned closer to Brune. "What do you think that's about?" The bear shrugged, clearly as uneasy as she.

"Don't know. But whatever the emperor's serving, I've a feeling I'll like it less than poison pie."

CHAPTER 40

The highest nobles in the land, all of them dripping in furs, jewels and the best silks coin could afford, milled around the private entry gate to the castle. They had disembarked from their carriages and now filed through the arches dividing the carriage yard from the inner castle court-yard. A checkpoint where castle guards searched visitors for concealed weapons slowed the tide to a trickle.

Ornox had, like everyone else, dismounted in the main yard and handed his reins to his servant. Sarkus, dressed in fine livery that Ornox had ordered, took his master's horse and cloak.

"Wait for me in the servants' quarters," Ornox instructed. Sarkus nodded, silent. He had seemed morose since their encounter with the toy seller, but Ornox didn't have time to indulge childish sulking.

Sarkus led the horse away, and Ornox turned to look up at the gates into Kalyun-eh's central yard.

The air was thick with anticipation, and Ornox felt it crawl along him like an unwelcome touch. Everyone was trading guesses as to who the emperor would declare his heir, many nobles no doubt hoping Dorgun would name them.

Ornox walked with head high, eyes alert. He could see the

guards ahead of him searching robes and boots for knives, dirks, even pins that might be used to harm the emperor. He felt the weight of the phoenix pendant around his neck, but forced himself not to touch it.

Several of the nobles, recognizing Ornox, tried to engage him in conversation, but he cut them short with the minimal amount of necessary politeness. Their offended looks didn't bother him. Soon, they would fawn over him.

As he neared the checkpoint, a guard in regalia seemed to recognize him and bowed deeply.

"Greetings, Lord Ornox, hero of Mankahar," the guard said. "I apologize for the search, but orders…"

"I understand," Ornox replied and held his arms out. "The emperor's life is paramount. He is right to be cautious with those who come near him."

The guard seemed relieved and patted him over the arms, the legs. He found no weapon, and he didn't even glance at the pendant on Ornox's chest. "Welcome to Castle Kalyun-eh, Lord Ornox. Enjoy His Eminence's hospitality."

Ornox nodded in thanks, and once he'd passed through, allowed himself a smile. The next time he entered these gates, he would be emperor.

* * *

THE BAND of seed sellers wound their way slowly through the city streets, ever toward the looming castle. Though Brune's bulk and sheer presence made the crowd around them melt away, Indigo still found their pace excruciating.

As they approached the castle drawbridge, Reenan motioned to them all to stay calm. "Smile, don't frown. We're here to make coin, not stir trouble."

Indigo swallowed and instinctively reached for her sword, but realized it wasn't there. She felt naked as she glanced at the wooden pushcart rolling along next to her, but she forced an easy-going smile that she hoped looked sincere.

They entered the castle grounds, where the guards patted each of them down to check for weapons. Indigo tried not to tense as one of the guards pulled up one of the push cart's wooden covers and plunged a hand inside. If he reached all the way to the bottom, he'd feel her blade, which lay buried, along with Brune's axe and three tubes of black snow, at the bottom of the seeds.

But the guard only skimmed the surface, picking up a palmful of seeds. He sniffed them, then popped them in his mouth and chewed. Seemingly satisfied, he waved them through, and Indigo hoped the guards didn't hear the collective sigh of relief that passed through their group.

They pressed through with the crowd of well-wishers and others with business inside the castle, before Reenan nodded to them and motioned to Manneki. The Grodlyn jumped onto Reenan's shoulder, and Brune discreetly reached into the push-cart and pulled out the three tubes of black snow. He passed them to Reenan, who deftly slid them into an inner coat pocket, and the man and Grodlyn made their way around the side, doubling around toward the gatehouse. Indigo silently sent a prayer to Aktu to help them and keep them safe. They would need to destroy the drawbridge chains to keep it from being drawn up, then collapse the gate arch to block any pursuing soldiers. Such timing would not be easy, but it was their best hope.

The remaining three walked into the castle's outer courtyard, where musicians were playing and citizens from all walks of life were dancing and making merry. Wine flowed freely from kegs everywhere, and Indigo could see that many were already giddy with drink. Great tables laden with foods sat at regular intervals, and rich and poor alike were helping themselves.

She had never been to Kalyun-eh, but it was impossible to not have heard of the emperor and his temperament. Indigo knew such a man couldn't be generous without good reason. If any of Kalyun-eh's inhabitants and visitors had the same concerns, they didn't show it, and busily indulged in the ruler's largesse.

A few approached to buy seeds, and Hizarah and Indigo dutifully filled paper cones for their customers. Before more could corner them, Hizarah patted Brune's shoulder to indicate that they should leave while they could. Indigo clambered up onto Brune's shoulder.

Brune pushed the cart into the next courtyard, where the crowds were thinner.

"The dungeons are on the west side," Hizarah murmured.

Brune turned west, and they passed through corridors lined with guards. One of them came forward, blocking their path.

"No outsiders beyond this point," the guard said.

Hizarah gave her best surprised expression. "But we were asked to bring food to the guards here, since they can't make it to the main courtyard. Orders of the household." She produced a seal from her pocket. Indigo knew it was supposed to be a replica of some sort of imperial pass. The guard hesitated, and Indigo could tell he didn't recognize it.

"Surely, you know the inner household's seal?" Hizarah said, gently enough to seem as if she was giving the guard a chance to save himself. "The chamberlain himself already paid us. I don't know what to tell him if I don't deliver. If I can't go in, at least let us give you a serving, so the chamberlain's coin doesn't go to waste."

He shook his head as she held out a paper cone, but jerked his head. "Go on then."

They made their way to a courtyard, then through another two baileys until they reached a guardhouse and gate. Here, two guards in armor stood with sheathed swords and leaned on long spears, laughing over something. Behind them, Indigo could see the dark throat of a stairway winding down.

Noticing the newcomers, the guards straightened. "Stop

there! No vendors in this part of the castle," the taller one called out.

Brune didn't bother answering, and instead, barreled straight into both guards, crushing them against the prison wall before either could bring their spears into play. They crumpled unconscious to the ground, their weapons clattering from slack hands.

Indigo scanned the area to see if there were other guards about, but in the din of the festivities, it seemed no one had heard. Hizarah and Brune dragged the two unconscious guards into the doorway of the prison, where Hizarah stripped the shorter guard and began changing into his clothing. Indigo flung open the pushcart lid, and Brune joined her. He shed his cloak and plunged a paw into the seeds, pulling out his axe and Indigo's sword.

"Ready?" He tossed her her blade.

The princess caught it. "Let's find Theo."

CHAPTER 41

Ornox strode off in the direction in which the other nobles were being ushered, out a connecting courtyard and into the ball field beyond. Trumpeters lined the far wall, with red and purple ribbons tied to their instruments. But the item that captured everyone's attention, including Ornox's, was the giant ship on the right-hand side of the field.

The ship was ornately carved, and as large as any sea-going vessel, but what made everyone gape was the sight of it hovering just above the ground, buoyed by a silk balloon that seemed to fill the sky.

"What in Blackhide..." Ornox found himself murmuring along with everyone else. A team of four workers fed wood into a chimney on the ship's deck, and the hot smoky air seemed to be what made the balloon fly. Six thick ropes anchored the ship to the ground and kept it from sailing up like some great bloated bird.

"Lords and ladies, the emperor invites you to join him," a herald wove through the crowd of onlookers, stopping occasionally to repeat his message. Ornox looked toward the tent, a pristine, white-silk affair on top of a wooden platform. Ornox walked toward it, ascended the steps, and entered.

The space was wide and laid out with tables arranged in a horseshoe so that all diners had a view of the game and the ship outside through the tent's one rolled-up wall. Ornate braziers in the corners burned sweet-smelling sage to perfume the air. At the bend of the horseshoe stood the emperor, greeting the well-wishers who approached to convey birthday greetings. No doubt all hoping to be the lucky heir, Ornox thought.

Ornox took his place in the queue, and when it was his turn, he bowed deeply. "A thousand well wishes for your day of birth, and may you rule forever more."

"Lord Ornox, the hero of Mankahar," the emperor said, bidding him rise. When he stood, Ornox made sure to avoid eye contact with Volchega, who stared ahead, blank, as did the rest of the imperial guard.

"Today is a momentous day," the emperor said to him, clasping his hand with surprising strength. "For both of us."

Ornox bowed his head, hiding the flicker of nervousness in him. If he was to wear the crown, he would have to keep his head.

* * *

REENAN WALKED SLOWLY against the incoming foot traffic until he reached the edge of the castle barbican. The guards were intent on those coming in, rather than those going out, so it was simple for Reenan to pause and lean against the castle's outer wall next to a bolted door, as if waiting for someone. Manneki scampered off his shoulder and up the wall, his paws seeming to find invisible footholds, until he disappeared over the edge.

Reenan waited, doing his best to look natural as he surveyed those around him. No one seemed to be paying attention to him in his plain coat and low-brimmed hat. The bolted door next to him opened, revealing Manneki, and Reenan took one last glance around before following the monkey in. They hurried up the stairs to where a door led onto the second story of the barbican.

They entered and surveyed the room, which was bare except for two giant drums wrapped with heavy chains, used to raise and lower the drawbridge. Each was shaped like a giant's spool of thread, with a hole through the middle. Reenan saw four murder holes in the floor along one side of the room, one of them half open, and went over. He peered through the open panel and looked down on the heads of revelers passing through the barbican below on their way into the castle. No one looked up.

"Just one of these would take two Reenans to wind!" the Grodlyn said, clearly still awed by the size and height of the drums.

Reenan tried to close the panel but soon realized it was stuck. Giving up, he went over to Manneki. "Good thing we don't have to wind them then," the man answered.

Each of the drums currently had only two wraps of the chains around them, as the bridge was down to allow a free flow of guests into the castle's outer keep. He now understood why no guards were stationed up here, for no saw nor blade could cut through such thick chains.

But black snow could.

"We better get ready," Reenan said and turned back to Manneki and the winding drums. Two drums. Two tubes. He handed his tube to Manneki, who carefully laid one in each drum's center hole, where it was sure to create the most damage.

Reenan drew out his flints and oil lamp, and lit it.

"Now what?" Manneki asked.

"Now, we wait," Reenan said simply, wondering how the thought of doing nothing could be so difficult.

They looked out the one square window that afforded a view of the crowded castle keep below, and waited.

* * *

THE DUNGEONS WERE dark and airless. Indigo led the way with her sword held out, moving along the corridor and listening for soldiers. Brune came next, while Hizarah brought up the rear. Though they expected to find other guards here, the place seemed deserted. They turned a corner into a long, dank hallway that ended in a circular space, where light from a grate above trickled in to reveal grimy wooden doors and blood-stained walls. A stench hit them, and they held their arms to their noses. Indigo tried not to think whether the blood might be Theo's, that part of the smell of death could be his.

They snuck along the hallway and noticed that to the left and right were doors with rectangular holes at Hizarah's head level that could open and shut.

"Theo?" Indigo called out, hushed. Then louder, "Theo!" *Please answer me.*

"Are you real?"

She knew that voice. Indigo looked at Brune, who seemed just as surprised. She whirled around, but there was no one there. "Orjo?"

A mirthless laugh answered her. "Yes, the Terrible. Though Terrible describes my physical state now more than my personality."

Brune moved down the corridor toward the voice and pulled the eye panel back on one of the doors. He looked in.

"He's in here," the bear motioned for Hizarah. "Any keys on that guard's belt?"

Hizarah began searching the ring of keys she'd lifted.

"We'll get you out, Orjo," Brune growled, examining the door for weaknesses.

"Forget that," Orjo said from within the cell. "Just find Theo."

"Where is he?" Indigo asked.

"The game, lass, the game. He's in the game."

"What game?" Could Orjo have lost his mind down here? It was not only possible, Indigo realized, but highly likely.

"The game," Orjo said impatiently. "The horseball game."

Hizarah looked up. "The emperor's horseball game. He often kills his enemies that way. It will be on the main playing field of the castle. You two go. I'll find the keys on the other guard and get Orjo out."

Brune looked unsure, but Indigo nodded. "Thank you. Free him and go to the drawbridge. We'll join you there."

Indigo gripped her sword and ran with Brune up the corridor back to the outside, where she could now hear the growing din of horses and horns.

Please, she begged the goddess Aktu, *please don't let us be too late.*

The nobles took their places at the long table, cooing their admiration for the carved ornaments that marked their seats. Each place setting had a small ivory carving of their family crest, to show where they should sit.

Ornox found the Vyad arms on a flat piece of ivory ten seats down from the emperor, on his right side. As Ornox sat, he studied the gathered nobles. The most powerful warlords were here, and by the curious looks they shot him, Ornox knew they were wondering if the hero of Mankahar would soon be ruler. A wiry man with a thick beard down to his chest raised his goblet toward Ornox in salute. Ornox recognized the seal of Harkwin and nodded in reply. The richest man in Mankahar would be his father-in-law if the emperor kept his word.

"Welcome."

To Ornox, Dorgun's voice sounded throaty and full of decay. Even so, everyone fell silent, not wanting to miss a word about who would become heir.

"A birthday is a special time, especially at my age. It pleases me to see all the noble houses of Mankahar here today for my birthday celebrations, and I intend us to celebrate in style."

Two servants entered, carrying a giant platter with a silver lid. They hefted it onto the table before Dorgun, as the emperor motioned to the servants waiting behind the guests. The servants stepped forward with pitchers of wine and filled everyone's goblets.

"But first, a toast," Dorgun said, raising his goblet. Everyone did the same, watching the emperor's every move. "To Lord Ornox of Vyad, who has rid us of Theo Griffinrider, the one many feared would bring down our great empire. The empire my ancestors established." Dorgun smiled and raised his glass. "To Ornox."

"To Ornox," everyone dutifully echoed and drank from their goblets. The servants slid forward immediately, refilling every glass. Ornox put his hand over his.

"Please, Ornox. I have been saving this tale for my birthday. Tell us how you slayed the Griffinrider."

Ornox kept his expression neutral. Why was Dorgun doing this? From the sour expressions of the other warlords, they clearly thought this an indication that Ornox might be pronounced heir due to his having killed the Griffinrider. But Ornox knew better than to assume game was meat before it had been killed.

"I wouldn't want to bore everyone," he protested politely.

The emperor tapped the table with his goblet and encouraged everyone else to do the same, until there was a chorus of whistles and table tapping. "We have been eagerly awaiting the story. Come, Ornox, tell it to us in every detail."

"There's not much to tell. I threatened Jaipri with destruction unless they gave me Theo Griffinrider, and so they did. I put my sword through him, and he died like the animal he was. Then I sent his body into the Jaipri river."

"Such welcome words," Dorgun said, raising his goblet again. "To Ornox, our hero for doing what no one else could."

The gathered nobles all smiled and echoed Dorgun's toast, but Ornox heard the ripple of hostility beneath it. They did not appreciate this homage to Ornox, seeing it as evidence that

Ornox was favored. Could it be that the emperor would simply hand over power? Could it be that easy?

"As you all know," Dorgun said smoothly, putting his goblet down. "I promised to announce my heir at today's feast." All eyes shot back to the emperor, and in the silence, Ornox thought he could hear the creak of the old man's bones as he shifted in his seat. "An heir to Mankahar must be strong, worthy. And who could be more worthy of a throne than the hero who killed the Griffinrider?"

There was an uncomfortable silence, a stillness as the nobles snuck looks at Ornox, trying to gauge the emperor's tone. Ornox felt a flicker of nervousness. The time had come. Was the emperor really going to name him? Had Ornox been paranoid for no reason?

"Given this, Ornox is the clear choice for my heir."

Ornox felt lightheaded. The emperor had spoken the words, and from everyone's reaction, they had heard them. There were clear hints of dissatisfaction from almost all except Harkwin, but no one protested. A few raised their goblets, and then everyone followed suit, ready to toast the newly named heir. Ornox dipped his head to accept the nomination.

"There's only one problem."

At Dorgun's words, Ornox stilled. The nobles held their goblets in midair, frozen.

Dorgun reached forward and lifted the silver lid on his platter. Lying there, bound and with a gag in his mouth, was a grey rabbit with unmistakable black eye patches and black paws.

A collective gasp circled the room. The nobles recoiled, their chairs scraping against the wooden floor. The rabbit took in everything around him, eyes wary.

"If you killed Theo Griffinrider, Lord Ornox," Dorgun asked, voice soft, "then why is he alive and on my table?"

Ornox didn't bother to stand up. He would not dignify this charade, for now was the time to hold firm against any sabotage. "It's a hoax, Your Eminence. I watched Theo die. This rabbit is a remarkable lookalike, an impersonator. And whoever is doing it is trying to discredit me."

"Guards," Dorgun commanded. "Take the rabbit to the game."

The guards came forward and pulled the trussed rabbit off the table, dragging him from the tent as the nobles muttered uneasily among themselves. As the rabbit passed Ornox, the warlord felt a pinprick of doubt. The rabbit could have been the twin of the one he had killed.

"Lord Ornox, you have lied to me, and to the empire," Dorgun said. "Such lies cannot go unpunished."

Ornox felt the air in the tent turn icy.

"Your Eminence, if someone has been feeding you this story—"

"It's not a story, Ornox," Dorgun snapped. "I found the Griffinrider myself, alive and well, in the heart of our city. In my home! You are a false servant and clearly fabricated these heroics to take the throne."

There were shouts of support at this, but Ornox raised his voice above theirs.

"I'm afraid you have lost your wits, Your Eminence."

There was a collective intake of breath. Ornox stood, his frame towering. It was time to show these sheep that he was not afraid of a weak old wolf. "This is your desperate attempt to keep power at any cost, and you're trying to discredit me so that you can sit on a throne you no longer deserve." He turned to the nobles. "It's time for new leadership. Mankahar needs it; you need it. All who join me now will be rewarded, and all who don't will suffer the consequences."

Dorgun's face twisted. "We now see your true colors, Ornox. Well, I know what to do with traitors." He clapped his hands, and two burly guards strode in, carrying a large square block of wood between them with handles on the sides.

Ornox bounded over the table. "Now, Volchega!"

It took him a moment to realize that the woman was moving not toward the emperor, as they had planned, but toward him.

His moment of surprise allowed enough time for Volchega and another of the emperor's guards to grab his arms, twisting them behind his back and forcing him down to his knees.

"Your mother will die for this," Ornox growled up at Volchega.

Her face crumpled for the briefest of moments before she regained control.

"Volchega's mother died this morning," the emperor said icily. "I had her killed. I told Volchega she could keep her head, but only if she delivered yours."

Ornox looked up at him, glowering. The bastard had known all along. Volchega kept a stony silence as the guards with the block set it down in the space inside the horseshoe of tables, and the guard with the curly hair reached under the table and pulled out a glistening new axe. He hefted it and strode toward the impromptu execution ground.

"Let this be a lesson to those of you who wish to defy your emperor," Dorgun said. "Lord Ornox of Vyad, you have been found guilty of treason, and I now accept your life as payment."

CHAPTER 43

*P*ozzi pressed himself against a wall as a crowd of revelers barreled down the street, uncaring of who or what they trod underfoot. He had lost count of how many times he'd had to duck, weave, or dive into an alley to avoid being trampled as he made his way to the city gates. This journey out was not without its dangers.

"Don't miss it. The most wondrous event in Mankahar's history is happening today. Those who remain indoors will regret it!"

Pozzi ignored the town crier and pressed on. He had passed many such criers, all urging people out of their houses and into the streets. He couldn't care less about what the wondrous event was. All he could think of was getting out of this city and back to Keeva and Walnut. Would they still be with Harlan? Joseb had told him the name of the town, and directions back. He had also given Pozzi a short knife.

"It's a dangerous road, full of slavers," the man had said simply.

Pozzi had reluctantly taken it, not sure he knew how to use it, but knowing Joseb was right that he needed some sort of defense if he were attacked. It had taken them six sunsets to get to the capital, but that was by cart. Pozzi would have a long, dangerous journey ahead on foot.

He turned a corner and caught a glimpse of the towering gates with metal studs that marked the city's perimeter. He broke into a run, threading between the boisterous children and their scolding parents. He was now only a stone's throw from Kalyun-eh's walls. He would be glad to be rid of this teeming city, with its stenches and the thick crush of people slowing his progress. He was still intent on the approaching gates when a figure came out of a laneway, directly into his path. He stepped to one side to go around, as he had countless times today, but the figure stepped with him. And that's when he noticed the shoes, the leggings. He'd seen them before.

Pozzi looked up and knew, even before he saw the figure's wooden mask and the disfigured smirk, that Sarkus had found him.

Pozzi tried to stay calm as the boy took one step toward him, then another. He had to buy time, not panic. But this was easier said than done, as he now realized that Sarkus had backed him into a deserted, narrow alleyway.

"Sarkus," Pozzi tried, holding up his paws. "I know you blame me for the crows, but I bargained for your and your family's lives."

The boy's lip curled. "Did you now? Is that why my mother and father are dead? Why my sister and I are orphans?"

Ghazan and Tansha, dead? "Argasar gave me his word—"

"And you actually believed him," Sarkus said, bitter. "You took the word of a wolf. And now my parents are dead. You ruined my face, and now you killed my parents. You let the wolves in, and I have lost everything because of you."

Pozzi tried to put the puzzle pieces together, but couldn't. And right now, none of it changed the fact that the boy before him hated him with a frightening passion. None of it changed the fact that Pozzi was now looking at a sharp, wicked blade in Sarkus's hand.

* * *

THEO'S ARMS ached from where the bonds held them, and the tight grip of his guards didn't help. As they exited the tent and crossed the yard toward the field where the horses were cantering back and forth, he took in the great ship and its billowing balloon.

A balloon. That's how the emperor was going to make it fly. And the hold was no doubt filled with pacification powder, to be dropped over the entire city, perhaps beyond. His heart sank as he twisted in his bonds, and the realization that he was completely helpless to stop any of this hit him like a punch.

He didn't know what his role was to be in this game that involved horses and riders and the rings at the end of the field, but he knew there was no surviving it. Some of the players were trying out mallets, while others were already mounting and trotting out to the field, but it wasn't this that made Theo's throat go dry. He saw guards similar to the ones who held him, holding down a familiar figure.

Xandru's scraped and bleeding face looked up at him, pale after his days without sunlight. The boy watched Theo approaching, and the rabbit tried to keep a brave face. He owed Xandru that much.

The boy lifted his chin and nodded to Theo. "I'd rather die like this than with the slavers."

Before Theo could answer, a hood was pulled over his head and tied at the back. This was the end.

* * *

ACROSS THE FIELD, Indigo and Brune emerged from the court-yard adjoining the dungeons. Indigo saw the familiar face just as the hood was pulled over it, saw a guard yank Theo to his feet and drag him toward a circle marked in white paint in the middle of the grass, where a line of riders on horses waited with long mallets.

She didn't realize she was running until all she heard was the blood pounding in her head, the rush of desperation in her veins.

* * *

INSIDE THE TENT, the emperor's demand for Ornox's head had been followed by a deathly silence, the nobles pinned to their seats in fascinated horror at what was about to come.

Ornox glared up at the surrounding nobles in the tent. He struggled against the guards holding him and shouted, "This is your chance to rise up, to overthrow this weak madman who rules you. Stand with me!"

There were only petrified faces, with one noble letting out a hysterical giggle before stifling it with a kerchief.

"Traitor!"

Ornox looked over. Harkwin was standing up, his expression stony. Soon others took up the cry, siding with the emperor and growing more strident. Ornox burned inside. A bunch of spineless sycophants, all of them. If he were emperor he would kill them all. Not if, *when*. He held this thought like a promise as he let himself go limp between the guards holding him, seeming to crumble under the barrage of abuse the gathered throng was now shouting at him. Each seemed eager to outdo his neighbor.

Ornox hung his head. Volchega and her companion lifted him to his feet to drag him the few paces to the block. The imperial guards never wore helmets, as a sign of their invincibility. This also meant their noses were unprotected.

In the moment before they made him kneel, Ornox threw his head back with all his might, and though his skull hurt on impact, he heard a satisfying crack as the man's nose shattered. The guard's grip on his right arm loosened just enough for Ornox to jerk his arm free and reach into his shirt for his pendant. He yanked it hard, snapping the string. Volchega tried to grab Ornox's free arm, but the warlord was faster. He wrapped his hand around the pendant and smashed his fist into Volchega's throat.

She doubled over, trying to breathe. Ornox took aim at the nearest brazier of sage, and threw.

The pendant spun in an arc, landing in the coals of the nearest brazier, just as the guard with the smashed nose tackled Ornox to the ground.

An explosion tore through the emperor's tent, but the guard's body shielded Ornox. Screams erupted as shards of metal and chunks of burning coal found flesh, and Ornox heard the guard on top of him cry out as he rolled off, his arm on fire. Ornox got to his feet, taking in the devastation through the ringing in his ears.

The tent roof was now reduced to shreds, the pieces floating back down from the sky. Panicked nobles scrambled to their feet, some flailing wildly to bat out the flames on their clothes. One of the emperor's guards was helping a lacerated and bleeding Dorgun to stand.

Ornox lurched toward the old ruler, when from the corner of his eye, he spotted the burly executioner bearing down on him, axe raised. Ornox grabbed the nearest noble, a disoriented man with an oiled beard, and pivoted. The axe sank into the noble's body, ending his feeble cry of surprise.

Ornox pushed the body to the ground. The executioner, instinctively holding on to his weapon, pitched forward with the weight of the man, exposing his back. Ornox landed two solid blows to the executioner's spine. The executioner let go of the axe and tried to swing around to defend himself, but Ornox's boot found his face first. The executioner's head snapped back, but not before his foot kicked out, connecting with Ornox's knee. Ornox heard several pops and hissed from the sparks of pain radiating through his leg. Ornox yanked the axe free of the noble and brought it down into the space between the executioner's neck and shoulder, killing his opponent instantly.

When he looked up, nobles were fleeing in every direction, limping off the shattered wooden tent platform and running across the horseball field. He caught sight of Dorgun, two of his remaining bodyguards flanking him, running as quickly as his old legs could take him toward the ship.

Ornox hefted his axe and gave chase.

* * *

THEO TRIED to struggle against his bonds, against the merciless yank of his captor pulling him to the middle of the field and to his death. He could hear the whinnying of horses and tried to focus. If he could shut out his fear, he just might be able to find a way to get his hood off. His breathing sounded too loud, the air was getting too close.

Just then, there was a roar like that of a griffin, and the sound of splintering wood. The whinnying changed to terrified shrieks, panicked footsteps, and Urzok screams. What was happening? The guards' hold on him slackened, and he was shoved to the ground. The hood ripped off his face and he looked up, expecting to see an Urzok, or worse, a mallet. Instead, he had never seen anything so welcome. *Indigo*.

"What are you doing here?"

"Saving you," she said, her voice cracking. The guards lay dead at her feet. "You have so much explaining to do."

Behind her, Theo saw Brune—Brune!—freeing Xandru, untying his bonds and pulling the boy to his feet. Dozens of horses were running panicked across the field, while distraught Urzoks, many bleeding through charred or ripped clothing, were fleeing in every direction, further spooking the already terrified game horses. They pulled at their reins and kicked at their handlers, their hooves catching some of the fleeing nobles.

"We have to leave through the main drawbridge," Indigo

explained, pulling Theo to his feet. "Manneki will make sure the drawbridge is down, but we don't have much time."

"Manneki's here too?" Theo asked.

Indigo nodded as Brune grabbed the reins of a fleeing horse and pulled it close. The bear pushed Xandru up into the saddle, then gestured at Theo. "Quick! Up on the horse, Theo!"

Theo looked over to the ship. Dorgun had almost reached its anchoring rope, and Ornox was in pursuit, axe in hand. The warlord was limping, he noticed, though it barely slowed him.

"You go. Take them out of here. I need to stop that ship."

"What? Why?" Indigo asked.

"It's full of pacification powder," Theo said. "If it flies over the city then everyone in it, Urzok or not, will be pacified."

"By Aktu," Brune grunted.

"I'll find a spear or arrow, and we'll burst the balloon," Indigo said, preparing to run.

Theo grabbed her arm, stopping her. "It's too late! It's already off the ground. If we do that, it'll crash and spill the powder everywhere."

Theo turned back. The emperor and his bodyguards were almost at the ship, with Ornox close behind. The half-dozen crewmembers on board were making ready to cast off the ropes holding the vessel down.

"Then we have to get on it," Brune growled as he began sprinting.

* * *

ORNOX WAS GAINING on his prey. The emperor cried out for a ladder, and the crew on the ship were lowering one. Ornox put in a burst of speed, axe raised, and cut the tethering rope closest to him. The ship's stern rose, and the ladder Dorgun had tried to reach floated just out of his grasp before it fell to the ground, the crew member having lost his grip when the ship jerked.

"Kill him!" Dorgun screamed to his bodyguards, and the two

turned to face Ornox, swords drawn. But Ornox could feel the battle rage in him, the cool calm that came when he was about to spill blood. He noted the two fighters' stances, the nervous grips on their weapons that betrayed their fear. He went for the larger of the two and, instead of aiming directly at the man's head or chest as expected, used the curve of the axe blade to hook the man's sword hilt and yank him close. Ornox smashed a fist into the surprised soldier's nose, then quickly cut down the second one whose courage had wilted, making his moves hesitant. Ornox picked up one of the discarded swords and advanced on Dorgun, slashing out as the emperor screamed for help.

His blade connected with the old man's flesh just as someone slammed into him from above, sending him crashing to the ground. A searing pain spread in his shoulder, and he bellowed as he rolled back onto the man who had jumped him.

Ornox reached out and grabbed his attacker by the leg to flip him. The man proved slippery, however, and evaded Ornox's attempts to unbalance him, instead bringing an elbow back into Ornox's face. The warlord reeled, but when the man turned to tackle him, Ornox had his sword ready and cut up from below, catching the man unawares and cleaving into his abdomen. He let the man's body slump to the ground.

He looked up and saw Dorgun clutching his bleeding arm, trying to grasp a rope ladder being lowered by the ship's crew.

"Dorgun!"

The emperor's head snapped around, and seeing Ornox, he hesitated, unsure. But as Ornox advanced, the emperor abandoned the rope ladder and began running as quickly as he could for the castle.

Ornox started after him, but then saw a flash of grey and black running for the ship, grasping the ladder that had been meant for Dorgun. The grey rabbit who looked like the Griffin-rider was trying to hold on to the ship, Ornox realized with incredulity, despite his size. A bear came barreling to his aid and pulled the rope, but the crew simply threw it overboard. The bear ran for one of the three remaining ropes that held the ship down. On the deck, the crew shouted to each other to cut all lines.

Against his better judgment, Ornox strode toward the grey rabbit. He had told Dorgun that this was a hoax, an imposter— and what else could it be? But he had to find out. He had to know that this was not some resurrected demon, for he had killed that enemy back in Jaipri, and this was impossible.

If he had to kill it again, he would.

He was halfway across to the rabbit when a voice from behind stopped him.

"Ornox!"

He turned and saw a white rabbit, her ears tattooed with blue swirls, sword gripped in both paws. "I killed your daughter Agacheta."

"No! Indigo!"

Ornox vaguely registered that the grey rabbit had shouted out, but the white rabbit's words had stilled everything, made time slip out of place. "What did you say?"

"I, Indigo of Alvareth, killed your daughter," the rabbit said, her sword drawn. "I put an arrow through her. I watched her die."

Ornox wasn't aware of making a decision. He felt the axe in his hand, and then he was hurtling forward, nothing but fury in his veins.

Theo didn't have time to rush to Indigo's aid. The remaining crew members on the ship had severed the other three ropes holding the ship down, and the stern was now lifting away, with Brune clutching one of the snapped ropes.

"Go!" Indigo shouted to him as she parried Ornox' first attack. "Stop the ship!"

Theo leapt up and just managed to grasp the tube strapped to Brune's axe harness before the bear rose off the ground and out of reach.

"Hang on!" Brune cried.

Theo heard the rush of an arrow and looked up. One of the crew was shooting at them, while another sawed at the thick rope holding them. Brune proved himself an expert climber, however, and within three quick pulls had them up to the ship's side, just as the crew severed the last of the rope and sent it flying away. Theo didn't dare look down, but he could tell they were rising, passing the low castle stables, then balconies. Brune leapt onto the ship's side railing, with Theo clinging to his back, and then they were on the deck. The bear grabbed one archer's bow and pulled him over the side, while the one who had cut the rope brandished his knife at the bear, his eyes full of fear.

Theo leapt down onto the deck, looking for a weapon. He had to settle for one of the logs that had rolled free from the wood crate where they were stored, and rushed to the chimney. There were only two crew members remaining, one holding a tangle of lines leading up into the balloon, and one at the oven stoking the fire. The rest had apparently fled before liftoff.

"Bring us down!" he shouted at the man working the oven.

The man was clearly fear stricken, and Theo wondered briefly if he recognized the Griffinrider. As they rose, the ship crashed into a castle balcony, throwing everyone off balance. Theo skidded to the floor, and the man leapt on him, all punches and kicks. Theo tried to lash back, but the man was much bigger than he was, and fueled by fear. Theo felt a fist connect with his face, then his arms as he tried to fend off the blows. He tried to roll away, but the ship lurched again, this time from colliding with a protruding turret, and began listing to one side. The man lost his balance. Toppling down the deck, he hit the railing and rolled over the edge, screaming. Theo went sliding as well and would have gone the same way if the log he was holding hadn't caught on the railing. Theo found himself dangling over the side of the ship. He looked down and saw they were nearing the top of the Kalyun-eh castle spires. The ship was still rising, despite its collision with multiple obstacles.

"Theo!"

A burly paw grabbed him by the arm, and he was forcibly hauled back onto the deck. Brune set him down. They faced the one remaining crew member, who clearly knew he was the last man on board. His face was scratched and bloodied, and his eyes darted about for an escape route.

"This ship is full of pacification powder," Brune growled. "Take the ship down."

The man hesitated, then ran for the ship's stern. And that's when Theo noticed too: they were headed for Kalyun-eh's highest spire.

"We'll never clear that!" Theo cried.

The man took a leap just before impact, landing on the sloped roof and clawing desperately as he slid down and grasped the guttering. Theo didn't have time to see if he survived or not, for the ship's hull was scraping the spire. He heard a horrible pop as the wood below gave way. Slowed but not stopped, the ship continued over the last castle spire, then onward over the city outside with its crowded streets.

* * *

INDIGO COULD FEEL HERSELF TIRING. Ornox was bigger, stronger, one of the best in the land.

She had been reckless telling him she had killed his daughter, but she'd had to divert him from Theo. Now he burned with a fire she knew only too well, a fire that made one not need food or drink or rest. Which was why the myriad cuts Indigo had managed to deliver to Ornox hadn't seemed to slow him in the slightest.

They had been fighting through the field and into the adjoining courtyard, the remnants of panicked revelers and nobles scattering as the pair cut and kicked their way through. Indigo took every chance to lead him away from the ship. She debated about escaping, but even this luxury was impossible, for Ornox was pressing harder now, bearing down on her with unrelenting force, giving her barely enough time to avoid injury, much less find an escape route. Because of his superior size and strength, she had to favor evasion over blocking his blows. Only by tiring him sufficiently could she contemplate attack, but at this rate, she feared the man had an unnatural stamina. Too late, she dodged a particularly vicious slice and felt the sting of his sword graze her back. Blood seeped, binding her shirt to her fur.

"Surrender," the warlord said. "And I may simply quarter you, rather than take a piece each day."

She gritted her teeth. "I did not surrender to your daughter. I certainly won't surrender to her old father."

The Urzok's face darkened, and he brought his sword down with brutal force. Indigo leapt to the side, but his free fist was waiting, ramming into her abdomen with bruising accuracy. She went airborne before crashing onto the hard ground. From here she had a view across the courtyard to the upper reaches of the castle gatehouse and saw a face there.

Manneki.

"Manneki!" she screamed as loudly as she could. "Now!"

She saw the Grodlyn disappear from view just as Ornox's foot smashed into her side, sending her flying again. She thought she felt a rib crack, and her head connected with a wagon wheel. Where was her sword? She scrambled under the wagon, temporarily protected, and pleaded with Aktu for her friends' help.

* * *

Up in the drum room, Manneki saw Indigo fall, then heard her shout as she ducked under the wagon just as Ornox's sword came down against it.

Manneki whirled to Reenan, who had been waiting with the oil lamp ready. "Fire now, Reenan!"

Reenan rushed his lamp to the first tube. But his rushing to the winding drum had snuffed the small flame, and now he had no fire to light the black snow.

"By Blackhide, no!" Tears of frustration beaded as he fumbled with his flints, trying to relight the lamp.

"Hurry! Princess will die!" Manneki shrieked.

"I'm trying!" Reenan snapped.

The flints sparked, died, sparked again. He finally held his hands still long enough to light the lamp, and, with a shout of triumph, he lit the first tube. Manneki pulled the tube from the second drum and thrust it toward Reenan to light. Reenan touched the flame to the wick.

"Hey! What are you doing?"

Manneki yelped and dropped the lit tube in his paw. Two castle guards stood at the open entryway, their halberds pointed toward him. The tube rolled away, then disappeared down the open murder hole to the barbican corridor below.

"Oh gods." Reenan breathed. Manneki's eyes widened.

"I said, what are you doing here?" the guard repeated. "Get out!"

But neither Reenan nor Manneki was listening, for both were sprinting for the window overlooking the keep, bracing for what was to follow.

* * *

INDIGO ROLLED out from under the other side of the wagon and spied a soldier's halberd with a broken handle on the ground. She swept it up and turned, just in time to block the shattering blow that Ornox dealt. She parried again and again, but felt the force of Ornox's sword wearing her down.

Where was the explosion? What was Manneki doing? He was either in trouble or hadn't seen her. She risked a glance toward the gate window and knew she had made a mistake. She missed seeing through Ornox's feint, and he flicked his sword upward, sending the halberd flying from her paw.

"Tell Agacheta her father loves her," he said, fierce.

Indigo tensed as Ornox aimed to sever her head. But suddenly, someone yanked her by her vest and pulled her up onto a horse.

"Hold on, Princess," Orjo crowed as he helped her onto the saddle in front of him. Indigo looked up and saw Hizarah in her stolen soldier's uniform, gripping the reins, Orjo riding in front of her. Ornox was giving chase, and Hizarah spurred the horse faster.

"Now, Manneki!" Hizarah shouted, "Now, now, now!"

The horse raced for the drawbridge. People scattered as she came barreling past, and Ornox plowed through anyone unfortunate enough to be in his way. The horse was just through the barbican, onto the other side, when a resounding roar sounded from behind. Indigo glanced back to see the gate arch buckle, then fall, great pieces of rubble caving inward in a maelstrom of dust.

The castle was barricaded.

* * *

"How do we stop this thing? Without pacifying the whole city?"

Theo didn't have an answer to Brune's question. "There's no place to land it without it breaking apart and spilling the pacification powder everywhere."

He had checked on the hold immediately after the last Urzok had abandoned ship, and seen the telltale remnants of white powder on the wooden floorboards. There was enough pacification powder to turn ten cities into mindless wastelands. And now they were sailing over the city, and Theo could see the crowds gathering below, cheering and pointing at the brightly colored balloon in the sky. Bells rang as town criers waved and shouted, the great spectacle drawing everyone out of their homes.

"Maybe we can clear the city, then put out the fire," Brune suggested. "That should deflate the balloon and bring it down."

Theo shook his head. "If the fire goes out, the whole thing will crash as well. It'll rain the powder everywhere, on everyone."

"We'll bring it down over a river then."

Theo saw a trail of something behind them and stood up to get a better look.

"Too late. We're leaking."

Brune joined him. "By Aktu." A long tail of white powder was drifting to the city below. "The spire. It must have punctured the hold."

"This will pacify everyone!" Theo began waving his arms, and Brune joined him, bellowing to those below.

"Get away!" the bear roared.

Theo cupped his paws over his mouth. "Run! Hide!"

But the cheering and the music below drowned out their voices, and the powder continued to fall in a deadly wake behind them.

"They can't hear us," Brune said, gripping the rail in frustration. He took something and threw it over the side, but the crowd only thickened, eager and reaching.

"They think we're giving out coin or food as part of the festivities," Theo said, putting a paw on Brune's arm to stop him. "It won't work."

"Then what will? We have to do something," the bear growled.

But what?

* * *

Ornox stood, looking at the blocked barbican, and screamed in frustration. When his anger had cooled enough, the pain in his knee brought him out of his vengeance fever and back to cold reason. He had lost precious time chasing his daughter's killer, and he had been forced to admit that he couldn't get to her once the castle barbican had collapsed. He would find that rabbit again and make her suffer for a very long time. But for now, he must remember, he had an empire to win.

He turned back and made his way toward the courtyard from which Dorgun had fled. The telltale drops of blood lay bright and cheerful on the dark stone, beckoning. Ornox followed them into the main castle foyer, then through to the courtyard that girded the emperor's private chambers.

Ornox looked up at the pyramid with its wide carved steps. The blood trail led up the stairway and into the chamber at the top. Ornox took the stairs two at a time, gritting his teeth against the pain in his knee, focusing instead on the thrill of the hunt. All animals went to their lairs, their safe places, to die. And Dorgun would be no different.

Ornox reached the balcony that led into the private chambers, and pushed on the glass doors. They were unlocked. He stepped in, scanning for signs of Dorgun, but saw no one. The bedchamber held a luxurious bed draped in silks and linens, and the walls were covered with priceless tapestries. Beyond, Ornox could see a bathing chamber and a foyer. But everything seemed deserted.

Ornox tracked the trail of blood straight to the middle of the room, where a gaping hole yawned. It was a circular door in the floor, swung open on an axis. Ornox cautiously stepped forward. Of course the wily old goat had a secret chamber. But even if it was an escape route, he was losing blood. The emperor could not go far.

Ornox peered into the hole and saw the stairs winding down. He let his sword go first, stepping silently on every step, then pausing to listen. By the time he had reached the bottom, he was sure the emperor had fled further in. There were a dozen or more doorways along a wide corridor, and he stepped to the first to peer inside. He could see shelves lined with volumes of bound paper. He paused, momentarily thrown. Why would the emperor have caught words? What was this place?

He saw a hunched figure in the middle of the chamber, a helmet on its head and a cloak around its shoulders. Ornox raised his sword.

"I'll make this quick, old one." He struck, but instead of the feel of flesh and bone, he heard a metallic crack. He yanked the cloak aside to reveal a stone pillar, with a helmet resting on top.

He turned and came face to face with Dorgun. He felt cold steel push past his ribs and into his chest, until his throat flooded and he couldn't form sounds.

The emperor's milky eye hovered over him as Ornox sank to his knees. And then the knife was flashing again. Ornox lifted his arm and tried to grab the blade, but instead stumbled forward. His palms were slippery with blood, and he tried to curse Dorgun but only gurgling came.

"You are a strong warlord, Ornox of Vyad, but you're not half as clever as I," the emperor said, watching the man slump to the floor. "Your death will be slow. I want my ancestor Dakus to enjoy this."

CHAPTER 45

From the deck, Theo saw a familiar face in the crowd. He squinted. The balloon was rising, slowly it was true, but the crowd was growing more distant. Could it be his eyes were playing tricks? But no, it *was* Xandru, sitting astride a horse, his face turned up toward the ship.

"Xandru!" Theo shouted with all his might. He could tell the boy saw him, but whether he heard him was another matter. *Think, Theo!*

He turned around and scanned the deck. There was nothing on the ship but broken pieces of rope and charred wood.

Charred wood. Charcoal.

"Brune! Help me break the decking." He gestured at Brune's axe and motioned at the ship's deck. At the bear's expression, he said, "There's no time! Just do it! Break a large wide piece of the deck, as wide a piece as you can manage."

While Brune hefted his axe and began hacking, Theo looked at the chimney and pulled out the thickest pieces of burning wood he could find. He stubbed out the flames against the chimney stove, making sure the sparks were all gone before bringing them back to Brune. The bear was prying up one end of the plank, and then began working on the other.

Theo knelt with the charred log and began filling up the whole width of the planks Brune was carving out with glyphs.

By the time Brune had the other end free of the ship and had pulled it up, they had a section three planks wide, and half the length of the ship. Theo hurriedly finished the last glyph.

"Now what?" Brune asked, puffing from the exertion.

"Help me tie rope around the ends," Theo said. "We have to lower it over the side, with the Forbidden Language facing out."

Brune helped him find two pieces of rope. Already, they were clearing the city spires, soon they would be too far up for anyone to see the planks clearly. When they had tied the rope to the ends, they dragged it to the edge. Theo tied his other end of rope through one of the portholes, and Brune did the same.

"On the count of three!" Theo cried. "One, two, three!"

He hefted his end, while Brune hefted his, and they heaved the plank over the side. The wood slid over, the ropes slithering with it, before the ropes pulled taut. The ship listed to the side as the weight shifted, and the plank swung in the breeze.

"Please, please, let it be visible!" Theo said under his breath, watching the gathered crowd below. The white powder was flowing fast and free now, and even from here, he could see some people doubling over as the pacification took effect.

He saw Xandru holding a hand over his eyes, gazing up at the plank. And then he began shouting, standing in his stirrups and gesturing.

Theo let out his breath. Xandru had been able to see "DANGER" written on the plank, and figured out what he was trying to say. By now, some of the crowd had realized that people were fainting and collapsing around them. There were screams and cries of confusion, and then Xandru was off the horse, clearly ordering people indoors.

People began to run, clearing the street, and only just in time. For there came a giant groan from the ship as the planking in the hull began to give way. The trail of pacification powder became a stream.

"We have to get the ship over the walls, before all of it falls on the city," Theo cried, and began shoving wood into the chimney. If they could get high enough and catch the winds, they might sail over the city walls and into the less inhabited countryside. There, they could at least minimize the effects of the powder.

Brune began helping him push wood into the chimney. The fire roared hungrily, and the balloon stretched as it tried unsuccessfully to rise.

"The plank!" Brune shouted. "It's acting like an anchor!"

Theo took over for Brune at the chimney, and Brune picked up his axe. He severed the first rope holding the sign, and the ship jerked up, buoyed. Brune cut the second rope, sending the plank whirling away from them, and the freed ship rose at an even faster pace. From up here, Theo comforted himself, the powder would at least be dispersed and less potent, taking longer to hit the city below.

Soon, they were over Kalyun-eh's outer walls, where those who were celebrating or sheltering pointed up and shouted.

"We've cleared the city, at least," Brune said, panting.

Theo brightened, pointing. "I see a river! It's not very near, but if we can change course and make it there, we can bring the balloon down. Once the powder's wet, it's harmless."

Brune nodded. "It's our best chance."

"I'll start damping the fire, we'll need to stop rising if we're going to bring it down there."

"And I'll see if I can figure out how to steer this thing," Brune said, heading for the stern.

* * *

Pozzi did the only thing he could: run.

He raced down the alleyway, looking for an open door, or window, anywhere he could hide. Sarkus was close behind him, gaining fast.

Somewhere in the distance, trumpets blared, and the city

seemed to take a collective gasp. A door ahead on Pozzi's right opened, and a woman stepped out cradling a baby. Pozzi made straight for the open door, and almost crashed into the woman's legs.

The woman shouted at him, making the baby wail. But Pozzi was already racing up a set of rickety stairs, which he soon regretted. The stairs led to a narrow child's room, with no escape except by way of one window in the sloped roof over the bed. He stood, debating, but could already hear Sarkus pounding up the stairs, and the young mother's shouts from below.

Pozzi gritted his teeth. He had to take the roof. He ran to the bed and jumped up to the window, unlatched it, and threw the shutters wide. He leaped, grasping the edge of the windowsill and pulling until his muscles screamed. He managed to swing himself up, over, and onto the roof just as Sarkus reached for him from the bed, one hand grabbing Pozzi's foot.

"Got you," Sarkus snarled, then howled as Pozzi pulled his knife free and sank it into Sarkus's hand. The boy let go, cradling his impaled hand, and Pozzi scrambled out onto the roof tiles, trying to maintain a grip on the sloped surface. Up here, two flagpoles held imperial flags out over the alley, their cloth waving lazily in the wind. His only escape seemed to be a drop to the alleyway below, a sure death if he fell.

He tried to look for a place to climb down when he noticed it: something large was rising into the sky ahead, and he could hear cheering. He squinted, unsure what he was seeing. The thing was closer now, and he could make out the deck of a ship. He could also just make out figures on the deck. He heard a grunt from the open window and turned to see Sarkus pulling himself out of the child's room. His hand was bandaged in a ripped sheet, and his other hand held his knife. The mother was right behind him, her chin reaching just above the window.

"Get out of here! I'll call the guards!"

Sarkus ignored her, all eyes on Pozzi. "There's nowhere to run, rabbit," he smirked. "It's my turn to draw blood."

The boy lunged. Pozzi almost fell, his quick movement having unbalanced him. He backed slowly toward the flagpole, noting that its flag flew quite close to the next building. If he could reach the pole and climb out on it, there was a chance he could swing over to the next rooftop, or even slide down the flag to what looked like an ajar window in the next building. But only if he didn't fall first, or lose his balance on landing. He had very few options, and none of them were good.

He heard shouts of alarm. The flying ship—for there was no other name for it—had drifted even closer now, and was only a few houses away. A curtain of white powder seemed to be trailing it, falling like snow on everyone watching. He could see a rabbit on the deck, and a bear, and something about the rabbit seemed familiar, but before Pozzi could work it out, he realized that the screams were a word, and he could make it out now.

"Pacification!"

A chill snaked through him. The trail of white blooming from the ship's hold was pacification powder.

"Get inside!" Pozzi shouted. The baby's mother was still at her roof window, though like Pozzi, she seemed to have been distracted by the ship. Pozzi shouted at her. "It's pacification, get the child inside!"

He pointed at the ship, then at the window, and fear sparked in her eyes. The woman retreated below, slamming the shutters closed behind her.

"We have to find shelter, Sarkus," Pozzi argued, "or we'll both be pacified!"

The boy smiled. "Your distractions won't work." He lunged again, swiping with his knife, and this time, Pozzi was too slow. A thin line of blood welled on Pozzi's right arm, darkening the patched fur there.

"Sarkus, listen to the shouts! Those are shouts of fear!"

The ship's shadow was over them now, and Pozzi glanced up, trying to see where the powder was. And as he did so, he could have sworn he saw Theo's face for an instant before it disappeared over the edge of the ship.

Was he imagining it? He had no time to dwell on it, for the curtain of white was drawing closer.

"Quick, cover your mouth!" he shouted at Sarkus. He began stripping his shirt. The boy ignored him, however, and instead rushed forward, knife raised. Pozzi lost his footing and slid down the roof and over the edge into the air, his fall only checked when he managed to grab hold of the flag.

He dangled there, trying not to look at the drop below. The curtain of white was closing. Soon it would be on them. With his free paw he ripped his shirt sleeve clean off and began winding the material around his nose and mouth.

Sarkus appeared over the edge, standing on the roof with a triumphant smile. From there, he couldn't reach Pozzi, but he could reach the flag that Pozzi was hanging on. Sarkus pulled the flag above Pozzi in one hand and pressed his knife against it with the other.

"I'll enjoy watching you die." The boy grinned from beneath his mask. He began to saw with his knife, and Pozzi felt the threads give. He hung there, heart hammering, too scared to even breathe.

All at once, the world turned white. The blizzard of pacification was upon them, drifting over their clothes, his fur, settling on Sarkus's hands and lips like ash. The boy's movements faltered, and his fingers trembled. The knife slipped from his hands, and Sarkus began coughing violently. He tried to crawl away up the roof. But it seemed his body wouldn't obey him, and before he had reached the window shutters, which were covered in powder, his foot slipped on one of the tiles and he slid unchecked toward the roof's edge.

Pozzi closed his eyes as the boy fell, and tried not to breathe as he heard the crack of bones. He listened for a moment, two, before opening his eyes again, and saw the boy's broken body in the alleyway, his limbs at unnatural angles and his mask split so that his disfigured face was visible to all. In the sky, the ship was floating on, approaching the city walls.

Pozzi heard a rip, and looked up. His flag was tearing. If he didn't hurry, he too would fall. He clambered paw over paw, until he had reached the flagpole. The exertion on his injured arm made him want to take deep breaths, but he forced himself to breathe shallowly. He didn't know how much his shirt would protect him. As soon as he was back on the roof, he ripped off his remaining shirtsleeve, then wound that around his nose and mouth too.

He looked back toward the ship, squinting. Theo couldn't really have been on that ship, could he? But what if he was? If he hurried, perhaps there was a way to follow the ship and discover whether he had indeed seen his childhood friend.

* * *

"WE'VE GOT A PROBLEM." The bear had returned from the stern, scowling. "I can't figure out how to change course."

Theo looked up from banking the fire. "There's no rudder?"

Brune shook his head. "No rudder, no helm. If there's a way to turn this ship around, it's not by usual means."

Theo stood and looked up at the balloon, and the ropes trailing under it. "It must use wind or heat." Theo looked out at the tiny sparkle of river in the distance. Already, it was disappearing as they drifted further and further away. He turned in the direction they were headed, trying to see if the river wound back ahead of them, but instead, he spotted something else in the near distance. He pointed. "Is that what I think it is?"

Brune turned. Approaching on the horizon was a large cluster of dwellings, smoke curling from chimneys. Already, they could hear the faint sounds of celebratory drums.

"A village," Brune said.

"They're right in our path." Dread pooled in Theo's belly. "They'll all be pacified if we don't change course."

"And how do we do that with no helm or rudder?" Brune looked about. "I've never seen a contraption like this, and I'm not sure I can learn to fly it in time."

Just then, there came a giant groan from the ship's belly, and Brune and Theo shared a look. "Was that the hold?" the rabbit asked.

Brune cursed and rushed to look over the edge of the ship. His expression turned grim. "The planks are splitting."

Theo looked out. The village was drifting closer and closer. The drumbeats were growing louder, and he could see children running about, some pulling brightly colored kites on the wind —wind that would soon rain pacification powder on them if Theo and Brune didn't stop the ship.

"There has to be something we can do!" Theo said, though he couldn't think what.

The bear pulled the tube from his back, and hefted it. "There's enough black snow in here to destroy the ship, the balloon, and everything in it. Burn it all before it hits the ground."

Theo swallowed. "Including us."

Brune fished in his holster and pulled out what looked like a whistle. "Not necessarily."

"What's that?" Theo asked.

"A gift from a friend," the bear answered. "Maybe there's a way we can get off the ship before we light the powder." He took a deep breath and blew on it, hard, but no sound came. "Maybe it's blocked," he muttered. Frowning, he wiped the whistle and blew again, hard and long, but the whistle stayed silent. Brune's face fell.

"What's it supposed to do?"

"I was hoping it would summon help."

A silence hung between them. "Brune..."

The bear hefted the tube and looked over at him, solemn. "Looks like you and I need to make a choice, Theo."

The rabbit nodded, throat dry. "You know my answer."

The bear smiled. "I thought so."

Theo nodded. "If it's the only way, we have to. Right? I've died before, it's not so bad."

This made Brune snort out a laugh before his expression turned serious again. "Eternal hibernation. Together?"

"Always." Theo forced a smile.

"Walk with Aktu, Theo Griffinrider."

Theo put his paw over Brune's, and the tube of black snow. "Goodbye, Brune of Hegg."

Together, they threw the tube of black snow into the chimney.

CHAPTER 46

$\mathcal{I}$ndigo, Orjo, and Hizarah had only just found Gerdene's mare and wagon by the gate when they heard the cheers of the people watching the balloon turn to terror.

"What's going on?" Hizarah asked, dismounting. Shouts of "pacification" rang through the streets, and citizens began to scatter in waves, rushing into any shelter they could find. The streets emptied and fights broke out as people tried to force their way into shuttered doors or cellars.

"They know what's in the ship's hold," Indigo said.

Gerdene pulled the covering off the wagon, revealing piles of fabric. "Quickly, make yourselves scarves, and give them out."

Hizarah and Orjo began ripping the fabric into long strips, and Indigo tied one around her nose and mouth before holding the rest aloft. "Cover your faces! Take shallow breaths!"

Soon their cart was surrounded as citizens rushed forward to snatch at whatever protective covering Gerdene offered. Hizarah and Orjo couldn't rip the cloth fast enough, and soon, the wagon was empty. A dozen or so people who hadn't gotten scarves were crying out for help.

"We'd best shelter soon," Orjo commented.

Gerdene stood and addressed the dozen people trying to clamber onto the wagon. "Help us turn the wagon over, and we can all hide under it."

Hizarah and three men from the crowd unhitched the horse, then pushed with all their might until the wagon tipped, then fell to the ground. Two of the men held one end of the wagon up while the rest of the people gratefully crawled underneath. They all sheltered inside, squeezed tightly together, until they managed to make sure everyone had torn cloth from their robes or jackets and made protections for their faces. They huddled there for a time, listening to the sound of running and shouts. Just as Indigo was about to insist she and Orjo, at least, venture out, they heard a familiar voice shouting over hoofbeats in a nearby street.

"It's cleared the walls! The ship's gone!"

"That's Xandru's voice," Gerdene said.

Indigo and two of the men lifted the edge of the wagon, and they all cautiously emerged. The air seemed clear, and here and there, doors cracked open, shutters were lifted.

Xandru, his nose and mouth covered in a scarf, appeared at the square, riding what appeared to be one of the emperor's horses. At the sight of Indigo pulling Gerdene out, he rode over and leaped down. The weaver and the thief hugged each other.

"Are you all right?" Xandru asked the old woman.

She nodded and spoke through the cloth wound around her face. "Never better."

Xandru surveyed the dozen people coming out from under the wagon. A few others had cautiously emerged from the houses and shops around the square, looking up at the skies. Xandru leaped up onto the bottom of the wagon, which was still upside down, and addressed the square.

"People of Kalyun-eh! Emperor Dorgun was going to pacify us all, his own people, on his birthday." He pointed up at the ship, which was floating beyond the city walls. More shutters opened, more faces appeared at windows, and the square began filling. Xandru continued. "If not for Theo Griffinrider who warned us, that ship would have been our doom. He came back from death and saved us all from the very empire that killed him." He jumped back onto his mare's back and pulled one of the horseball clubs from its sling on the saddle. "Ride with me into the castle! Today, we tell the emperor we will not be pacified!"

The square reverberated with shouts, as the people gathered roared their anger and support. Some ran to find weapons, others flooded behind Xandru's horse, empty-handed, while others brought forth kitchen knives, staves, and anything else from their shops or households that could be used as weapons.

Indigo took Xandru's hand and climbed up on his horse, then helped Orjo up behind her, while several citizens righted the wagon. They all rode together toward the drawbridge, where even now, a group of men was hauling away the rubble blocking the barbican. The few remaining castle guards on the walls tried to put up a fight with their bows and arrows, threatening to shoot anyone who entered, but the tide was too strong, and some of the people had soon worked out a way to shield them from the soldiers' arrows using ripped off doors from neighboring buildings. They soon had the rubble cleared, and Xandru led the people of Kalyun-eh across the beleaguered barbican.

They flooded into the main courtyard, where Indigo began shouting instructions. "Orjo and I will find the emperor. Xandru, we need to secure the armory. Reenan and Hizarah—"

A roar louder than any griffin rent the air. Its sound and force seemed to swallow everything around it, and the residents of Kalyun-eh looked up as a giant sun seemed to appear out of nowhere, a ball of flame and fluttering silk exploding just outside the city walls. Everyone froze, stunned. All eyes watched the flaming balloon break into tendrils of flame. There was a moment of silence.

"Theo." Indigo's heart lurched.

Orjo gave her a push. "Go. I'll see to the emperor and all this."

She nodded, and rushed back the way they had come.

* * *

DORGUN MADE his way up the library stairs, determined to ignore the pain in his arm. He had left Ornox's body to bleed in his library, which was fitting. For now, he had matters to attend to, such as his balloon and its path. He crossed his bedchamber to the doors that led out onto the balcony, but then paused. There was a strange sound coming from beyond the courtyard.

He frowned, listening. It was like a roar of water, but he knew that was impossible. He stepped out onto the balcony to hear better. He took a few steps down the pyramid stairs, looking for guards he could call to, someone to command. But none of his servants were in sight.

As he approached the gates that led to the outer courtyards, he realized why. The roar he had heard was the shouting of thousands of people, all pushing their way into the castle. He first saw a dozen people running past the open archways, then more, all with makeshift weapons and all chanting a single word.

No, not a word. A name.

"Theo! Theo! Theo!"

Dorgun quickly turned and made his way back to the pyramid stairs. As he went, he heard a bone-rattling roar and looked up in time to see his balloon burst into flames in the sky, like some giant exploding sun.

Blackhide curse it. His beautiful ship, that he had meticulously planned, was gone. And the city did not sound pacified. Far from it, in fact. The thunder of hundreds of feet and their cries convinced him to turn and make his way back up the pyramid stairs and into his private chambers. He shut and locked the doors, pulling the curtains across, then brought a low table over for good measure. He checked that all the other doors were locked as well. Satisfied, he fled down into the library, locking the secret door behind him.

All he needed to do was wait here until his guards could restore order. For they would restore order, they had to. A bunch of drunk riff raff from the street could not overpower his royal imperial arms.

He simply had to wait it out.

* * *

ORJO AND XANDRU, followed by the twelve men and women who had sheltered under the wagon, rode through the courtyard and into the central part of the castle. Xandru dismounted before the pyramid and led his group up the steps, then tried the doors. When they wouldn't give, he and his companions kicked at the handles until it gave way, then pushed the table aside and opened the doors. They entered the opulent private chambers of the emperor, but found them empty.

"Wily old bat," Orjo muttered, squatting by the mosaic that led to the Library. "He's under this."

Xandru looked over his shoulder, confused. "Under the floor?"

"In the Library," Orjo said, running a paw over his whiskers as he looked at the tiles. "There's a password, we just need to—" Orjo stopped and began laughing.

Xandru frowned. "What?"

"I'll be. The password is 'Calgornan'."

"Who's Calgornan?" Xandru asked.

"The best bard who ever lived. Now come on."

* * *

DORGUN HEARD the sound of the door scraping open and froze. From where he sat at his desk—the very desk where he had drawn the plans for his beloved ship—he could distinctly hear several pairs of feet descending the steps.

He watched as they entered the room, a dozen of them in all,

319

youngsters every one. They looked like rabble—one even had half-grown-out hair that showed he had once been a prisoner. Dorgun glared at them.

"I am the last omatje of Mankahar. Kill me, and you will lose the power of the Library forever."

At this, another figure emerged from behind them, a much smaller figure that the emperor immediately recognized.

"You're not the last omatje, Dorgun," Orjo said, chortling. "Far from it, in fact."

The one with the stubble on his head gave an insolent grin. "We will all become omatjes, and this Library belongs to Mankahar now."

* * *

INDIGO RAN FASTER than she had ever run in her life.

The streets sped by in a blur, the walls of the city couldn't appear fast enough. She kept seeing the ball of fire in the sky, still felt every fiber in her scream at the thought that Theo and Brune might be there, in the flames.

Though many had taken shelter when they had realized that pacification powder was raining on them, the streets were now busy again, full of angry citizens on their way to the castle, their faces covered with scarves.

Her lungs burned and her feet ached by the time she reached the city gates, which were open and unguarded, the threat of pacification apparently having scattered any remaining troops.

She sprinted as fast as she could toward the fading plumes of smoke in the distance. She searched, growing more desperate, but could find no sign of the balloon, or any wood from the ship. The explosion had annihilated it, leaving not one scrap of wreckage.

Indigo felt the strength seep out of her legs. She sank to the ground, numb. History was repeating itself. Theo was gone once more, without a trace.

Someone put a paw on her shoulder, and she instinctively grabbed his arm to throw him.

"It's Pozzi, Princess!"

She let go, looking up at the black and white rabbit, his face covered in a ripped fabric. "What are you doing here?"

"I was going to ask you that as well. I thought I saw Theo in the ship. The one that exploded. I came to see if I could find him."

Indigo looked out over the wreckage. "Me too."

"No one could have survived this though," he said softly.

She shook her head, tears stinging. "No. No one could survive this."

The sun went dark as a shadow passed over her. She looked up, frowning, and saw a giant beast whose wings were so large they seemed to swallow the sky. Recognition flickered as the giant beast circled once, then landed some distance from her.

"Morr?"

The great dragon stood on three legs, while the foreclaw held Brune. The giant bear climbed out, and Indigo stumbled to her feet when she saw the inert figure he carried.

She ran to them as Brune lay Theo down on the ground. She knelt to cradle his limp head in her arms, and tugged her scarf down from around her nose and mouth.

"Morr came as fast as he could," Morr said.

"It's a silent whistle. Can you believe it?" Brune said, wiping his wet eyes.

"Morr saw them fly out of the exploding ship," Morr said, then added softly, "But Morr was too late."

Indigo looked down at the bruised and bloodied face in her arms. Something had cut him across the cheek and just missed his eye, which was swollen. She ripped the scarf from under her chin and bandaged his eye, knotting it behind one ear.

"I'm sorry, Indigo," Brune said. "I didn't expect to live."

"Theo," Indigo whispered, holding him against her. "You can't go. You can't. Come back. Come back, and I'll do anything.

Learn the Forbidden Language. Didn't you want to teach me that? I'll do it."

"You promise?"

In her imagination she thought she heard him. Then from the whoops of delight that Brune, Morr, and Pozzi let out, she realized she hadn't imagined it. She looked at Theo and saw his un-bandaged eye was open and looking at her.

She felt the tears come then, and she was kissing him. She didn't care who was watching, or whether it was against Alvareth laws, and only pulled away when Theo winced as her arm grazed his side.

"Let's get you to a healer," she said.

Theo turned his eye to Pozzi, incredulous. "Is that you, Pozzi?"

The black-and-white patched rabbit nodded and squeezed Theo's paw. "You're sure a welcome sight, chum."

Morr bent and let them climb on, with Brune cradling Theo, and Indigo and Pozzi clambering up alongside him. And then they were airborne, flying toward the spires of Kalyun-eh.

CHAPTER 47

In the days that followed, there were contradicting accounts on the order of events. But the biggest event, the one that Pozzi was sure would be sung about for ages to come, was that the castle had been forcibly taken by the common folk of Kalyun-eh. When they had learned of their emperor's plan to pacify them all, they had rebelled. Some of the guards had tried to resist, but once they realized the emperor had been captured, they had agreed to surrender.

In the absence of a clear ruler, Indigo and Brune held the castle with Xandru and Morr's help, and tried to maintain some sort of order to prevent looting and chaos. Many of the nobles who had attended the birthday celebrations had died during Ornox's fight, but those who had survived were unwilling to risk further bloodshed by fighting the new commanders of Kalyun-eh, and instead barricaded themselves in their homes to see which way the political winds would blow.

Two days after Feast Day, Indigo and Brune were relieved to receive Lord Noshi at Kalyun-eh's castle. The old leader had arrived with what remained of the Order's forces.

Pozzi could barely believe his eyes when he heard someone

among the Order's arrivals shouting his name, and saw two familiar figures run toward him.

"Keeva! Walnut!" Pozzi cried, crushing them in his arms. "I worried Harlan had done something terrible to you both."

"I'm so sorry." Keeva's eyes were full of tears. "Whatever happens, wherever we go, we are not traveling with Harlan. I'm sorry I didn't see through him sooner."

"But how did you come here?" Pozzi asked.

"I suspected Harlan wasn't telling me the whole truth, so I plied him with wine one night and found out what he'd done," Keeva explained.

"We decided to come fast as we could to Kalyun-eh, and met Lord Noshi on the road," Walnut added.

"They kindly offered us protection."

"Is it true that Uncle Theo is alive?" Walnut asked, eyes bright.

Pozzi nodded.

"Can we see him?" Walnut pleaded.

"Not yet," Pozzi said. "He's recovering."

* * *

THEO WAS KEPT in the infirmary for the whole of two days and saw no one but Indigo, Brune, Orjo, and the team of healers who attended him, for his injured eye required rest and repair. The only other visitor allowed to see him was Noshi, who was shown in soon after arriving in Kalyun-eh. He entered with a smile and sat down next to the rabbit's bed.

"It's good to see you, Theo."

"As it is you, Lord Noshi. I'm sorry I didn't tell you I was alive."

The old man waved a hand. "No need. I understand the whys. I am glad Orjo protected you so fiercely. Well, Theo Griffinrider, how does it feel to have brought down an empire?"

"It hurts," Theo said, indicating his wounded brow. His eye

was still swollen, but he could see, and the healer had assured him there was no sight damage.

Noshi chuckled. "All of that can be fixed."

"What happens now? Now that you're here?"

Noshi drew a breath. "The nobles are willing to work out a truce. The laws are that with my brother Dorgun deposed, his crown passes to the next of kin."

Theo frowned. "But that's—"

The old man nodded. "Me. Yes."

"So you will become emperor?"

Noshi shook his head. "I think the days of an emperor are over. Dorgun made sure of that. No, I think Mankahar needs joint rule. Rule where non-humans also have a say. I'm going to recommend that the animals nominate a leader to rule with me over a Council, which will be formed by members that the nobles and the animals jointly choose." Noshi paused. "You know they will likely put your name forward?"

Theo hadn't thought of this. "Is that wise?"

Noshi smiled. "I believe you have come to be seen as wise. And Mankahar needs wisdom now, perhaps more than ever."

"I'm not sure I'm the right one," Theo said.

"Give it some thought," Noshi answered.

Theo nodded out of politeness, then changed the subject. "Is the Library safe?"

A cloud passed over Noshi's face. Seeing Theo's look, he gave him a reassuring nod. "The Library is fine, and guarded to make sure it stays intact."

Theo tried to think of a delicate way to ask, but couldn't find the words. "What will happen to Dorgun?"

"I will speak to him and see if he will unconditionally surrender and perhaps live in exile. I might be able to do that for him." Noshi paused, thoughtful. "I still can't believe that our father told him about the Library, and not me."

"Mankahar's fate might have been so different if you had been given the Library."

Noshi nodded. "Perhaps. But there's no point in wishing for what could have been." He sighed. "And now I should leave you to rest. I have much to do, starting with my brother."

* * *

THE GUARDS BOWED to Noshi and stepped aside to allow him into the stairwell to the dungeons.

The old leader passed the long row of cells until he reached the end. A guard nodded to Noshi and was about to open the eye hatch when Noshi motioned at the door.

"I wish to go in."

The guard looked unsure, but Noshi nodded to reassure him. The guard took out a set of keys from his belt and unlocked two locks on the door, then opened it.

The inside was bare, dank, and above all, dark. The only light came from the torches in the hallway, silhouetting a hunched figure on a bench shoved against the wall. He held up one arm to ward off the light.

"Hello, brother," Noshi said.

Dorgun's arm fell, and he turned to his visitor, blinking. His milky eye had no reaction to the light, but his one good eye squinted, as if even this dim flame from the hallway pained him. When he caught sight of Noshi, he laughed softly in contempt.

"Welcome home," Dorgun said. "You've come down here to gloat, have you?"

The old leader of the Order shook his head and took a seat on the bench opposite Dorgun. "I have come to offer you amnesty, a chance at redemption." His voice was quiet and deeply sad. *Aktu, give me strength*, he thought. Two seeds from the same source, they should have loved each other instead of spending decades hating each other over a divide that could not be mended.

Dorgun gave a hiss of disgust. "I don't need your pity, or your amnesty, big brother. This is why Father never told you about the Library, never wanted you to be emperor. Because you never had the spine to do what needed doing."

"And what do you think I should do now? With you?"

"Kill me," Dorgun said evenly. "For if you don't, you can be sure I'll find a way to put a knife in your back."

"And for that, father loved you." Noshi said it not as a question, but almost as if it was a realization.

Dorgun leaned forward at this, stony. "I had the iron to rule Mankahar as he saw fit, and he knew you didn't."

Noshi nodded. "You're right. You and Father believed in ruling with your fists. And I believed in ruling with my mind. The last thing I can offer you then, as your brother, is a choice as to how you'd like to exit this life."

"Poison," Dorgun said without hesitation. "And bury me with our ancestor Dakus's helmet."

"Very well."

"Promise me you'll bury me with the helmet."

"I promise," Noshi said, solemn. He stood. "I will be back on your execution day to say goodbye."

Dorgun leaned back against the wall. "If you wish, brother. Remember me when you're rotting in your own idealism. Power favors the strong and the ruthless."

"Perhaps," Noshi agreed, pausing in the doorway. "But that was yesterday. Not today."

CHAPTER 48

The day of Dorgun's execution dawned, pale and new.

Noshi insisted it be a private affair, for even in this, he was determined to be a good brother and give Dorgun some dignity. A small group of nobles and Order members, including Theo, Ingido, and Brune, were there to see Dorgun drink the poison concocted for him, and to dress his body and bury it, with Dakus's helmet, in a modest, unmarked grave outside the city walls. The event held no joy for Theo, despite his thinking it would help him find closure over his grandfather's death, and he knew it held even less joy for Noshi. Upon Dorgun's death, Noshi spent two full days accepting pledges of allegiance from all the noble houses of Mankahar, and holding council with them to assure them that they would not be robbed of their lands or punished for their roles in the war against the Order.

The day after the burial, the castle and the Order's forces busied themselves with the impending vote on who would be Council leader. Theo had been uncomfortable with the numerous well-wishers who made clear that they would be voting for him. As he dressed for the day's event, the rabbit looked critically at his reflection in the mirror. He was scarred and hardened compared to the youth who had fled Willago two years ago, not to mention his eye was still tender and swollen.

He took a breath and tried to rehearse the words he'd practiced last night, but they still felt odd to him. The meeting of the Council was today, where the animals of Mankahar would choose a leader to work with Noshi to create something new out of the empire's fragments. So far they had managed to maintain peace between the humans and the animals, but Theo suspected Noshi was right when the man said there would be many disgruntled Urzoks who would miss their way of life, and perhaps even fight to restore it. It wouldn't be easy convincing them that they had to share power, and the path forward would be fraught.

A knock sounded on the door.

"Come in," Theo called, expecting the servant Noshi had assigned him. Theo was uncomfortable with the idea of someone waiting on him, but Noshi had insisted.

Indigo poked her head in. She had, like him, dressed with care, he saw. She was in formal Ihaktu clothing, her snow-colored fur brushed to a high sheen, her boots newly oiled. The sight of her still sent his nerves tingling, but he remembered with a pang that they were not to be together. Despite the kiss they'd shared on the field.

"You look...regal," she said.

He decided to keep his observations of her to himself. "I'm not sure how regal I look, given this..." He gestured at his eye. He hadn't given it a thought when he'd been allowed to see Pozzi, Keeva, and Walnut. In fact, the young rabbit had seemed in awe of Theo's wounds, and even disappointed to know there wouldn't be much of a scar. But Indigo's presence made Theo acutely aware of his appearance.

She came forward and looked at it, her expression playful. "Gives you a hardened air befitting the Griffinrider."

He smiled ruefully. "I think my Griffinrider days are over."

She nodded. "There's much to adjust to, isn't there?"

They were silent, unsure how to discuss the past, much less the future. They hadn't had time to talk about anything personal, occupied as they were with physical recovery, and the changes all around them. In this rare quiet moment together, Theo realized with a stab of guilt that he had been avoiding Indigo, dreading this conversation and the truths they would have to bring out. And worst of all, his having to hear about her impending marriage to a prince.

"Why didn't you tell me? About being alive?" she said at last.

"Orjo said it was our best defense," Theo said slowly. "That if the Urzoks thought me dead, they wouldn't be looking for me, much less expecting me in Kalyun-eh."

Indigo considered this. "It was a hard time."

"For me as well," he answered truthfully. "Though I'm glad for your future happiness."

Her brow furrowed. "What's that supposed to mean?"

"I hear you're to marry a prince. Someone worthy of you." The words cut him, but she deserved happiness, not guilt about his feelings. He had concluded that her kissing him was simply a heat-of-the-moment action, a leftover judgment from a previous time.

She flushed. "You heard about that?"

Theo forced down his emotions. "I congratulate you, and wish you every happiness."

She was about to reply when his servant, a tall, lanky badger, entered. "Master Theo, the Council is gathering. Both of you are requested."

Theo smiled at Indigo, trying to dispel the ache in his chest. "Shall we?"

Indigo looked torn, then glanced at the badger. "We can't keep the Council waiting, can we?"

* * *

THEY WALKED TOGETHER through the castle, silent. Theo wrestled his thoughts away from his conversation with Indigo and tried to remember the words he had rehearsed for this moment. He would have to know what to say when—if—the Council nominated him. And maybe they wouldn't. Maybe Noshi was wrong.

When the doors opened and he and Indigo walked in, everyone was busy finding their seats in the amphitheater. But at their entry, all paused and began stamping their feet in approval. Indigo nodded politely, while Theo felt like he wanted to slip quietly away somewhere and hide. The badger ushered them to their seats, two places on the front bench, then retreated from the room. Theo looked around at the faces of the Order, some familiar but most not. There were Wortimer and Olea, whom he remembered from the Battle of Ralgayan, and Tarq the wise commander. Brune sat on the opposite side and gave him an encouraging grin. Theo couldn't help feel a pang of sadness noticing how diminished the Order's numbers were, compared to just a year ago.

At that moment, a herald announced Lord Noshi, and the man entered and motioned for everyone to take their places. A hushed but excited silence fell.

"Welcome, members of the Order," Noshi began. "Today is a momentous day, a day where we move forward into a future where power is shared, not hoarded. Where our land is for all, instead of for the few, and where everyone has a voice, and no one must be silent."

At this, the gathered throng stamped their feet, and Noshi allowed the audience to express themselves before continuing.

"We are here to replace an emperor, an arbitrary single figure of power, with a shared, respectful Council. But every ship must have a captain, every pack must have an alpha, and so must every council have its leader. We are here to decide who will act as leader of the Free Council. This leader will not be your ruler, but your mouthpiece. Your voice, your hammer, and your friend, in negotiating with the humans of Mankahar. These humans will be led by me, as per the old imperial rules."

At his use of the word *humans*, there was a murmur throughout the crowd, but Noshi raised a hand and the hubbub ceased. "The word 'Urzok' has always been one of contempt. If we are to proceed as equals, as allies, regardless of religion or species, then we have to abandon these words." He let this sink in. "Now, we will vote on who you wish to nominate as your leader. Those in favor will stand up. Our first nominee is no surprise. Many of you have voiced your wish that Theo Griffin-rider represent you."

Theo's throat went dry. He couldn't quite understand the idea that he was being nominated to lead all of Mankahar's free beasts, but here he was. Almost everyone stood up. Barely a soul remained sitting as Noshi surveyed the room. Theo looked around, until his gaze fell on Indigo, who was also standing.

"You'd make a fine leader, Theo," she whispered. "And it would be an honor to serve you."

Noshi's gaze swept the room before turning to Theo. "Well, Theo Griffinrider, you have nearly the entire room's vote, which puts you in the lead without even considering other candidates. What say you? Do you accept this nomination?"

Theo took a deep breath and stood. There was silence as the chamber waited, and for a moment, Theo thought his words wouldn't come. He cleared his throat.

"I am honored, and humbled, that you would place your trust in me," Theo said. "I am but a rabbit—"

At this, there were cries of protest, and thumping, and Theo sheepishly held up a paw in surrender.

"Indigo has also tried to school me in the fact that there is no such thing as 'just a rabbit.' I'll rephrase. I have done many things that I thought I never could do. Not least of all, dying and coming back to life."

There was quiet laughter at this.

"I've had a lot of time to think about what leadership is, and what Mankahar needs. For a long time, I felt that Mankahar needed a great weapon, one that could destroy the Urzok—I mean, human." He nodded to Noshi, catching himself. "Destroy the empire. I thought it was the *Book of Cures*, something that could reverse pacification. But I've learned that the greatest weapon in Mankahar is not a single book in a library. It never was." He paused, smiling at how blind he had been. "It was the Forbidden Language itself. That is and will be Mankahar's greatest weapon, tool, and teacher." He paused, remembering the recurring dream he'd had of being in the Library, and the books turning into identicals of him. He finally understood what the dream was trying to tell him. "The Forbidden Language is what saved me, and saved Kalyun-eh. And if you and the leaders of Mankahar will let me, this is what I'd like to continue to do. Teach the Forbidden Language to anyone who wants to learn." He turned to Indigo. "Indigo is the natural leader here. She is a fair queen, a selfless warrior, and she will lead you like no other can. Certainly, a thousand times better than I could. I believe Indigo should be the leader of the Council. And I hope all of you will join me in voting for her as well."

There was a moment of silence, as even Indigo seemed thrown.

Theo caught sight of Brune, who cleared his throat. "By Aktu, he's right." The bear looked around at everyone gathered. "Indigo has led us to victory through multiple battles. She uses her head as well as her sword. I vote for Indigo as leader of our new Council."

One by one, and then as a wave, the other animals stamped their feet, voicing their support. Soon, Noshi was calling for a vote, and everyone remained standing in support of the princess of Alvareth.

Indigo looked stunned, but Theo smiled encouragingly, and leaned toward her. "You will make a fine leader, and it will be my honor to serve you."

CHAPTER 49

The next week passed in a dream-like blur. It seemed Indigo was flooded with visitors and supplicants, all trying to plead their cases or argue for their causes. She had alliances to forge and parties to please, plans and laws to draft.

For his part, Theo was no less busy—many wanted to meet the Griffinrider, and when news spread that he would teach the Forbidden Language to anyone who wanted to learn, a trickle of applicants turned into a stream, and a stream turned into a tide. Unpacified animals, hearing that Kalyun-eh was no longer under empire rule and that indeed, the empire had disintegrated, were flocking back to the capital city.

In the midst of this, Theo was able to enjoy precious snippets of time with Pozzi, Walnut, and Keeva. He heard about their running into Harlan, and though he was angered by what his brother had done to his friends, a part of him was relieved to hear his brother was alive, that Theo had not guaranteed his death when he exiled him from Ralgayan. He was especially joyous when he learned that Pozzi and Keeva were to be married. While they enjoyed a meal together, Pozzi had shyly shared the news, and Theo couldn't help but throw an arm around his friend.

"So…no hard feelings then?" Pozzi asked, clearly remembering their youth and Theo's infatuation with Keeva.

Theo smiled. "This is the happiest news today."

Pozzi hesitated. "Are you sure? I know you and Keeva—"

"My feelings for Keeva are part of childhood." Theo couldn't help his gaze wandering to the table at the opposite side of the dining hall, and though Theo looked away, he knew his friend had caught his glance.

Indigo sat at the far table, hosting Wortimer and Olea and several other members of the Order who were eager to be with the new Council leader. "Oh, Theo, chum," Pozzi said, looking from Theo to Indigo. "I didn't know."

"I truly am happy for you, Pozzi."

"Does she know?"

"Yes, but it doesn't matter. She's destined for greater things."

Pozzi snorted. "There's no greater rabbit than you, Theo. Haven't you heard?" Pozzi toasted him with a tankard of ale. "Perhaps greatest fighter that ever was, if you listen to the songs."

"The greatest after me, that is," a voice interrupted, and Orjo sat down heavily on the bench next to Theo. "Can't have you replacing me, Griffinrider."

Theo's heart gladdened at seeing the muskrat. Orjo walked with difficulty now, one of his limbs having never quite healed properly after being thrown in the Forgetting Well.

"And what will you do, now that the war's over and you're no longer an exile?" Pozzi asked Orjo.

"Still haven't gotten used to it," the muskrat grumbled. "Being infamous and feared had many advantages."

"I have a task for you," Theo offered.

Orjo looked at him, amused. "Aye? Does it involve liquor?"

"It might," Theo said. "Stay in Kalyun-eh with me. The Forbidden Language—"

"It's not forbidden anymore, remember," Orjo corrected him.

"True. But while it was forbidden, no books were made.

That's a lot of missing history, and knowledge. The Library could use your contributions."

"That sounds like a lot of hard work and very little gain," Orjo snorted.

"I would campaign for there to be generous funds to support your work. Very generous."

"I'll think about it," Orjo responded.

Theo nodded. "Good, I'd…" He noticed rabbits filing in on the other side of the hall, and he fell silent. Seeing his look, Pozzi and Orjo followed his gaze and watched the towering rabbit, Prince Ebben, enter the hall with his retinue. The Irontail went straight for Indigo, unheeding of those waiting their turn, and everyone around her melted away to allow him through.

Theo couldn't hear what was said, but he also knew he didn't want to.

"Time for my class," he said abruptly and stood. He avoided looking in Indigo's direction as he left the hall and went to find the chamber they had set up as a classroom for the Forbidden Language. Not forbidden anymore, he reminded himself and tried to take joy in this new change. But somehow, his heart wouldn't rise from where it had sunk after seeing Ebben and Indigo together.

* * *

HE WAS SO LOST in thought that he barely heard his name.

"Theo! Wait!" the female voice cried.

He turned. Hizarah and Reenan strode toward him, with Manneki perched on Reenan's shoulder.

Theo broke into a smile despite himself. The trio had been keeping spirits high in the castle, composing victory songs and putting on plays depicting the storming of Kalyun-eh.

"We came to say goodbye," Reenan explained.

"You're leaving?" Theo asked, surprised. "Why?"

"Because Manneki is Magnificent!" the Grodlyn crowed.

Theo smiled. His old friend had discovered a love for being the center of attention.

Hizarah gave the Grodlyn's tail a playful tug. "Full of yourself, aren't you?" She turned back to Theo. "We've decided to tour Mankahar."

At the rabbit's confused look, Reenan added, "We're doing shows about the emperor's fall and the Order's rise, and Noshi thought it would be good to spread the word through stage and song. So we must be away."

"Can't you stay and perform here?"

"And miss this chance at greatness?" Reenan asked, smiling. "No. Kalyun-eh needs its leaders, and Mankahar needs its storytellers. We each have our roles."

Theo nodded. "We'll miss you," he said, his voice tight.

Manneki scampered down and gave Theo a hug with his skinny, red-furred arms. "Manneki will come back."

Reenan smiled. "As will we."

They each embraced, not without tears, and Theo watched them saunter back down the corridor until they had disappeared around the corner.

We each have our roles.

He turned and continued the other way, to the guest solar on the northern wing of Kalyun-eh castle. Not for the first time, he paused in the doorway and admired how the room had been repurposed.

Sunlight flooded in from the balcony windows, as well as from the skylight above. One wall had been stripped bare of its tapestries and replaced with a large rectangular slate. Boxes of charcoal pieces sat on small square tables around the room, and each table had its own slate piece on it.

"I tried to get the extra supplies you asked for," Brune said, appearing by his side. "Though we may still be short. Looks like there are more today than yesterday."

He pointed at the students entering from the opposite door and taking places at the tables. Theo was pleased to see there were humans and animals. Xandru and his crew had spread the word to every corner that Theo was teaching the Forbidden Language to anyone who wanted to learn. Most were curious enough about what had saved Mankahar to come and listen, if not participate.

Soon every chair and cushion was taken. Brune looked around, then nodded to Theo. "I'll leave you to it."

The bear saluted a few in the room whom he knew, and took a position at the back. Theo looked out at the faces, some old, some young, some jaded, some eager. But they were all here because they wanted to learn the Forbidden Language, about the skill Father Oaks had passed to him. The skill everyone had once called a curse.

He wished his grandfather were here to see this. He pushed sentimentality aside and took a breath.

"Welcome," he said. "Today, we'll..."

He'd had a lesson planned, but he suddenly couldn't remember it. For Indigo had entered the room and stood leaning against the doorway, watching him.

Theo felt the familiar squeeze in his heart and worried that today's lesson was just about to get more uncomfortable. He cleared his throat. "Welcome, Head Councilor. Can we help you?"

"Like everyone else, I'm here seeking answers." She took a seat on a cushion at the back, and murmurs rippled around the room. The loudest murmur was probably in Theo's head, for he knew she had always refused to learn the Forbidden Language. Through everything, there had always been a part of her that viewed his ability as sorcery—a sometimes useful sorcery, but sorcery nonetheless. She had promised to learn on the field that day, but Theo had relegated it to the same place as her kissing him—a momentary impulse.

He retreated back to the head of the classroom and tried to marshal his thoughts. He began writing glyphs on the large rectangular slate that was propped against the wall. "For those of you joining us for the first time, these are the building blocks of the once forbidden language, please use your slates to write them down."

Everyone dutifully picked up their charcoal pieces and began writing.

"Now, before we—" He turned back to the class, and paused.

Indigo had her arm raised.

"Yes, Councilor Indigo? You have a question?"

"I do."

"I've only just begun the lesson, can it wait?"

"No. I really don't think it can."

She rose and walked to the front, stopping beside him. She picked up a nearby piece of charcoal and wrote one glyph on the slate. At Theo's look of surprise, she smiled. "Xandru taught me a few basics."

"That's…excellent," Theo said. "And so what was your question?"

"This," Indigo turned back and began writing on the slate again, her brow furrowed in concentration. When she was finished, she looked over at him.

He stared at the words, dumbfounded.

"Well?" She glanced from him to the slate, as if to make sure the words hadn't disappeared.

"That's your question?" Theo asked. He caught the words twice, then three times, just to make sure he hadn't misunderstood.

"Yes," she answered, voice soft. "Marry me?"

The class seemed to realize what was going on, and from the corner of his eye, Theo could see Brune watching, holding his breath with everyone else. When the silence stretched she flushed. "So…is that a no?"

"No! I mean yes," he managed to say, then took a breath. "A thousand times yes."

Her eyes sparked with happiness, and her ears flushed. The

rest of the class rose, stamping their feet and shouting out congratulations.

Theo held out a paw, and Indigo took it. He pulled her close, feeling her curl into him. He folded his arms around her and wished he never had to let go.

ACKNOWLEDGMENTS

It takes a village to raise a child, as the saying goes. A book is no different, so there are many to thank at the end of a trilogy!

Thank you first and foremost to all the readers who have followed Theo's journey through these books. Your support, not just in reading but in spreading the word, ensures more stories in the future.

Thank you also to the team behind the book's actual process: Sam, for being my unflagging alpha reader and always seeing exactly what work is needed where. Thank you to my editor, Shelley Holloway, and my cover designer, Monika Zec. Thank you also to my wonderful ARC team and other supporters: Cecilia Sutton, Vanessa Church, Prencella, Kelly Ortig, Terry Adams, Melissa Steele, Maya Reid, and Johnette Blanc. You all rock.

And lastly, thanks to my children, Artemis and Evander. You're constant reminders of why we need good stories, now and forever.

ABOUT THE AUTHOR

Melanie was born in Canada but raised in China, and now lives in Ballarat, Australia with her husband and two children. She loves to read, write, and laugh. She also makes movies.

www.melanieansley.com

facebook.com/melanieansleyauthor
twitter.com/writingrooster
bookbub.com/profile/melanie-ansley

www.ingramcontent.com/pod-product-compliance
Lightning Source LLC
Chambersburg PA
CBHW030933120726
47906CB00002B/567